# JENNIFER RYAN and the
# WILDES OF WYOMING

"I love cowboy romance and Jennifer Ryan is one of the best at writing it. Sexy hero. Strong heroine. Unbridled passion. The perfect mix!"
—Donna Grant, *New York Times* bestselling author, on *Chase Wilde Comes Home*

"Filled with heart and the warmth of home, Jennifer Ryan delivers! A must read for fans of western romance!"
—Maisey Yates on *Chase Wilde Comes Home*

"Chase and Shelby stole my heart. Broken and battered and both ready to heal, I could not put down this heart-stopping romance yet never wanted it to end!"
—A.J. Pine, *USA Today* bestselling author, on *Chase Wilde Comes Home*

"Fast-paced and filled with heartfelt emotion, this book kept me up late into the night! . . . Poignant and heartwarming, with characters that come to life. I thoroughly enjoyed this book!"
—Victoria James, *New York Times* and *USA Today* bestselling author, on *Chase Wilde Comes Home*

# By Jennifer Ryan

*Stand-Alone Novels*
THE ONE YOU WANT • LOST AND FOUND FAMILY
SISTERS AND SECRETS • THE ME I USED TO BE

*The Wyoming Wilde Series*
SURRENDERING TO HUNT • CHASE WILDE COMES HOME

*The McGrath Series*
TRUE LOVE COWBOY • LOVE OF A COWBOY
WAITING ON A COWBOY

*Wild Rose Ranch Series*
TOUGH TALKING COWBOY • RESTLESS RANCHER
DIRTY LITTLE SECRET

*Montana Heat Series*
TEMPTED BY LOVE • TRUE TO YOU
ESCAPE TO YOU • PROTECTED BY LOVE

*Montana Men Series*
HIS COWBOY HEART • HER RENEGADE RANCHER
STONE COLD COWBOY • HER LUCKY COWBOY
WHEN IT'S RIGHT • AT WOLF RANCH

*The McBrides Series*
DYLAN'S REDEMPTION • FALLING FOR OWEN
THE RETURN OF BRODY MCBRIDE

*The Hunted Series*
EVERYTHING SHE WANTED • CHASING MORGAN
THE RIGHT BRIDE • LUCKY LIKE US
SAVED BY THE RANCHER

*Short Stories*
"Close to Perfect" (appears in SNOWBOUND AT CHRISTMAS)
"Can't Wait" (appears in
ALL I WANT FOR CHRISTMAS IS A COWBOY)
"Waiting for You" (appears in
CONFESSIONS OF A SECRET ADMIRER)

# Surrendering to Hunt

A Wyoming Wilde Novel

# JENNIFER RYAN

AVONBOOKS

*An Imprint of* HarperCollins*Publishers*

SURRENDERING TO HUNT. Copyright © 2022 by Jennifer Ryan. All rights reserved. Printed in the United States of America. No part of this book may be used or reproduced in any manner whatsoever without written permission except in the case of brief quotations embodied in critical articles and reviews. For information, address HarperCollins Publishers, 195 Broadway, New York, NY 10007.

First Avon Books mass market printing: August 2022
First Avon Books hardcover printing: August 2022

Print Edition ISBN: 978-0-06-311142-4
Digital Edition ISBN: 978-0-06-309463-5

*Cover design by Nadine Badalaty*
*Cover photograph by Rob Lang/roblangimages.com (couple)*
*Cover images © iStick/Getty Images; © Shutterstock*

Avon, Avon & logo, and Avon Books & logo are registered trademarks of HarperCollins Publishers in the United States of America and other countries.

HarperCollins is a registered trademark of HarperCollins Publishers in the United States of America and other countries.

FIRST EDITION

22 23 24 25 26 BVGM 10 9 8 7 6 5 4 3 2 1

*For all those fearless hearts who surrender
to love and do so with wild abandon.*

# Acknowledgments

Thank you to my Western Romance Café Facebook group for helping me name a couple of characters.

Jennifer Jefferies—Rad was the coolest name for a very bad guy.

Sandra Baker—Lana Joy is the brightest joy in Cyn's world.

# Surrendering to Hunt

# Prologue

*The moment a woman came between Hunt
and his best friend . . .*

Willow Fork police officer Hunt Wilde drove down
Rad's driveway with the lights swirling, siren blaring,
and skidded to a stop. Rad stood outside of his home,
squaring off with the purple-haired beauty who glared
at Hunt every time they crossed paths. Granted, he was
usually issuing her a ticket at the time, because the
hairdresser thought laws were mere suggestions and
warnings were simply permission to go ahead and do
it again. Speeding, public intoxication, public nudity,
trespassing on private property: The woman lived up
to the sound of her name. Cyn.

Why the hell was she here?

Causing trouble, he was certain. It seemed that's all
she ever did.

Hunt stepped out of the car, but before he broke up
the argument between Rad and the wildcat talking with
her hands, her whole body illustrating the fury coming
off her, something up by the house caught his eye. Cyn's
sister, Angela, cowered behind a tree, tears streaming
down her face.

Cyn lived her life out loud.

Angela's quiet and subdued nature had landed her in a bad relationship with Rad, who dominated her life.

"Finally," Cyn shouted. "About damn time, Wilde." And there was the glare she gave him every time they met.

"Get her off my property," Rad yelled at him. "She's trespassing." Rad took a menacing step toward Cyn.

Hunt instinctively put his hand on his gun, because he and his fellow officers had been called out here too many times for domestic abuse. He didn't know what Rad was capable of anymore. "Back off, Rad. Let me handle this."

Cyn's glare turned icy. "Like you did the last time this asshole hit my sister and you let him go?"

Well, damn. First his brother's fiancée, Shelby, accused him of not doing his job weeks ago when her biological father made a nuisance of himself and now Cyn was doing the same. Like he told Shelby then, he couldn't go around locking people up without cause. Or in Rad's case, Angela's cooperation. She refused to press charges and even backed up Rad's account that she tripped and hit her face on the counter.

He knew it wasn't true. Angela knew he didn't believe her. But no amount of coaxing or promising that he'd protect her if she told the truth convinced her to hold Rad accountable for hurting her.

Rad held his ground up in Cyn's personal space. Hunt gave her credit for holding her own. But Hunt didn't like Rad that close to Cyn. It did something to his gut to see a man threatening her. As it should. But there was something more tweaking him that he continued to ignore every time they crossed paths.

He was here to do his job.

Of course Rad had an excuse. He always did. And turned to Hunt to spill it. "Angela and I were hanging out, and then little-miss-know-it-all showed up, saw Angela crying and demanded her sister leave with her." Rad turned on Cyn again. "Stay out of my business. Angela is with me"—he pointed his finger in Cyn's face—"and there's nothing you can do about it. So stay the hell away from us."

Cyn's sneer turned into a frown when her gaze shot to her sister. Her resigned expression of sadness combined with weariness tore at Hunt. He'd seen Cyn exuberantly happy dancing at the bar, funny and playfully tipsy, and drunk and singing at the top of her lungs without an ounce of self-conscious hesitation. Hunt had seen her be sexy and seductive when flirting with a guy—giving Hunt another unfamiliar feeling when it woke up a jealousy he'd never experienced with any other woman. But seeing her in this depressed state made him want to put the smile back on her face, even if that smile was never directed at him.

Angela had stepped out from behind the tree. She stood looking fragile and lost, her arms wrapped around her middle. "You shouldn't have called the cops. I'm fine." She looked anything but okay.

Hunt closed in on his friend. "Rad, step away from Cyn. Let's talk."

Cyn's eyes pleaded with her sister. "Please. Come with me. I will keep you safe."

Angela held herself tighter. "He doesn't mean it. He loves me."

Hunt had done this enough times now on the job and with Rad and Angela to know how this played out and pinned Rad with his sharp gaze. "Did you hit her?" Hunt didn't see any marks on Angela. This time. But just because he couldn't see them didn't mean they weren't there.

"No," Rad scoffed. "We argued. She said some things. I said some things. It got heated. I knocked something over and it broke. I slammed a couple doors. I tried to storm out, but she got in my way. She fell. It was an accident." Rad held Angela's gaze the whole time, silently letting her know she better back up his story.

Hunt had seen him do it before, but asked Angela anyway, hoping she'd tell the truth, and not just Rad's version of it. "Is that what happened?"

"Tell him the truth, Angela," Cyn pleaded. "Please. You don't need to stay here. I will take care of you."

"I take care of her," Rad snapped, stepping toward Cyn.

Hunt planted his hand on Rad's chest and shook his head in warning.

Rad stared down at Hunt's hand on him, then met Hunt's gaze. "Really. You know me. But you're going to believe *her*," he scoffed.

Hunt tried to reason with Rad. "I know her, too. And how many times have the police been called out here?"

Rad pointed at Cyn. "If she'd stop calling the cops for no reason, you wouldn't need to come here at all."

Hunt stepped closer to Rad. "Angela is crying. You're trying to bully Cyn to leave. And we both know something happened or Cyn wouldn't have called for help. So stay put right here. Shut up. And let me do my job."

"I really wish you would." Cyn glared at him again.

He ignored her as much as he could, because when Cyn was near, he couldn't not pay attention to her. He approached Angela, waving his hand out so she'd walk away from their audience and he could speak to her without being overheard.

Hunt stared down at the top of Angela's bent head. "Are you really okay, Angela? Did he hurt you?" He spoke softly, like he would to his niece, Eliza.

"I should have been more careful. I got distracted watching a movie and I left dinner in the oven too long. It burned. He worked all day. The least I could do is put a proper meal on the table."

Hunt's gut tightened as he heard Rad's accusing words in Angela's explanation. A simple accident had escalated to this. Other victims had rambled off scenarios like this on other domestic disturbance calls. Something innocuous got blown up into something more important than it ever was and someone got hurt, because abusers liked to make people pay.

That made Hunt confront the very uncomfortable reality that his best friend had turned into a dangerous man. He'd seen Rad's quick temper flare several times over the years. It started in high school. But his anger always seemed justified. Until recently. But maybe Hunt had never really wanted to look too closely at how Rad never seemed to be able to walk away from an argument or fight—and escalated things sometimes for no other reason than he couldn't control his temper.

"You know, if you didn't have that smart-ass mouth on you," Rad spoke to Cyn, "you'd be a nice piece of ass."

*Fuck you* was the comeback Hunt expected, but Cyn held her tongue, until Rad opened his big mouth again.

"Maybe I chose the wrong sister. Getting you in line might actually be a hell of a lot of fun."

Hunt turned just in time to see Cyn's lips curve into a deceptively sweet smile. "I'd rather be set on fire than let you put one fingertip anywhere on my body."

Rad sneered. "You're always such a fucking bitch."

"You're a coward who beats on women to make your small self feel big and strong and powerful, but we all know you're"—Rad started for her, Hunt rushing to close the distance, knowing he was too far away to get there in time to stop it—"just compensating for a tiny—"

Rad backhanded the rest of Cyn's words right from her lips.

Hunt grabbed Rad by the arm and kicked him in the back of the leg, sending Rad to his knees as Hunt shoved him all the way to the ground, pulling his arms behind his back and cuffing him before his friend knew what hit him.

"Fucking let me go," Rad bellowed, struggling to move, but Hunt pinned him down.

Cyn sauntered close, stared down at Rad, wiped the blood from her split lip and gave him that deceptively sweet smile again. "Enjoy your time in jail, asshole."

"I'll fucking kill you for this. You'll be begging before I end you."

Cyn finally met Hunt's gaze for the first time. "Add the death threat to the assault charge."

Hunt sighed, shaking his head at Rad. "Why the hell couldn't you just let me handle this?"

"You can't fucking arrest me. She provoked me."

"And you hit her. In front of a cop." Hunt hauled Rad up to his feet and kept hold of his arm, because he didn't know what Rad might do next. The guy he used to share

Ho Hos with in grade school wasn't the man standing beside him.

"You can't fucking arrest me. We're friends. Do something."

"As a cop, I have to follow the law. As your friend, I'm advising you to keep your mouth shut and get a lawyer to plead this down to a lesser charge and stay the hell away from Cyn and her sister from now on."

"No fucking way. Angela is mine. And if you do this, you're no friend of mine."

Then it worked out, because Hunt didn't want to be Rad's friend anymore. Not when he'd broken the law and abandoned his morals, hurting two women all to bolster his overinflated ego.

Bullies and abusive partners were the worst kinds of humans.

"You're going to pay for this." Rad spit at Cyn, missing her by mere inches.

All Hunt could do now was read Rad his rights and take him into the station.

But he had a strange premonition this wouldn't be the last time Cyn taunted Rad to retaliate against her and Hunt would be caught in the middle again.

# Chapter One

*Seven months later . . .*

Hᴜɴᴛ ᴡᴀʟᴋᴇᴅ into Cooper's bar. He'd spotted his brother's truck in the parking lot. At ten thirty at night, Chase should be home with his beautiful fiancée and their little girl. He hoped Chase and Shelby were out on a date and his brother hadn't fallen off the wagon. But then he spotted Shelby at a table with the last person he wanted to see.

Gorgeous, tempting, not-for-him Cyn.

He didn't think the purple-haired party girl and his reserved soon-to-be sister-in-law had anything in common or that they even knew each other. But everyone in town knew Cyn. Every man wanted her. Many had the pleasure of her company and a wild tale to tell about it. Though Hunt suspected a lot of what was said about Cyn was wishful thinking and exaggeration on those guys' parts.

Still, what the hell was she doing with Shelby?

In his police uniform, he attracted a lot of attention as he made his way through the crowd toward the two women who probably wouldn't be happy to see him.

He'd been hard on Shelby this past year. He'd wanted her to make Chase better. He'd wanted her to somehow erase Chase's PTSD and prescription drug addiction. It wasn't fair to put that on her, but the anger, resentment and blame he'd put on Chase unfairly spilled over to her.

He'd apologized. He'd do so again if need be, because he liked Shelby. More than that, he liked who his brother was with her, sober and happy.

As for Cyn . . . she hated him, even though he'd arrested Rad and severed all ties with a guy he'd once considered his best friend. Rad did what Hunt had advised and pleaded the charges down, so he basically got a slap on the wrist. It was a first offense, and he had no priors because Angela, and any other woman Rad might have hurt, hadn't filed charges against him.

Angela took Rad back the second he got out on bail.

Cyn blamed Hunt for that, too.

Yes, he knew her anger was warranted, but she'd aimed it at the wrong person. Much like he'd done with Shelby about Chase. And though he and his fellow officers had been called out to Rad's place on numerous occasions by Cyn before the arrest she instigated, they hadn't been called out since.

And, well, Cyn had cause to loathe him more because he'd written her a total of five speeding tickets over the past seven months alone. The last one she still hadn't paid.

Not that he was keeping track, or anything.

He didn't like the hold she seemed to have on him.

She liked speed, a good time and skirting the law and outright breaking it every chance she got. Though it had been quite a long time since one of his brethren had issued her a citation. Either she had tamed her wild ways, or more than likely she simply hadn't gotten caught.

Folks in town and down at the station still talked about how she and some drunk cowboy got caught skinny-dipping in Mrs. Thompson's pond. Mrs. Thompson discovered her teenage son watching the couple get it on in the shallow water.

He'd bet a month didn't go by without one of the guys at the station talking about seeing her in her drenched clothes, looking like the winner of a wet T-shirt contest.

He understood why. He'd never seen a more beautiful woman.

Steps away from Shelby and Cyn's table, he stopped short when Rad appeared out of nowhere, drunk and stumbling to a stop, hands planted on the wood surface, his face a foot from Cyn's scowling one.

"Fuck off." She glared, not giving a damn Rad had hit her in the past and her words and attitude could provoke him to do it again.

Hunt's gut tightened and his fist clenched. One wrong move and Hunt would put Rad down on the ground again.

Rad grinned and his gaze roamed over Cyn's face and dipped to her chest before he met her angry gaze again. "Why do you have to be such a bitch?"

"I wouldn't be if you treated my sister with respect. Especially now." Cyn rose and planted her hands right in front of Rad's on the table and leaned in close to him. "She needs to be treated with care."

Rad scoffed. "She won't let me near her."

Cyn's lips curved into that smile that taunted. "Good."

"She's mine."

"She has something more to live for now than spending every waking moment trying to make you happy."

Shelby stood and put her hand on Cyn's shoulder. "Let's go."

Rad turned his gaze to Shelby. "Who the hell are you?"

Hunt stepped in before things escalated and his brother's fiancée ended up in the middle of what could turn into a very bad situation. "Shelby, honey, back away from the table. Cyn, you, too."

Cyn didn't move an inch. "Rad and I were just talking. This is none of your concern."

"Did you actually call the cops?" Rad's bloodshot eyes narrowed.

"You're an idiot," Cyn snapped. "I've been right in front of you the whole three minutes you've been taking up my time. And how the hell would he get here so fast?"

Hunt put his hand on Rad's shoulder and pushed him back up to standing. "No one called the police. I came in to see Shelby."

"Me?" Shelby asked, surprised.

"Actually, I saw the truck, thought Chase was here, so I came in to make sure he was okay."

Shelby nodded, understanding in her eyes. "He's home with Eliza. It's girls' night. I'm supposed to be Cyn's wing woman, but we've been having too much fun together for me to find her a proper date."

"He doesn't have to be too proper," Cyn teased. "I like them a little untamed."

"Well, then come on. If your sister won't put out and you're always ready . . ." Rad slurred those words through a lecherous smile.

Cyn cringed. "Just the thought of you makes me feel like I need a monthlong scalding-hot shower."

Rad lurched toward her.

Hunt shoved him back. "Enough. Do you have a ride home?"

"I can drive." Rad swayed on his feet, taking a swig from the nearly empty beer bottle in his hand. Then to prove Cyn's point that he was anything but desirable, Rad belched long and loud.

Disgusted and wanting out of this situation, Hunt waved his hand, got the bartender's attention and mouthed the word *taxi*. The bartender nodded.

Not half a minute later, the bouncer showed up and took Rad by the arm. "Let's go, man. Time to go home."

Rad tried to pull away but the bouncer was six and a half feet tall and a good two-fifty of nothing but muscle.

Rad pointed the beer bottle at Hunt. "You turned out to be a real asshole."

"Back at you." Hunt kept an eye on Rad as the bouncer led him out, then turned to Shelby. "How is Chase? Is he all healed up?"

Chase had gotten stabbed in the shoulder and back by Shelby's biological father nearly a month ago. Though he'd gotten through the surgery and rehab without narcotics, Hunt worried Chase would relapse and fall back into his addiction.

Shelby touched his arm. "He's fine, Hunt. Mostly healed. He's been working at the ranch this past week, but not riding horseback or doing any heavy lifting until I tell him he can. He comes in for physical therapy at my office three days a week. I'm working with him on getting his strength back." As a physical therapist, if Shelby said Chase was better, she meant it.

Cyn had taken her seat and sipped a whiskey on the

rocks a waitress had dropped by while he and Shelby spoke. She looked both irritated and suspicious of him.

"What?" he finally asked, wondering what was going on in her head. The woman always looked one second away from raging at him and hell if he knew why. He hadn't done anything to her. Except issue her tickets when she broke the law. Otherwise he left her alone and hardly ever thought about her. Mostly. Because damn if she didn't pop up in his mind once in a while. Not that she'd know about it. He replayed the scene between Cyn and Rad a dozen different ways in his mind and he was always too late to stop the assault from happening.

Maybe she blamed him for not arresting Rad sooner for how he treated Angela. But damnit, he was restrained by the law. And if Angela refused to cooperate, she tied his hands and Rad got away with being an abusive ass-hole.

Now he was mad about his lack of action and Rad's continued bad behavior.

Cyn's gaze took nearly a full minute to rise to meet his. "I didn't say anything."

"You didn't have to," he shot back grumpily.

"Hey, I was just sitting here with my friend, minding my own business, getting the scoop on how hot things are with Shelby and her Wilde man, when that scum interrupted us. I didn't invite him over. I didn't provoke him. I didn't do a damn thing."

She shot back the rest of the whiskey and stood and faced Shelby. "Sorry my sister's dickhead ruined girls' night. I'll make it up to you. Let's call it a night and head home."

Shelby let out a disappointed sigh. "It's all right. I'm

sorry we didn't get to finish our conversation. I really did want to help take your mind off your sister's troubles."

"Is everything okay?" Hunt asked, concerned.

Cyn pressed her lips tight. "She lives with a self-centered jerk who doesn't care about her feelings and mistreats her. But she loves him," she gushed with a false saccharine lilt to her words.

"It's frustrating to see it happening to someone and they let it because they're either too afraid to do something about it and leave or they think they deserve it. You can't help someone if they aren't willing to help themselves." Hunt had felt that way when it came to Chase and his addiction.

"Yeah, well, I guess you see it a lot on the job. Still, I'd like to give her a big ol' shove out the door of that place and show her that she doesn't really love him. She's clinging to an illusion that will never be reality. He will never treat her the way she deserves to be treated because he is a piss-poor example of a man. And of course she chose badly, what with our own father running out on us. If you've never seen a good man, how the hell are you supposed to recognize one?" Cyn turned to Shelby. "They exist, right?"

Shelby smirked. "I found one. You will, too."

Hunt hooked his hands on his gun belt. "Take my advice. Steer clear of your sister's boyfriend, so you'll live long enough to find out."

Cyn walked right past him and said over her shoulder to Shelby, "I'll meet you at your truck."

Shelby gave him a sympathetic look. "See you soon."

He followed the two women out of the bar and caught up to Shelby. "Go home to Chase. I'll drive Cyn home."

Cyn glared at him like always. "The hell you will. I'd rather walk."

Hunt rolled his eyes. "I'm here," he told Shelby. "You've got a long drive out of town. Chase will be desperately waiting for you to get home."

Shelby blushed under the bar's neon lights. "I don't mind taking her."

"And now you're both talking about me like I'm not here."

Hunt turned to Cyn. "I'm just trying to do my brother a favor." There'd been some bad blood between them for a long time. Because of their mother. Because of Chase's addiction. But they were trying to move on from it. And Hunt wanted his brother to be happy, especially after how many times he'd nearly lost his life. If he'd died before Hunt fixed things, Hunt would have never forgiven himself.

Shelby made Chase happy, and so Hunt could do this small thing to get Shelby back to him tonight a little sooner rather than later.

"Fine," Cyn said, exasperated. "Go home to your Wilde man. We'll have lunch later this week."

Shelby embraced Cyn in a big hug. "He's a cop, doing his job. And a good man. He cares, even if he doesn't show it sometimes." Shelby released Cyn and walked past him with an all-too-knowing grin and a sparkle in her eyes that Hunt didn't even try to read.

"You coming?" Cyn called as she walked toward his patrol SUV.

He had a feeling he'd follow her into hell just to keep her from taunting the devil and getting herself into more trouble.

# Chapter Two

CYN SAT in the front seat of the patrol car for a change. Usually she ended up in the back seat. She ignored the big, broody man beside her, until he turned down the wrong street. "Where are you going? I thought you were taking me home?"

"I am. You live on Spruce. Right?"

"Uh, no." How did he know that? Probably from all the times he'd checked her driver's license to issue her a ticket. "I rented Shelby's old place."

He shot her a sideways glance. "Since when?"

"I moved in the week after your brother proposed to her."

"Oh."

She didn't know if that meant he was okay with her living there or not. And what did it matter? She loved the quaint little two-bedroom house. She could walk to work when the weather was nice. It was much quieter than her old apartment, where she could hear her neighbors arguing and fucking at the top of their lungs. And don't get her started on smelling everything everyone cooked, not to mention her chain-smoking pervert of a downstairs neighbor who liked to sit out in the court-yard and stare up at her through her window. Gross.

"Why did Rad come at you like that?"

"He was drunk tonight, but he's always stupid," she replied.

Hunt actually chuckled.

"I'm surprised you find that amusing. I thought you two were best buds." She didn't know how two men so different could be friends, especially when one was a cop and the other a rage-induced murderer-waiting-to-happen.

"I haven't hung out with Rad since I arrested him." Hunt rubbed his hand over the back of his neck. "Longer than that, really. The job makes people distance themselves. Ever since I became a cop, Rad looks at me like he's waiting for me to accuse him of something."

"Guilty people feel guilty sometimes, I guess. Though he doesn't seem to give a shit about how he treats my sister. Oh, sure, he apologizes up and down, but what good are words when you don't back them up? What the hell does a promise mean if you don't follow through? *Sorry* is just a word if you don't mean it."

"Tell me how you really feel."

"I don't say things I don't mean. I don't treat people like shit because I feel like it. I don't hit the people I care about. He's not a man, he's a little boy acting out, thinking he's big shit when he's less than most of us."

"How is your sister?" Hunt's voice was warm and coaxing.

"She's trapped and she doesn't even know it. Even more disturbing, she thinks she's in love. And it will only end one way. Badly. I just hope I get her out of there before it's too late."

"No one from the department has been called out there in a long time."

"Because the last time a cop showed up"—meaning him—"he beat my sister bloody. Worse than he ever hurt her before. I don't call the cops anymore. I go and pick her up and put her back together only to watch her go right back to him."

"Cyn." Just her name and the world of feeling he put behind it. Frustration. Resignation. Understanding. She hoped the regret she heard was genuine and he really did care about what happened to her sister.

She sighed. The whole situation made her tired. "I know Shelby is right. You did your job to the best of your ability, but that doesn't mean I'm not pissed off that when it comes to domestic abuse, the system works far better for the criminal than it does the victim all too often and the victim pays an even higher price. I'm tired of watching my sister suffer for what she thinks is love but is nothing more than that asshole tearing apart her heart and soul. Who my sister used to be is fading away. I don't think she even recognizes herself anymore.

"I know it's not her fault. He's made her afraid. She believes his lies that she's inadequate and does everything wrong. And if she's not good enough for him, she's certainly not good enough for anyone else. He made her believe that he's the only one who'll want her. I've tried so hard to erase that from her head, to show her that I love her more than anything. But she doesn't hear the words. She only hears him in her head now."

"I wish there was something I could do." Hunt pulled

up in front of her cute little home, the place she'd hoped her sister would come and live with her.

"I'm not sure there's anything anyone can do at this point. And right now, she's deep in depression and just existing day to day. I've tried to get her to go back to the doctor, but she won't." She shook her head. "Sorry. I'm sure you spend your day listening to other people's problems, you don't need me adding to it."

"It's okay." He shifted to face her across the console and the computer between them and studied her. "I've never seen you like this."

"That's because I'm usually a happy drunk. He killed my buzz, the asshole."

Hunt chuckled. The deep rumbly sound made her stomach flutter. And what the hell was that about? Obviously, she'd been without a man too long.

"I'm sure you'll go back to yelling at me the next time I catch you speeding."

Damn right. "You could just let me go, you know."

"What fun would that be? You're entertaining as hell when you're irritated and know you're in the wrong but want to get away with it anyway and think every man should let you."

"You're just not any man, are you?"

"No. It's my job to uphold the law. And I'll remind you, I did give you a warning."

"One time."

"A warning means consequences are coming the next time you do it."

"Ugh! You're irritating."

"You're obstinate," he shot back. "How do you and Shelby even know each other?"

Cyn sat up straight. "What? I'm not good enough for your brother's fiancée? Seems to me you didn't like her much either a while back."

"I always liked her," he corrected.

"You have an odd way of showing it."

"Things between Shelby and me got complicated because of Chase and her biological father. We're all good now. But you two seem so different from each other."

"We are. And we're not." She shot him an accusing glare. "She doesn't judge. She sees more than just the stupid things I've done." With that, she hopped out of the patrol car and headed for her front door.

Hunt's rich voice followed her, though she wanted to smack him upside the head for his words. "Don't forget to pay your speeding ticket. I wouldn't want to have to haul your ass off to jail."

She bet he was looking at her ass right now. No man could resist her in a tight little black leather skirt.

Though she doubted the by-the-book cop would ever admit to liking anything about her.

She kept walking, held up her hand and flipped him off.

"See you soon, Cyn."

They both knew it wouldn't be long before she was in trouble for something again. Sometimes she couldn't seem to help herself. She didn't apologize or feel the need to reel herself in when life was meant to be lived, not wasted.

She hoped her sister figured that out before it was too late.

# Chapter Three

❧

HUNT STOOD in Mrs. Phelps's kitchen, staring down at the eighty-three-year-old, who was sitting at the breakfast table holding an ice pack to her swollen face. He'd been called out for a home invasion and felt terrible seeing the poor elderly woman in such a state of panic.

She'd lost many precious items in the robbery.

At least she hadn't lost her life.

The asshole who broke in had pistol-whipped her.

Who does something like that to someone who looks so fragile a strong wind might blow her over? She used a walker, for goodness' sake.

This was the third home invasion in two weeks in Willow Fork. He'd gotten reports from surrounding towns that they'd also seen a rise in break-ins and small businesses being hit that dealt in a lot of cash.

"Won't you sit down? You're so tall, looking up at you is putting a crick in my neck."

Hunt pulled out the chair next to her and sat. He put his hand over hers on the table. "Are you up for answering some questions?"

"I'm old. Not feeble. Go on with you."

He grinned, liking her spunk. "How did the man get

into the house?" Hunt noticed no signs of forced entry on the front door. The one behind Mrs. Phelps looked to be in working order, too.

Mrs. Phelps bowed her head. "I met the mailman out front. Jim knows I can't make it to the end of the drive to get my mail, so he brings it all the way up to the house. It's quiet out here. No one else really comes around. I sometimes forget to lock the door." She fisted her hand and pounded it on her thigh. "I should have known better. My daughter has been begging me to come stay with her now that my husband is gone. She said I shouldn't be out here all alone. But this is my home. This is where I've lived for the past sixty years." She sighed with such anguish Hunt felt it roll off her. "He took my wedding ring."

She pulled the ice pack from her face and stared at her ringless hand. "After he knocked me down, he quickly went through the house, snatching up what few valuables I own. He found my jewelry box on the bedroom dresser and took the whole thing. I'd hoped to leave it to my daughter and granddaughter."

Hunt felt sick over her loss. "What else did he take?" Hunt wrote down the list of items Mrs. Phelps rattled off, her eyes misty with unshed tears.

"Before he left, he threatened to hit me again if I didn't tell him where I kept my money. I told him I didn't have anything more than what was in my purse in the kitchen." She notched her chin toward the coatrack beside the back door where her purse hung. Her wallet lay open on the hardwood floor. "He didn't believe me. I was lying on the floor just inside the front door where he'd left me after he hit me the first time. He kicked me in the thigh and asked about the money again." She pressed her lips tight. "I didn't want to tell him . . . but I did." She glanced at the empty coffee can and lid on the counter.

"How much was in the can?"

"Everything I'd saved for a rainy day and a trip to see my daughter and granddaughter. About twelve hundred dollars."

"How much was in your wallet?"

"Maybe forty dollars at most." She let out another weary sigh and hung her head. "What am I going to do now?"

"What do you want to do?"

"I don't want to leave my home. But I don't feel safe here anymore."

Hunt sympathized. He'd seen it a lot. When someone broke into a house, it made the residents feel violated and unsafe. Home was supposed to be where you could let your guard down. When that sense of security was taken away, it took a long time to get it back.

"I'm scared," Mrs. Phelps whispered. "I've never been hit before. It came out of nowhere. And what did I do that he needed to hit me like that?"

"Nothing," Hunt assured her. "And we will do everything possible to find the person who did this to you."

"He's a mean man." Mrs. Phelps shivered.

"Can you describe him for me?"

"Tall. Slim."

"How tall?"

Mrs. Phelps sized him up. "A few inches shorter than you. Not as wide in the shoulders. Lean. Not with all your muscles."

Hunt tried not to smile at Mrs. Phelps's gleam of approval that came into her eyes as she roamed her gaze over him.

"What color hair?"

"Not sure. He wore a black hooded mask with a white scary face on it."

"Like a ghost face?"

She nodded. "I guess that's what it was. Looked like a Halloween mask of some kind."

"It's a very popular one." Which meant he wouldn't get anywhere trying to trace it to a particular buyer. Other victims had reported the mask, too.

Mrs. Phelps filled in the other details. "He wore a black sweatshirt with a hood, black jeans, black boots and gloves. I don't know if he was white or something else. His voice just sounded like a man, but like he was trying to make it sound deeper." She shrugged. "That's not much help, is it?"

"If he wore gloves, we won't find any fingerprints. With the mask over his head, probably no stray hairs. He was careful."

"He's done this before."

Hunt nodded. "There have been other break-ins here and in other nearby towns. It sounds like the same guy." Hunt needed to check those other cases to see if the guy used a gun in every one and if he'd assaulted other individuals. Was the guy escalating? Breaking into occupied homes was a risk in and of itself. Why not wait for the occupants to leave? Then again, hitting a senior citizen's home probably felt like a low-risk opportunity.

"Put the ice back on your face," he coaxed, not liking the extensive bruising blooming on her face and around her eye. "I'll take a look around the house, see if I can find any clues." He doubted the guy had left any trace of himself behind, but Hunt would look and hope he found something, because he really wanted to get this guy.

Mrs. Phelps patted his hand. "Thank you for your help."

"I wish I could do more."

"You're here. You make me feel safe. The stuff I lost . . . Well, it's just stuff. Right? I have my memories. I'm thinking staying with my daughter isn't such a bad idea. I'd get to be with my granddaughter and make new memories with her."

"I think that's a great idea. I have a niece. Eliza. We have a weekly Pancake Tuesday breakfast, but I wish I had more time to spend with her."

"Make time. You never know when it's going to run out." She pointed to the goose egg on her head.

"You sure you don't want me to call an ambulance?"

"I can't afford one. I'm okay."

"Just to be sure, I'm going to take you to the emergency room myself. I'll bring you home, too."

"You're a good man, Officer Wilde."

"Would you like me to call your daughter and tell her what happened?"

She shook her head. "I'll do that while you look around."

Hunt grabbed the cordless phone from the kitchen counter and handed it to her. "I hate that this is what made you decide to go. I hope you'll be happy with your daughter and her family."

"I will be. It's been lonely here. I've just been stubborn

and a little scared of leaving what I've always known. But I know I'll be happy with them."

Hunt left Mrs. Phelps to make her call and looked around the house. The guy who did this was methodical. He started in the bedroom where he knew most people—women in particular—kept their jewelry and cash, though he'd been right in assuming a lot of people stashed cash in the kitchen. He'd left closets open. Probably looking for a hidden safe. The medicine cabinet was closed, but Hunt checked inside and found several pill bottles. The guy wasn't looking for drugs. He wanted the quick money. Cash and jewelry he could pawn or exchange at one of the many cash-for-gold businesses that had popped up everywhere over the last few years. Those places made it near impossible to track down stolen items.

Mrs. Phelps would probably never see her wedding ring or any of her other valuables ever again.

Unless Hunt tracked down the guy doing this and got to him before he had a chance to get rid of the evidence for the cash he really wanted.

Hunt made his way back to the kitchen, noting the intruder hadn't left any clues inside the house. He'd check for footprints out front.

Mrs. Phelps was just finishing up with her daughter. "Yes, I'm going to have my head examined. Officer Wilde is taking me. I'll call later to let you know everything is all right. Just like I said. I'm fine." Mrs. Phelps listened, then sighed. "I'm looking forward to seeing you, too, sweetheart." Her eyes glassed over. "Yes. The room sounds lovely. I'm sure I'll be very comfortable there. We'll talk tonight."

Mrs. Phelps ended the call and looked up at him.

"She and her husband renovated their house recently. They turned a downstairs living room into a bed and bath for me. They planned to ask me to move in again over Thanksgiving. I had no idea."

"They wanted to make sure you knew you were wanted and they had a place just for you." Hunt had moved out of the Split Tree Ranch main house and into one of the cabins on the property. He'd renovated it and made it his. But he missed seeing his dad and brother in the morning and at night and knowing they were right there if he needed them. He missed spending time with them.

Short-staffed and underfunded, the police department kept him working long hours, which meant he hadn't helped out on the ranch in too long to even remember the last time he did. He missed working alongside his brother Max and their dad.

The rift between him and Chase the last year hadn't helped.

But they were all trying to put the past behind them and move forward.

Still, Hunt spent more time in his patrol car and at the station than he did at his place. And he couldn't remember the last time he went on a date, let alone spent the night with a woman.

The closest thing was bringing Cyn home from the bar three nights ago. He could still conjure the memory of her in that tight leather skirt, hips swaying as she walked up to her door, and how she flipped him off. Perversely, he loved her sass and how she disliked him. He didn't really take it personally. She simply didn't like him imposing rules on her.

"You okay?" Mrs. Phelps asked. "You look like you'd rather be somewhere else, too."

Maybe with someone else. He wouldn't mind being wrapped up in some good trouble with Cyn, but that was never going to happen.

He didn't answer Mrs. Phelps. "Let's get you to the hospital and checked out." He grabbed her walker and helped her up. After he picked up her wallet, put it back in her purse and draped the bag over her shoulder, he walked with her to the front door and out onto the porch. "Did you happen to see what kind of car he was driving?"

Mrs. Phelps pursed her lips and looked off in the distance. "A gray four-door of some kind. I think it had a broken bumper. It hung kind of lopsided."

Hunt made note of it. "Give me a second before I help you to the car." He walked down the two porch steps and down the paved walkway to the dirt-and-gravel driveway. He spotted where the car had been parked and the deep grooves the tires left when the guy peeled out of the driveway. He had some tire impressions and one good shoe print. Maybe a work boot of some kind.

"Let me just take some pictures of this." He went to the back of his patrol car and pulled out a ruler. He laid it out next to the tire impression and took several close-ups of the tread marks. He did the same with the shoe impression. Then he took pictures of the wider view of the scene. He'd already photographed everything inside Mrs. Phelps's home. He'd add them all to her case file and hope he found some evidence that was tied to her assailant, so he could lock the guy up for hurting such a nice woman.

Finished with the task, he helped Mrs. Phelps down the steps and to his car. He made sure she was comfortable in the front seat and got behind the wheel.

He pulled out onto the main road and headed to the hospital.

"Are you married, Officer Wilde?"

"No. My older brother just got engaged," he offered, making small talk to take her mind off what happened to her.

"That's wonderful. I miss my husband something terrible. Especially now. It's a hard thing to lose someone you loved nearly your whole life."

"But what a gift to be with someone that long, too."

"Are you seeing someone?"

He shook his head, not wanting to think about his empty bed and lonely cabin.

"Find someone who gets you. Someone who makes you happy when you just look at them. Someone who takes care of you in small ways. Because I can tell you it's not the big things that you'll want back when they're gone, but the little things you'll miss. My husband used to bring me coffee in bed in the morning because he knew I was slow to rise and I liked that quiet time. He made sure my car always had gas, so anywhere I wanted to go, I was ready. And every night when we went to sleep, he'd hold my hand as he drifted off. Sometimes, I can feel his hand in mine when I lay in bed at night."

Hunt hoped one day he found a woman who wanted something as simple and meaningful as all that.

And damn if his gaze didn't go right to the purple-haired beauty walking down the street toward her hair salon. For whatever reason, she turned and stared at him, a look of horror on her face as he passed by.

He stopped at the light and Cyn ran up to the car and knocked on the glass on the passenger side.

He rolled down the window, but didn't get a chance to ask what she wanted when she blurted out, "You're arresting old ladies now?"

He scowled at her.

"Mrs. Phelps, what's happened?"

Mrs. Phelps patted Cyn's hand. "Oh, dear, I'm okay. Just some trouble at the house."

"What?"

Mrs. Phelps turned toward Cyn, and he saw the look of pain on Cyn's face when she spotted Mrs. Phelps's injury. "Oh my God."

Mrs. Phelps frowned. "Officer Wilde is taking me to the emergency room to get it looked at."

Cyn's gaze met his again, but she didn't look apologetic for accusing him of arresting little old ladies. "I see."

Hunt wondered if she'd ever see him as more than just a cop. "Light's green. Step back. We need to go."

Cyn put her hand over Mrs. Phelps's on the door. "Do you need me to drive you home after you see the doctor? I'd be happy to do it."

Hunt shook his head. "I'll stay with her at the hospital and make sure she gets home."

Cyn eyed him again, like she couldn't believe he'd do such a thing.

"Protect and serve," he said, reminding her of the police motto. And in a small town like this, everyone helped everyone out. And he was a nice guy. He wanted to see Mrs. Phelps home safe and sound.

"You let me know if you need anything," Cyn told Mrs. Phelps. "I'll call and check on you tomorrow."

"Thank you, dear. You've such a good heart."

Cyn backed away from the car, then stepped close again. "If you get called away for something and can't take her home, call me. I'll do it."

"Thank you. But my shift ends in half an hour, so it shouldn't come to that."

"But if it does . . ."

"Okay," he assured her. He liked seeing this compassionate side of her.

He waited for Cyn to move back onto the sidewalk before he pulled away.

"She's very pretty." Mrs. Phelps pointed out the obvious.

He wasn't blind. And he wasn't stupid enough to open this can of worms.

"Did you know she picks up several of us who don't drive anymore once a month and brings us down to the shop?"

That surprised him. "She does?"

"Yes. We all live alone. But she brings us together, so we can get our hair done up all nice and gossip together. It's very kind of her to think of us."

"Yes, it is."

"She takes care of people." Mrs. Phelps gave him a pointed look as he pulled into the emergency room parking area and shut off the car.

"I've issued her numerous speeding tickets, reprimanded her for jaywalking twice and pulled her out of two altercations at Cooper's. She looks at me and sees a badge and the guy who ruins all her fun. She's looking for a good time and I want . . . ." Her. But he said, "More." Because he didn't want some casual fun. He'd done that enough. He wanted someone to spend his off time with, his nights, someone he looked forward to being with at the end of a long shift. Someone who understood his job took a lot out of him, and wanted to make him feel good again after a long day. Someone like Mrs. Phelps described, who didn't sound like a description of Cyn. Though she was a beautiful, and apparently thoughtful and caring, woman.

She still wouldn't give him the time of day.

He'd be happy if she ever simply smiled at him.

But why would she? She didn't like him one bit.

"I think there's a spark there," Mrs. Phelps said, breaking into his thoughts. "You may not see it, but it's there."

"Everything I know about her says she's looking for a good time and nothing else."

"Are you sure about that? Maybe she just hasn't found the one who makes her want more. Everyone wants to be loved."

He thought of how happy Chase and Shelby were together with their little girl. Rehab, therapy and the right medication had saved his brother's life, but love had made him want to live and he was happier than Hunt had ever seen him.

Hunt felt as if his life had shrunk to endless days and a lot of nights filled with work and little else. He was tired and restless and wanting more.

He opened his car door and looked back at Mrs. Phelps. "Let's get you checked out and back home."

"All right. But just one more thing. If something

does come of that spark, don't try to tame her. Leave her wild, like she is. She'll make your life interesting and keep you on your toes. A man like you, steeped in responsibility, needs to cut loose once in a while. She'll help you do that and be happy about it. She'll remind you how to have fun."

Hunt couldn't remember the last time he'd had fun.

Cyn would probably laugh in his face if he asked her out on a date.

# Chapter Four

CYN PULLED into the driveway where her sister lived with Rad and immediately spotted his truck. "Damn my luck." She didn't want to get into anything with him. She just wanted to check on her sister and beg her one more time to leave the scumbag and come home with her.

It hadn't worked the first time Rad hit her, or the last time. Cyn didn't expect it to work today. But she'd keep trying and hoping that one day soon her sister chose a better life.

Which reminded her of her phone call with Mrs. Phelps this morning. She'd checked on her the last three days after her harrowing incident with the intruder in her home. She'd spent all those calls recounting how kind and wonderful Hunt had been to her.

Cyn had no reason to disagree that he'd been very helpful. It was his job, after all.

Still, she did give him credit for going the extra mile, not calling an ambulance that would have cost Mrs. Phelps an arm and a leg and probably her other foot to pay. He took Mrs. Phelps to the hospital himself. He'd stayed with her the whole time, and when the doctors gave her the all clear to return home, he drove her back.

Before he'd left, he'd checked all her doors and windows to be sure they were securely locked. And he'd even given her his cell number, just in case she got spooked or something happened.

Cyn wasn't immune to the man. His good deeds melted her heart.

She'd laughed out loud when Mrs. Phelps said, "You should climb that tall drink of water and guzzle him down."

It still made her smile.

But she'd told Mrs. Phelps, "The last thing I need in my life right now is a guy who thinks everything I do is scandalous, or at the very least too uncivilized for him."

"That man could use a reckless escape once in a while."

And that was the thing. She was tired of being someone's wild night.

She wanted to be someone's safe place.

Yes, she wanted passion and wild abandon, but she also wanted comfort and safety and someone to talk to and be with in quiet moments of togetherness. She wanted someone to binge-watch TV with and share a meal where they talked about their day. Someone she could tell all her hopes and dreams and who stood by her side while she made them a reality. Someone to tell her secrets to and know that he'd keep them for her.

Hunt was not that man.

Even if she had seen a different side of him.

He was her best friend's soon-to-be brother-in-law. There were rules against that. Right?

Didn't matter.

She wasn't interested.

*But you do think he's hot. That's why you're thinking about him.*

She hated that little voice in her head.

She liked it a lot better when it told her, *Chocolate cake for breakfast is perfectly fine.*

And what the hell did Mrs. Phelps know about men? She'd been married to the same one forever.

Cyn sighed. What would it be like to love someone so much you didn't want to spend a day without them?

Her sister opened the front door and stood there with her unhappiness showing in her dull eyes and barely believable grin.

Maybe you can't choose who you love, but you can live without them, especially when they ruthlessly treated you like crap and didn't deserve your love.

If she could get her sister away from Rad for a week, two, maybe it would be enough time for her sister to see that life didn't have to be this depressing and hard. Love should be easy. It should make you wake up happy to be with the person you get to be with one more day.

Cyn doubted Angela had woken up feeling that way today or at all in more than a year, and it broke Cyn's heart.

She climbed out of her car and met her sister at the porch. "Hey. Is the baby awake or asleep?" She really wanted to get her hands on her six-week-old niece.

"Asleep." Angela shrugged. "Sorry."

Disappointed, Cyn held up the box of fresh donuts she'd picked up on her way over. "Did you eat today?"

Angela's favorite treat brought another halfhearted smile to her sister's haggard face. "I had some cereal just before you arrived, but I'll definitely take one of those."

Rad came out of the house and up behind Angela and smacked her on the butt. "This gets any bigger you won't fit through the door."

Angela's gaze dropped to her feet.

"You're an asshole," Cyn spat out.

"What? She knows I'm kidding." Rad took the box from Cyn's hands.

She let him take it, angry that he made her sister feel bad about wanting a treat and making her think something was wrong with her shape. He should appreciate having a woman as kind and loving as her sister in his life. Instead, he shredded her self-confidence and made her sister try really hard not to care about anything so she didn't have to hurt. But it was always there now.

Cyn wrapped Angela in a hug and poured all her love into it, hoping it made a difference for her sister.

Angela held on to her for dear life. She hadn't done that in a long time. She was always so ready to let go and try to hide how she really felt. But Cyn felt her pain and anguish and a raw need to be held and comforted.

"I love you, sis. So much. I'm here for you. Come away with me."

"He'll never let me go now." Angela held on tighter. "I've been so stupid. I should have listened to you."

Cyn blinked back tears. "Then hear me now. You can come and stay with me. I will take care of you and the baby. You know I will. I want to. We can take care of each other. I need you, too."

Angela gripped Cyn's hair and turned her lips to Cyn's ear and whispered, "He's been leaving every

Monday and not coming home until late Tuesday night from his parents' place. Those are your days off, too, right?"

Cyn nodded.

"Be ready tomorrow. I'll call you when I'm ready to leave. It probably won't be until the afternoon. I'm never sure when he'll go or be back, but if we time it just right . . ."

"Let's do it right now," Cyn pleaded.

"It'll be better if he's not here. In town . . . at your place . . . he can't do what he does without someone seeing him there. Please, Cyn, trust me. This is the safest way. I can't risk—"

"Okay." Cyn held her sister tighter. "I'm so proud of you for making this really difficult decision. I know you've wrestled with it a long time."

"It's not just about me anymore."

"Everything will be better when you're away from here. I promise. And if he won't stay away, we'll make him." If she had to go to Hunt and beg him to help her get a restraining order, she'd do it. Though after seeing him with Mrs. Phelps and how he'd helped her, maybe she wasn't giving him enough credit for caring about the people he served.

She needed to find a good lawyer. Maybe Hunt could point her in the right direction for that, too.

She could ask Shelby to ask him for her.

Because ever since the other day when she ran up to his patrol car and discovered she'd completely made a fool of herself, and especially since her calls with Mrs. Phelps and what she said about Hunt, Cyn felt the need to show Hunt she wasn't who he thought she was.

And that could only mean one thing. She wanted him to like her.

And what the hell was that about?

Angela stepped back and waved her to come inside the house. "Stay a bit. I don't want him to get suspicious."

Cyn followed Angela into the house, noting the bottles by the sink, dishes in the strainer and the basket of folded laundry on the table. Her sister had come out of her funk and cleaned up since the last time Cyn was here. A good sign her sister's depression had waned.

She took a seat at the table across from Angela. Cyn couldn't help but glance at the haphazard stack of mail in front of her. The past-due notices interspersed with the junk mail caught her eye.

Rad walked up and dropped the donut box on top of the mail. Four donuts were missing from the box. He had glaze stuck to the corner of his mouth. "Nice of you to bring those." He sounded suspicious. "But you could have gotten more than just glazed ones."

"Those are Angela's favorites." *As in, I brought them for her, dumbshit.*

Cyn stood and went to the counter, grabbed a couple of paper towels off the roll, dropped one in front of her sister, placed a donut on it, then sat and did the same for herself.

"Make yourself at home," Rad bit out.

She glanced up at him. "I thought I was welcome in my sister's home?"

"This is my place. She lives here with me and follows my rules."

"Is there a rule against having company over?"

"Company is usually polite and minds their own business."

She cocked an eyebrow. "Have I not been polite? I brought my sister a treat for having me in her home."

He narrowed his gaze and seethed because she hadn't said *his* home.

"I've held my tongue and not said ninety-nine percent of what I'd like to say to you."

"I'd like to shut you up and put that devilish tongue to much better use."

Cyn sat back in the chair and glared up at him. "I'm confused. You say stuff like that, which makes me think you want to fuck me, but you're constantly antagonizing me and telling me to stay the hell away, like you can't stand me. So which is it? Because it's a real shit thing to want to fuck your girlfriend's sister, not to mention saying it right in front of her, even if you are thinking it. I mean, that's just not polite." And she'd rather swallow nails and be doused in acid than be with him.

"I don't have to like you to fuck you."

"Which proves my point that you don't give a shit about Angela. I respect and love my sister. The last thing I would ever do is have sex with her man. But let's get one thing straight. I would never, ever, invite you to put a hand on me. I would rather—"

"Be set on fire," he bit out, fury in his eyes. "Yeah. So you've said, you stuck-up bitch."

"I'm glad we're clear on that." She took a bite of her donut, not taking her eyes off him. She wanted it to look like she didn't care, but her heart pounded in her chest. She'd really made him angry and maybe poking the rattlesnake was not a good idea, but she loathed him so badly she couldn't help herself.

"Careful, Cyn, or you'll get what's coming to you and I will burn your ass."

Angela had sat across from them, perfectly still and watchful, but the threat made her lean forward. "Aren't you supposed to be at work soon?"

"Should you be telling *me* what to do?"

"I didn't," her sister quickly said, lowering her head.

Rad snatched the donut box, grabbed his keys and walked out the front door, slamming it so hard the picture on the wall rattled.

She and Angela sat in silence until they heard Rad's truck start up and him peel out of the driveway.

"Well. That went well." Cyn sighed out her relief that he left. "At least we didn't have to call the cops this time."

Angela traced her fingers along the wood grain on the table. "You shouldn't taunt him like that."

"I stated the facts. But he's got his own version of reality going on in his head."

Angela looked directly at her. "I don't want anything to mess up my plan for tomorrow."

Neither did Cyn. "Do you want to load some things into my car right now?"

Angela shook her head and started bouncing her leg on her toes beneath the table. A habit she started after the anxiety kicked in, living with Rad. "I want to do it all last-minute. I don't want him to suspect anything. He comes home and it's like he sees every little thing I've done. Or haven't done," she added, biting her thumbnail.

Cyn didn't want to push. This was the first time her sister had ever agreed that she needed to get out of here.

That she had some sort of a plan already in mind bolstered Cyn's excitement that this was finally happening.

Angela could finally live her life the way she wanted to live it and not be stuck under Rad's thumb. She and the baby would be safe.

"I don't have any money," Angela blurted out.

"I've got you covered," Cyn assured her sister.

"I don't want to be a burden."

"You won't be. You're not. I make decent money and I've been saving up. I can't wait for you to see my new place. It's two bedrooms. The one you'll be in was my friend Shelby's nursery for her daughter, Eliza. There are cute woodland creatures on the walls in different places so that it looks like they're popping out of a baseboard or walking across a bookshelf. If you don't like it, we can change it. Shelby told me to make the place my own. The crib is still in there, and I've added a double bed and a dresser. It's not much, but we'll get you whatever you need."

"I don't want you to have to support me."

"It's only until you're back on your feet again. For right now, I'm here to help. You'll have the rest of your life to pay me back, though I don't expect you to, Angela. You're my sister. More than anything I want you to be safe and happy. And you will be with me."

Silent tears slipped down Angela's cheeks. "You've been begging me to do this for so long."

"It's okay," Cyn assured her. "You weren't ready."

"I was an idiot thinking he'd change."

"I'm sorry you had to learn the hard way that people are who they are. Believe me, I've been disappointed, too, by someone I thought I could trust or possibly love or wanted to be my friend. It's not easy to give up on hope that they will be the person we thought they'd be."

"I thought he'd surprise me." The wistfulness in Angela's voice broke Cyn's heart because she wanted her sister to be loved. She wanted Rad to have been the guy who changed because she mattered enough to him to do it.

She thought of Hunt, the guy who always seemed hell-bent on laying down the law, but who turned out to have a real heart and genuine concern for others, even if the law sometimes got in his way of helping in the way she'd needed his help.

Damn. *Why do I keep thinking about him?*

Mrs. Phelps had planted that little seed in her head and the damn thing was sprouting, trying to show her that there were more layers to Hunt than an onion.

She didn't want to like him.

She just wanted him to help her sister.

Angela fidgeted. Her leg was still bouncing under the table. "You should get to work. I need to decide what I'm taking and what I can just leave. I want to be out of here quickly once he's gone tomorrow."

"If you want to walk out with nothing but your purse, I'm happy to buy you whatever you need so long as you never come back here to him. And he's going to try to make you come back. Oh, he'll say some pretty words and make you promises, but he won't mean them, Angela. You have to know that by now."

"I do."

"Good. Because then he's going to threaten you. And I want you to know that I'm ready to hire an attorney. We can file for a restraining order."

"I just want to leave and be done with it."

"I know. But he's not going to let you do that, not without us fighting him every step of the way. And we will. Together. I promise you won't have to do this alone."

Angela stood and so did Cyn. They met in the middle and shared another big hug. Angela buried her face in Cyn's neck. "Thank you. I love you so much. I don't know what I'd have done these last many months if I didn't have you checking on me, making sure I was all right and always reminding me that someone really did care about me. I mean, Mom is not very . . . motherly. She's kind of useless when it comes to us and what we need."

"I will always come for you. I will always be there for you. You are never alone."

Angela hugged her tighter. "I have the best sister ever."

Cyn couldn't wait for Angela to move in with her tomorrow. She didn't expect it to be easy. Rad would put up a fight. Cyn would be ready for him. She'd done her homework. When a domestic abuse victim left, it could be the most dangerous time in the relationship.

They'd do it while Rad was away.

They needed to be very careful tomorrow and get away clean.

There was too much at stake now. Lives were on the line.

And maybe she needed to take her own advice and ask for help.

# Chapter Five

Hᴜɴᴛ ᴅʀᴏᴠᴇ by Jerry's Body Shop, where Rad had worked since high school. Even as a kid, his buddy had loved to tinker with engines. Rad had helped Hunt out with the equipment on the ranch and his own vehicles over the years, and Rad had started working there as a teenager.

Rad wasn't a bad guy back in the day. He could be a hothead, sure. But he hadn't been abusive. Not the way he was with Angela. There was a time when, because he'd always had to be in control, he'd generally held it together. But this was another level of violence altogether.

Hunt needed to face the fact that his friend had serious issues.

No one in the department had been called out to the house for another domestic disturbance call in a while, but Cyn told him Rad took out his frustration and anger on Angela after the arrest. It turned his gut sour. So he was stopping in to check on Rad and see if he could get a read on how things were going now. He didn't like that Angela, especially, and Cyn were in danger every time Rad couldn't control himself.

He parked around back of the shop where they kept

customers' cars until they worked on them. He stepped out of his vehicle and headed for the big open bay door, but something caught his attention. Parked behind Rad's truck, Hunt spotted a tilted back bumper on a silver car. He backtracked to take a look, something in his gut telling him this could be the car Mrs. Phelps had seen when she'd been pistol-whipped and robbed.

"What are you doing?" Rad asked, coming up behind him.

Hunt barely spared Rad a glance before he walked to the driver's side door and peered into the vehicle. He didn't see anything incriminating. That would be too easy. "Whose car is this?"

"I'd have to check the sheet."

"Do you know how long it's been here?"

"I parked it back here a few days ago."

"And no one's driven it since?"

Rad shrugged. "As far as I know, it's been sitting right there where I left it. What's this all about? Why are you so interested in this car?"

Hunt noted the uneasy look about Rad and wondered why he was being so cooperative when last they'd seen each other he'd wanted to give Hunt a good ol'-fashioned beat-down for breaking the bro code and not having his back.

Hunt rubbed his hand over the back of his tense neck. "A witness saw a car like this one at her home when she was robbed."

Rad stuffed his hands in his front pockets and shifted his weight side to side, his voice rising when he said, "There's probably a dozen cars just like this one in town."

"Probably," Hunt agreed. A gray or silver four-door sedan was too common, but the broken bumper made Hunt believe he might have found the right vehicle. It may not be conclusive, but he felt like he was on to something. "Mind if I take a look inside?"

"Not my car, man. You'll have to get the owner's permission. Or a warrant," Rad added, like that sounded like the better idea.

Hunt grew more suspicious of Rad's odd behavior. He hadn't even asked why Hunt was here. "Can I get the owner's information?" He could look it up using the vehicle plate and registration, but he wanted to see if Rad would give it to him.

Rad took a minute to think about it, then shrugged. "Let me ask Jerry if he's cool with that."

"Okay."

Rad frowned and turned to the garage bay. "You look like shit," he tossed out.

"Thanks. I feel like it. I've been on duty nearly twenty-four hours." One of the guys' wives had gone into labor and he'd covered his shift, then there was a four-car accident that took forever to clear.

Rad walked up to a bearded, potbellied guy in grease-stained coveralls. "Jerry. Cops want to check out that silver Honda out back with the busted bumper. Can I give him the owner's information?"

Jerry wiped his hands on a rag and looked Hunt up and down. "Got a warrant?"

"No." Hunt waited, noting Jerry just wanted to push back against the law coming into his place of business. He got the same reaction all the time from people who felt like the cops were trampling their civil liberties. All

Hunt wanted to do was uphold the law and keep the peace.

Rad continued to act all jumpy. Maybe because of the arrest, Rad didn't know how to act around him anymore.

"Owner's name is Steve Thompson. Lives out on Deer Oaks Drive." Jerry dismissed him and bent over the car he'd been working on when they walked in.

"Any idea how the car got damaged?" Hunt spoke to Jerry's back.

Jerry didn't bother to turn around, but answered, "Got rear-ended in a parking lot."

"And he was okay leaving the car here for days?" Most people needed their car and didn't want to wait days to get it back. They hadn't even started working on it.

Jerry turned around, clearly exasperated by the conversation. "His wife is a writer and works from home. He said he'd use her car until I fixed his. Said he wasn't in a rush when I told him I had several other vehicles ahead of his." Jerry shrugged. "It's not like there's a lot of places around these parts to get it fixed, so he was happy to leave it with me. I'm busy because I'm good." With that, Jerry turned his back and dismissed him again. "Get back to work on that tire rotation, Rad."

Rad walked over to the car up on the lift.

Hunt followed. "How's Angela?"

"Same as always."

That didn't really answer Hunt's question.

"Probably telling her sister a bunch of lies as we speak. I hate it when those two get together. That bitch Cyn is always filling Angela's head with ideas about leaving. That's not going to happen. Not now. Angela knows her place. She knows what'll happen if she steps out of line."

"What will happen?"

Rad seemed to suddenly comprehend he wasn't spouting off to a friend but a cop. "Nothing. Stay out of my fucking business. You've made it clear we aren't friends anymore."

"*You* broke that bond when you gave me no choice but to be a cop instead of your friend."

"Yeah, well, you've got no cause to be sniffing around me. What the hell are you even doing here?" Finally, Rad asked the question Hunt expected him to ask the second he saw him.

"I came to see if the guy who used to be my friend had come back. But it feels like he's gone for good. And it's too bad. Because I liked that guy. And Angela deserves better than what you've become."

Rad fisted his hands at his sides and squared off with Hunt. "You don't know anything."

"I know beating up your girlfriend, scaring her, making her feel less than, is the lowest thing a man can do."

"What did you say?" Jerry asked, standing by the other car, pointing at Hunt with a wrench in his hand.

Rad glared at Hunt. "You just had to run your fucking mouth."

Jerry took a menacing step forward. "You hit that sweet woman?"

"Angela is fine," Rad assured his boss. "It's not like what happened to your daughter."

"No?" Jerry asked, taking another step closer. "You didn't get angry and take your frustrations out on her?

Did you leave bruises on her? Did she bleed? What could she have possibly done to make you do something like that to her?"

"We argued. It got out of hand." Rad read Jerry's simmering rage and rightfully kept his answers short, so as not to antagonize the man.

Hunt readied himself to intervene.

"Some women are filled with passion and fire. They can be wild with it." Jerry seemed to appreciate those traits.

Hunt thought of Cyn, not Angela, when he heard those words. Angela was softer, quieter. Which made Hunt believe that even if Angela had tried to stand up for herself, she still wouldn't have been a match for Rad's temper. Not the way Cyn could hold her own against him. He wondered if he hadn't been there that day he arrested Rad if Cyn would have hit Rad back for daring to touch her.

Angela probably would have tried to protect herself, but he doubted she would have fought back. Not like Cyn.

And that wasn't a recrimination against Angela. She knew how to survive. That took its own kind of strength.

Jerry's voice turned deceptively soft yet determined. "Men should appreciate a woman's spirit. They should worship a woman for their comfort, caring and strength. A man is luckiest and blessed when a woman allows them into their heart and their arms. Women hold men up, and we should never tear them down for doing so."

"Jerry. You don't know what happened. Angela and I are good together. She loves me. You know that. You've seen her with me."

"I saw my Katie with the man who said he loved her.

But I didn't see the truth she tried so hard to hide from me because she was scared and ashamed." Jerry turned thoughtful. "And now I remember Angela, standing in here with you, her eyes downcast, her fake smile falling when you spoke for her instead of letting her talk." Jerry shook his head and pointed the wrench at Rad. "I see you now. And you're not welcome here anymore. Collect your things. I'll pay you what you're owed. You're fired." With that, Jerry turned and walked into the nearby office.

Rad turned on Hunt. "You fucking asshole. Look what you've done. Arresting me wasn't enough, now you got me fired."

Hunt had tried to keep his conversation with Rad private, but in the huge open room, voices carried. "I didn't mean for that to happen. I just wanted to see if everything between you and Angela was better and know that she was safe with you."

"Safe. How am I supposed to pay the rent and buy food when I don't have a job? Things were already tight. I've been trying to get some money together— You know what? Fuck you. You ruined everything. Again." Rad stalked off to the office, presumably to collect his final check.

Hunt left, not wanting to make things worse. And he needed to get an address on Steve Thompson and check out the story about the car. Because that was his job. Trying to fix things with Rad and assuaging his guilt about getting him fired seemed like a lost cause, and Hunt would have to live with it.

# Chapter Six

---

Lyn LOCKED the front door of the salon and headed down the street toward her house. She loved that she could walk to work, though tonight the weather was chillier than she expected. She pulled her sweater around her and stared up at the setting sun, wishing she had someone to help warm her up when she got home. Unfortunately, she'd been going home to an empty house for a long time now.

She could go to Cooper's and see if there were any hot cowboys looking for a good time, but she'd done that often enough to know it was fun in the moment, occasionally ended with sex, but rarely started something worth holding on to for even a few months.

She wanted something real. Something solid. Something that would last.

That led to several blocks of imagining walking up to her door, opening it and seeing the man she loved at home waiting for her with a smile and kiss that buckled her knees.

Wouldn't that be nice?

But when she opened her door and stepped inside her cute little rented house, the only thing that greeted her was silence.

"I need to get a cat," she grumbled to herself. At least she'd have something to come home to.

But then she let herself feel the excitement she'd put off all day. Tomorrow, her sister would move in with her, filling the house with love and laughter and a sense of home Cyn had been missing for a long time.

She hadn't let herself think too much about Angela today while she cut, curled, dyed and primped her customers' hair, because in the back of her mind lingered the niggling feeling things were going to fall apart. Again. Angela had made noises before about leaving Rad. Granted, this time she sounded sincere and ready, so Cyn remained cautiously optimistic. But she knew not only could Angela back out, but Rad could do something to stop Angela from leaving. What if Angela gave herself away tonight or in the morning before Cyn got there?

Cyn stopped herself from letting those thoughts choke her with fear and spin out until she was a mass of anxiety.

"It's going to be okay," she said to the empty room, catching herself. "Great. I'm talking out loud to myself now."

It wasn't like she didn't talk to people all day. She was hardly ever alone at work. But it wasn't the same as having someone in her life to share her hopes and dreams and fears. Because right now, she was terrified something bad would happen when Angela left Rad.

She dumped her purse on the table by the sofa and pulled out her phone. She hoped Shelby wasn't in the middle of dinner or putting her little girl down to bed, but took a chance and called her.

"Cyn! It's so good to hear from you."

Relieved her friend was happy for the call, Cyn blurted out, "I need to ask you something."

"Sure. Anything."

"Are you comfortable giving me Chase's brother's cell number? I need his help."

"I'm sure Max would love to help you. Is there something that needs to be fixed at the house?"

"No. The house is perfect. Everything I wanted in a new place. But it's not Max I need to talk to, it's Hunt."

"Oh. Um. I thought maybe you didn't like him. Is everything okay?"

She didn't want her friend to think she didn't like Shelby's future brother-in-law. "I like him. Well, I don't really know him. But I don't dislike him." She was talking too fast. "I need his help with my sister, but I don't want to officially call the cops. But I need a cop. I know that doesn't make sense, but . . . I don't know. Maybe it's too much to ask. I'm probably making something into nothing and everything will be fine. But it would be nice to have some backup. And I thought maybe he could, you know, stand there with that intimidating look on his face and make sure everything is okay. I mean, I just want Angela out of there. And get her over here. So maybe he could do that." She sounded like a lunatic.

Shelby paused for a moment, then said, "Cyn. Hunt is a good man. He will help you. All you have to do is ask."

"You're sure? Because I don't think he likes *me*. I'm pretty sure he thinks I'm off my rocker." The scene with her accusing him of arresting old ladies and acting like a maniac in front of Mrs. Phelps played in her mind.

"I'm sure that's not the case. I just sent you his contact information."

Cyn's phone beeped with the incoming text. She sighed with relief.

"Call him. If he can't help because of work or something, you let me know and I'll ask Max to help you out. If this is about your sister, I don't want you going there alone. I know it's usually fine, but still I'd feel better knowing you've got someone there just in case something goes wrong."

"Thank you, Shelby. I really appreciate this."

"You might let Hunt know you appreciate his help instead of glaring at him all the time because he wrote you a ticket."

"Many, many tickets. The man never lets me off with a warning."

"Did he *ever* give you a warning?"

Cyn glared at her phone before reluctantly answering, "Yes."

Shelby chuckled. "Stop driving like you're in NAS-CAR."

"Whatever. I can't help it. And now that I walk to work most days, I've gotten less tickets."

"Didn't you get one like three months ago for doing ninety-something on the freeway?"

She ignored that altogether. "Are we still on for lunch on Wednesday?"

Shelby chuckled. "Of course we are."

Cyn grinned. She really loved talking to Shelby. It was so easy to open up and just be herself. "Thank you again. You're the best."

"Be safe."

Cyn saved Hunt's contact card, debated for a moment whether to simply text him or call him. In the end, she decided that something like this required her to actually speak to the man.

She put the call through and waited, holding her breath, unsure if he'd even speak to her, let alone help her. Three rings in, she thought maybe she'd get voice mail, but then he answered.

"What do you want?" Hunt grumbled in that deep sexy voice of his that always sounded irritated when he spoke to her.

She wished he didn't sound so displeased to hear from her.

"Hello. Who is this?" This time he sounded half-asleep.

"Hey, Wilde. It's Cyn. Are you sleeping?"

"Not anymore," he grumbled again. "What time is it?"

She checked her phone, wondering why he didn't do the same. "Six twenty-two."

"Why are you calling so early?" He slurred the words like he really wasn't awake.

"It's the evening."

"It is?"

"Yes."

"Sunday evening?"

"Yes," she said impatiently. "Wake up. I need to talk to you."

"How did you get my number? Never mind. Shelby." Well, he was starting to be coherent.

"Why are you asleep? Are you sick?"

"I just got off a twenty-six-hour shift an hour ago."

He groaned, obviously unhappy to have been woken up after so little sleep.

"Oh. I'm sorry. I didn't know. I'll call you back in the morning." She was about to hang up when she heard her name.

"Cyn." The deep resonance of it made her go still and focus on him on the other end of the line. "I'm awake. Obviously you called for a reason. Are you okay? Can I help you?"

She found some deeper meaning in those questions because the voice inside her spoke up, saying, *No, I'm not okay. I'm lonely. And yes, I need your help. I want you to make everything all right again. I want you to make Angela safe again. The way you make me feel safe right now.*

*I'm really fucking going crazy.*

"Cyn. You there? You're starting to worry me."

"Um. Sorry. This isn't as easy as I thought it would be."

"Just talk to me."

What a wonderful idea to just lay her problems out for him. Deep down, she felt like just telling him everything would make it all feel better, or at least like she didn't have to carry the load all by herself.

"I . . . It's not easy for me to ask for help." She wasn't sure how to begin. "Angela is going to leave Rad tomorrow. He usually spends time at his parents' place on Monday and Tuesday, so Angela thinks it's the best time to get away without a confrontation. The plan is that she'll call me as soon as he leaves and I'll drive out to pick her up and bring her to my place. I was wondering if you'd meet me there just in case."

"Fuck. I wasn't thinking after I left Rad this afternoon. I'd been on duty for more than the double shift they put me on."

"What are you saying? You saw Rad today? About what?"

"It's not important why I was there, but that while we talked, his boss overheard me asking after Angela and telling Rad that he ruined our friendship because of how he treated your sister. Apparently his boss's daughter had been in an abusive relationship and his boss got pissed that Rad had mistreated Angela, so he fired him on the spot."

"What? When?"

"Today."

"What time?"

"I don't know. Around two, I guess."

"I have to go. There's no telling what he did to her when he got home." She didn't think. She just hung up, dialed her sister's cell, grabbed her purse and ran out the door. She had her keys in her hand the second an incoming call interrupted her sister's voice mail message. She ignored it, knowing Hunt was calling her back. She jumped into her car and left her sister a voice mail. "Angela, it's me. Call me back right now!"

She hung up and called again.

She peeled out of her driveway and headed out of town like the NASCAR driver Shelby accused her of driving like, headed straight for her sister, ignoring the incoming calls and texts from Hunt.

The drive seemed to take forever. She got her sister's voice mail six times before she gave up, pushed the gas pedal to the floor and tried to hold herself together and brace herself for whatever she found when she got to Rad's place.

HUNT SWORE, JUMPED out of bed naked, pulled on a pair of worn jeans, a T-shirt he picked up off the floor that probably needed to be washed, and stuffed his bare feet into his work boots. He ran through the house, grabbed his wallet and keys off the table and made it out the door in record time. He climbed into his truck, tore out of his driveway, still trying to call Cyn, but the damn woman wouldn't pick up.

He hated to think the worst, that she'd barge in on Rad and Angela and discover her sister had been hurt because Hunt was a dumb shit. He'd been so exhausted he'd never even thought Rad would head home, pissed off, and be looking for someone to take it out on.

He smacked his hand on the steering wheel when he got Cyn's voice mail again. He needed to beat her there, but doubted he could. Not the way Cyn drove like a bat out of hell on a normal day.

This was anything but a typical situation.

He'd be glad to see her in one piece and not roadkill because the woman didn't know the meaning of slow down.

The drive took an eternity. All he wished was for her to be safe and unharmed and that they got Angela out of there before things got worse.

CYN JUMPED OUT of her car the second she slammed it into Park and shut off the engine. She ran for the porch steps and burst into Rad's house without knocking.

"Angela! Angela, where are you?" She didn't see her

in the kitchen and turned to the living room, the sound of the TV drawing her attention, but it was Rad rising from the couch, a half-empty bottle of whiskey in front of him, his eyes dark with fury.

"What the hell are you doing here?"

She ignored him, turned for the hallway, looking through every open door until she reached the master bedroom and rushed in, hoping to find her sister but not seeing her. She looked at the open closet, the dresser, into the bathroom, and didn't see any sign of her sister packing anything to leave.

He didn't know.

At least she hoped not.

But where was her sister?

Driven by fear and fury, she rushed back into the living space and found Rad standing between the kitchen and living room. "Where is she?" This time she noted the scratch marks welling with dried blood on the side of his neck. It looked like her sister had raked her fingers over his skin. "What did you do to her?"

"Get out!" Rad bellowed at her.

"Where is she?" The desperation clawing at her insides sprang up as tears in her eyes.

Something feral came over Rad and he stalked toward her, his mouth drawn back in a snarl. He hooked one hand at the back of her head, braced his other arm against her chest, shoved her back into the entry wall and held her there, his face inches from hers. "I am so fucking tired of you coming in here making demands. She's not here. And if you don't leave, you'll join her where she is."

She sucked in a gasp, surprised he'd say such a thing,

but hearing the truth in his words all the same. The tears fell despite the rage exploding inside her.

Rad turned as a truck came to a jarring stop in the driveway, the headlights spotlighting them. He pulled her close. "You fucking called the cops. Again." He shoved her into the wall again and her head smacked against the drywall and bounced back, making her see stars for a second. "If you don't get rid of him right now, you'll never find her."

"Just tell me where she is? Is she okay?"

"Fix this, and maybe I'll tell you." He shoved her toward the door.

She had no choice and let her fury fly at the wrong man. "You did this," she accused Hunt.

He abruptly stopped in his tracks the second her words hit him. "Are you okay? Your head . . ."

"She's fine," Rad said. "She was just leaving."

Hunt pinned Rad in a death glare. "I wasn't talking to you."

She turned to Rad and did something she never thought she'd do with any man. She begged. "Please. What happened? Tell me where she is." She could feel Hunt come up behind her.

Rad looked past her at Hunt. "I arrived home this afternoon, thinking my girlfriend would be here waiting for me, ready to sympathize about how *you* got me fired," Rad seethed. "But did she sympathize? Did she console me? Did she offer any kind words of encouragement that everything would be all right?"

"What did you do?" Hunt asked.

"*Me?* What did *I* do? How about what *she* did?" Rad took a menacing step closer to Cyn and stared down into her eyes. "Your bitch of a sister didn't do anything. She just sat there looking at me like it was all my fault. Like I deserved it. For what? Putting her in her place when she got out of line or fucked something up? Again. Because a guy who used to be my best friend betrayed *me*? Not once, but twice." Rad pinned Hunt in his gaze, then turned that hate-filled gaze back on her.

"What did you do?" She repeated Hunt's question on a breathless whisper.

Rad didn't answer the question. "She should have known better."

Those ominous words froze Cyn's heart and she knew that terrible thing she'd always feared had come true.

Rad nodded at her like he'd read her mind. "She never did anything right. She wanted a fight. She got one." Rad's seething gaze went to Hunt. "So you'll get the fuck out of here, my official statement is this . . . We had an argument. Things got heated." Rad turned so Hunt could see the scratch marks on the side of his neck and jaw. "She left and she's not coming back."

Cyn turned to Hunt. "She wouldn't just leave. Not alone. She'd come to me. She was supposed to come to me. We had a plan."

Rad folded his arms over his chest and glared at her, but didn't say anything. He didn't have to. He knew. Whatever argument he had with Angela had ended with her telling him she was leaving.

And oh God . . .

Cyn bent at the waist, feeling her sour gut pitch with the god-awful truth.

She was never going to see her sister again.

She whipped her head up and pinned Hunt in her gaze. "Arrest him. He killed my sister."

Sympathy warmed Hunt's blue eyes. "We will start searching for Angela immediately," he promised her.

"Arrest him. Make him tell you where he hid her body."

Rad held his arms out wide and silently dared Hunt with a go-ahead look.

"Cyn, I . . ."

She slammed her hands against his chest. "Arrest him!"

Hunt took her face in his hands and held her still. "I can't."

She shoved him away from her. "You won't."

Rad actually came to Hunt's defense. "He can't because there's no evidence I did anything wrong. As you can see, her car is gone. She left."

"You killed her!" Cyn tried to go after Rad, but Hunt wrapped his arms around her middle and held her back.

"Stop," he ordered, his lips pressed to her ear. "This is not the way to do this."

"If you won't do your fucking job, then I'll see justice done my way." She struggled to get free of Hunt's hold but he was just too strong.

Rad sneered at her. "Careful, Cyn. I might take that as a threat and file charges against you."

She stopped fighting Hunt's hold and looked Rad in the eye. "You will pay for this. I will find them."

Hunt went still at her back. "Them?"

Rad's gaze narrowed. "She's mine."

Cyn gave him a very insincere smile. "Prove it. I

made sure Angela never put your name on the birth certificate. With your record for assault, the numerous domestic dispute calls the police were called here for and the fact that you're now unemployed . . . I'll have no trouble getting custody of her."

"Did you and Angela have a baby?" Hunt asked, putting the pieces together. "When?"

"Six weeks ago," Cyn answered, never taking her eyes off Rad. "And this asshole spent the last six weeks angry that Angela was exhausted, suffering from postpartum depression and doing her best to take care of an infant on her own because he couldn't be bothered to lift a finger to help."

Hunt had loosened his grip on her, though he still held her against him. Maybe to offer comfort that right now she didn't want because she was too angry and devastated and anxious to know where Rad took her niece because while she believed him capable of killing Angela, she didn't want to think him so callous, coldhearted and evil that he'd kill an innocent baby.

"Where is she?" Her voice went raw, she screamed it so loud.

Rad shrugged. "Maybe she's with Angela. Maybe she's somewhere else. Either way, it's none of your fucking business where my kid is."

Cyn tried to go after him again, but Hunt held tight and lifted her right off her feet. She kicked and squirmed and tried with all her might to get loose.

"Stop it, Cyn. You're not going to get what you want this way. He wants you to do something stupid so I'll have no choice but to arrest you."

"She kicked an officer of the law," Rad pointed out.

"I'd say assaulting an officer is a serious offense. One you should absolutely arrest her ass for and take her the fuck away from me."

"See?" Hunt whispered in her ear. He let her go, turned her to face him and pulled her back and away from Rad. "You're too smart to fall for his game. We need to do this the right way so that he pays for whatever it is he did."

"He killed her and took the baby somewhere. Probably his parents' place."

"I'll have an officer go there and do a well-check, then. We'll file a missing person report on your sister and start investigating. We'll find the evidence we need to put him away."

"You want me to just leave here without knowing anything?"

He gave her a pained look. "I wish I could get you the answers, but he's not going to just admit what he did. He is the baby's father. We have to assume either your sister did leave and took the baby with her, or more likely he did something to your sister and took the baby to someone who would take care of her. But until we have proof, we can't arrest him. Not on a hunch."

"Lana," Cyn told him. "Her name is Lana Joy *Wilson*." Not Harmon, like Rad.

He cupped her face again, swiped his thumbs across her wet cheeks and stared into her eyes. "I won't stop until I find them."

She didn't like the idea of leaving without answers and Rad behind bars, but she did believe Hunt would live up to his name and do everything in his power to find her sister and niece.

"Fine. But you have to send someone to his parents'

house. If I know the baby is okay, maybe I'll be able to breathe without feeling like I'm drowning."

Hunt hugged her to his chest and pulled out his phone.

Rad paced back and forth by the porch, unable to hear them from where Hunt had pulled her down the driveway.

"Hey, it's Hunt." He paused to listen. "Yeah, I know I'm supposed to be off duty and sleeping."

That reminded Cyn that he'd been up more than twenty-four hours. He had to be exhausted. And now that she checked his haggard face, he looked it.

"I need a well-check on the Harmon family out on Pinecrest Road. Specifically, I'm looking for a six-week-old baby girl named Lana Wilson. If she's not there, interview the Harmons and anyone else on the property to determine when they last saw their grand-daughter. If Lana is not there, we'll need a missing person report and possibly an AMBER Alert for her. I believe the father, Rad Harmon, may have harmed or killed the mother, Angela Wilson. I want a BOLO put out on her, her vehicle, and a missing person's case opened. She's been missing since around three p.m. this afternoon. She drives an old green Subaru Outback. You'll find the details in the system. I'll send over photos of Angela and Lana in a few moments. I want this spread throughout the state ASAP to all law enforcement. I don't think Lana's been taken out of the state."

Neither did Cyn. Rad hadn't had enough time to drive that far and come back and be here when Cyn arrived.

She appreciated that Hunt had taken charge, thought

things through, even on no sleep, and was doing something to help her.

"I want an officer out at Rad's place." Hunt rattled off the address. "Because of my personal involvement, I'll leave it to one of the other officers to question him about his girlfriend and daughter's disappearance. Expect him to be uncooperative."

Hunt listened for another minute or so, making Cyn's insides tense with anticipation. She just wanted this to be over. She wanted her sister back. She wanted her niece to be safe and loved and away from the man who had tormented her sister and changed her into someone Cyn didn't recognize but always loved. She didn't want her niece to grow up with him taunting and ridiculing and controlling her.

Hunt rubbed his hand up and down her back, soothing her.

It was then she realized she was pressed up against him, her hands fisted in the sides of his shirt, holding on to him like a buoy in the turbulent sea her life had become. She released him and stepped back.

He frowned and held her gaze, but continued to listen to whoever was on the line with him. "Four minutes out. Great. I'll take Angela's sister home. She can give a statement tomorrow morning at the station and we'll move on whatever information we gather tonight." Hunt listened again. "No. I doubt he's going to give permission to search the home and property here. We'll need a warrant and right now we don't have enough to get one."

Cyn spoke up. "I was in the house. There's nothing that indicates a struggle. No blood. The only thing that points to her not leaving of her own free will is that her stuff is all inside the house. Her clothes, the baby's stuff, everything. Her car is missing, but her purse is hanging on the coatrack."

Hunt relayed the information to the officer on the line, then hung up and stared at her for another long moment.

"We had a plan." Her bottom lip trembled, but she held it together. Barely.

"I know. I'm sorry."

"You know, just like I do, she's not coming back."

Hunt didn't say anything.

"I need you to find them."

"I won't stop looking until I do," he promised her a second time.

She needed to hear it again, more for reassurance, because she believed him the first time.

"No matter what the outcome, Cyn, you will be okay. But I need you to let me do my job. Please don't make me come after you."

She didn't say anything to that because ever since she stepped away from him, she wanted to be right back snuggled up to him, to find the comfort she hadn't felt in a long time.

A patrol car pulled into the drive.

Hunt gave her one more long look, then went to speak to the officer who'd arrived to do what Hunt had recused himself of taking on so that Rad wouldn't be able to accuse Hunt of a personal conflict or vendetta.

Rad rushed toward Hunt and the officer. "You can't arrest me. I didn't do anything."

Hunt finished saying whatever he'd been quietly talking to the officer about, then looked at Rad. "I'm not arresting you. But this officer is going to ask you some questions about your missing girlfriend and daughter. I suggest you answer truthfully and tell him where Angela and Lana are so that we can confirm they are alive and well. If not, you'll be looking over your shoulder until I find them." Hunt turned and walked back toward her.

She wanted to stay and get the answers, but Rad had already dug in and was yelling at the top of his lungs that he was being harassed by the police and hadn't done anything wrong.

Hunt put his hand to her back to nudge her to turn around and walk away.

It was the hardest thing she'd ever had to do.

"I'll follow you back to your place."

She stopped beside her car and looked up at him. "You're beyond exhausted. Get in. I'll drive you home."

"I'm fine."

"Your shirt is not only on backward but inside out. You don't have any socks on and you didn't even tie your boots. You look like breathing is too much to do right now."

Hunt glanced down at himself, surprise and dismay lighting his eyes, then he planted his hands on his hips and stared at her. "Cyn. I can't do this with you right now. I need my truck to get to work in the morning. Just get in the car, and let's go."

"You can't what with me?"

"Argue. Defend myself against accusations you know aren't true, but want to put on me, anyway. We can go back to that tomorrow, but right now, I just want to get you home where you'll be safe and out of trouble. Can you do that for me? Please. Just this once, don't make me be a cop and let me just be your friend."

She fell back against her car, completely taken aback by his words and seeing the raw need he had for her to let him take care of her.

"No."

His shoulders slumped.

"You're right. I've given you a really hard time about doing your job. And then I called and asked you to help me in that same capacity. After the way I've treated you, I'm surprised you said yes."

He opened his mouth to say something but she held up her hand to stop him.

"I'm also not surprised at all that you agreed to help me. It's your job and you're good at it."

"That's not the only reason I agreed." He took a step closer. "Or why I rushed out here to catch up to you."

She heard something new in his voice. "Because you want to be my friend?"

He sighed. "That would be a good start."

She tried to read the almost desperate look in his eyes. "Because of our connection to Shelby, or something else?"

Hunt took another step closer, his gaze direct and locked on hers. "Something *more*."

She didn't know what to do with that at the moment. "Okay. I'm going to just let that simmer for now."

"I've been doing that for a while, Cyn."

She really liked the way he said her name like that, all deep and impatient and needy.

Hunt leaned in a bit closer. "I'm kind of hoping now that you know, you'll want to catch up."

"I definitely need to catch my breath."

Hunt backed up a step. "Fair enough."

She nodded her thanks that he gave her some time and space to take this all in. "So friends. Which means you're going to let me drive you home because I'd never forgive myself if you came all the way out here to help me and ended up crashing and dying because you were too hardheaded to let me drive you home."

A hint of a grin tugged at his lips. "Name-calling is not that friendly, Cyn."

"I'll work on it."

"Do that. Let's go." Hunt walked around to the passenger side of her car. She slipped in behind the wheel. He folded himself into the seat, then pushed it back as far as it would go to accommodate his big frame.

"Comfortable?"

"Never when I'm around you."

She was about to take exception but stopped herself when he shifted in the seat and tugged his T-shirt down over the bulge in his jeans.

"Interested in something, Cyn?"

She didn't even think, just answered with the only thing that popped into her head. "Maybe."

Hunt closed his eyes and grumbled, "Drive."

She backed out of the driveway onto the main road and drove on autopilot.

Nothing tonight had gone as she expected. She felt sick and heartbroken. The worry ate at her insides. She desperately wanted to find her sister and niece and felt inadequate and helpless to do so.

Hunt's hand gently enclosed hers on the steering wheel. She released it and Hunt immediately laced his fingers with hers, the back of his hand resting on her thigh.

"It's too far and too late to drive to the ranch and back to your place. I'll stay at your house tonight. Make sure you're safe. And not alone."

She glanced over at him. He hadn't even opened his eyes.

She squeezed his hand. "Thank you."

"It sucks being alone," he admitted.

She wondered if he was just too tired to guard his words, because she'd never heard him talk like this. Of course, she was always in his face about giving her a ticket she deserved, the grief he'd given Shelby about Chase and whatever else she wanted to accuse him of, like Mrs. Phelps, without giving him the benefit of the doubt.

"Hey, Wilde."

"Yeah?"

"I'd like to be your friend."

Again Hunt didn't open his eyes but drew her hand to his lips and kissed the back of it. "Sounds like a good place to start to me." He put his hand back on her thigh. She gave it a squeeze, then focused on the road and getting them home.

No, not home. Not their home. But to her place. Yeah. That was it. Where he'd stay with her tonight because he didn't want her to be alone.

"I like the sound of that."

# Chapter Seven

THE LAST thing Hunt remembered from last night was falling onto Cyn's too-short sofa and finally letting sleep claim him, despite how desperately he'd wanted to make sure Cyn was okay. It couldn't have been an easy thing to do, leaving Rad's place without knowing what happened to her family. Hunt did everything he could, short of beating the answers out of Rad, which would have gotten him what he needed for Cyn, but also landed him in jail and out of a job.

He'd woken up before her and couldn't help but smile that she'd pulled off his boots, covered him with a blanket, left him a bottle of water on the coffee table and his phone charging on the kitchen counter. After a quick shower—because how could he not when she'd left a towel, new toothbrush and toothpaste for him in the guest bath?—he called Max, who wasn't happy at all about the predawn wake-up, and asked him to bring Hunt's uniform and drive him out to Rad's place to pick up his truck.

For all her grumbling about him and glaring at him all the time, she still made him feel welcome in her home.

Feeling better after seven solid hours of sleep, he'd snuck a peek at Cyn in her bed, the covers in disarray, looking like she'd had a hell of a time falling asleep. And no wonder with so many unanswered questions about Angela and Lana. Then he left to get his truck and head to work.

On his way, he couldn't stop thinking about her in that skintight black tank top and those tiny little shorts and all that creamy skin. But once he arrived at the office, it was all business. He'd gone in to read the reports and statements from the officers who interviewed Rad and his parents. Rad gave basically the same statement he'd given to Hunt last night. The officers didn't find Angela or Lana with Rad's parents, who were dismayed and upset to discover they were both missing. They blamed Angela, said their son would never hurt anyone and demanded the cops find Angela and bring their granddaughter home immediately.

He'd only been in the office twenty minutes when he heard Cyn call out, "Wilde, where are you?"

He stood and went to the office doorway and stared at an aggravated Cyn holding a foil-covered plate in one hand and a large coffee in the other.

"Wilde," she called again.

"Right here."

Her eyes scanned over him in one hot sweep before her eyes narrowed into that annoyed glare she always gave him.

What would it take to actually make her happy to see him?

"Why did you leave this morning without waking me

up? You could have at least said goodbye and told me why you left so early."

Two of the women in the office glared at him. The other three male officers snickered and looked expectantly at him for an answer.

He wondered how long it would take her to figure out they all thought he and Cyn slept together last night and if she cared. Apparently she didn't even give it a thought as she closed the distance between them, giving him a better look at her in dark denim jeans, a white see-through crisscross top over a black bra, all those sexy curves and that wild purple hair. He wanted to slide his fingers through the strands and pull her in for the kiss he'd been dreaming about sharing with her for too long.

"Did you even get enough sleep after you'd been up for so long?"

The guys' eyes went wide with knowing and amusement. The ladies gave him a good long look of appreciation, since they thought he'd spent the night making Cyn happy, even if he'd left early.

Cyn stopped right in front of him.

He looked down into her blue eyes and read the surprising concern there. "Good morning, Cyn." He'd like to say that to her on another morning. While they were in bed together. Right before he really did make love to her.

Her lips scrunched. "I wanted to make you breakfast and thank you again."

More chuckles from the peanut gallery.

He leaned in close, so only she'd hear him. "You do realize that you've made everyone here think I left you in bed after we had some wild night together."

"I realized a long time ago that it doesn't matter what I say or actually do, people will always assume and tell tales about me. Ninety percent of it is bullshit. If I actually slept with all the men in this town who claim to have slept with me, I'd never get anything else done."

"Well, there's at least one here who did sleep with you." And it irritated the living daylights out of him to think a guy he knew and worked with had been with the woman he'd wanted for more than a year.

She didn't hesitate or break eye contact when she simply said, "No, there isn't."

"Are you sure?"

"That I know all the men I've slept with and who they are? Yes. I'm sure. But thanks for that dig. I'm sure I deserve it after the way I've treated you, but . . . really?"

Hunt spared one second of a glance for Officer Reid, then wrapped his arm around Cyn's shoulders as she was trying to walk away from him, steered her into the office and slammed the door.

"I only meant that maybe you hadn't seen all the men out there, particularly the one who likes to tell tales about his nights with you."

Cyn stared up at him, not a trace of embarrassment or deception in her eyes. "I have not slept with any of the three men out there. And if you want to know about my past, then ask. I have nothing to hide. I don't apologize for having healthy relationships with men I wanted to be with for however long or short it lasted. I do expect a level of privacy from them I don't always get, which is one of the reasons why things didn't work out. I don't want to be someone's conquest or bedmate and nothing more. I know the truth. The people who really know me know who I am and what matters to me. I don't care what anyone else thinks."

"You care what I think, or you wouldn't have given me that explanation."

"You said something last night . . ."

"That I want us to be more than friends," he finished for her because it seemed like maybe she didn't believe him or she needed to hear it again.

"Yes. That. Are you sure?" Disbelief shone in her eyes.

"That I want you? Yeah. Definitely sure about that."

"Do you even like me?"

He chuckled. "Yes. You're a handful, that's for sure. But you also care deeply about the people you let in. Like Shelby and Mrs. Phelps. While your love for speed and cutting loose once in a while gets you in some minor trouble, you'd never do anything to purposely hurt anyone. While people love to talk about you, I've never heard you talk about anyone else. In fact, I know that you go out of your way to be nice to people who feel ostracized or like they're an outcast. I've seen little girls run up to you because they like your hair and makeup and clothes. You always stop and chat with them like they're your best friends."

She tilted her head. "Are you stalking me, Wilde?"

"It feels that way sometimes, because lately everywhere I go, there you are."

She smiled at that. "Are you getting tired of finding me everywhere you go?"

"Only when I find you shoved up against a wall by a guy we know is an abuser at best and more than likely something far worse. You scared the hell out of me last night." He rubbed his hand over the back of his tense neck so he wouldn't reach out and pull her close again. Where he desperately wanted her.

"Sit down, Wilde. Eat this. Drink this." She set the plate and coffee to-go cup in front of him. "Now tell me what you know about my sister and niece. I know you left early because you hoped you'd have good news for me, but you don't, or you would have come back and woken me up."

Hunt avoided thinking about how he'd like to have woken her up and pulled the foil off the plate and stared at the food, inhaling the delicious aroma. "Did you make this for me?"

"Yes."

"Why?" He couldn't believe she'd gone to all the trouble to make his favorite breakfast.

"To thank you for coming to my rescue last night and reining in my crazy. If I'd killed Rad the way I wanted to and intended to after what he said to me, then I'd probably never find my sister."

"What did he say to you?" Hunt dug into the pancakes topped with fresh strawberries and drizzled with honey because he was starving, she'd made it for him and there was no way he was letting her effort go to waste.

"Basically, he said if I didn't get rid of you and fix the situation I'd never find my sister."

Hunt went still with a forkful of fluffy scrambled eggs with diced tomato and chopped green onions in them an inch from his mouth. He set the fork down and stared at her.

"You caught it, too. Not that I won't *see* my sister

again, but that I won't *find* her." Cyn fell into the chair across the desk from him and wiped the tears from her pale cheeks and under her bloodshot eyes. "I'm headed over to my mom's house. She needs to hear it from me. You think I'm nuts? This will be a whole other level of denial and grief and blaming me for . . . everything."

"I'm not blaming your sister. She was in a dangerous situation. But she chose Rad. How is that your fault?"

"Welcome to my world. I get blamed for a lot of things I didn't do. Like Rad saying it's my fault this happened. If I'd stayed out of his and Angela's relationship, all would have been just dandy while he beat her. My mom . . . she's not really the hands-on type and always left me to take care of my sister. If something happened to Angela, Mom will blame me."

Hunt took a sip of the coffee, noting she'd added milk to it. How did she know that's how he liked it? "By your logic, if you're to blame, then so am I. Rad was right about me getting him fired."

Cyn rolled her eyes. "He got fired because his boss didn't want to keep an abusive asshole on the payroll."

Hunt leaned forward, desperate to believe that's how she really felt. "So you don't blame me for not thinking about him going home and taking out his anger and frustration on your sister?"

Cyn leaned on her arms on the desk. "No. And I'm sorry I lashed out at you last night and made you think I do blame you. I can be a hothead sometimes."

He grinned. "Really? I hadn't noticed."

She sat back again. "What happens next?" She didn't mean between them.

"We've got a large geographical area where her cell

phone last pinged between three cell towers. It's off the highway and remote. Thick forest and hills with a river winding through it. We're getting search teams together and dogs. We'll start in a couple of hours, go until nightfall, then start all over again tomorrow until we're satisfied she's not there."

"But it's likely she is."

"For all I know, Cyn, she did leave in her car with the baby and is holed up in a motel somewhere hiding."

Cyn shook her head. "She doesn't have a job or any money of her own. She'd come to me."

"I know you believe that. I think it's the most likely thing, too, but if he threatened her and you, maybe to protect you and the baby, she ran as far and as fast as she could."

"I want to believe that."

"I know you do." But Angela still would have called Cyn to let her know she was okay.

"What about her car?"

"We're looking for it. Every law enforcement agency in the state has the vehicle description and license number. She didn't have an antitheft tracker or a service that can locate the car for us."

"It was old and on its last legs. I thought about giving her my car. It's newer and would have been perfect for her and Lana. I'd get something new. Lana would grow up happy with her mom and auntie watching over her."

"We don't know if Lana is with your sister, or if Rad stashed her somewhere else."

"Where? She's not with his parents. Who else would he take her to?"

"We're checking with all his relatives and friends."

Cyn crossed her arms and hung her head. "It feels like the longer we don't know anything, the worse it gets."

"We are doing everything we can right now. I swear to you, I won't stop until I find them."

She sighed and leaned forward again. "Thank you. Know that I appreciate it even when I don't show it."

He stared down at his half-eaten plate of food. "You have a really nice way of showing it. I can't remember the last time someone cooked me a meal that didn't come from a restaurant."

"Then I'm happy to be that person. Someone needs to look out for you. You work too much."

"We're short-staffed due to a couple of retirements and officers leaving to take jobs in bigger cities for more pay."

"And you've barely slept the last two days."

"Worried about me?"

She gave him a half grin. "Mildly concerned," she teased.

"I'll take it." He dug into the food again, because he'd need the sustenance to get through the grueling search later. "Do you want me to go with you to your mom's place?"

Cyn stood. "Thanks for the offer, but we haven't even had a first date and I don't want to scare you off this soon in our relationship."

He met her amused gaze. "I don't scare that easily, sweetheart."

"You haven't met my mother." She planted her hands on the desk and leaned in close. "Thank you for coming to the rescue last night, but if you ever risk your life like that, driving while you're that exhausted, I will not be happy about it and you will not be happy with how I express it."

Hunt stood, matched her position with his hands planted on the desk, his face close to hers. "I will always come when you call. No matter what. And when you need someone, I don't care when or why, you better call me."

She put her hand to his jaw, her thumb across his chin, her index finger to his lips. "You might regret it when I do."

He kissed her finger, then took her hand and planted another kiss in her palm. "I don't think I ever will."

"Text me the location of where the search will begin. I'll be there."

"Cyn . . ."

She squeezed his hand. "I need to do something."

"What about your job?"

She tilted her head and gave him a sassy half grin. "It's not like I'll get fired. I own the place."

Hunt stood to his full height. "I didn't know you owned it."

"I bought it outright last year. I'm opening a second location in Blackrock Falls. I secured the location last month and the remodel starts in a couple weeks."

*Damn. Go, Cyn!* "Congratulations."

"Thank you."

"You've got a lot on your plate."

"Yeah. And I need to hire a lawyer."

That piqued his interest. "Why?"

"I don't believe Rad hurt the baby. My sister . . . Yeah, I can see him losing his shit and killing her. But a tiny little helpless baby . . ." Cyn shivered. "I want to be prepared to take custody of her."

Something Cyn said last night crept to the front of his mind. "Why did you tell Angela not to put Rad's name on the birth certificate?"

"Because she didn't have to do it. Because if something happened, like she finally decided to leave him, he'd have to fight to get custody of Lana."

He understood now. "One more roadblock to him doing that. He'd have to request a court-ordered DNA test."

"He doesn't have a lot of money. Lawyers cost a fortune. He'd be ordered to pay child support. I hoped he'd give up and eventually leave Angela alone to raise the baby. Angela could have worked for me at my salon. I could have helped support them." Cyn sighed and her shoulders slumped, her gaze found his. "All this time, I begged her to let me help her. I had the will and the means to take care of her. All she had to do was get over her fear. I know that was asking a lot from someone who knew the consequences of leaving. The possibility and potential for even more violence." She gave him a sad smile. "I'm sorry to say, but this relationship may very well end with you saying goodbye to me through bars, because I really feel like I'm going to kill him."

Hunt took her hand and pulled her around the desk and right into his arms. He hugged her close and pressed his cheek to her soft hair. "Then I'm going to do everything I can to bring him in myself. I don't want to lose you and what's just starting to get good between us."

Cyn squeezed him tight. "Just find them for me. I don't think I can live with not knowing what happened to them." She released him all at once and turned for the door and left him worried about her but also impressed with how well she was holding up under the immense circumstances. The woman had the strength and will of ten people.

He didn't want to ever see her break.

So he got back to work, doing what he could and what she'd asked to find her sister and niece.

To help with that, he called in reinforcements for the search later today and someone in particular Cyn would be happy to see.

# Chapter Eight

"**W**HAT ARE you doing here so early in the morning?" Her mom stood smoking a cigarette in the kitchen. She leaned against the stove wearing a hot-pink baby doll nightie top and cotton polka-dot boy-short undies. The creases around her lips and eyes stood out as she took another drag off the cigarette and blew smoke to the nicotine-stained ceiling.

Cyn didn't bother to acknowledge stepdad number three sitting at the table eating greasy eggs and sausage while he scrolled through iFunny on his phone. Ed would eventually head off to whatever job he'd be fired from next. Probably some job on a road crew or something in construction, judging by the worn jeans and bright orange T-shirt. Then her mom would have to come to her for "just a little something" to get them by until he found another job he'd suck at and lose.

"I came to talk about Angela and Lana."

"I hope Angela's behaving herself. She needs to take care of her man, not rile him up all the time."

Cyn looked at Ed's plate, remembered the one she'd made for Hunt this morning and thought, *At least I'm doing a better job of taking care of my man than Mom.*

"I don't care if Angela served him dog food for breakfast, there's no excuse for him hitting her. Ever."

"Sometimes men are . . . demanding. Aggressive. Passionate about the things and women they want." The appreciative glance she gave Ed made Cyn's stomach roll.

Her mother had been in a few rough relationships. She liked to argue. She liked to be manhandled once in a while. Hell, the woman liked to poke at men just to see them snarl. But what she really liked was to watch them come at her with wild abandon to shut her up with one surefire way that always worked. Kinda. Because her mom liked to get loud during sex. She and Angela had fled the house more times than they could count because no child should have to endure that kind of raw and uncensored life experience.

She cringed at even the memories of it.

Ed, like all the other men her mom brought home, didn't want any part of this family thing and headed back to the bedroom.

She wanted out of the smoke and this house.

"Mom. Please, sit down. What I have to tell you is . . . very difficult."

Her mom waved the cigarette back and forth in front of her. "It can't be that bad. What'd he do this time? A black eye? Busted lip? Broke her wrist again?" Her mother seriously didn't think any of those things were that bad to happen to her daughter.

Cyn wanted to punish Rad tenfold for everything he'd ever done to her sister. "What would it take for you to think that Rad hurting your daughter was bad?" She could feel the anger building inside her like a living thing stretching and spreading through her.

"Oh, come on. I didn't mean it that way."

"What way did you mean that it didn't much matter to you if she had another black eye, busted lip or broken arm? What if he beat her so bad she was more black and blue than pale skin like he did when she was just a couple months pregnant? Would it be okay with you if he backhanded Lana across the face and busted her lip?"

Her mother's mouth drew tight into deeper creases. "She's just a baby. What would she do to get him to hit her?"

"Cry. Not do what he wants. The same things he hit Angela for. But you know what? I'm not sure what's worse. Him for hurting her. Or you for being so apathetic and blaming Angela for what he did to her."

"I told you to put a stop to it."

Cyn scoffed, held her arms out, then let them drop. "Now it's my fault."

Her mom drew in a long drag on the cigarette, eyes narrowed on her. "What do you want from me?"

"I want you to care!"

"I do care. But you've said it a million times. She needs to decide she's had enough and leave. You've begged her countless times and she won't do it. So what do you want me to do about it?"

Cyn held back the scream of anger. "There's nothing to do now. She's gone."

Her mom's eyes lit up. "Great. Where did she go?"

Cyn shook her head. "No, Mom. She's gone. For all I know, they're both dead."

Her mom shook her head. "No. That's not true. You're lying."

"He got fired yesterday. Guess who he took out his anger and frustration on."

"He wouldn't do anything like that. They argue. They fight. It gets out of hand sometimes, but he loves her." She seemed so sure about that when all the evidence and history told her otherwise.

"No," Cyn snapped, pissed off her mom still didn't get it. "He used her as his punching bag. He made her feel worthless and unlovable and then he hurt her again and again because he wanted to feel in control and like a big man, but he's a worthless piece of shit who killed her." There, she'd said it out loud. And, oh God, did it hurt.

Her mother wrapped one arm across her chest, the smoking cigarette in her other hand, her face pale, eyes filled with defiance and fear that Cyn was right. "No."

"I went there last night to get her. She and Lana weren't there. But he was, with scratch marks on his neck."

"See? She took the baby and left."

"No, Mom. You can't possibly believe that."

"She left him." Her mom nodded, like that would make it true. "Just like you wanted."

Cyn huffed out an exasperated breath. "Then tell me where she is. Where would she go with a six-week-old baby if she left him?"

Her mother's gaze bored into her and she pointed the cigarette at Cyn. "She's not gone."

"Everything she owned, her purse, were all in the house. Her car is missing. The police are looking for her, the baby, the car. But Rad told me I'd never *find* her. Not without him telling me where she is."

It took her mother a long moment to speak. "And the baby?" Her voice trembled, the first crack in her this-can't-be-real shell.

"It is my greatest hope that he stashed Lana somewhere with someone he knows will take care of her until he can go to her. His parents were questioned. They don't believe he did anything. They believe Angela left with the baby of her own free will. But you know, Mom. You know the only place she'd go."

"To you," her mom finally admitted, then burst into tears and crumpled to the floor, crying.

Ed walked in, pulled her into a hug and looked up at Cyn. "Look what you've done."

God save her from people who blamed everyone but the person responsible. She wanted to let all the pent-up angry words in her head out.

But now wasn't the time to explode with all the blame she'd like to heap on her mom.

Cyn squatted and put a hand on her mom's bony knee. "The police have filed a missing person report on both Angela and Lana. The police have figured out where Angela's cell phone was last sending a signal, but it's a big area. They're beginning the search today. I'll be there. I have a friend in the police department. He'll keep me up-to-date on what they're doing and what they find."

Her mom gripped Cyn's arm so tightly her knuckles went white. "You need to find them. And then you need to make him pay." The vehemence in her mother's voice and the fury in her eyes matched the ferocity of the rage inside Cyn.

"I will." She stood and looked down at her mom and Ed. "I'll be in touch." She headed for the door.

"You get him, Cyn," her mother shouted. "You make him pay!" Her anguished sobbing followed Cyn out the door.

She climbed into her car and sat in the quiet for a moment, then let loose with her rage and screamed and hit the steering wheel, kicking the floorboard as the tears fell and the overwhelming rush of emptiness and grief hit her again.

The phone in the dash holder dinged with an incoming text. She sucked in a breath, wiped away her tears with her fingers, then picked up the phone and sighed that she'd missed a bunch of texts.

Grief gave way to hope that her sister and niece had been found.

She tapped the screen and pulled up Hunt's texts first.

HUNT: Thank you for breakfast. I loved it and spending time with you.

She didn't think she had a smile in her, but she found one for that sweet message.

HUNT: Nothing new in case. Sorry ☹
HUNT: Search teams are gathering.
HUNT: Meet me here.

The next text was a map location with a pin in it. She knew exactly where to go.

HUNT: We'll find them.

She appreciated his optimism and commitment. She didn't know Hunt well, but it occurred to her she wouldn't want anyone else by her side for this. He had a tenacity and drive she admired. And through Shelby's eyes and stories, she'd learned he had a deep love of his family, doing what was right and protecting those he loved. That protective streak extended to his community. He might be the most honorable man she'd ever met.

It made her wonder what he saw in her, because she tended to shirk the law when it suited her. She thought of what he'd said to her this morning. She was a handful, but he liked it because she cared about people and wasn't out to hurt anyone.

They had those kinds of core values in common.

She needed to stop thinking about him and get moving, but first she pulled up the other texts from her best friend.

SHELBY: Are you okay?
SHELBY: Heard about your sister. I'm so sorry. I'm here to help with whatever you need.
SHELBY: Hugs. ♥♥♥

Cyn wiped away the tears that slipped down her cheeks, then texted Shelby back.

CYN: I'm not okay but I'm holding on to hope.
CYN: We'll talk soon.
CYN: And I definitely need a hug. ♥♥♥

Her phone chimed with an incoming text, but it wasn't from Shelby.

HUNT: How did it go with your mom?
HUNT: You still there?
HUNT: Rad's parents got him a lawyer. He's not talking. We had to let him go.
HUNT: I'm sorry.

Cyn fumed, but it wasn't Hunt's fault. He was bound by the law. She wasn't.

CYN: My mom knows.
CYN: Happy to be done with that madness for now.
CYN: Headed your way after I pick up some stuff at my place.
CYN: Need anything???
HUNT: YOU!!! Safe and in my sight.

Cyn started the car and pulled out of her mom's place and headed home even though she wanted to go right to Hunt and fall into his warm embrace and shut off her head and heart and just let him hold the world at bay for a while.

But that wasn't going to happen. She had things to do. Starting with searching for her sister. Because Cyn knew she was out there somewhere. Rad didn't have enough time to take her far. She imagined he'd been in a hurry, out of sorts, not thinking clearly. He'd have wanted to ditch the car and hide the body. The woods were a good place to start. And she'd scour every inch of them, turn over every rock and pine needle, if that's what it took to find her sister.

She had to believe her niece was safe somewhere else.

Because down the path where Cyn didn't get either one of them back lay madness. And if Rad did that, he'd see what kind of wrath she'd bring down on him.

# Chapter Nine

A WAVE of relief washed over Hunt the second Cyn's car pulled in behind all the other vehicles clogging the recreation area parking lot that hikers, mountain bikers, horseback riders and ATV riders used. Today they were all here to help find Cyn's sister.

They'd triangulated Angela's cell phone to this geographic location filled with hiking and hunting trails, campsites and fishing holes along the river. There were no motels in the area. The best they could hope for was to find Angela's car and her and the baby in it.

Alive and hiding from Rad, Hunt hoped.

It was a place to start.

Astonishment and surprise filled Cyn's eyes when she got out of her car and saw how many people showed up. They'd put the call out to their regular volunteers and nearly everyone showed up with a few extras, too.

And he'd called in his own backup.

The second Shelby spotted Cyn, she ran for her. Cyn met his soon-to-be sister-in-law halfway across the lot. They embraced and held each other tight.

Another wave of relief swept over him. She was safe

and leaning on a friend. He'd like her to rely on him, but for now, she got what she needed.

His brothers, Chase and Max, leaned against the horse trailer.

Chase eyed him. "That's an intense look you've got for Shelby's friend."

Max pushed off the trailer and took two steps toward Cyn. "I think I'll go see if she needs some consoling."

"Take another step, little brother, it will be your last."

Max grinned. "You owe me ten bucks," he said to Chase, who pulled out a bill from his pocket and handed it over.

"I knew it was a sucker bet when I made it. I just love seeing the look on Hunt's face."

Hunt glared at them. "You guys are assholes. We're here to find her missing sister."

Both his brothers sobered.

Chase slapped his hand on Hunt's shoulder. "We know that. But we can still poke at you while we do it."

Hunt wanted to thump his brother in the head, but refrained because it had been too long since things felt like old times between them. And he appreciated that Max and Chase had both dropped everything to come out here to help him today.

"We've got serious things to do right now. The fourth team just headed out. We need to get on the move. We're burning daylight." He turned to Cyn as she and Shelby approached them.

Cyn had changed clothes since he saw her this morning. She wore a pair of worn denim jeans, a black T-shirt that made him laugh and a pair of hiking boots. She'd tied a fleece jacket around her waist for when the temps dropped later. She carried her backpack in her hand.

"What's so funny, Wilde?"

"Is that your search and rescue shirt?"

"Yep." She gave him his first real smile.

He chuckled again at the picture of a bottle of wine being poured into a glass with the words *I just rescued some wine* over the picture and *It was trapped in a bottle* beneath it.

"It's so you," he said, then closed the distance between them and softly asked, "Everything okay with your mom?"

"As expected, she took the news hard. Ed was with her when I left. Maybe he'll prove he's useful for something and keep her from going off the deep end. If not, you'll arrest her for Rad's murder and we'll all be happy." She did something completely unexpected and dropped her forehead onto his chest. "I can't bear to go back and see her until I find Angela."

Hunt rubbed his hands over her shoulders and slid his fingers into her hair and held her against his chest just like that. "Then let's find her together."

Cyn looked up at him, her eyes filled with sadness. "What if she's not out here?"

"What did I tell you?"

"That you'd never stop until you found her."

He held her gaze. "Do you believe me?"

"Yes."

He kissed her forehead, then looked down at her again. "Good. Let's go." He took her hand and led her to the trailer where Shelby and his brothers waited.

"Uh, when did things change between you two?"

Shelby pointed from him to Cyn and to their joined hands. "And how come no one told me."

"Last night," Hunt admitted.

"It could have happened sooner, but instead of asking me on a date he kept writing me tickets and acting like every jealous girlfriend dumping drinks on me was my fault."

Hunt stared down at her, shocked. "You'd have actually said yes to a date?"

"You're a walking sex dream in a uniform." She gave him a duh look and glanced at Shelby for confirmation that he was stupid for not knowing this.

Chase stepped in, but was no help. "He's a little slow. Hi. I'm Chase. I've heard a lot about you. Sorry about your sister, but Max and I are here to help."

"Hey, Max," Cyn said, like they knew each other.

"Hey. We need a rematch soon."

Cyn smiled. "Any time you want me to beat your ass, I'm in."

"What?" Hunt looked from one to the other.

Cyn eyed him. "Do you have something you want to ask me before your head explodes with whatever you're thinking?"

"Did you . . . with my brother?"

She nodded. "Yes. I played pool with him at the bar and won a hundred and twenty bucks off him over the last year and a half. But I didn't sleep with him."

Max shrugged. "I don't know why I keep playing with you."

"Because I'm good company and we always have a great time."

Max nodded his agreement. "You're a good friend."

Hunt didn't feel jealous. He liked that Max found something besides a hookup with Cyn. Hunt sometimes worried Max had given up wanting something more with a woman after his breakup with the last woman he'd actually had a relationship with.

Cyn took them all in with one sweeping glance. "I only ever had my sister to have my back. Thank you all for coming here today to help me look for her. I really appreciate it. And I see why Shelby loves you all so much. You've taken her in as your own. Thanks for showing up for me today."

Hunt appreciated so much that she understood they'd come at his request but also saw that they understood why he'd asked them to be here. Because she was important to him.

He hooked his arm around her and pulled her back to his chest. He leaned down and whispered in her ear. "You matter to all of us."

She put her hands on his arm over her chest and tilted her head into his chin. "Let's go find my sister."

"Do you ride?" Hunt asked her.

"Not in a while, but I'm decent enough."

Chase led Lady over to her. "She's a sweet girl. Minds well. You'll do well on her."

Hunt held the reins while Cyn stuffed her jacket into her pack and put it on her back, then mounted. He handed her the reins. "You good?"

"Ready to go."

Hunt mounted his horse and led their group of about fifteen riders down the fire trail. They scanned the area as they went, looking for any signs that someone had either driven this way or walked, though there was a lot of traffic on the fire road between hikers, bikers and all the rest. As they came to other trails, the searchers split off from them in groups of three and four until Hunt found the trail he thought Rad might have used. He dismounted and unhooked the chain blocking the trail with a sign that said No Trespassing Forestry Road. It was wide enough for an ATV or even a car, though the grass and brush had thickened over the last many months the trail hadn't been used.

"Isn't this where you and Rad used to ride and hunt?" Chase asked.

"Hunt Wilde would never break the law and trespass," Cyn said in mock shock.

He didn't look at her. "My dad's friend worked for the forestry service and gave me permission to use the trail."

"Of course you asked permission." Cyn smiled at him.

He liked it so much he wasn't even embarrassed about her teasing him about being responsible.

Chase stopped, dismounted and squatted by a large bush and some soggy ground. "A vehicle went through here recently." Chase pointed to a broken limb and the tire impression in the mud.

Hunt asked Chase to come because he'd learned a lot of tracking skills in the military. Hunt was good. Chase was better.

"Let's ride single file down the center of the path," Hunt suggested. "Chase and Shelby, you watch to the left. Max, Cyn and I will take the right. If you spot anything, point it out and we'll mark it." Hunt pulled the yellow flags out of his saddlebag and marked the potential evidence they'd found and took a couple pictures.

He'd have the crime scene guys come out later and cast the tire impression.

Cyn called out to him. "Is this the only place in the search area you and Rad used to go together?"

Hunt shook his head. "No. There are three other places. One's a trail that leads to a big open field where we used to hunt. Another is a fishing hole on the river, but it's a popular spot, so I doubt he'd have gone there to . . ." He left off *hide a body*. "I have groups checking those two spots just to be sure." For all Hunt knew, Rad took Angela's body, waded into the river at their favorite fishing spot and let her go. They could find her a mile downriver, twenty, or maybe never locate her body and never know for sure that's what he'd done.

"And the third spot?" Cyn glanced back at him.

He mounted his horse and followed behind their group this time.

"Yeah, Hunt? What's the third spot?" Max needed a good thump in the head for taunting him.

"It's a place we liked to camp," he said dryly.

"With girls," Cyn asked, grinning back at him.

"It was high school. Bonfires, booze and girls," he confirmed.

Her smile faded. "He wouldn't take her there. Those were probably happy memories. He wouldn't want to taint them. He'd want her far away from all the fun he had."

Damn, she was smart. "Which is why we're taking this trail."

Her gaze sharpened. "What happened down here?"

Hunt didn't want to think about how his friend turned into someone he didn't know, but it started on this trail.

At least in Hunt's mind, because it was the first time he'd ever wanted to hurt his friend.

"Wilde," Cyn called to him. "What happened?"

"We got in a fight. Words were said, punches were thrown, and that was the beginning of the end that came years later when I arrested him for hitting you. I thought that was the worst that could happen between us. I was wrong."

Cyn stopped her horse and he rode up beside her and stopped his as the others continued on down the long and winding trail.

She reached out and took his hand. He felt her gaze on him, but didn't look at her. "That was the first time you saw him hit a girl."

"Her name was Lori but we called her Sprite because she was so lively and flitting about like some fairy. She was sweet and happy all the time. She didn't have a mean bone in her body. They ducked away together with a bottle of Wild Turkey and a blanket. I was . . . distracted."

Cyn squeezed his hand. "What was her name?"

"Kelly. We dated for two years."

"Your first?"

"Nope," he said with a grin, though his sweet memories clouded with what happened when Lori came running back. "I don't remember how long they were gone. Half an hour, maybe more. She came out of the trees at a dead run, her shirt gone, bra smeared with the blood from her busted lip. Rad ran after her. I didn't think, I just ran straight for him and tackled him to the ground before he caught her. She ran into Kelly's arms, and I held Rad off from going after her, but it didn't stop his mouth from running. He accused her of being a tease and saying that she shouldn't have started something she didn't intend to finish." He turned to her then and held her gaze. "I was so stunned he spun out of my hold and went for her again. He was in such a rage. He didn't care that she was crying and bleeding and so scared. I'd never seen anyone that scared." He rubbed his hand along the back of his neck. "He snagged her arm and tried to yank her away from Kelly. I grabbed him and clocked him right in the jaw. He stumbled and went down to his knees. We argued. He got pissed I took her side and blamed him for hitting her when he swore it was an accident and Lori vehemently accused him of backhanding her because she told him she didn't want to go all the way. I believed her. And Rad came up punching. I put him back on the ground, gathered the girls, and we left Rad there and I took the girls home."

"What happened when Lori told her parents what happened?"

"She didn't tell them. She wasn't supposed to be out with boys. She lied to her parents that she was staying overnight with Kelly, then she snuck out to meet us. When she got home, her story was that she tripped on the back porch stairs at Kelly's house and busted her lip on the bricks.

"When she saw Rad at school the next day, he tried to apologize and tell her that it was the alcohol, he'd had too much to drink and that wasn't him. She basically told him to fuck off."

"But you and he remained friends?"

"Rad came to me, too, apologized for what happened, said it would never happen again, he didn't know why he'd acted that way. He seemed really sorry and upset about it. I'd never seen him be that out of control. He had a mouth on him that got him into trouble and a few scrapes, but that was different than what he'd done to Lori. He seemed genuinely contrite. So I gave him a second chance and watched him with other girls. He wasn't that popular. Yeah, he'd joke around with the girls who hung out with Kelly, or whoever else I was seeing, but they mostly steered clear."

"I bet they sensed something about him."

"Maybe. Probably." Hunt frowned. "Word gets around. But Rad learned to be charming—as he got older he definitely got smoother, which made me think the thing with Lori was an isolated incident. Until Angela."

"Others probably left before it got as bad."

Hunt agreed with a nod. "Angela's beautiful and sweet. Her instinct is to nurture and soothe."

"It didn't work on Rad. There's no sense in why he treated her the way he did."

"Abusers don't need a reason," Hunt said sadly. "I'm just saying that maybe Angela wanted her goodness to fix Rad. He's the only one who can change who he is."

"It's too late for him to change. The only thing left for Rad to do is pay for hurting my sister." Cyn kicked her mount to catch up to the rest of their group.

Hunt followed, wondering if he'd end up between Cyn and Rad again. No question, he'd take Cyn's side, but would he have to put Rad back on the ground or six feet under to stop him next time?

# Chapter Ten

‹───✦───›

Cyn had never felt more tired, desperate and conflicted in her life. She wanted to find her sister, but she didn't want it to be out here in the woods. She also couldn't stand the thought of Angela out here alone. Dead or alive. The thought of her sister being missing, her fate undetermined, for the rest of Cyn's life . . . It would haunt her forever.

And while she loved being back on a horse, this was no pleasure trail ride. They'd been searching the forestry road, going slow, being observant of everything around them, and her ass hurt.

She hoped she wouldn't embarrass herself and not be able to walk when she got down off the sweet but uncomfortable animal the next time they took a break.

When they'd stopped a little while ago to eat and Hunt had checked in with the other teams on his radio, her legs had already been wobbly. She'd stretched her sore legs and continued to scan the area on foot, looking for any sign that someone came through this seemingly little-used path. In her mind, she hoped to find some kind of bread-crumb trail her sister left for her to follow. But all she really had was some notion Hunt had that

Rad would go somewhere he knew if he wanted to hide a body.

Oh, Hunt didn't say it in so many words, but they all knew that's what they were out here looking for and it threatened to break her the longer they went without finding anything.

Half an hour into their resumed ride and search efforts, Hunt reached out and took her hand. "I know this is hard. If you want to turn back and let us finish—"

"No. I'm fine. I can do this. We have the trail, if that's what it is, to follow." They'd marked several places that looked like fresh tire tracks. Were they from her sister's car or Rad's truck? They wouldn't know for sure until the police investigated further and compared them. For all she knew, they could be following the last forestry truck that went through here, or some hunter's vehicle who'd trespassed and used the trail.

She could see exactly why they'd risk it. So far, she'd spotted about a dozen deer along the way.

If they weren't out here for the reason they were, it would be a really pleasant ride. She loved nature and seeing the woodland creatures scampering about the damp leaf-laden forest floor and up in the tall trees.

"The river is not that far ahead. That's my end point for today." Hunt glanced up at the sky. "We're a little behind my schedule, but we should be able to make it back before full nightfall."

She asked the hard question. "Do you think he dumped my sister in the river?"

Hunt squeezed her hand, their thighs touching as they rode their horses side by side. "I don't know, sweetheart. All I know is her phone was in this general area before it was shut off or the battery died. Most of it isn't accessible by car or ATV. Rad doesn't own an ATV or a horse, so my best guess is he came out here in your sister's car."

"How did he get out of here and home?"

"Again, my best guess... Someone helped him. Someone who I hope is taking care of Lana."

She hadn't thought of that, but it made sense. "What kind of person helps hide a body and takes care of a baby that's not theirs after they know the person who asked for their help killed someone?"

"Someone who doesn't know that's what happened. Rad probably lied and came up with a plausible story. He'd say they fought. Angela scratched him. His wounds were deep. She fought hard. So he tells this person what he told us. She left him."

"And this person buys that?"

"Until they find out the authorities are looking for them. Then, hopefully, they do the right thing and bring the baby back."

"If that's even what happened," she said skeptically.

"The best lies are the ones that stick closest to the truth."

She shrugged. "Is that the river I hear?" The roaring sound had gotten louder the last few minutes.

"Yeah. We're close."

Chase headed back toward them. "We spotted something." He held her gaze. "You might want to wait here."

Her stomach dropped. She kicked her mount forward. "There is no way I'm coming all this way and waiting."

Chase turned to Hunt. "We'll need to keep the horses back a bit so we don't disturb the scene."

Hunt caught up to Cyn just past Chase's mount. "Wait a second, Cyn. We'll tie off the horses here and walk in. We need to do this right so the evidence sticks and Rad goes away for this."

She sighed and unclenched her hands from the reins. "Fine." She dismounted and nearly fell on her ass, but Hunt caught her.

"Get your legs under you."

She stamped her feet to get the blood flowing.

Hunt rubbed his hands up and down her arms and kissed her on the head, then dipped low and whispered in her ear. "Whatever we find up ahead, know I'm here for you."

"I can do this." She said it as much to reassure herself as him.

"I know you can." He took her hand and led her down the path to where Chase, Max and Shelby had dismounted and left their horses.

Shelby gave her a weak smile. "We don't know anything for sure yet," she warned.

Cyn walked toward the edge of the rise, following the very distinct tire tracks that went right off the cliff over the river embankment. Her stomach knotted as dread filled her heart. Hunt walked beside her, making sure they didn't trample any evidence. He stopped her a mere foot from the ledge and they stared over it at the rushing river. At first, she didn't see anything as she scanned the bank closest to them. Then Hunt's hand squeezed hers and she glanced up at him, then followed his gaze further downriver to the barely-there hint of the back corner of a car sticking out of the water. A green car. It would have been difficult to see without the sunlight glinting off the red brake light. In another few minutes as the sun descended, they might have missed it.

She didn't think. She let go of Hunt, found a somewhat negotiable path down the steep incline to the edge of the river and started ripping off her clothes.

Hunt grabbed her just as she let her shirt drop on top of her jacket and she reached for the button on her jeans. "What the hell do you think you're doing?"

"I have to know if she's in that car."

"That water isn't even fifty degrees. You'll freeze and drown."

Chase and Max showed up with a rope.

"Then you'll have to pull me out, but I am going in that water."

Hunt held her by the shoulders. "I'll call in the search and rescue divers. They'll check the car and we'll hook it up and haul it out of there."

"I'm not waiting. I have to know now." To prove it, she pulled off her hiking boots, socks, and stripped off her jeans. Standing there in a black bra and panties, it didn't even register that she'd stripped in front of everyone there, because the only thing that mattered was knowing if her sister and niece were in that car.

Hunt held tight to her arm. "Cyn, please. You don't have to do this. I'll go."

She shook her head. "I'm a good swimmer. Captain of my swim team. State champion. I can hold my breath for three minutes. At least I used to be able to. I'm going. Besides, I'd never ask anyone to risk their life for me."

Hunt didn't let her go. "I'll do it, Cyn."

She put her hand on his chest and felt his heart racing

beneath her palm. "I trust you to hold on to me and not let me go. I need you to do that for me."

Hunt sighed. "Damnit, Cyn. It seems I'll do anything for you, even if it's crazy."

Chase and Max came to her to secure the rope around her, both of them focused on the task. She raised her arms out to the side and Chase wrapped the rope around her and tied some intricate knots so that the rope went around her shoulders and arms and waist and ended up at her back, so that when they pulled, she wouldn't come out of the rope even if she was unconscious. She didn't want to think about that or how cold that water was going to be.

She stood at the edge of the rushing water, her feet already burning with the cold.

Shelby gave her a hug. "Are you sure you want to do this?"

"Yes." She didn't take her eyes off the spot where the car had sunk.

Hunt turned her to him. "Try to go straight out toward the center here, then let the current take you downriver until you hit the car. Get some extra breaths, then go under. One tug on the rope means you need more slack. Two tugs and we'll pull you out. If I think for one second you've been under too long, I'm pulling you out."

"Okay." She reached up and touched his face. His eyes filled with concern. "And if this goes very wrong, just know that I really wanted to find out—"

He crushed his lips to hers. "Nothing is going to go wrong. You trust me to hold on, well, I'm not letting go. So get used to it." He kissed her again, but this time it was soft and tempting and a promise for something more. He ended the kiss with a brush of his lips against hers. "This is crazy."

She didn't know if he meant her going into the freezing water or them.

"Come back to me."

She squeezed his arm. "I will."

Hunt growled deep in his throat, then took hold of the rope. "If you're going to do this, be quick."

Shelby stood nearby with a blanket she must have gotten from one of the saddlebags. "You've got this, Cyn. They won't let you go."

Cyn glanced at the three strong men, Hunt up front of his brothers, holding the rope, then turned to the river. She sucked in several deep breaths to raise the oxygen in her system, and walked out into the rushing water. She had a purpose and that helped her to ignore her body's immediate response to the cold and do what needed to be done.

The swift current quickly grabbed hold of her. She hadn't made it to the center of the river before it swept her under. She had to use all her strength to kick and stroke to get above water and on course. Before she knew it, she slammed into the side of the car. The water pushed against her back as she braced herself with her feet and hands on the vehicle.

She could hear someone shouting something to her, but it was too hard to hear over the rushing water. The cold was quickly sapping her energy. She needed to do this fast.

One tug for slack, two for help, she reminded herself

as she sucked in two big gasps of air, prayed for the car to be empty and dove under the water.

She used her hands and feet to keep her steady and against the car so she didn't get dragged over or under it by the current. She felt along the roof, down to the windows. She peered in through the back. Though the water was a bit murky, she could make out the empty back seat. She pulled herself down deeper into the water to the open driver's door window. A rush of relief came when she didn't find her sister in the driver's seat, but that quickly faded when she realized the passenger window had also been either broken out or left down so the car would sink.

Desperate for air, she tried to push off the car to get to the surface, but because of the cold sapping her energy, making it hard to even think, let alone move, she miscalculated and her legs got pushed through the driver's window. She grabbed hold of the top of the car to keep from being pushed all the way through the car and downriver, but she didn't have the strength to hold on, nor could she let go to reach for the rope to tug on it.

She felt her muscles losing all strength and her lungs burning for air. Just as everything was about to go black, a sharp yank on the rope drew her away from the car. Then another and another. They were pulling her out. She wanted to kick her legs and move her arms to help get her to the surface faster, but her body wouldn't work.

It felt like forever by the time her face broke the surface and she got her first desperate gasp of air, but it was quickly stolen when the water swallowed her again.

Something hit her in the head. Her leg caught on something, holding her back from being pulled out further, but then another hard yank freed her, but damn, it felt like icy claws scratching her leg. Her head hurt just about as much as her lungs, and just when she thought she'd be free of this icy hell, she blacked out wondering if she'd ever find her sister and niece and get to kiss Hunt again.

# Chapter Eleven

HUNT PRESSED his lips to Cyn's frozen ones and breathed into her mouth. He'd been giving her CPR for what felt like forever but had only been a minute or two. "Damnit, Cyn. Come back!"

He gave her another breath, everyone watching and waiting with their own breath held, hearts pounding, and finally she spit up a bunch of water and coughed until everything was out of her lungs.

Shelby handed him the blanket. He laid it against his chest, hooked his hands under Cyn's arms, pulled her back up against him and wrapped her up and held her close. "Damnit, Cyn. You fucking died on me. Don't do that ever again."

She shivered in his arms, her teeth chattering. Max was at her legs and pressed a thick gauze pad to the gash bleeding everywhere.

Chase put Cyn's socks on her and rubbed her blue-tinged calf and thigh to get the blood moving down to her extremity.

Hunt rubbed his hands up and down her arms and made sure the blanket was tightly wrapped around her. "Come on, baby, say something to me."

"I knew y-you'd s-save me."

He hugged her tighter and felt her head press to his cheek. "Don't make me do that again."

"I can't promise anything." She coughed again and burrowed back into him.

He wanted to smile at her teasing, because where the people she cared about were concerned, she'd do just about anything to help them.

"Everything h-hurts."

"I know. It's the hypothermia. I've got an ambulance standing by roadside, and one of the other officers is coming with a truck to take you out of here. We'll crank up the heater and get you warm. I couldn't get a helicopter in here with all the trees, so you have to hang on until I can get you the help you need."

Shelby kneeled down beside them. "Okay, Cyn, you win for craziest stunt. I'm going to make you a huge pot of hot stew. You'll sit by a fire. And you'll let Hunt do all the detective work from now on."

Cyn still trembled in his arms, but she managed to grin at Shelby. "I think I need a hospital first. My head hurts. My vision is all wonky."

Shelby brushed Cyn's hair away from her neck, then looked up at him. "Turn her a bit."

Hunt adjusted Cyn in his arms and looked down. He thought the wetness soaking his shirt was from her hair, but he was covered in blood.

Shelby's eyes went wide. "There's a huge cut on the back of her head and neck." Shelby turned to Max, who had the medical kit. He handed her some gauze pads and she pressed them to Cyn's deep wound.

Cyn squirmed, trying to get away from more pain.

"I've got you, sweetheart. I know it hurts. The truck just pulled up. Help is coming."

"Don't l-leave m-me."

"No way. Not going to happen, sweetheart."

She passed out on him again.

He tried to see it as a blessing as they strapped her into a basket stretcher to carry her up the hill. They placed her in the covered bed of the truck, opened the window between the cab and the back so the warm air from the heater could work its way back to her. They also put a bunch of hand warmers along her body and wrapped her in three dry blankets, hoping to raise her body temperature.

The head wound soaked through pad after pad. Her leg wasn't as bad, but it would require stitches, too.

He didn't know how extensive the head injury was, but hoped it wasn't as severe as it looked. Head injuries tended to bleed a lot. But he wasn't sure if she had a concussion or worse.

The drive to the parking area where the ambulance waited seemed to take forever, though they drove as quickly as they could over the rough terrain. He didn't worry about the evidence they'd marked and photographed on the forestry road. If it all got contaminated or destroyed, it didn't matter now. They knew Angela's car had been driven down that road. What mattered most was Cyn's life.

What he didn't know was if Cyn found her sister and niece in the car.

It only took a few seconds to transfer Cyn from the police truck to the ambulance where the paramedics were set up to run an IV into Cyn. Her color already looked better.

Hunt held her hand under the blanket, keeping one of the hand warmers between his palm and hers. She didn't wake during the whole ride to the hospital. By the time they got there, his concern was off the charts.

Her eyes fluttered for a moment and he leaned in close. "Cyn, baby, can you look at me? Let me see those beautiful blue eyes."

She didn't open them, but he felt a soft squeeze of his hand.

"There you are. I felt you. You're going to be okay. We're just about to take you into the hospital."

She whispered something.

He leaned in close. "I can't hear you, sweetheart. Say it again."

"No car seat. No Angela. Front windows open."

He kissed her on the forehead. "Okay, sweetheart. The baby probably wasn't in the car because she'd have been in her car seat. Rad probably took it and her out before he sent the car into the river. And your sister wasn't there, so more than likely she wasn't in the car either. Unless she was swept out the window."

She squeezed his hand again, letting him know he'd understood what she was trying to tell him.

"Could you see if the seat belt was fastened even though she wasn't there?"

She didn't answer right away and he thought maybe she'd passed out again, but then she whispered, "Not fastened."

He kissed her lips. "They're going to pull the car out tomorrow, but I'll tell the guys working the case what you told me. She's still out there somewhere. We'll find her." He helped the paramedics take her gurney out of the ambulance and walked beside her into the emergency room. The badge allowed him to stay with her as they wheeled her into a room, transferring her onto a bed. A nurse covered her in blankets from a warming cabinet.

Cyn groaned and tried to open her eyes, but the light seemed to hurt them, so she closed them tight.

The doctor issued a bunch of orders to the team around Cyn, then asked, "How long was she in the water?"

He answered. "Four minutes, twelve seconds. When we pulled her out of the water, she wasn't breathing. No heartbeat. I gave her CPR for approximately two minutes before she spit up a bunch of water. At that point, she was breathing on her own, though it was shallow and uneven until we got her warmed up enough that her whole body wasn't shaking violently. There's an eight-inch gash on her right shin, along with some other scratches. I think her leg got caught on some rocks. There's another severe wound on the back of her head and neck, left side. She said her vision was wonky and her head hurt."

The doctor nodded. "Do we suspect any other head or neck trauma?"

"She was able to move her head and limbs."

The doctor ordered a neck brace until they got her scanned and X-rayed to be sure there wasn't anything wrong.

"Thank you, Officer, we'll take it from here."

Hunt wanted to use his authority to stay with her, but he knew she was in good hands. "Doc, she's . . . my girlfriend, and I'll be waiting to see her as soon as possible."

The doctor nodded. "Any known allergies or medications? Drugs? Alcohol? Medical issues we should know about?"

"No drugs or alcohol. I'll call her mom right now and find out the rest, though she lives in town so her medical records are probably on file here. She's strong. Spirited. She's a fighter. She knew the risk going into that water and she did it anyway."

"I'll keep you posted."

"I need her back as soon as possible."

"I understand. We'll take good care of her." The doctor brushed her hand over Cyn's hair. "You hear that, Cyn? Your guy wants you back ASAP."

Cyn's lips twitched into a soft grin. She whispered, "He's bossy."

He slid in between the doctor and a nurse and bent over her. "Damn right. I'll be waiting for you, so hurry the hell up."

One side of her mouth lifted into a real half smile. "I'm just going to rest a bit first."

"Of course you are. You always do what you want to do." He kissed her right there in front of everyone. "Don't keep me waiting too long." He pressed his forehead to hers for a moment and did the hardest thing he'd ever done and left her to go and sit in the waiting room.

Shelby showed up first, since his brothers were taking care of the horses they'd ridden today. "How is she? What have they said?"

"Nothing yet. I'm waiting for an update once they've done their scans and X-rays. I called her mom. She's a mess. One daughter missing, another in the hospital. I expect her to arrive soon, though I don't know that Cyn will be happy she's here. You know anything about their relationship?"

"It's complicated. Messy, from what I understand."

"Okay. That's not a lot of help."

"Cyn needs you, Hunt. Someone who cares about *her*. Do you get that?"

"Yes. I like her. I want to be with her." He shot up from his seat and paced, then stopped in front of Shelby. "I can't stand that she's back there somewhere and I'm not with her. Do you have any idea how it hit me when I pulled her out of the water and practically her whole body was blue and she wasn't breathing? She had no heartbeat. She was dead, Shelby." He rubbed his hand over his neck.

Shelby stood and put her hands on his chest. "And you saved her. She's alive. She's going to be okay."

"Not good enough."

"What more do you want?"

"Her. With me. In perfect condition. Right here. Right now."

Shelby smiled and patted his chest. "You really care about her."

"Didn't I say so?"

"Yes. I think you've made it perfectly clear. She knows it, too. I know people think she's just out for a good time, but she's just like everyone else. She wants someone to want her."

"Everyone wants her. Max's eyes popped out of his head when he saw her strip down. Chase wasn't much better," he grumbled.

"She's a beautiful woman. And she has a beautiful

heart she wants to share with someone who sees more than the package it's wrapped in, Hunt. Don't be the next guy who just wants her. Be the guy who loves *all* of her."

"I never said I was in love with her."

Shelby took her seat again and stared up at him. "Your actions speak louder than anything." She grinned at him. "Hunt, who can't stand that she's somewhere in this hospital without him by her side."

He fell into the chair beside hers and kept his mouth shut.

Shelby leaned into his side. "She likes red wine. Mostly merlot. Pasta is her favorite. Any kind. Spaghetti, Alfredo, pesto, whatever. Pizza is a very close second. You can probably guess her favorite color."

"Everyone would think purple because of her hair, but she loves to wear blue." Most of her tattoos were blue butterflies.

Shelby bumped her shoulder into his. "You really have been paying attention. She loves to be outside."

"I see her walking in town all the time."

"She likes country music and classic rock the best. I'm pretty sure Aerosmith is her favorite band, though I've heard her singing Heart when she thinks she's alone in her shop. She's got a better than decent voice. But you know what I like best about her?"

"What?"

"That she knows how to have fun. I think a lot of people lose that as they get older. I think a lot of people in this town see her doing what she likes to do and are jealous that she goes about it with a carefree spirit they've lost. They can't get out of their heads and stop worrying about what people might think and just cut loose once in a while like she can. I'd hate to see someone try to rein her in when they'd probably be better off themselves joining in."

"Are you saying I don't know how to have fun?"

"I think you'd do well to let yourself have some fun." Shelby met his gaze. "I can't imagine all the things you see on the job. Today was hard, being out there, looking for clues and searching for someone we all think is probably dead. I hated watching Cyn go into that water, knowing the risk she took, but also thinking that she might find her dead sister and niece in that car. It took guts to face that. I'm so glad she didn't suffer that trauma, but that means you'll still be out looking for them, along with facing everything else you deal with on the job. I think you need someone like Cyn who can bring happiness and fun into your life."

"Part of what's drawn me to her is her bright spirit. And I even like her snap-at-you-when-she's-mad mouth, because she's not mean. She's spunky. And I just want to be with her. I want to know everything about what makes her so . . . her. I want to be the guy she likes. And wants."

"If she doesn't feel that way, and I really do think she does, then she'd be missing out on a really great guy. And I'll be the first to tell her that."

"Thank you. That means a lot, especially since you and I have had our differences."

"Your heart was in the right place with Chase and my biological father. And Eliza thinks you're an exceptional uncle."

"I love that girl."

"I know you do. It shows. You're a good man, Hunt. Cyn knows that, too."

They both stood when the doctor walked in with a soft smile on her face. "Officer Wilde, if you'll come into the hall with me. Cyn is awake and doing better than expected now that we've got her body temperature back to normal. She asked me to update you and gave me permission to speak about her injuries."

Shelby touched his arm. "I'll wait here."

Hunt followed the doctor down the hall to an area where they had some privacy. "She has a mild concussion. We believe she hit her head on a log or piece of wood in the water. We took out several splinters from the gash on her head and neck. We've stitched the wound. Her scans and X-rays show no broken bones or internal bleeding. Though she suffered severe hypothermia, she only suffered stage II frostbite on her feet. She's got some blistering on her toes, but it will heal quickly. You got her warm in a timely manner to stave off the worst of things."

"What about her leg?"

"She's got contusions and scratches on a lot of her body. We've stitched the majority of the gash on her shin and bandaged the whole thing. We're giving her IV antibiotics and will prescribe some for her to take for the next ten days at home along with putting topical ointment on her head, neck and shin to prevent infection, too. Any questions?"

"She swallowed a lot of water. Her heart stopped. Is she really going to be okay?"

"Her lungs looked clear, but we'll keep her here overnight and into tomorrow to recheck them and be sure she doesn't develop pneumonia. Her heart looked good on the scan. The cold prevented swelling in her entire body, so that helped a lot. Otherwise she's strong, like you said. She's in good health and we'll probably send her home sometime after lunch tomorrow if all stays looking as good as it does now."

He let out a sigh of relief. "When can I see her?"

"She's in room 302. I've let the nurses know you'll be up soon."

"Thank you."

"You're welcome. I have her mother's contact information. I understand she's on her way as well. I'll call and update her."

"Great. I'm going to see Cyn now."

"I'm surprised you were this patient." She gave him a knowing smile.

"Thank you for taking care of her."

"She's going to be fine. And with you looking out for her, I bet she'll recover even more quickly."

Hunt thanked the doctor again, then stopped by the waiting room just long enough to see his brothers had arrived and to tell them and Shelby he was going to see Cyn.

They followed him up to the third floor, but let him go in to see Cyn alone.

She was lying in the bed, eyes closed, a bandage wrapped around her neck, the blanket covering her all the way up to her chest. Her hair was dry and in wild disarray, but her cheeks were pink, her lips a deeper berry color and chapped from the cold water.

He leaned over without touching her and whispered in her ear, "I'm here, sweetheart."

She leaned her face into him. He kissed her forehead. "Rest, sweetheart. I'll be right here beside you."

She pulled her hand out from under the blankets.

He took it and kissed her palm. "Sleep," he ordered.

"Bossy," she whispered, and settled, her breathing soft and even.

He pulled the chair beside the bed closer so he could hold her hand and just be with her.

Shelby peeked in the door. "Everything okay?"

He nodded and pressed the back of Cyn's hand to his cheek. "It is now."

"We're going home. Do you want us to bring you anything in the morning?"

"I've got everything I need right here." He stared at Cyn, then turned back to Shelby. "Thanks for being here with me."

"She's my best friend. And I love you."

"Love you, too, sis."

Shelby smiled, understanding he really did feel like they were family, then backed out of the room, letting the door close softly.

The quiet settled around him. He found comfort in holding Cyn's hand and knowing she was going to be all right.

But the peace and quiet he wanted for her broke into chaos the moment her mother rushed through the door. The scent of cigarette smoke and Cyn's stepfather following her in. "Oh, my baby!" She flung herself toward Cyn's chest to hold her, but Hunt was quick enough to slip his arm between them and hold her off.

Cyn's mom pressed her hands on the bed and glared at him. "This is my daughter."

"I don't care. She's hurt. You have no idea how bad and you were just going to touch her without any consideration for her injuries."

"The doctor said she's fine."

"She will be, but—"

"Hunt. I've got this," Cyn rasped out, her voice thick with sleep.

"Are you warm enough? Do you need some more pain meds? The nurse is supposed to be here in"—he glanced at the whiteboard where the nurse had written the schedule—"twenty minutes."

"I can wait."

"Why is *he* here?" Cyn's mom asked.

"Because I want him here," Cyn snapped at her mom.

"But you don't want me?"

"I didn't say that." Cyn rolled her eyes, then squeezed them shut because the movement didn't agree with her concussion. Her blood pressure rising with her mom's appearance probably didn't help either.

Hunt studied her. "Sweetheart, you need to stay calm and get some rest."

"You don't get to tell her what to do." Cyn's mom folded her thin arms over her chest.

"Mom, give him a break. He saved my life. He's just looking out for me."

"Well, it was a stupid thing you did going into that water."

"You wanted me to find Angela and Lana."

"I want you to kill that asshole who hurt them. Did you do that yet?"

Cyn sighed. "Mom, you can plainly see the badge on Hunt's waist. Putting out a hit on someone is against the law, so you might want to shut up."

"Well, you didn't find them, so now what?" she asked him.

"Mrs. . . ." He didn't know her last name because he knew she'd married twice after Cyn's dad left them.

"Terri. Just Terri, since you're sleeping with my daughter."

"God, Mom, just stop talking already."

Hunt squeezed Cyn's hand, then met Terri's expectant gaze and short-tempered expression. He stuck to the matter at hand and not his relationship status with Cyn. "Angela and Lana are still missing. As far as we can tell, the baby wasn't in the car when it went into the water. We believe Angela wasn't in the car either, though it looks like Rad wanted us to believe she was and got swept away by the current. He's being brought in for questioning again this evening. We will continue to do everything possible to find Angela and Lana and bring Rad to justice for any and all crimes he's committed."

"And until then, you'll keep this one"—Terri pointed at Cyn—"from doing stupid things."

"Didn't you just say that I have no say in what she does?"

Terri fumed and turned to Cyn. "Maybe this one can rein you in."

"I intend to let her be as wild and free as she is, otherwise she just wouldn't be Cyn. And I like her just the way she is."

"Then you're a damn fool."

"I appreciate a good thing when I see it." He held

Cyn's gaze and watched her blink back tears when she smiled up at him.

"So you're not still mad about the dying-on-you thing?" She cocked an eyebrow.

He gave her a mock glare. "I'm relieved to have you back."

"So what now?" Terri asked.

He let Cyn rest and answered for her. "We'll continue the search for Angela and Lana. Cyn should be released from the hospital tomorrow afternoon. I'll take her to my place to recuperate."

Cyn opened her eyes again. "Hunt, you don't have to do that."

He squeezed Cyn's hand. "I want to take care of you, but if you'd rather go home . . ."

She shook her head.

"Okay, then. That's the plan."

"I guess I don't get a say," Terri grumbled.

"Mom. I know you're upset about all this, but I'll be fine in a few days."

Terri crossed her arms, then dropped them again. "Is there anything you need me to do for you?"

Hunt jumped in on that. "Shelby is picking up some clothes and things from Cyn's place in the morning."

Cyn sighed. "I'm good, Mom. Thank you for coming. I appreciate it. But right now, I just want to get some sleep. I'll call you in the morning."

Terri brushed her hand over Cyn's hair, in what had to be a rare show of gentleness and motherly love because Cyn looked stunned for a moment. "You sure you're okay?"

"I'm okay." Cyn squeezed his hand to let him know

he was part of the reason she was okay. "Just exhausted. Go home. Eat something. Get some rest. You look tired, too."

"My girls are trying to give me a heart attack." The rebuke was gentler than before, and Terri backed up toward her husband, who spoke for the first time.

"Be good. Do what the doctor tells you."

"I will."

Hunt waited for the couple to leave before he stood and leaned over Cyn.

"So, that's my mom."

He chuckled at her sardonic tone. "She's interesting."

"That's a word to describe her."

He brushed his fingers over her soft cheek. "You actually called me Hunt."

"That's your name."

"You always call me Wilde. And most of the time it doesn't sound pleasant. Hunt sounded good coming from your lips."

She gave him a soft smile. "Kiss me good night, Hunt."

He did. And it was soft and sweet and nothing like what he craved but everything she needed right now. He guessed they both did because it soothed him in a way nothing else could.

But he couldn't stop thinking about her mom either. "Is she serious about wanting you to kill Rad?"

She sighed out her frustration. "She's not exactly the most stable person in the world, in case you didn't notice."

"You didn't answer my question."

"She's as serious as she gets. But that doesn't mean

I'm out to do him in because she commands it. If he killed my sister and niece, or just one of them, I'd like to see him rot in a cell for the rest of his life. I'd like him to regret what he did and miss every moment from now on in Lana's life, knowing I'm the one raising her and that I will never allow him to see her. I want him to suffer the way I'm suffering without them." She broke down in a fit of tears that wrenched his heart.

"I'm sorry, sweetheart. I know how much you miss them and not knowing where they are or if they're safe is killing you." He held her close, his face in her neck, her arms around his shoulders until, exhausted, she fell back into a fitful sleep until the nurse came in, shot her full of narcotics, and Cyn got the respite she needed from all the trauma she'd suffered.

Hunt planned his next move to take down Rad and stop him from hurting anyone else, including Cyn, ever again.

# Chapter Twelve

RAD AND his lawyer sat next to each other at a scarred table, waiting for Officer Reid to come in and conduct yet another interview. Rad had heard about the search for Angela on the local news. He'd wanted to help, but his lawyer and parents told him to let law enforcement handle it. He looked guilty no matter what, so he decided to sit it out rather than spend the day with everyone around him judging him.

The stress of the situation wore on him. He didn't need this.

Officer Reid made him and his lawyer wait a good twenty minutes before he walked in the tiny room carrying a thick folder with his name on it. Just a trick, he told himself. *He wants to intimidate me.*

Rad fumed. Every second he sat here his lawyer racked up more money on the bill. His parents were helping him out, but their generosity only extended so far.

And they were on his case big-time about Angela and Lana. They'd outright asked him if he did anything to Angela. They begged him to bring Lana home.

As if he could.

He planned to keep his mouth shut from now on.

He'd given his statement the first time he got dragged down here and he didn't want to add anything to it. He wasn't stupid.

His lawyer broke the silence. "We've gone over Mr. Harmon's statement twice now. If you have no new questions or information, then my client has said all he knows about the disappearance of his girlfriend, Angela, and their daughter, Lana."

Officer Reid leaned in. "We have some new information."

"What?" Rad asked without thinking, but caught himself before he jerked forward and demanded to know exactly what they knew.

Officer Reid eyed him. "The police department, in conjunction with other law enforcement agencies along with Search and Rescue, conducted an extensive search today in an area about twenty miles outside of town. One of the teams, led by Officer Wilde, located Angela Wilson's vehicle."

Rad leaned forward. "How did he find it?"

Officer Reid held his gaze. "You sound surprised?"

"What? I'm not." He sat back and wiped his hands on his thighs. "It's just . . . That was fast."

"Your tax dollars at work. And Officer Wilde seems to have a personal interest in the case."

"Let me guess . . . Cyn." He thought he caught something going on between them when Hunt showed up after Cyn busted in on him at his place. That girl was like a dog with a bone. She'd never stop coming after him.

Officer Reid didn't answer him. "You and Officer Wilde were friends since grade school until you had a falling-out when he arrested you for assault."

That bitch deserved a good smack in the face for taunting him. She never knew when to shut up. Not like Angela. Well, except the last time he'd seen her.

"Then shouldn't Officer Wilde recuse himself from this case?" his lawyer asked.

"Officer Wilde was simply assisting with the search for two missing people. It seems he had a sixth sense for where the car might be, based on his knowledge of the area."

Rad fisted his hands, his mind going back to the days when he and Hunt did everything together and had each other's backs. Then his buddy went and made something of himself on the police force and Rad found himself stuck in a garage fixing cars and scraping by.

"Hunt's lived here his whole life. Of course he knows all the back roads and places to go," Rad grumbled.

His lawyer gave him a look to shut up, then asked, "You said you found the car? Did you find Angela or Lana?"

Rad flinched because he should have asked that question the second they said they found the car. He leaned in to the cop, who held him pinned in his gaze. "Well?"

"I'd have expected you to ask, seeing how you've been so concerned about finding your girlfriend and daughter. I mean, you must have called us . . . Oh, wait, you haven't called a single time to see if there's any word on them. You didn't file a missing person report. Not even on your daughter."

"Because I expect Angela to show up groveling that she wants me back, she didn't mean to leave with my kid, and begging me to forgive her."

Officer Reid sat back. "Your kid goes missing, her

mom's not answering the phone, no one, including her sister, who is very close to her, knows where they are and you just sit back and wait?"

Rad folded his arms across his chest. "You don't know me or how things were between me and Angela."

"I've got a good guess based on the domestic disturbance calls and the assault on Cyn Wilson." Officer Reid leaned in. "Just tell me what happened the other day when you came home angry you'd lost your job and you took it out on Angela."

"I've already told you everything. We fought. She got her licks in." He pointed to his scratched neck. "She took the baby and left. I haven't seen or heard from her since. Now, was she in the car, or not?"

"You mean were *they* in the car?" Officer Reid gave him an I-know-you're-lying-and-you-suck-at-it look that went with the smug I'll-get-you-for-it smirk.

Rad smacked his hand on the table. "Just tell me."

"No. *They* were not in the car."

He sighed and sat back. "Did *they* get swept away by the current?"

"Funny thing about what we found in the car. Or I should say, what we didn't find in the car."

"What?" he asked, because this was taking forever.

"No car seat. Not the base or the infant carrier."

"Couldn't they have been swept out of the car by the raging current?" his lawyer asked.

"Not likely, because they would have been strapped in with the seat belt. Oddly enough, the front windows were rolled down about three quarters of the way. On both sides. Strange since it was only a high of seventy-one the day Angela . . . left your place. Now, if she had a newborn in the back seat, it's extremely unlikely she'd have the windows down."

"Maybe the heater was on the fritz and she rolled the windows down because the car got too hot." Rad offered the plausible explanation.

"You're a mechanic. I'd think you'd have kept her car in tiptop shape."

"Things happen." He sounded stupid to his own ears.

"Then there's the thing with her seat belt."

"What about it?" he asked, trying to look bored.

"It wasn't buckled. It's the law. Now I know some people don't always remember, but her car has one of those reminder signals in it. Plus, with a new baby, you'd think she'd take all precautions."

"She was in a hurry when she left. Maybe she forgot and ignored the warning buzzer."

"Perhaps. But you know what I find the most interesting about us finding the car?"

"What?" he snapped.

"That you knew we found it in the water."

Sweat trickled from his armpits down his sides. "You said you did," he shot back.

Officer Reid shook his head. "No. I never did. So why don't you tell me how you knew it was in a fast-moving river that could have swept them away."

His lawyer looked at him.

He blurted out the first thing that came to mind. "I guessed. I assumed. That's all. I didn't do anything to them. You need to find them."

His lawyer put his hand on his arm. "Don't say anything more."

"If your client won't help himself and tell us what he really knows, then the DA is going to go after the maximum penalty for the charges coming his way. If he tells us where they are, maybe that helps his case."

"Are you charging my client?"

Officer Reid stared at him while Rad held his breath. "Not at this time. But I would advise your client to come clean about what he knows and tell us where Angela and Lana are before it's too late and the full weight of the law comes crashing down on him."

"My client has been advised."

"I'm sure we'll speak again soon, Mr. Harmon."

"So I'm free to go?"

"Yes. Just remember, it's a small town. Angela and Cyn are well regarded. And a missing infant . . . Well, that's just unthinkable. Everyone will be waiting for their safe return. And watching your every move."

Rad hated Officer Reid.

He stood and walked out without looking back and got into his truck.

His lawyer knocked on his window. "We need to talk."

"Tomorrow." He turned on the truck, backed out of the parking space and drove out of the police station lot, hoping he didn't have to ever go back there and knowing Hunt wouldn't stop coming for him.

Not now.

His life was royally fucked. He wouldn't be able to go anywhere without this hanging over his head.

He slammed his hand on the steering wheel several times until his palm ached and the rush of adrenaline and rage washed through him.

"Fucking Hunt!" He pulled his phone out of his back pocket and made the call with vengeance in mind.

"Cyn nearly died today because of you." Rage filled Hunt's voice, but it was nothing compared to how Rad felt.

"We used to be friends. Now you're coming after me and ruining my life. I'm going to make you pay, and I'm going to use her to do it."

# Chapter Thirteen

HUNT PULLED into his driveway at dusk with Cyn in the passenger seat beside him. It took longer than expected to get her out of the hospital because she'd experienced some dizziness and cognitive issues that cleared up the longer she was awake, but the doctor ran more tests and scans to be sure everything was okay, especially with the concussion. He'd waited in her room, pacing like a caged animal, hoping everything was all right.

"I told you to take me home."

He glanced over at her, looking so beautiful in a long blue dress that skimmed her curves and looked soft and comfortable. And it didn't press on the stitches running down her shin.

"You shouldn't be alone."

"Shelby volunteered to stay with me."

He narrowed his gaze. "I thought you wanted to come here with me."

"You're the one who looks like you'd rather me not be here."

He reminded himself that the stressful day brought only good news. She was okay. Some minor side effects of the hypothermia that the doctor assured them would clear up over the next couple days as her brain and organs recovered from the shock and cold. Her heart was fine. Her blood work came back normal. Her blood pressure was a little high, but that was understandable given all she'd been through.

But he couldn't get Rad's warning and threat out of his head.

"I'm sorry, sweetheart. It's been a long couple of days and I guess it all kind of hit me that you're okay now, but it could have been so much worse."

She leaned across the seat. "I appreciate that you're worried about me. But you need to tell me what's really wrong with you. Because there's something. And if it's not about bringing me to your house when we've barely started this thing between us—"

He kissed her to stop her from saying anything more about him not wanting her here. He kept the kiss soft and tempting and promising so much more to come. He brushed his lips across her cheek and whispered in her ear. "I brought you here because it's where I want you." He drew away a few inches so she could look in his eyes and see the truth. "I just want you, Cyn."

"I'm here with you, exactly where I want to be."

He brushed the back of his fingers over her cheek and tucked her hair behind her ear. "I don't want anything else to happen to you."

"I promise not to jump into the river again."

"Except if it's for your sister or niece, right?"

"You already know me so well."

"I've been paying attention," he admitted, letting her know again that things between them may have started off with him laying down the law when she broke it, but he'd always been intrigued and drawn to her.

And because he was really starting to understand what drove her, he knew she'd jump into the fire for the people she cared about. Which meant she'd put herself in danger and not think of the consequences if it meant saving her sister and niece.

"Will you promise me something?"

"I won't take my clothes off in front of your brothers anymore. Probably," she added, teasing.

"That's a start. But this is important."

"My being naked in front of your brothers isn't important to you?" The teasing grin didn't distract him from getting her to promise what he wanted.

"I'd really prefer the only one you get naked with from now on is me."

"Do I get to see you naked? Because it seems wholly unfair that you've gotten an eyeful of me and I got nothing."

"Cyn, I'll strip bare if you promise me this one thing."

Cyn relented, dropped the teasing grin and looked him in the eye. "Just ask, Hunt. The last thing I want to do is upset you."

"I know I can't stop you from doing anything and everything possible to find your family, but will you please promise me that if you chase after anything that you think will lead to Angela and Lana, you will let me know so that I can, if not talk you out of it, at least chase you down and be sure you have backup?"

She tilted her head and studied him for a moment. "Do you think I'm reckless? Or is there something you're not telling me?"

"Not reckless. Driven. And willing to put yourself at risk for others. And yes, there's something else." He needed to tell her about the threat so she'd be careful and look out for herself when he couldn't be with her.

She put her hand on his shoulder and squeezed. "What is it?"

"Rad."

"He's an asshole and quite possibly a murderer. Believe me, I won't underestimate him."

"He called me last night." He traced his finger along the side of her face. She leaned into his touch, making him want to kiss her again, hold her close and keep her safe. "He threatened me with harming you."

She gasped. "What did he say exactly?"

"That I ruined his life and he'd pay me back for going after him by going after you, basically."

"The fucking coward. You're too hard a target, so he comes after me because . . . what? Not because I've pestered him about my sister, but because he thinks I'm important to you?"

He kissed her quick and hard. "You *are* important to me. Damnit, Cyn, this is no idle threat. He hit you once. We think he killed your sister and possibly his own baby. He knows we found the car and are on to him. I spoke to Officer Reid, who interviewed him last night. Rad made a mistake. He knew we found the car in the water without Officer Reid mentioning it."

"Did they arrest him?"

"No. It's not enough. We need more evidence, not just what we think happened."

"You can't let him get away with this."

"He won't. There's nowhere he can go that this won't

follow him. Then there's the other thing I'm investigating that led me to him, too."

"What other thing?"

"I'm still looking into it. It's an open investigation. I got distracted by your sister's disappearance, but if I'm right, Rad is facing even more charges."

Cyn shook her head. "It doesn't surprise me."

"He knows he's about to lose everything, including his freedom. If he has Lana, there's no way he can just bring her home and raise her without a lot of questions about Angela."

"Okay. I'll contact a lawyer tomorrow and get started on whatever needs to be done for me to have custody of her when we find her."

He rubbed his thumb over her cheek. "I don't know how you stay so positive and take this all in and keep going."

"For my sister. For Lana. And because I want that asshole to pay." She squeezed his shoulder again. "But I will be careful and tell you before I rush into danger again."

He half frowned and shook his head at her. "At least you're honest that you'll be putting me through hell again."

"I hope you think I'm worth it, because you asked me to stay here with you tonight. I haven't dated in quite a while. Truthfully, I'm tired of not getting what I want."

"And what's that, Cyn?"

She looked at him, her eyes filled with uncertainty about revealing her needs. "What Shelby has with Chase. A committed, exclusive, all-in relationship. Not let's-have-fun-and-see-where-this-goes, like most of the men I've seen think is what I want, and yeah, maybe that's my fault for not being clear up front. So I'm doing that now, because Shelby is my best friend and she's marrying your brother and that could get complicated, but I hope it won't because I'm interested in a lot more than just getting naked with you. The last few days, you've shown me that you care about me and want to be with me."

"I do. I'm not a serial dater anymore. Haven't been in a long time. When I go out with someone, I'm looking for a connection. I feel that with you. Yes, you're beyond beautiful and I want you desperately, but I also want to know you."

"You said something like that before, and I appreciate you letting me hear it again, because it's important to me to start this with a clear understanding that there's a level of commitment between us."

"You have my undivided attention and understanding that this is a monogamous relationship and that, like you, I hope this turns into something deeper and lasting."

"Then we're on the same page."

"Honey, I've been waiting for you to catch up."

"Well, you weren't exactly sending out the I-want-you vibes when you issued me those tickets, and I did get hit in the head."

He chuckled. "I was being professional while having a dozen fantasies about you. And I'm sorry you got hit in the head. I should have never let you go into the water."

"You know you couldn't have stopped me, right?"

"I know. Still . . ."

Cyn sat back in her seat and reached for the door handle. "You ready to go in and see what happens next?"

"I know what's going to happen. You're going to sit on the couch and rest in front of a fire."

"Sounds cozy."

"It will be," he promised, because he couldn't wait to hold her close and just enjoy some normal quiet time with her.

They both got out of the truck. He held her bag in one hand and wrapped his other arm around her waist just in case she got dizzy again as they walked up the stairs. Plus, he just wanted to keep her close.

He didn't even get the door open when Shelby pulled into the driveway and gave a double-tap to the horn, smiling at them through the windshield.

They waited for Shelby to get out and retrieve the pot from the back seat floorboard. She held it up and walked toward them. "As promised. Stew."

Cyn was about to head down to meet Shelby, but he held her close. "You're still a bit wobbly. Let her come up."

Shelby eyed Cyn up and down. "You look a lot better."

The dark circles under Cyn's eyes were gone. Her skin was back to having a warm, rosy glow to it. Her eyes were clear and bright and focused most of the time. She limped on her hurt leg, but she didn't seem to be in a great deal of pain. Probably because he'd made sure she took her meds before they left the hospital a little while ago.

"I feel better. Where's your Wilde man?"

"At home with Eliza. She's come down with a cold."

"Oh, no. I hope she feels better soon."

Hunt unlocked the door, pushed it open, then let the two ladies go in ahead of him.

Shelby tapped him in the gut with her elbow, but spoke to Cyn. "Looks like you've got your own Wilde man taking care of you."

Cyn grinned. "If he keeps doing a good job, I'll keep him."

"I'm all yours, sweetheart." After their talk in the truck, he wanted her to know he meant it and had no problem saying it in front of Shelby. She would no doubt tell Chase, who would tell Max and his dad, and everyone in town would probably know tomorrow that he and Cyn had shacked up at his place.

Let them talk.

He'd been just as honest as Cyn had been about what he wanted.

That didn't mean he wasn't trying to navigate this next step with a lot of consideration for her condition while he also figured out how fast or slow she wanted to move this forward. Either way, he walked into the downstairs bedroom and put her bag on the dresser. No matter what, he wanted her in his bed tonight. Even if he wasn't in it with her.

He found Shelby and Cyn in his kitchen off the open living room.

Cyn smiled at him. A big, open, happy smile. "I love your place. Outside, it's got this old-fashioned charm with all the wood and black-framed windows, but inside, it's a more rustic modern feel."

This pleased him so much that he smiled and his heart soared. "I'm glad you like it."

"My favorite part is the wall of windows off the back

overlooking the pastureland. Nothing but trees and wide-open fields. It's gorgeous."

He loved it here. "This is the backside of the ranch. Don't be surprised if you wake up to cows mooing, though I think Max and Chase moved the cattle to another pasture last week. I don't know, I've barely been here, it seems, with all my double shifts. I used to work a four-hour shift early in the morning at the ranch, then head into town for my shift on the force. Now, it's double shifts and more most days."

"When do you have to go back to work?" Cyn asked.

"Tomorrow. Unless you're not feeling well, then I'll stay home with you."

Shelby raised a brow. "I don't go in until late tomorrow, so I can always come by."

Hunt thought of Cyn's concussion. "Chase and Max will be on the ranch anyway, so I'll ask them to keep an eye on Cyn."

Cyn shook her head. "You guys are sweet, but I'm okay. I spoke with my assistant at the shop. She's got things covered, but I really need to go in and make sure everything is running smoothly."

Hunt closed the distance to her. "Cyn, you need to rest, sweetheart."

"I need to run payroll, do a couple other things. I won't stay all day. I'll probably sleep in and go in late."

He eyed her, but ultimately let it go. He couldn't keep her here, even if he wanted to wrap her in bubble wrap, lock the doors and keep the world away. "Remember what we talked about outside?"

She gave him a firm nod. "I'll be careful and stay in touch with you."

"I'd really appreciate that."

Shelby beamed. "Look at you two working together."

Hunt rolled his eyes. "I'll start a fire." He went to the hearth and stacked the wood and kindling while Shelby heated the stew on the stove and chatted with Cyn. He couldn't hear what they were saying. He assumed they were talking about him. He got the sense the two seemingly different women were really close.

Cyn always called Chase Shelby's Wilde man. He'd like to be Cyn's and hoped them spending time alone tonight would bring them closer together. He didn't expect things to go anywhere in the bedroom while she recovered, but he hoped to find a kind of intimacy in being alone with her and just talking and being close.

He lit the match and set it to the paper and kindling. In seconds, the fire grew and caught the dry split logs.

"You two enjoy dinner and have a nice night," Shelby said as she walked from the kitchen toward the front door. "I'll see you both soon."

And just like that, he was alone in his house with Cyn. She came around the counter and into the living room space toward him. "Okay, Wilde, you said if I made you a promise you'd get naked."

He saw the teasing light in her eyes, but wasn't about to renege on a promise. He stood with the fire behind him, grabbed the back of his thermal over his shoulder and pulled it up and over his head.

Cyn's eyes went wide with surprise and lust. "Good God, Wilde. Damn." Her eyes wandered over his chest, down to his abs and over his arms. He tried really hard not to flex and look like an idiot.

He reached for the button on his black jeans and popped it just to see what she'd do.

The damn woman bit her bottom lip and her eyes lit up with anticipation.

If she wanted a show, he'd give it to her, because he was hard and aching for her, standing there in her body-skimming dress with her breasts mounded at the top of it, all those curves just waiting for his hands and lips and tongue to explore.

But just before he slid the zipper over his thick cock, she closed the short distance between them and put her hand on his chest. A bolt of electricity shot through him as her skin met his.

"I know I started this . . . God, you're hard to resist with your clothes on. With them off . . . there's no possible way to not want you desperately." Her gaze slid over him. She took him in with a look of such desire and need and appreciation that his cock twitched and he fought not to grab her and make love to her.

He'd known she was teasing when she made the comment about him getting naked, so he let her off the hook, cupped her face in one palm and smiled at her. "I was just going along because I promised you. I knew you didn't really mean it and was about to stop anyway."

"I do want it," Cyn said, her gaze on his hard length pressed against his fly.

He brushed his thumb over her cheek. "Enough said, Cyn. Another time. Let's eat." He went to put his shirt back on, but she closed the distance between them, pressed her breasts to his chest and kissed him softly.

He wrapped her in his arms, his shirt dangling over

her ass and down her legs. They fell into the moment and lost themselves in dozens of kisses, his tongue sliding over hers, her hands wrapping around his neck and holding on as she pressed close to him. He'd let her have her fill and end things when she was ready. She ended up with her cheek pressed to his chest, his arms banded around her as he held her close, his chin atop her head.

"I've never felt anything like this."

"Like what?" he asked.

"Safe. Like I'm not going to lose this moment if I let go."

He pressed his lips to the top of her head. "We're just getting started."

"If it feels this good now, what's it going to be like down the road?"

He leaned back, cupped her face, kissed her softly and said, "Better," believing it with his whole heart.

# Chapter Fourteen

CYN COULDN'T quite believe she'd ended up in Hunt's house, eating dinner, then lying on the sofa with him behind her, a pillow and her between his legs, his fingers brushing through her hair. He'd lulled her into a relaxed state nestled in his warmth while he watched a movie she hadn't paid any attention to because she was too busy enjoying the fire and the closeness she felt. But it was getting late and the movie credits were about to roll and she needed to decide what came next, because ever since he'd made it clear he wanted her and she'd seen him with his shirt off, she wanted to get her hands on him.

"Hunt?"

"Yeah, sweetheart? You okay?"

"You should take me to bed now."

"Sure, sweetheart. You can have my bed down here. I'll sleep upstairs."

She shifted so she could look up at him. "That's not what I said."

His gaze held hers. "What are you asking me for, Cyn? To share a bed and hold you while you sleep, or more?"

She didn't hesitate. "All of it. Everything."

He brushed his hand over her hair. "It doesn't have to be tonight."

She sat up and faced him. "After what I've been through, what *we* went through at the river, I don't want to waste precious time. We agreed to be together, so let's *be* together."

He hesitated.

She pushed to let him know she really meant it. "Wilde, make love to me."

One side of his mouth kicked up into a half grin. "Now who's bossy?"

She rose from the sofa, giving him a good glimpse of her cleavage as she did so.

"That's so not fair."

"You want it? Come and get it." She held her hand out to him.

He took her hand, turned the TV off with the remote, checked to be sure the fire had died down enough to be left unattended and followed her as she turned and walked toward his bedroom.

"Your ass is perfection."

She gave him a seductive grin over her shoulder. "Yeah? I can't wait to get my hands on yours."

Hunt snuggled in close behind her when she stopped at the foot of the bed. He put his hands on her hips, pulling her back and wedging his thick erection in the crevice of her ass. His warm lips pressed to the place where her neck met her shoulder, his tongue sweeping out to taste her as he kissed her there. "Are you sure you're feeling up to this? You're not sore or too tired?"

She leaned back into him and rubbed her ass against

his thick cock. "I'm hurt and tired and sad and angry and the only thing I know for sure right now is that you are the best thing in my life. I want to wrap myself around you and feel you move with me. I want to let everything else slip away until there's only me and you and this crazy magic between us." She turned in his arms and stared up at him. "Be with me, Hunt, in this moment we make for ourselves, because who knows if we'll ever have it again."

He cupped her face. "I won't let anything bad happen to you."

She hooked her hands on his wrists. "It already has. It will again. So let me have you and tonight and however many more moments we can share together."

"All you want, Cyn. Everything you want. However you want it." He kissed her soft and sweet and with a promise that this was just the spark. "Give me a second to light the fire. I want to see you." He kissed her again. Took his time. His lips brushing hers, building that spark into a flame as his tongue swept over hers and he claimed her mouth.

He ended the kiss on a soft groan, released her and moved through the dark room to another beautiful stone fireplace where he lit a match and set it to the already prepared wood and kindling.

Behind him, she pulled the comforter and blankets down on the bed, slipped out of the comfortable maxidress and her bra, climbed onto the soft mattress, wrapped her arms around her bent knees and took in the gorgeous man lit up by the fire. The flames highlighted his dark hair and the scruff along his jaw. He sat on his heels, his jeans pulled taut over well-defined thighs. She'd seen what was under that thermal earlier and wanted to kick herself for not taking advantage. But now she was glad they'd waited a bit longer.

She appreciated that he'd taken the time to set the romantic mood. The fire made the room feel cozy. But the man made her feel safe and wanted in a way she'd never experienced.

"You are without a doubt the sexiest man I've ever seen."

Hunt turned from the fire to look at her sitting in his bed and caught his breath. "Cyn." Her name came out like a prayer. "It's not enough to say you're beautiful. You take my breath away." He rose and came toward her, pulling his shirt off and letting it drop to the floor. His gaze was hot and focused on her when he pulled off his work boots and socks, undid his jeans and shoved them down his long legs, leaving him standing in only his boxer briefs next to the bed with his hungry gaze devouring every inch of her. His thick erection poked out of the waistband, straining against the constraint. He leaned over and pulled open the drawer by the bed. He rummaged inside, then tossed a packet of condoms on the bed.

She watched it land next to her, then met his gorgeous blue eyes.

"What do you want, Cyn?"

"Everything. All of you."

Hunt crawled onto the bed as she lay back into the pillows. He softly kissed a particularly bad bruise on her calf and another on her thigh. She'd gotten banged up in the river. "I'll try to be careful with you, Cyn, but you tell me if I'm hurting you and I'll make it better."

He planted a kiss on her hip as he moved his way up her body, then his wicked tongue flicked over her tight nipple.

"I'll come back for this. Right now, I'm desperate to taste you."

She expected another deep kiss, but the man sat back, slid his hands beneath her knees and pulled her legs up and out so she was completely open to him. He spared a glance for her wrapped leg with the stitches, then slid down, wrapped his arms around her thighs and licked her already wet folds from the bottom to her swollen clit. He took his time, licking and plunging his tongue inside her, tasting her until she lost all control and thrust against his mouth, wanting more and hoping he never stopped. She slid her fingers into his silky dark hair and held him to her as he took her up to the edge, back down again, then back up but never let all that pleasure explode on the orgasm she desperately craved.

"Hunt, please."

He raised his head and rubbed the pad of his thumb in soft circles over her clit. Her inner muscles clenched, wanting that release he held back even as she rocked into his touch.

"I love touching you, feeling you wanting me."

"I do want you. Inside me."

He pressed his thumb harder against her clit and lapped his tongue over her sensitive folds. "Soon. I could do this all day." To prove it, he slowed things down again, sliding one finger into her and stroking her in long slow glides in and out, his tongue softly sweeping over her clit again and again. Then it was two fingers and that wicked tongue of his, and the tempo built subtly at first until she was writhing again, her fingers clenched in his hair, her legs spread wide and her man making her soar.

She was still quaking with her release when he slid his tongue ever so slowly over her again and she sighed with the sheer pleasure of it. She stared down at him and met his hungry blue gaze.

He planted a kiss just below her belly button, then another above it, then between her breasts, on her chin, then he took her mouth in a searing kiss, his tongue plunging deep. She tasted herself and all the desire he unleashed on her. He vibrated with it. But he still managed a soft caress of his fingers up her arm, down her chest, until his big hand settled over her heavy breast, her tight nipple pressed to his palm.

He gave her one more deep kiss, their tongues tangling, before he trailed kisses down to her free breast and he took her hard nipple into his mouth and suckled it deep. She arched into his touch and slid her hands over his wide shoulders and the strong muscles in his back, then swept them back up and into his hair.

He used the hand on her breast to pluck at her tight nipple and sent a bolt of heat down low in her belly. She rolled her hips up but he was holding himself mostly off her and she let out a disgruntled groan. He answered it by releasing her breast and kissing her hard and deep as he plunged two fingers deep into her wet core. Those fingers worked in and out of her and the heel of his hand pressed against her clit. This time he didn't make her wait and sent her flying again.

The kiss they shared turned into a soft sweep of his tongue along hers in a much slower, leisurely pace and those fingers still in her eased out, then back in like he had all the time in the world to just keep touching her and making her feel heavenly blissful.

She brushed her hands up and down his back, broke the sweet kiss and looked up at him. "I want to touch you."

"Later. Right now, I just want you to lay there and enjoy this as much as I am." He pressed a soft kiss to her cheek, then the other, on her forehead, all the while he played with her in the most sensual way. He went back to her breast, licking and sucking her nipples, teasing her into another lull before the storm he liked to build in her, until finally he grabbed the condom and tore it open.

He rose above her to slide it on, but she beat him to his thick cock and wrapped her hand around it, feeling the silky warm skin stretched taught and the hardness as she stroked him from base to tip and back down.

He hissed and thrust into her hand. "It's not been easy to wait this long, Cyn. You keep that up, it's going to be over the second I'm inside you."

She stroked him one last time, soft and slow the way he'd teased and tempted her, then took the condom from his hand and rolled it on him herself.

He settled between her thighs, finally putting some of his weight on her as the wide head of his penis brushed against her damp folds and he glided into her in one smooth stroke until he was deep and snug and finally a part of her.

He kissed her softly. "You feel incredible."

She slid her hands over his rock-hard ass, spread her legs wider and pulled him in deeper.

He groaned. "Damn, Cyn, I really wanted to make this last."

"I want to feel you let go."

He gave her what she wanted and pulled out nearly all the way, then slammed back into her in one powerful thrust that made her inner muscles quake.

"Yes," she moaned.

As if she'd unleashed him, he let loose and fucked her hard and fast and she matched him, meeting his thrusts, her fingers digging into his hips as she pulled him in, and the world fell away. She lost herself in the lust-fueled desire pouring out of him and into her.

Hunt shifted just enough to hit that spot he had no trouble finding and her core tightened around him.

"Yes," he cried out.

She went off like a rocket and Hunt thrust deep one more time, spilling himself inside her. He crashed on top of her and it was the most wonderful thing to feel his weight sink her into the bed and to hold him while his and her breathing slowed. She drew lazy swirls and lines with her fingertips on his back and loved how close she felt to him, lying skin to skin, feeling like they'd shared something extraordinary.

"You okay?" he whispered at her neck.

She realized she was smiling. "Better than I've ever been."

He planted his hands next to her shoulders and pushed up just enough to look down at her. "God, you're beautiful. Especially when you smile."

"I'm very happy here with you like this."

He brushed his fingers along the edge of the bandage on her neck over the stitches. "I didn't hurt you?" He glanced down at her leg.

She cupped his face and made him look at her. "You only make me feel good."

He pressed his forehead to hers. "That's all I want to do."

"You did. Multiple times. You're better than any drug."

He brushed his nose against hers. "Good. I'll be right back." He pulled out of her and left her feeling empty and desperate to have him back. She'd never felt that way with anyone before, but with him, she craved that closeness and connection.

He slid out of bed and went into the bathroom to deal with the condom. She stared at the fire, watching the flames dance, knowing something happened while she made love with Hunt. Actually, it probably happened the night he'd come racing to her rescue at Rad's place and she'd seen the deep concern in his eyes. She'd seen it again when she woke up on the riverbank freezing and stared into his frightened eyes. He'd thought he lost her. She'd thought she'd almost missed her chance with him.

She'd fallen for Hunt and had her very own Wilde man.

He slipped into bed next to her, pulled the covers over them, slid his arm beneath her neck, careful to avoid her injury, hooked his arm over her hips and held her close as the fire died down and the darkness crept back into the room.

"Hunt."

"Yeah, sweetheart."

"Thank you for taking care of me." Tears filled her eyes. No one had ever taken care of her the way he did and she didn't mean the outstanding, mind-blowing sex.

He pulled her a bit tighter to him. "Always, Cyn." He kissed her shoulder and was still holding her later when she woke from a nightmare of her sister dead and drowned in the car, the icy water trying to swallow Cyn, too. He soothed her back to sleep with soft, reassuring words, his body pressed along the back of hers, his arms holding her secure.

He made love to her again in the dim light of dawn when she'd felt his thick erection pressed to her bottom and couldn't help but rub her ass against it. His hand had slipped between her legs, the other around her back and up between her arm and ribs to cup her breast. Then he'd rolled to his back, bringing her on top of him, lying down his length, her back to his chest, her head on his shoulder. She planted her feet on the bed near his thighs and spread her legs wide so she was open to his fingers fondling her soft folds, plunging deep inside her and rubbing against her clit while he pinched and played with her nipple with his other hand and rubbed his hard cock on her ass. He made her come twice before he shifted her back onto the bed, grabbed another condom and made love to her slow and sweet and like he had the rest of his life to do it and would willingly forget everything else to be in bed with her.

He slipped out of bed again, and she fell into a deep sated sleep and woke up alone, but she felt him nearby and smiled because that was new, too, and she liked it.

So she went in search of her Wilde man, knowing he hadn't gone far.

# Chapter Fifteen

❧

Hᴜɴᴛ ꜰᴇʟᴛ her before he saw her coming out of his room. Damn, she looked good wearing his thermal shirt from yesterday and a pair of socks bunched up at her ankles. The bandage circling her calf didn't detract from her spectacular legs. Her purple hair was a mass of wild waves around her beautiful face. Her blue eyes narrowed on him the second she spotted him across the room.

She pointed an accusing finger at him. "That is not cool."

He shifted toward her, but didn't stand from the desk chair. "I was just about to come and wake you, sweetheart." He hated that she'd woken up alone, but he'd had some files to go over from the forensics on the car used in the home invasion at Mrs. Phelps's place.

She waved her finger side to side and shook her head. "No way do you get to taunt me with that uniform *and* glasses. Come on, Wilde, that's too damn much sexy for one woman to resist."

He full-on busted up laughing.

She turned disgruntled and closed in on him, then straddled his lap and cupped his face. "What do I have to do to get you to wear those to bed?"

He chuckled again. "You can have me right here, right now, but make it quick because I've got to go to work."

"Challenge accepted." And then she kissed him like her life depended on it and rocked her hips into his thickening erection, and he thought he was joking about them having a quickie before he left but now he was dead serious about getting her naked again.

He slipped his hands under the way-too-big-for-her thermal and cupped her bare breasts, stroking and fondling and squeezing her nipples between his fingers as she sighed into his mouth and kissed him deeper.

She didn't waste time tackling the button and fly on his jeans. The second she freed him, her hand wrapped around his aching cock and she stroked him to a hard and throbbing rod. "Condom," she said between kisses.

He hated to release her spectacular breasts, but had to use one hand to pull his wallet out of his back pocket, unfold it on the desk and find the condom he handed her because he loved watching her roll it on him.

She did it in two seconds flat, jumped off his lap, spun around toward his desk, pulled the shirt up over her bare, lush ass, planted her hands on the wood and looked over her shoulder at him with a sexy come-and-get-me smile.

He palmed her ass in both hands, squeezing the cheeks, then slid one hand down over the blue-and-black butterfly tattoo, followed the tiny tattooed dash lines down her ass and swept his fingers over her soaking wet soft folds.

"Damn, you weren't kidding about the uniform and glasses turning you on."

"And I'm not kidding about you fulfilling my little

fantasy right now, Wilde." She pushed her ass into his hard cock and half groaned, half begged, "Now."

He took her by the hips and thrust into her, pushing her into the desk.

"Yes."

He loved being inside her, but she rocked him back on his heels when she slid her hand down to where they were joined and bracketed his cock between two fingers as he pulled out, then thrust back into her. The feel of her surrounding his hard length deep inside her and those fingers adding just the right amount of grip and he lost all thought of control and slammed into her again and again, and just when he was close, she moved those fingers up to her clit and stroked herself as he thrust deep inside her and they both came on jagged pants and desperate need until ecstasy overtook them and he ended up bent over her back trying to catch his breath and wondering how this woman made him want her so damn bad and love it.

He slipped his arms around her under her breasts, pulled her up and hugged her to him. She leaned her head back against his shoulder and tilted it into his jaw.

"Cyn. You are so fucking amazing."

"You liked that," she teased.

"I'm barely standing after that."

"You said I had to hurry, so I had to figure out a way to speed things along to both our satisfaction."

Which made him think she'd never done anything like that with anyone else. He didn't ask. He didn't want to know. He held on to the fact that this was something special between them.

She put her arms over his and snuggled into him. "Thanks for chasing the nightmares away last night."

"How are you feeling today?"

"Lovely right now. Content." She held his arms tighter. "But I'm so worried about Angela and Lana. It's overwhelming—all the what-ifs make me afraid and angry and I feel helpless."

He kissed her on the head. "I know. I hope we uncover something solid today to help us find them. Until we do, know that I'm here for you."

She settled back into him and he kissed her soft hair. They stood like that for a few minutes before she glanced up at him. "Don't you have to leave?"

"I do. But I like this. You and I together, looking out the window at the cows." It hit him all at once. "Oh, shit. Cows. My brothers are here." He scooped up Cyn and carried her away from the large windows and back into the bedroom where he set her on the bed. "Bad move. You. A bed. Those legs. That ass." He groaned. "Those breasts." He shook his head.

"Anything else you like about me?"

He leaned down and looked her right in the eye. "Everything. All of it. You."

She kissed him softly. "That's really sweet."

"Will you do something for me?"

"Maybe."

He even liked that she was honest and didn't say yes when she didn't know what she was saying yes to. "Stay here today. Watch TV. Rest. Heal. The search teams will still be out looking for your sister and Lana in and around the area where we found the car."

"Where will you be?"

"I'm following another lead on a home invasion that happened last night."

She tilted her head. "Like what happened to Mrs. Phelps?"

"Yes. You can call or text me whenever you want. Just know if I don't pick up or text you back right away it's because I truly can't because of whatever I'm doing on the job. But I'll get back to you as soon as I can."

She kissed him again. "Be safe."

"Cyn?"

She gave him a half grin. "I will stay here today."

"My brothers will be keeping close today."

"You asked them to come babysit me."

"I did," he confessed. "And I'm hoping they didn't see the whole show when they arrived with the cattle."

She blushed. "I was too busy loving on you to notice."

"Whenever you're around, you have my full and undivided attention, too, sweetheart. The house is yours. Do you need anything before I go?"

"I'll just be waiting for you to come home."

He leaned in and touched his forehead to hers. "You have no idea how good that sounds to me."

Her eyes went wide. "I—"

He kissed her, long and deep, until she had her arms wrapped around his neck and was trying to pull him down on top of her on the bed. He pulled back, reluctant to let her go, knowing he needed to get to work. "I'm going to take what you said with me today and be happy to know you're here waiting for me."

She gave him a sweet smile and nodded. "Okay."

"Okay." He brushed his fingers down her thighs as he stood. "Your meds are on the kitchen counter if you need them."

"I feel better today. I think you're right, though, a day

of rest will do me good. And maybe just some ibuprofen to ease the pain where I'm stitched up."

He gave her a nod, then went into the bathroom to clean up before he left for work. He found her in the kitchen with a cup of coffee, looking in his fridge.

"You are a healthy eater."

"I try to be."

She looked over her shoulder. "Please tell me there is something chocolate in this house."

"Check the pantry. I usually have some cookies in there. If not, text me what you want and I'll pick it up on my way home."

She tilted her head. "Really? You will?"

"Sure," he said, wondering why she didn't think he would.

"That's very sweet, Hunt."

He shrugged. "It's not a big deal."

"It is to me." She looked down into her coffee mug, but he caught the sincerity in her eyes.

He closed the distance between them. "Anything you want, Cyn, just ask."

"You've done so much for me already, coming to my rescue at Rad's place, searching for my sister and niece, giving me an amazing night and morning. Holding me when I needed you last night. Asking your brothers to watch over me today."

"I just want to keep you safe."

She studied him for a second. "You're worried Rad will make good on his threat and come after me. Here."

"Here would be a real *fuck you* to me. Hurting you in my house, on my land, when I'm not here . . . Yeah. I'm worried. And I wouldn't leave you if the department wasn't shorthanded and I didn't have a lead that could help me put Rad behind bars or at least give me some leverage to make him tell us where Angela and Lana are."

"What lead?"

"Right now, it's just a hunch. I need some solid proof."

"Then go get it. I'll be fine. Especially if there are chocolate cookies."

He gave her a goodbye kiss that was more a promise of what was to come when he got home tonight.

He tore his lips from hers, turned and headed to the door before he couldn't leave her at all. "Please, for the love of God, put some clothes on, woman." She was still wearing only his thermal and nothing else.

Her giggles followed him out the door.

He stopped in the driveway when Chase called out from the side yard. "Looks like you had a good morning."

Hunt groaned. He knew his brothers had to have seen him with Cyn. "Jealous?" he tossed out, not wanting to say anything that would have them razzing him even more.

Chase chuckled but his expression said it all. "Nope."

"Fuck you both," Max grumbled. Apparently he'd woken up alone.

Chase grinned at Hunt again. "Just happy to see you happy, man."

"Keep her safe and I will be the happiest man alive."

His brothers both gave him a firm nod.

Hunt drove to the station, his gut in a knot that wouldn't unravel until he was back with Cyn again and she was safe and sound and in his arms.

# Chapter Sixteen

Hᴜɴᴛ ᴡᴀʟᴋᴇᴅ into the quiet station and smiled at the receptionist. "Morning, Marcy. Is William over his cold yet?" She had the cutest chubby toddler.

She smiled at him. "He's feeling better and finally slept through the night again last night."

He continued past her to his office. "Good to hear."

"How's your girlfriend? Is she still in the hospital?"

Hunt stopped and turned to Marcy. He didn't feel the need to correct her on the girlfriend thing. He and Cyn were . . . getting there. It felt like they were there. He didn't want to presume. But after what they'd shared last night, yeah, it felt right to have some claim to her. "Cyn's feeling better. The side effects of the hypothermia seem to have subsided, though we'll see how she does today. Thanks for asking."

"It was brave what she did, going into the water like that. If it was someone I loved . . . I'd want to know one way or another if they were in that car."

He nodded and turned back toward the office, not wanting to let the fear and memories of waiting those four minutes and twelve seconds for her to come out of that water. Not to mention the other couple minutes he had to give her CPR. He shook off the thoughts, dropped into the seat behind his desk and booted up his computer.

He'd been trying to compile information from all the home invasions and break-ins in Willow Fork and the surrounding towns but Cyn had distracted him in the best way this morning from finishing his task.

He grinned at the memory of her shaking her finger at him about his uniform and wearing his reading glasses.

Officer Reid leaned against the doorframe. "I bet Cyn put that grin on your face."

Hunt went perfectly still and stared at his friend and fellow officer.

"Have you counted the butterfly tattoos? All twenty-two of them."

He'd kissed all twenty-*six* of them last night.

"Did you look closely at them? They've got the names of all her favorite lovers in the wings."

"You shouldn't talk about things you know nothing about." He eyed Reid. "You've never seen all her tattoos, despite the stories you like to tell about being with her. We both know you've never been with her."

"If she said otherwise, she's lying."

"Is it really that easy for you, and I'll bet a lot of other guys in town, to pretend you slept with her, and then call her a liar when she says she didn't sleep with you?"

"The girl likes to fuck."

"So does most everyone. That doesn't mean you were with her."

"Whatever. She'll move on to the next guy soon and you'll be the one with the memories of tapping that."

Hunt never really paid attention to the guys talking in the office. But now realized that Officer Reid was usually the one instigating the locker-room-type talk.

Hunt leaned back in his chair. "You and I are going to have a real problem if you don't drop this."

"Whatever."

"Let me make myself clear. You will never speak about Cyn in that way ever again. You will not lie about being with her ever again. If you do, I'll tell everyone you lied. You won't be able to back up your stories, because I know more about Cyn than you ever will."

Officer Reid hooked his hands on his gun belt and shrugged. "Fine." He turned to leave, but shifted back around. "Is she okay?"

"A little banged up and sore, but better today. Thanks for asking."

"She's a little crazy, you know."

"She's Cyn." He liked her just the way she was.

"She makes a man want to sin, that's for sure."

Hunt couldn't help the grin, because Officer Reid spoke the truth. He changed the subject. "Do you have an update on Rad?"

"We had an officer on him after he left the station and went to work, but the officer got called away for an accident. By the time he made it back to the garage, Rad had left. He didn't go home, though. He's not at his parents' place either."

"Shit. We need to hire more officers."

"The city needs to increase the budget if we're going to keep the officers we have and find new ones."

"Wait. You said Rad went to work at the garage?" That couldn't be right.

"Yeah. Why?"

"Because he was fired a couple days ago."

"Then what was he doing at the garage?"

Hunt had a hunch, but didn't know if he was right. Yet. "I'm looking into a home invasion where I found the car seen at the crime parked out back at the garage. I had it processed. Rad's prints were found inside."

"He works at the garage, probably drove the car in and out of the bay to work on it, or at least that's what he'll claim."

"Exactly. But there was another home burglary last night. I was just going to pull the information for any and all vehicle descriptions in the various cases here and in neighboring towns and see if I can trace them back to the garage."

Officer Reid nodded. "I see where you're going with this. Definitely sounds promising. Let me know if you need help. I'm heading out to check in with the search teams. I'll let you know if there's anything on Angela or Lana. If I'm honest, since they weren't in the car, I'm betting they're nowhere near that area."

"You think he just ditched the car there." Hunt thought the same.

"The missing car seat gives away that he didn't drive the baby out there. He's got a car seat in his truck. He said their parents bought them each a car seat when Lana arrived."

Made sense to have one in each of their cars, just in case. Chase and Shelby each had a car seat in their cars for Eliza.

Hunt hated that they didn't have anything solid on Rad. The guy wasn't that smart, yet he'd gotten away with whatever he'd done to Angela and Lana so far. "Listen. I planned to tell everyone today at the daily briefing, but you should know Rad threatened Cyn."

"Did you arrest him?"

"It was real but vague." So it didn't meet the criteria for an arrest.

"Does Cyn know?"

"Yes. My brothers are watching her today. I'll do my best to make sure she's never alone, but she likes her independence, and where her sister and niece are concerned—"

"She'll do anything to get that bastard."

"Exactly. So if she calls in and needs help . . ."

"All of us will be all over it," Officer Reid assured him. "Tell everyone at the meeting. I'll make sure to spread the word to the officers conducting the search."

"Thank you."

Officer Reid turned serious. "She's really important to you."

"Yes."

"Then I've got your back and I'll shut my big mouth."

"I appreciate both. And so will Cyn."

"Forget all the rest. I like her. She's . . . unique."

He thought she was pretty damn special.

Officer Reid turned to go. "Let me know what you find out about the cars," he called over his shoulder.

Hunt finally pulled all the information he needed on

the vehicles used in the burglaries, went to the daily briefing, told his boss what he was investigating and headed down to the garage to talk to Jerry.

He stopped outside the garage and surveyed the parking area. He spotted the white Corolla he suspected had been used in last night's home burglary.

Before he went in, he texted Cyn.

HUNT: How are you feeling?
CYN: Lonely for you. ☻

He couldn't help it and smiled.

HUNT: Miss you, too.
HUNT: Any side effects this morning?
CYN: Got a little dizzy when I stood up too fast but otherwise no.
CYN: Still tired.
CYN: But that could be because I was in heaven and not sleeping most of the night.

He grinned again.

HUNT: Happy to take you there again.
CYN: And again. And again. And again. ☺
HUNT: YES!!!
HUNT: Gotta go hunt down some evidence
HUNT: Be good. REST!
CYN: Be SAFE!
CYN: ♥♥♥
CYN: P.S. I'm cooking you dinner tonight
HUNT: Can't wait

HUNT: I'm looking forward to dessert
CYN: ☙Me too!❧
CYN: Also you left 1 chocolate cookie in the bag.
CYN: 1! Who does that!

Hunt busted up laughing. It hit him all at once that he hadn't smiled or laughed this much in a long time. God, she was good for him.

HUNT: Sorry. I'll bring more home tonight.
CYN: And I will reward you

Oh, the images and thoughts that text brought to mind.

HUNT: Stop! I have to work and doing it without a hard-on would be better.
CYN: Sorry not sorry
CYN: Go be a cop then come home and be with me
HUNT: Best thing I've ever heard
CYN: UR sweet

He liked making her happy. It made him feel good to know that she was probably sitting on his couch, watching TV and smiling because of him. He worried about her dizziness. He'd keep an eye on her. If it got worse, he'd take her back to the doctor. They'd cleared her to go home, but if something was still wrong . . . He didn't want to even think it could be something serious.

Folder in hand, he got out of the car and headed into the big open bay door to find Jerry. "Hello."

Jerry slid out from under an old Nissan truck. "Officer Wilde." Jerry stood and wiped his hands on a rag. "What can I do for you?"

"Did you happen to rehire Rad in the last day or so?"

"No. I don't want someone like him working for me. I don't condone hitting anyone, especially women."

"Are you aware that Angela and Lana are missing?"

Jerry pressed his lips into a sad half frown. "The whole town knows, and I feel terrible about it. I should have known something like this could happen. My daughter tried to leave her abusive ex. He got very angry and hurt her. I sometimes feel it's my fault for not protecting her."

"It's not your fault," Hunt assured him. "The terrible truth is that if an abuser wants to get at his victim, he'll find a way. And you have to believe that Rad is responsible for whatever happened between him and Angela as well. Your firing him wasn't what caused it, and if he hurt Angela or the baby, then that's on him." Hunt held up the folder in his hand. "And that's kind of why I'm here. I've been investigating another case."

"The one about the car you found here."

"Yes. Rad was questioned at the station night before last. After he left, an officer followed him here. The officer thought he was coming into work. But I think he came here to take another car. The white Corolla out front."

Jerry frowned. "Damnit. I forgot to ask him for the shop keys back. He probably walked right in, grabbed the keys from the office, took the car and returned it without my knowing anything."

"Do you have any surveillance cameras inside here?"

"No. But I'm thinking I might need to change the locks and add some security. I've been broken into before. But it was minor stuff. Someone looking to make a quick buck off the tools and car parts. I have insurance. But I heard that burglaries are on the rise because of the poor economy. Desperate people do stupid things."

"I see it all the time. Do you mind taking a few minutes to look through your records for cars you've serviced to see if any more of the vehicles were here at the garage and match vehicles seen at a crime?"

"Sure. Whatever I can do to help."

Hunt followed Jerry to the office. "I'll also need our forensic team to check the Corolla outside."

"No problem. The customer parked it out front. I haven't touched it."

Hunt wondered if Rad left any evidence behind this time, or if he'd wiped the vehicle clean. Either way, they'd process it and see if any evidence could be used against Rad. It wasn't so farfetched to think he was the one committing the home burglaries and had hit Mrs. Phelps.

"I appreciate your cooperation."

"If you've got a lead on a good mechanic, I'd love to know about it."

"I'll keep an ear out for anyone looking for work."

"Appreciate it." Jerry sat at the desk and booted up the newer-looking computer. "My daughter set this up for me to help make billing and ordering supplies easier. It took me a while to learn the system, but now I'm good at it." Jerry looked up at him. "What do you need?"

Hunt pulled out the spreadsheet he'd made of the vehicles and the dates of the crimes. "Can you look up the vehicles you had here a few days before and on the day of the crime?"

Jerry shrugged. "What is he doing with the cars? He's already suspected of killing his girlfriend. God help him if he hurt that baby, too."

"Looking at it that way, this is less bad. I suspect he's been breaking into people's homes and burglarizing them. In a couple of instances, he pistol-whipped the victims who were home during the robberies."

"He's been complaining forever about how tight things have been financially. I told him Angela should go to work with her sister, like she wanted to, but he wouldn't allow it. He didn't like Angela being with her sister."

"That's because Cyn hates Rad for what he's done to Angela and was trying to convince Angela to leave him."

Jerry worked at the computer, looking up dates of service and matching up the cars to the best of his ability. In most cases, all Hunt had was a white four-door or a blue compact or whatever vague description was given. But if he could get close and gather enough evidence to prove Rad was involved, then he'd build his case one step at a time to take him down.

"Looks like I found cars that match the description for all but two of your robberies." He pulled the papers off the printer with the car and owner information and handed them to Hunt.

"Thank you, Jerry. This is a huge help. Can you give me the contact information for the person who owns the white Corolla out front so I can get their permission to search the vehicle and let them know it's suspected of being used in the burglary?"

"Sure." Jerry pulled that information from the many sheets of paper on the desk and handed it over. "Tell Cyn I'm real sorry to hear about Angela and I'll be thinking of her and Angela and that sweet baby, hoping they come home soon."

Hunt clapped Jerry on the shoulder. "Thank you. She'll appreciate it."

"You need anything else, you let me know. I'm going to call a locksmith now and get the locks changed so Rad can't come in here and steal vehicles anymore. You going to add that to his charges if you can link him to the car out front?"

"Yes. That's the plan."

"I'm here if you need me."

Hunt headed out to his car to call the owner of the vehicle and get the forensic guys to look it over. They had a small department and were lucky to have a couple of guys trained to do the forensic work. A lot of small towns out here had to do that on their own. Luckily, their long-standing mayor fought for and the city council funded public services like that to protect and help keep the citizens safe.

It took a few hours to get the forensics done, check in with the search teams out looking for Angela and Lana and take a few emergency calls before he was able to stop at the store to get Cyn her treats, then finally head home.

He pulled into his driveway and smiled at his dad, who pulled in right after him and met him at the porch. "What are you doing here?"

"Shelby had to get home a little while ago for dinner with Eliza and Chase. I told her I'd come by, introduce myself to your girl and make sure everything was still quiet out here. But I guess you're home, so I don't need to stay if you don't want to introduce her, and all."

Hunt hadn't made it a habit of introducing the women in his life to his family. But Cyn was different. "Come inside and meet her. You'll like her."

They walked up the steps. Hunt opened the door to the smell of spaghetti sauce and garlic and Cyn lying on the sofa watching a *John Wick* movie. She spotted them, smiled, sat up and stood in one fluid motion, then put her arms out and fell sideways onto the coffee table, nearly falling off the other end.

# Chapter Seventeen

CYN DIDN'T know what happened. One moment she was up on her feet, happy to see her Wilde man, and the next he was grabbing her arms and pulling her into his chest.

"Are you okay?" Desperation and concern filled his deep voice.

She gripped his biceps and a wave of panic rushed through her. "Hunt. I can't see."

He had his hand on the back of her head as he held her against him, then let her loose so she could look up at him. "Sorry. I didn't mean to shove your face into me."

"No. I really can't see. Anything." She gripped his arms tighter to keep her balance.

"But you saw me come in, right?"

"Yes. But the second I stood up, I lost all sense of balance and everything went dark." Her heart thundered in her chest. "What's happening?"

"I don't know, but I'm taking you to the hospital." He let loose his grip on her.

She panicked. "Don't let go."

He scooped her up into his arms. "I've got you. It's going to be okay."

"I'll take care of everything here," Mr. Wilde said.

She'd seen him many times around town, but they'd never officially met.

"Go, son, get her to the hospital. Could be from that knock she took on the head or something."

Hunt didn't waste time; he rushed her to his car, gently set her on the seat, buckled her in and kissed her quick when she wasn't expecting it, which meant she didn't really get a chance to kiss him back. Then he slammed her door and she heard the driver's one open and Hunt start the engine. She expected the car to move, but Hunt hit the gas so hard she jerked forward against the seat belt as he reversed out of the driveway, then fell back in her seat when he accelerated forward.

Her stomach went queasy. "Slow down. You're going to make me sick." She put her hands on the dashboard to steady herself.

Hunt took her hand and linked his fingers with hers. "Sorry, baby. Any other symptoms right now, or earlier today?"

She sat back in the seat and tried to relax and focus on Hunt's hand in hers. "I told you. Dizziness. Which happened when I stood up too fast." She thought of the rest of her day, lounging on the couch. "I don't know if this is anything, but I've had to pee a lot today. I've been really thirsty. I have a headache, but I thought that was from the head injury, but maybe it's something else."

"Why didn't you tell me about all of this?"

"Because I just thought it was symptoms of what happened and I needed rest, so I did. I only got up to get something to eat and make dinner to thank you for letting me stay with you."

"You don't have to thank me. I want you with me."

She sighed and closed her eyes because trying to see and not being able to was making her more anxious and scared. "What if this is permanent? What if it's something really bad?" She pulled Hunt's hand to her chest.

"I can feel your heart racing. Take a few slow deep breaths, sweetheart."

She did as he asked, because she felt a little light-headed still. After a few minutes, she felt steadier. More calm.

Hunt stopped the car. "We're here. Stay put. I'll come around and get you." It only took him a moment to open her car door. He took her hand again and slid his other hand behind her neck. "Get out slowly. Make sure you've got your balance."

She opened her eyes because it seemed the thing to do when she moved, and gasped. "I can see you now." In fact, the bright lights from the emergency room entrance hurt her eyes and she squinted.

Hunt cupped her face and made her look at him. "You can really see me."

"Yes." She saw all the concern and panic in his eyes.

"We're still getting you checked out." He slammed the car door, put his arm around her waist and walked her into the emergency room.

The badge, uniform and gun got them some stares, but it also got the receptionist's immediate attention. "Officer Wilde, how can I help you?"

"This is Cyn Wilson. She suffered hypothermia and a head injury a couple days ago. Thirty minutes ago, she stood up, lost her balance and suddenly went blind. Her eyesight came back a minute ago. We need to get her checked out to be sure the head injury isn't worse than initially thought."

The receptionist turned to her. "We have all your information in the system. Are you currently taking any medication?"

"Antibiotics. Also, I took two ibuprofens for my headache and the pain from my two stitched cuts but they didn't really help."

Hunt stared down at her. "Why didn't you take your pain meds?"

"Because they make me feel funny and I thought the ibuprofen would be enough. I . . ." She pressed her fingers to her ears and rubbed them, then looked up at Hunt.

He was saying something to her but she couldn't hear him.

He must have seen the panic come over her again because he mouthed, *Can you hear me?*

She frantically shook her head.

The receptionist stood and called out to someone. Then it was chaos for a moment when two nurses rushed to her side, helped her into a wheelchair and then pushed her down the hallway. She turned and reached for Hunt, but one of the nurses held him back, saying something to him to make him stay. He did not look happy about it.

She could only hope they were taking her for some tests and he'd be allowed to be with her again because she did not want to be alone. She needed him.

But a devastating thought creeped into her mind. What if something was terribly wrong and she didn't see him ever again? What if she never discovered what happened to her sister and niece?

# Chapter Eighteen

Hᴜɴᴛ sᴀᴛ in the waiting room, his patience wearing thin. He wanted to tear down the walls to get to Cyn, but they'd taken her away, fearing she might be having some kind of stroke or something. He had no idea what happened to her after he was forced to let her go and could only hope that she wasn't scared out of her mind and wanting him beside her. Because he couldn't stand being separated from her like this again.

His father had called, along with both his brothers and Shelby. He told them exactly what he knew. Nothing.

He should call her mom. But what could he tell her? What could she do? Sit here and go out of her mind with worry, too? She had enough to deal with, with Angela and Lana missing.

A nurse walked into the room. "Officer Wilde. She's asking for you. If you'll follow me."

"Is she okay?"

"She's resting in a room. The cardiologist will be in to see her shortly."

"Is there something wrong with her heart? I thought it was her head."

"The doctor will fill you and Cyn in as soon as he arrives. I'm sorry, but that's all I can say."

He knew the privacy rules all too well. He'd only been told about Cyn's condition last time because she gave permission. "Can you at least tell me if she got her hearing back?"

"Oh, yes. That came back during the MRI scan, though I think she got a bit scared when she all of a sudden heard the loud knocking noise it makes."

Okay. They'd done an MRI. That should give them some idea about what was happening to her.

"Here we are." The nurse opened the door to Cyn's room. "Don't get up," the nurse warned her.

She was lying in the bed, the lights in the room turned low, an IV line in her arm.

"Why the IV?" he asked the nurse.

Cyn answered. "I was dehydrated, even though I drank a lot of water today."

"The doctor will be here in a few minutes. I saw him down the hall." The nurse left him alone with Cyn.

He took the seat beside her and held her hand. "Can you see me?"

She smiled. "You are a sight for sore eyes. They took me away and I couldn't hear what they were saying around me. It was really scary."

He could tell by the death grip she had on his hand. "Do you know anything?"

"You're gorgeous and sweet and I'm so glad you're here."

He tried for a smile but it didn't come because he was too upset and concerned about her. "Cyn."

"They did a CT scan and an MRI, took some blood and gave me a thorough once-over from head to toe." She tugged on the hospital gown she now wore. "As far as I could tell, the cuts on my leg, head and neck don't show any signs of infection and are healing well. When I was able to hear, I answered all their questions, including doing simple math."

"Okay. So they don't know what's wrong?"

"I think I can answer that," the doctor said, coming into the room with a tablet in his hand. "I'm Dr. Smythe."

"Why does Cyn need a cardiologist? Did the hypothermia damage her heart?"

"No. Her symptoms point to something else."

"What?" Cyn asked, impatient as Hunt.

"Basically your autonomic nervous system isn't working properly, brought on by the hypothermia you suffered. Most likely, it's temporary, due to the tremendous stress your body was under and you continue to have due to the disappearance of your family."

"Doc, I'm not following." Hunt felt out of his depth and he desperately wanted to know if Cyn was going to be okay and what he could do to help her.

"Basically, all your autonomic systems—breathing, heart rate, digestion, sight, smell, hearing, diaphragm, anything that your body does without you having to think about—is controlled by this system. When working, you feel like everything is fine. When it's not, you feel the symptoms of whatever system is being affected. You were thirsty and dehydrated because your kidneys weren't functioning properly. The headache is another symptom. Migraines are common. Dizziness. Loss of smell, hearing, eyesight when your system is over-whelmed."

"Are you saying her autonomic system shut those things off because it got overwhelmed?" Hunt asked.

"Essentially, yes. Once her heart rate and blood pressure were regulated again, she regained them. Think of the body as a symphony. When one section isn't playing, the song sounds close to the same but something is off. It's not quite right."

"Could this kill her?"

"People live with the more chronic condition, known as dysautonomia, and manage the symptoms. But I don't think Cyn's condition is permanent," he rushed to assure them. "The hypothermia disrupted your body's natural functions. While your body recovers, your system is trying to get back to working in harmony. You'll want to take precautions, of course. Don't stand too quickly. Drink more water than you think you need. Balance that with added salt in your diet to keep your electrolytes up. If you feel your heart slowing down, or you feel faint, then sit. If it doesn't pass within a minute, call for help. If your heart is racing, take deep, slow breaths to regulate it again."

"I did that in the car and my vision came back."

The doctor nodded. "It's the sudden shock to the system, however small it used to seem to you, like standing up quickly, that makes the autonomic system respond to what is most pressing. Pumping your blood versus being able to see, for example."

"You're sure this has nothing to do with her concussion, or something in her brain?" Hunt asked to be clear.

"The scans of her brain show the concussion is healing. No bleeds. The swelling the last scan showed has significantly decreased."

"Okay. So she's okay, but will have to manage her symptoms until, hopefully, they disappear, or she'll have to learn to live with this and minimize it to the best of her ability."

"Yes. I'd like to see you in two weeks to assess how you're feeling. It would be helpful if you kept track of your symptoms and when and how they happen if you can."

"Sure," Cyn agreed.

"That will also help you determine what might be triggering a symptom and help you avoid it."

"Can she drive? Go to work?" Hunt asked.

"I'd avoid driving the next few days while you rest and allow your body to recover so this will resolve itself more quickly. You need to avoid stress." The doctor held Cyn's gaze. "I caution you to be aware of how you're feeling and to do what is necessary when you feel a symptom coming on to keep yourself safe. It is common for people with the condition to take a fall because of dizziness. Don't rush yourself through a symptom like dizziness. Give your body time to fully recover before you attempt standing or moving again."

"Does she need to stay in the hospital tonight?" Hunt asked.

The doctor shook his head. "Rest is the best medicine right now. And home is where she'll get it. I've already signed the discharge. You're free to go as soon as you finish the IV."

Cyn sighed out her relief. "Thank you, Doctor. I'll be sure to take precautions until I feel better."

"If you have any questions, please don't hesitate to call. Your discharge papers include an appointment time. If it doesn't work for you, please contact my office to change it."

"She'll be there," Hunt assured the doctor. He'd take her himself and make sure he knew what to do for her if things didn't get better.

The doctor left them alone.

Hunt stood and kissed Cyn on the head, then looked down at her beautiful face. "I'm so sorry, sweetheart. I should have never let you go into that water."

She gripped his hand in both of hers. "Hunt, baby, I'm going to be fine. This is not your fault. I was going in that water whether you liked it or not. You know that. You saw my determination. I had to know if they were in that car."

"And look at the price you're paying for it."

"For the hope it gives me that maybe there is some small chance, however improbable it may seem, that they're still alive, I'd do it again."

He hugged her close, needing to feel her against him and reassure himself that she was okay. He gave her a soft kiss, then sat back in the seat. "I hate this."

A soft chuckle burst out of her. "Me, too. Being blind and deaf for even that short time scared me half to death. I felt lost and helpless."

"No driving. At least for a few days until you figure out how you feel and if it's safe."

"Okay. But I need to pick up my car from where I left it at the search site. And I need to go into work."

"My brothers drove out to get your car. It'll be at my house when we get home. Shelby and I can take you where you want to go, but I would really like it if you did what the doctor said and rest."

"I will. But he didn't say I needed to stay in bed. I'll be careful and aware of how my body feels. I won't work full-time, but I have some clients who have appointments coming up that I don't want to cancel. Plus, I need to check on the new shop and be sure the contractor is ready to start the remodel on time."

"Cyn . . ."

She squeezed his hand. "I know you're worried. So am I. But I have to live my life, Hunt, and that includes being with you without you treating me like I'm about to die."

"You couldn't fucking see."

She slid out of bed and into his lap, dragging the IV line with her. "I know. But I'm okay now. I'll follow the doctor's suggestions to keep it from happening again. I'm talking a couple hours at work here and there over the next few days. The rest of the time, I'll chill. I promise. But I am not glass. You don't have to handle me with care. I proved that to you this morning."

He'd taken her in a rough and wild way. "Can you just let me do it for a few days until I know you're okay?"

"We'll see how it goes."

He rolled his eyes, knowing that was the best he was going to get.

"Tell me about your day," she prompted, changing the subject.

Since he had her in his lap and arms, he settled her against him. "It started off with a bang this morning," he teased. He traced one of the butterfly tattoos that looked like it was fluttering across her wrist. He'd seen all of them last night because he'd made a point to search them all out on her body. This one had a pair of scissors held in its little legs. "Why butterflies?"

"I thought we were talking about your day."

"Indulge me. I want to know about you."

"I love butterflies. They start as one thing and transform into something else. It reminds me that nothing stays the same. Something beautiful can come from something ordinary."

"I never thought about it, but yeah, there's beauty in that."

She grinned. "The tattoos started with a guy."

Hunt groaned and rolled his eyes. "Never mind. I don't want to know."

Cyn kissed his neck. "Listen."

He gave her a soft squeeze to let her know she had his full attention.

"He was the first boy I ever loved. Or at least what I thought was love at the time. I wanted to be a hairdresser to the stars. He wanted to be a singer-songwriter. Man, he had such a great voice. And the broken kind of soul that made his lyrics deep and edgy and heartwrenching."

"What happened to him?"

"He self-medicated his depression, even though I begged him to talk to a counselor and see a doctor. He called me one night, drunk and whatever and crying, telling me he couldn't take feeling lost and alone and empty anymore. I told him he had me. He had my heart. But then all I heard was deafening silence." She wiped a tear from her face. "He hung himself wearing the butterfly pin I'd stuck on his shirtsleeve one day at school.

He'd worn it on his shirtsleeve every day after that." She tugged down the gown to show him the butterfly on her arm. "So I tattooed one on my arm with a red heart in one wing and his name in the other."

He looked closely at the blue butterfly. The red heart was easy to see. But the name written in black ink within the blue was harder to make out.

"Leo," she said. "I've heard the rumor, Wilde. That the tattoos all have my lovers' names in them. The truth is, I never slept with Leo. I regret that we didn't share that before he was gone."

"How old were you?"

"Sixteen."

"I'm sorry that happened to you." He held her a bit tighter. "You must have been devastated."

"I still miss him. I think about what his life could have been. Every year on his birthday, I send his mom and dad a birthday card to let them know I still think about him and them. Leo has not been forgotten. He's part of my story."

Hunt kissed her on the head. "That's really sweet."

"Who told you the rumor about the tattoos?"

Hunt shifted beneath her. "It doesn't matter."

She cocked an eyebrow and held his gaze. "Apparently it does because you asked me about them."

"I was curious before I heard the rumor."

"Would it bother you if I did have a bunch of guys' names tattooed all over me?"

"Honestly. Yes."

"Me, too. That's just . . . too much. I mean, I liked all the guys I was with, but I really don't want to be reminded of them like that all the time."

Hunt grinned. "Neither do I."

She lifted her foot to show him the tattoo on her ankle. "When I got my cosmetology certificate." The butterfly was standing atop a rolled paper.

She pulled the other side of the gown down to show him the two on her other arm. A large butterfly with a smaller one standing atop one of the bigger one's wings.

He spotted the names in the wings easily. "Angela and Lana."

"Angela wanted a big family. I hoped she'd one day have lots of little ones fluttering about her."

She held up their joined hands to show him the butterfly with scissors on her wrist.

"When you opened your shop," he guessed.

"Yes. Some of them are to commemorate a special thing in my life. Others I got just because I liked them. They're whimsical and have meaning for me."

"They suit you. My favorite is the one on the back of your neck. The tiny black butterflies flying out of the dandelion."

"You certainly enjoyed kissing the kaleidoscope of the ones flying over my hip."

"Is that what a group of butterflies is called?"

She nodded. "Isn't that fun? That's why I had them done in all different colors." She touched her fingers to his scruffy chin. "You're the only one who knows the real truth about them. Most of the time I blow off people's questions with the simple answer that I like butterflies. *You* know it's more."

"Thank you for telling me."

"It's easy to share things with you. Like butterflies have a very short life span. They remind me to live while I can. So while your instinct is to keep me safe, you also have to let me live my life, Hunt."

"If Rad hadn't threatened you the way he did, I'd be happy to let you do whatever you want and enjoy watching you do it. But he is a real and present danger to you, Cyn." He cupped her face and looked her deep in the eyes. "If something happened to you . . ." He shook his head, unable to find the words to tell her what that would do to him. "I nearly had a heart attack tonight when you couldn't see or hear me."

She turned into him and wrapped her arms around his neck. "I know. I spent the day really thinking about who you are and what you do. You're a cop. You face danger on a daily basis."

"It's not that bad. Most of the time."

"Still. I couldn't help thinking about it and what that means for me."

"What are you saying?"

"That it was hard not knowing if you were coming home or not. And I know I have no right to—"

He kissed her, long and deep, then pressed his forehead to hers. "If you feel half of what I feel for you, Cyn, you have every right. I hate it every time the doctor or nurse has said they can't tell me something about you because I don't have the right to be included in what they're doing for you and telling me how you are when I'm desperate for any scrap of confirmation that you're okay."

"Well, then I guess you won't care that I listed you as my emergency contact and that you can receive my personal and private information and make decisions for my care. Just in case. I mean, this is the second time

I've ended up here in as many days and Rad is a problem I'm not ignoring."

"You did that?" He couldn't believe the trust she'd put in him.

"Yes." To lighten things, she gave him a funny grin. "You've met my mother. Do you think I want her to be the primary source of what's best for me?"

He chuckled. "No."

"Which is why you didn't call her and tell her I'm here."

"I wanted to wait until I knew what was going on."

"Wise choice. I'll call her tomorrow and tell her what happened, so she doesn't hear that I was back in the hospital from someone else."

"I just want to take you home. I want you to be okay."

"If these symptoms don't go away, I'll learn to manage them."

"And you'll take my advice about protecting yourself until I can put Rad behind bars."

"I love that you call it advice when we both know you're just telling me what to do."

"I wanted to soften it, so you'd be more amenable to doing what I say for your own good."

"I will do my best to follow your *advice*." She kissed him to stop him from saying more, then leaned back and stared up at the IV. "It's done. And I have to pee. Help me up?"

He sat up and took her by the hips. "Stand up slowly. Give yourself a second. Let me know if you're dizzy."

She braced herself with a hand on the IV stand. "I'm okay. I feel fine."

He still walked behind her to the bathroom, keeping

his hands on her hips just in case. He left her alone, pushed the call button for the nurse and waited outside the bathroom door for Cyn to come out.

The nurse walked in just as Cyn returned. "Everything okay?"

"Her IV is done."

"Excellent. Any more episodes of blindness or going deaf?"

"No. I feel fine." Cyn sat on the edge of the bed.

"Great." The nurse took the needle out of her arm and covered the puncture mark with a cotton ball and some tape. "Go ahead and get dressed. I'll be back in a few minutes with your discharge papers."

"Thank you." Cyn waited for the nurse to leave, then pulled the hospital gown off.

He handed her the stack of clothes he found in the cupboard by the bed.

She was only wearing a pair of black panties that barely covered her bottom. She slid her bra straps up her arms, connected it in the back, then leaned forward and adjusted her boobs in the cups with a little wiggle.

"I like watching you get dressed almost as much as I like undressing you."

She grinned. "Hand me my shirt."

"Do I have to?"

"Wilde, you can tear all my clothes off when we get home and are alone."

He frowned. "You should probably get some rest."

She met his concerned gaze. "You should give me what I want."

He handed her the shirt that read The Snuggle Is Real. "What do you want?"

She grabbed him by the front of his shirt and tugged him close. "You." Then she put her shirt on, grabbed her black leggings, pushed her feet into them, pulled them up to her thighs, then jumped off the bed to finish shimmying them over her hips, when she lost her balance and nearly fell sideways.

Hunt caught her and growled. "Slow down. The doctor told you not to stand up so fast."

She held his arm in a death grip. "I'm okay. Just a tiny bit dizzy."

"Can you see?"

She looked up at him. "Yes. I recognize that disgruntled frown."

"Sit on the bed. I'll help you with your shoes." He turned to look for them.

"I wasn't wearing any when you picked me up and carried me out to the car."

He faced her again. "Oh. Okay."

Someone knocked on the door.

"Come in," she called.

The nurse walked in with her papers, pushing a wheelchair. "Here you go. The information for your next appointment is included. Do you need anything else?"

"No. I'm ready to go."

Hunt helped her slowly stand, walk to the wheelchair and sit down.

She looked up at him. "I'm sorry about dinner."

"I spoke to my dad a little while ago. He put it in the fridge. We can eat when we get home." Hunt held her hand as the nurse wheeled her out of the room and they rode the elevator down to the lobby and outside to the curb where his police SUV was still parked.

He helped her into the front seat and buckled her in, then went around the car and climbed behind the wheel. Just before he was about to pull out of the hospital his phone rang.

"Wilde," he answered.

"It's Reid. There's been another home invasion."

# Chapter Nineteen

CYN TOOK the jacket Hunt handed her and draped it over her legs and feet. She snuggled into it and stared at the farmhouse twenty yards in front of the car. The glass in the front door had been broken. It stood open now as one officer dusted the doorknob for prints while another took photos of the man lying just inside the entry on his back. She could only see his worn cowboy boots. The older couple had been in town for dinner, then arrived home to find the front door busted open. The man went in to investigate and found the robber. The man was shot. The woman pistol-whipped outside on the porch when she ran to help her husband.

The house had been ransacked for cash and valuables. A man lost his life, a woman her beloved husband, all because some selfish asshole wanted to take what didn't belong to him and didn't care about the people he hurt.

"Are you sure you're going to be okay out here? I can call Max to come and get you and take you home."

It was late. She didn't want to wake his brother, who would more than likely be babysitting her again tomorrow. "I'll be fine," she assured Hunt. "But you could have just dropped me at my place when we passed it."

Not that she wanted to be alone. She wanted to be with Hunt.

"I'm not leaving you alone. For all the reasons we've already discussed. Not to mention, you just got out of the hospital. Again. If you're not with me, then I want you with someone who can watch over you just in case."

"I'm fine."

He tucked the jacket around her. "Are you still cold?"

She smiled, enjoying him being sweet and attentive. "I'm better. Thank you for the jacket." She inhaled his scent off it. "But if you wouldn't mind checking on me once in a while? Just in case." The fear from earlier when she'd lost her sight and hearing sent a shiver through her.

He put his warm hand on her cheek and gave her a soft kiss. "Of course I will. And I won't be long. I just want to see if this matches the other cases I'm investigating. The guy I'm looking for has hurt others in the past, like Mrs. Phelps."

She winced. "This time, he killed someone."

Hunt glanced up at the house and the ominous sight of the man's boots.

She waved him off. "Go do your thing. Figure out who's doing this. I'll be right here. Maybe sleeping." She felt drained from all the stress. "It's just the anxiety hangover from earlier." She notched her chin toward the house. "You'll be right there if I need you."

"Officer Wilde, you want to take a look at this?" one of the other officers called out to him.

"Go, Wilde. The sooner you get this done, the sooner we can eat. And despite the macabre circumstances here, I'm starving."

He hung his head. "I wish I hadn't dropped the bag of goodies I bought you at the store in the entry when I got home."

She sat up straighter, surprised and touched. "You bought me a treat?"

"Double chocolate chunk cookies and brownies from the bakery."

She melted into the seat. "That's so sweet. I can't believe I used to think you were an asshole."

Hunt chuckled. "Again, I was doing my job and you were breaking the law."

"Yeah. I know. And you really are a good guy."

"Wilde," the officer called again to get his attention, which hadn't strayed from her at all.

She took his hand and squeezed it. "I'm not going anywhere. Nothing is going to happen to me. You can go do your job and not worry about me."

He kissed the palm of her hand. "Not going to happen. But I'll be back soon." He tucked her hand back under his jacket, kissed her quick, closed the door so she'd stay warm and walked up toward the house, only looking back twice to be sure all was well with her before he conversed with the officer who'd been waiting for him.

Cyn watched him, standing on the porch, the picture of confidence and strength. He concentrated on what the other officer was saying and spoke to him like he knew exactly what he wanted to say, whatever it was. He had a sense of command about him as he gestured to the door and then the empty spot in the driveway the other officer had been scanning earlier.

Hunt checked out the front windows and walked all

the way around the house, using a flashlight to search the ground and surrounding area.

When he walked into the house, she snuggled into his coat and closed her eyes. She couldn't look again and feel the pain and anguish for the people who lived here and the ones she loved, too.

She came awake with a start when the light inside the car flashed on.

Hunt's big hand pressed to her chest. "Easy, sweetheart. It's just me."

She sucked in a breath. "You startled me."

"Sorry that took so long."

She brushed the hair from her face. "I fell asleep."

"It's okay. You need it."

"Did you find any evidence to prove who broke into the house? Did the homeowner get a good look at the guy?"

Hunt started the car and cranked up the heat. "No one has gotten a look at the guy's face. He wears a mask."

Something niggled in the back of her mind. "Like one of those ghost Halloween masks from that movie?"

Hunt's eyes narrowed. "Yeah. How did you know that?"

"Because I saw a mask just like that in the laundry basket at Rad's house the last time I saw my sister."

"Did she say why it was in the laundry?"

"I didn't ask. I just thought it was weird she had it out when Halloween is still a few weeks away."

Hunt pressed his lips tight. "That is strange."

"But maybe not," Cyn prompted, thinking the coincidence was just too much to ignore.

Hunt gave her a look that confirmed he had his own

suspicions about Rad and these burglaries. "The mask is so common we can't trace it. And the guy uses a different car each time."

She considered that for a moment. "Rad worked at a garage. He'd have access to all the cars that came in to be serviced."

Hunt grinned at her. "You're really smart."

She beamed. "You already suspected him. Because of some other evidence you can't tell me about, right?"

Hunt shrugged. "Even with the cars coming from the garage he has access to and the mask, it's still not enough to tie him to the burglaries."

Another thought occurred to her. "He's robbing people's homes, taking their valuables."

"Yeah. What are you thinking? Do you know something else?"

"Cash for gold."

He shrugged. "We assume the burglar is pawning or selling the items for cash."

"I thought it odd that there were so many envelopes in their mail stack that were from cash-for-gold businesses. I mean, I get those advertisements, too, but these were envelopes with those business names and return addresses. He's sending in the stolen jewelry and just waiting for the checks to arrive. That's why there were so many different ones. He couldn't trade in all the stuff through one place. That would look suspicious."

"Up until recently, he had a good job. Why would he do this at all?"

Money. "Rad and Angela were barely scraping by on what he earned. They lived paycheck to paycheck. Any little thing going wrong put them further into debt. Like when the refrigerator went out three months ago. They didn't have the money to replace it. I helped them out."

Hunt raised a brow. "I take it you helped them out more than once."

"Rad told my sister not to ask me for money, he'd take care of her. With his credit cards maxed, he had no choice but to take the money from me or ask his parents again. He hated doing that. It made him feel like a failure. He hated that I gave them money. He hated that they didn't have more. Most of their fights were about money. And then they got hit hard with the medical bills for the delivery and Lana's well-checks. He was responsible for taking care of Angela and a baby now and sank deeper in debt. I'm sure that weighed on him. Maybe this was his way of trying to get them out of a hole and then some. Fast, easy cash."

"And he gets to take out his anger on unsuspecting homeowners."

"He's been cultivating that mean streak for a while now." Cyn settled deeper into her seat. "Is there any way to connect him to the robberies through the sale of the jewelry? There's got to be some sort of reporting those places have to do if they suspected the items they were buying are stolen."

"Not really. The likelihood the police will spend any amount of time trying to trace items like that is fairly low. We just don't have the time and manpower to do it. Plus, there are too many businesses to check. Stolen property like that isn't usually recovered unless we find the thief before he's had time to convert it to cash."

"Well, that's just sad." She hated to think the victims

would simply have to come to terms with never getting back their treasured items and heirlooms.

"It's reality. I tell people who have had jewelry and valuables stolen to check local pawn shops, but thieves are sometimes clever and drive further away to pawn the stuff, or they take the easy route like Rad is presumably doing and send it through the mail."

"Well, you should arrest his ass and stop him from doing this to anyone else."

"I'm working on getting some concrete evidence. All I have on Rad is your say-so on the mask and cash-for-gold payouts. For all I know, he's been pawning his grandmother's jewelry to make ends meet and wanted to dress up as that ghost character for some upcoming costume party." Hunt glanced back up to the open front door of the house and the man's boots. "Now we have a bullet we can match to a gun. But I've never seen him with a gun and he doesn't have one registered to him."

Frustration exploded inside her. "Why the fuck does he get away with everything?" She sucked in a breath to ease the wave of anger that came over her. She thought about her sister and niece and let the tears fall. "Someone needs to stop him from hurting and killing people."

"I'm trying, sweetheart." He put his hand over her fisted one in her lap.

"I know you are. I'm sorry. It's just so damn frustrating that all we've found is her car and no sign of her or Lana. Where are they? If she's dead, why hasn't anyone found her body? Is the baby really alive, or am I just deluding myself into thinking he's not that kind of monster?"

"I wish I had some answers for you. My hope is that I can get him on the home invasion burglaries, assaults and now murder, and use those charges to get him to talk to me about Angela and Lana."

She stared out the side window as he drove them back to his place and thought the one thing she didn't want to say to him. *I feel like I may never know what happened to them.*

# Chapter Twenty

༺───༻

Hᴜɴᴛ ᴘɪᴄᴋᴇᴅ up his office line at the station, hoping he didn't have to go out on another call. He really wanted to go home and check on Cyn. She'd had a rough night after the hospital visit, waiting for him outside the latest house Rad had burglarized, then getting hit with another wave of grief over her missing sister and niece. It was all he could do to coax her to eat the lasagna and garlic bread dinner he reheated when they got home. She barely said good night before snuggling into him in bed and falling into one nightmare after the next.

He thought he felt rough when he woke up this morning, but it was nothing compared to seeing her with the dark circles and haunted look in her eyes.

He wanted to make her promises but couldn't.

He tried to make her smile, but even the glimpse of a grin she gave him left her lips as quickly as it had appeared.

It had only taken him asking her to stay at his place and not go into work or anywhere else for her to agree. He didn't like her easy capitulation when not so long ago she'd been stubbornly insisting she'd live her life the way she wanted to.

He needed to get home and check on her. But instead he picked up his ringing phone. "Officer Wilde," he said to the caller.

"Hello, Hunt. This is Jacob Harmon."

"Mr. Harmon. It's been a while. I hope you and your wife are well." He started with the pleasantries with Rad's father. He'd been welcomed in the Harmon house since he was a boy, and he hated that they were on opposite sides now.

"As well as can be expected under the circumstances, what with Angela running off with our grandchild."

Hunt gave it to Mr. Harmon plain. "I don't think that's what happened. I don't think you believe it either. Not after I arrested your son for assaulting Angela's sister."

"You mean the woman everyone is talking about you seeing now?"

"Cyn and I are together," he admitted. "That's a recent thing. Your son has a long history of domestic abuse with Angela. It's no leap to tie her disappearance to him."

"That's why I'm calling. My wife just heard from Rad. He said Angela called him this evening and told him she and the baby are fine. They're in Idaho with some friend of hers. She says she's not coming back."

"I'd like to hear Mrs. Harmon's account of the call. Maybe ask her some questions."

"I was listening in. I heard everything."

At this point, Hunt had to take his word. "Okay, then, did she tell Rad what city she was in or how he could get in contact with her in the future?"

"Not that I'm aware of." Not surprising.

"Did she say that Rad or you could go and see the baby?"

"He said that they talked about shared custody and that she'd let him see the baby soon." Vague.

"Did Rad say he was going to Idaho to see her?"

"He told his mama he'd bring the baby to see her soon, so I'm guessing he plans to bring her home for a little while before he returns her to Angela."

That didn't make much sense since Angela was breastfeeding the baby, according to Cyn. "Where is Rad now?"

"He didn't say. We haven't seen him in several days."

"He hasn't been at his place in the last few days either. If he's not home or staying with you, where would he go?"

"Don't know. He's a grown man. He doesn't answer to me anymore." That came across as defensive.

"Your son is suspected of killing Angela and Lana."

"Sounds to me like Angela took off with his kid without telling him."

"But she didn't take anything for herself or Lana from the house. Her car was found submerged in the river, like someone wanted to either hide the vehicle, or make it seem like she and the baby were washed away in the current."

"Maybe she did that to cover her tracks and her friend picked her up and drove her to Idaho." Mr. Harmon was reaching. And wishful thinking.

"And Angela called her abusive boyfriend to tell him she and the baby are okay but didn't bother to call the one person she's closest to in this world, her sister. Come on, Mr. Harmon, you're smarter than this. And so am I. Maybe you want to believe that bullshit story Rad fed you because you don't want to think your son capable of the things I know he's done. But I've seen the proof of it on Angela's face. And Cyn's. And on the other people I believe he's hurt."

"Who?"

"That's another thing Rad is going to answer for. But don't put yourself in the position of being charged with accessory after the fact. If you know where he is, you need to tell me before things get worse."

"Has he been charged with a crime?" Mr. Harmon was holding out hope this was all going to go away.

"Not yet. But don't think for a moment that I'm going to let this go."

"You two used to be such good friends."

Hunt didn't need the reminder. "Yeah. Right up until I watched him backhand a woman I care about. That's the kind of man your son turned into. Don't let him take you down with him. Now tell me where he is before it's too late."

"I don't know," Mr. Harmon said, his voice low and resigned. "His mother asked him twice. Both times, he changed the subject and didn't give her an answer."

"Do you know anywhere he might be?"

"At this point, I don't think I know anything about who he's become or what he's doing. All I want is my granddaughter back. She's just a baby. Where is she?" Fear and deep concern filled his voice. Despite the story his son had told him, he truly didn't have the answer to those questions.

"I hope she's in Idaho like Rad said, but I'm guessing she's not."

"Will you let me know if you find out anything about them?"

Hunt appreciated that Mr. Harmon wasn't only concerned about Lana. "I will. But you need to promise me you'll contact me if you hear from Rad again. This is very serious, Mr. Harmon. I will do my job no matter the connection I have to you and your family."

"I know it. Rad knows it, too, or he wouldn't have skipped out like this."

"He's guilty, Mr. Harmon. Of what exactly is what I'm trying to find out. All everyone wants is for Angela and Lana to be found safe. If he's done something to them, the best we can hope for is to give the families peace by figuring out what happened to them."

"I never thought this would happen."

"Unfortunately, this happens all too often in domestic abuse cases. If you talk to Rad, the best thing you can do is convince him to come forward and tell me what happened. I will make sure he's peacefully taken into custody. I will hear him out. But I will not stop looking for him until I know what happened to Angela and Lana."

"If he calls, I'll do my best. I'll try to get his mother to do the same, but she'll have a harder time of it." Mr. Harmon hung up.

Hunt dreaded telling Cyn about Rad's call. He'd ask about any friends Angela might have in Idaho. Didn't matter. She'd see right through it. But she'd hope it was true, that there was some explanation for her sister leaving the state and going to Idaho and staying with a friend. She'd want to explain away the cell phone not being used since, her sister leaving without any possessions, not even a change of clothes it appeared, and not calling her to tell her they were safe.

But Cyn would know, like he knew, that Rad was lying through his teeth, trying to buy time. For what, Hunt didn't know. But if he was in contact with his parents, maybe he was scared enough to come in and tell them what happened.

There was no way he was getting away with anything.

# Chapter Twenty-One

CYN MET Hunt in front of the diner in town. She'd followed him in her car. Finally after two days of resting at his place and no new episodes of her body doing weird things, he agreed to let her drive and go into work.

She'd never been in a relationship like this. Of course they all started with a spark of interest and a healthy dose of lust. But with Hunt, she found herself opening up about so much more than she'd shared with anyone else.

They sat by the fire the last two nights talking. He opened up to her about his past. She knew a little about his mom's death from cancer. He told her how Chase had taken their mother away because she wanted to die on her terms and in her own way. By the ocean she'd never seen in person. She hadn't wanted her beloved husband and sons to watch her die. Hunt resented Chase for a long time and blamed him for taking her away, though it was their mother's wish.

She'd felt his sorrow and regret that he hadn't been able to give his mom what she needed in the end. He'd begged her to fight, not realizing how much pain she was in and how much she wanted peace for herself and all of them.

Hunt said he and Chase had made up, but because of the rift that tore apart even more because of Chase's addiction and Hunt having to push him into rehab with Shelby or end up arresting him, things were still not back to normal. Hunt wanted them to be close like they used to be. And they were slowly getting there.

"Hey, sweetheart, everything okay?" Hunt held out his hand to her when he stepped onto the curb from the parking lot to join her.

She took his hand. "Just thinking about how nice it's been the last few days with you."

Hunt tugged her into his side and wrapped his arm around her shoulders as they walked into the diner. "I like having you close all the time. Sorry I got pulled away to work yesterday. I really did want to have a marathon movie day with you on the couch."

"Another time," she said, stopping in her tracks when she spotted Mr. Wilde, Hunt's brothers, Shelby and Eliza at a table.

"What's today?" she asked, then answered her own question. "It's Pancake Tuesday." Shelby and Eliza's tradition of going out to breakfast every Tuesday at the diner for pancakes. When Shelby and Chase got together, finally, everyone else joined in.

"Come on. I'm starving. Someone wanted my attention twice this morning and I don't think there are enough pancakes in this place to replace the calories I burned with you in bed and in the shower."

She blushed because his family was watching them, though they couldn't hear Hunt. She hoped the others waiting to be seated didn't hear him either.

He took a step forward, and she grabbed his arm and

pulled him back. "Hunt, this is a family thing. I don't want to intrude."

Hunt turned to her, blocking her view of his whole family waiting on them. "If I didn't want you here, I wouldn't have asked you to come with me. And let me make it clear. I want you sitting at that table with me, my family and your best friend. If I'm going too fast for you, I'll make an excuse and we'll go somewhere else."

She stared up at his earnest eyes.

"What's it going to be, Cyn?"

She'd wanted something special for a long time. Hunt was offering her more than she'd ever imagined in that dream.

"You. And me. And Pancake Tuesday."

The smile on Hunt's face lit up her heart. "Then let's go."

Hunt held her hand as they made their way into the dining area. The Wilde men stood when she reached the table and Hunt held a chair out for her.

She sat beside Shelby and bumped shoulders with her. "Is it smart to collect all the handsome Wilde men in one place? They might start a stampede."

Shelby laughed. "I'm so happy Hunt brought you with him."

Eliza jumped off her dad's lap and ran to her. "Aunt Cyn, can you make my hair pink?"

Cyn picked up Eliza, plunked her on her lap and looked her dead in the eye. "Yes. I can. But why would you want to turn this beautiful hair a different color?"

"I want to be pretty like you."

Cyn's heart melted. "You already are, sweetheart. Just the way you are."

Shelby bumped shoulders with her again.

Then she looked up and caught the intense look in Hunt's eyes. "You look really good with her," he whispered, so much meaning in those simple words.

"Eliza and I are best friends."

"Just like you and Mommy."

"Yep." Cyn snuggled Eliza and looked across the table at Mr. Wilde and Max. "It's nice to see you both." She turned to Chase, who had his service dog, Remmy, with him. "Thanks for sharing Shelby with me the last couple days."

Shelby had stopped by while Hunt was at work and kept her company. It had been nice to sit and chat and have a glass of wine with her friend.

"We've been worried about you. Any more strange episodes?" Chase asked, though everyone at the table waited for her answer.

"I've been doing what the doctor told me. Lots of rest and drinking a ton of water, making sure I get enough salt to balance that out. If I wait too long to eat, I kind of feel off." She shrugged. "Hunt watches me very carefully."

Hunt leaned in and kissed her on the side of the head. "I don't like seeing you scared, like when you lost your eyesight."

"That was something," Mr. Wilde said. "You turned white as a sheet and your eyes were huge with shock. Scared me, too."

"Thank you all for worrying about me, but I'm going to be fine. I'll meet with the cardiologist in a couple weeks and he'll reevaluate me. He says it's most likely temporary."

"If it's not, we'll manage it," Hunt assured her, his hand brushing back and forth on her back. "This morning we'll do that with a big breakfast. What are you getting?"

The waitress arrived at the table and glanced at her.

"I'll do the pancakes, scrambled eggs and bacon plate." She tickled Eliza in her lap. "What do you want?"

"Smiley-face pancake and eggs." Eliza's enthusiasm was infectious.

"Scrambled eggs," Shelby clarified for the waitress, then placed her order, along with all the guys at the table.

Max leaned in and caught Hunt's attention. "When do you think you'll have time to spend at the ranch? We could use your help."

"Everyone's busy with the searches, so I'm covering patrol and emergency calls. But I hope soon. I miss working the ranch in the morning. I'd like to take Cyn riding again when she feels up to it."

Max looked at her. "Any word from your sister?"

She appreciated that he asked like her sister could still be out there. "Hunt spoke to Rad's father the other day. He said Rad told them Angela called from a friend's place in Idaho and said she wasn't coming back, but Rad could have visitation with Lana."

Max looked at Hunt. "Do you believe that?"

Hunt shook his head. "No. It doesn't make sense at all when you account for her car in the river, her cell phone being off for so long and that she never contacted Cyn, who is her go-to person for everything, especially when it came to Lana."

Cyn hugged Eliza, needing her sweet spirit to bolster her own. "I think he told his parents that because he has Lana somewhere and wants to bring her home."

Shelby sighed. "You think someone is watching her and this is his way of saying Angela let him have his visitation time, so it makes sense that he has her?"

"Yes. And then he'll come up with some story that Angela is sick and can't take her back right now, or she's found a job and needs time, or simply that she doesn't want Lana back so he's keeping her. Whatever he comes up with, I won't believe, because Angela loved that baby. She wanted a whole bunch of little ones. And if she'd had a good guy, one who loved her and took care of her the way she deserved, she could have had the family and life she desperately wanted and tried so hard to make a reality with Rad. I hate thinking about how she twisted herself up to make him happy, hoping it would all magically be the way she saw it in her head. I hate she never got the chance to live that dream."

Eliza sat up in her lap, turned to her and wiped her tears. "Don't cry, Aunt Cyn."

"You make me smile, sweetheart." Cyn gave her a smacking kiss on the cheek and handed her off to Shelby when their food arrived.

The guys settled into a discussion about hockey. She didn't know Hunt liked hockey and found it fascinating to listen to him talk about the game and players with his brothers. Mr. Wilde talked to Eliza about her favorite horse on the ranch. She begged him to let her ride it alone. Chase, Max, Hunt and Mr. Wilde all told her no. Not until she was bigger.

She and Shelby talked about Cyn going back to work today and made plans to meet for their weekly lunch on Wednesday to talk about Shelby and Chase's wedding plans.

Hunt held her hand practically the whole time they sat together. She bet he sensed how being with his family like this meant so much to her. She'd never had this growing up. Her mom was . . . her mom. The men she'd dated and married were never much interested in Cyn and Angela. She didn't have a relationship with her own father; he'd left and never come back. But she and Angela were always close despite how different they were from each other.

She would have loved to create this kind of tradition with Angela and Lana. It broke her heart, because she believed, deep down, that they'd never find Angela alive.

Hunt leaned in and kissed her on the head. "Eat your bacon, sweetheart. You need the salt."

She'd already eaten all her pancakes because they were her favorite, especially when smothered in butter. She took a piece of bacon and bit into the salty yumminess of it, smiling at Hunt. "Better?"

"Yeah. This is really good." He didn't mean the food. He meant having her here with him.

"I couldn't agree more." Because she loved being with him.

But something sad came over him when he read an incoming text on his phone, then looked at her.

She immediately started shaking her head, trying to deny whatever put that look on his face.

He hooked his hand at the back of her neck. "There's nothing for sure," he assured her.

"What is it?" She didn't really want to know.

He pressed his lips tight, sighed, then spit it out. "They found the body of a woman. She's not been identified," he quickly added.

"Only a woman's body?" She couldn't seem to ask if they'd found a baby's body out loud.

"Yes. Only one person."

"Where did they find her?"

"Three miles outside of the original search area. She matches Angela's physical description. Because we don't know what she was wearing at the time she disappeared, they're unable to say if it's for sure her until they run her DNA."

The search area had covered at least thirty square miles. They'd been searching the area for a week.

Hunt wouldn't let her go back to help. It was too strenuous and stressful and potentially dangerous with her condition. He gave her updates several times a day. She'd gotten used to him saying they had nothing to report. No evidence Angela had been anywhere near the area where they'd found the car or further away in the search area.

She'd held out hope, however infinitesimal it might be, that Angela was out there somewhere.

Definitely not in Idaho.

Cyn couldn't think of a single person from Angela's past that she'd even sporadically had contact with that lived in Idaho.

"Cyn." Hunt brushed a tear from her face. "We don't know if it's her."

"Then we need to go find out."

"Are you sure you're up to doing that?"

"It needs to be done. Let's go."

Hunt put his hand on her shoulder. "Hold on a second." He rose and went to the waitress station and grabbed a large to-go cup and came back, poured her water into it and put the lid on, then poked the straw from her glass into the cup. "Take this with you." He was always thinking about her needs.

"Thank you." She turned in her seat and hugged Shelby. "I'll call you later."

Shelby brushed her hand over Cyn's hair. "I want good news for you."

"Me, too. But I'll take the truth and knowing she's not out there somewhere undiscovered and alone."

"He'll pay for this." Shelby echoed Cyn's looping thought.

"Yes, he will." She took Hunt's hand, remembered that she needed to get up slowly so she didn't jar her system into moving before it was ready to support her efforts with all systems working together. She turned to Hunt's family. "Thank you for a really lovely breakfast. I'm so glad you included me."

"You're always welcome," Mr. Wilde said. "You take care. Anything you need, just call."

Hunt glanced at his whole family. "I'll be in touch. And thanks," he said, letting them know he appreciated them accepting Cyn with him.

They walked out of the restaurant to the parking lot together, but she pulled her hand free when Hunt turned for his police SUV. "I'll drive."

She shook her head. "I'll take my car, that way if you need to stay and help with the investigation or something you don't have to worry about me."

"Cyn. I know you've got to be reeling by this news."

"I am trying to hold it together and not fall apart on you. I know what you need me to do when we get there. I can do this. I have to. For her."

Hunt cupped her face in his hands. "You can let go

with me any time you need to, Cyn. I know how strong you are. I know how hard this is for you. I also know that it's taking a toll on you to hold it all together and get through another day not knowing what's happened to them."

"I don't want it to be her," she confessed.

"Neither do I. And if you want to stay here with Shelby, I'll go do this for you."

"I need to do it. If it's her, I need to see her, so I'll know it's real and true."

"What if something happens while you're driving?"

"You'll be leading the way. You'll know if something happens. But it won't. I feel okay. If I start to feel off, I'll pull over."

"Promise me."

"I promise."

He kissed her, then reluctantly let her go.

She walked to her car, got in and drove out of the lot behind him, her heart in her throat and her mind taking a dark and twisted road she didn't want to go down but had to face all the same.

"Please, don't be Angela."

# Chapter Twenty-Two

CYN STOOD with her back against Hunt's police vehicle, her arms crossed. Her gaze was fixed on the group of officers standing under the command-center awning. She'd been here for over two hours waiting for them to carry the deceased down from the rugged terrain where she'd been found.

Another family had arrived fifteen minutes ago. Mom, dad, brother and a bereft boyfriend all hoping the body didn't belong to a hiker who went missing a couple days before Angela disappeared.

A car pulled in beside her, breaking hard and fast, the couple jumping out and ready to rush toward the officers.

Cyn stopped them. "They're still bringing her down," she told Mr. and Mrs. Harmon. "What are you even doing here?"

Mrs. Harmon stared wide-eyed at her. "We came to see if Angela and Lana . . ." She burst into tears.

Cyn held hers back with her anger. "I thought you believed she went to Idaho," she accused.

They didn't say anything to that because their presence here told the truth.

"They only found the woman. If you want to know where Lana is, ask your son. He knows. Make him come forward and do the right thing."

"He doesn't know," Mrs. Harmon wailed, pressing her face into her husband's chest the second he reached for her.

She met Mr. Harmon's resolute stare. "He knows. That's why he's hiding. That's why he gave you that bullshit story about my sister being in Idaho. She doesn't know anyone there. The only person she'd go to for help is me."

"We just want to resolve this." Mr. Harmon's words meant nothing.

"Tell him to turn himself in and confess what he did to them. You know what he did, you just don't want to face the fact the boy you love turned into a monster."

"He's not," Mrs. Harmon spat back at her.

"You know he is or you wouldn't be here to confirm that's my sister they're bringing down. You wouldn't be crying like that if you believed she was in Idaho, happy with Lana and away from your son." She bounced off the SUV and took two steps toward the Harmons and looked Mr. Harmon in the eye. "You know your son."

"I do."

"Then you know where he'd go if he was in trouble and can't go to you. It would have to be somewhere he'd feel safe and sure no one would look for him there. Somewhere he could come and go without raising suspicions because he knows the cops are looking for him and his truck. You know. You're just too afraid to face what happens if you tell and the consequences come crashing down on him. I know you want to protect him. He's your son. But what about Lana? She's out there somewhere. Is she safe? Is she warm? Does she have everything she needs to thrive? My sister was breastfeeding her. Did he get her any formula? Does he have any idea how much milk she needs and how often?"

"He'd never let anything happen to her. She's just a baby."

"And my sister loved him, and he treated her like shit. He made her feel small and unlovable and afraid. He hit her. He lost his patience and his morals when he got angry with Angela. What happens when he's faced with a crying, screaming infant and he doesn't know what to do?"

The Harmons looked stricken.

"You can't hide behind ignorance. You knew what he was doing to Angela. You know what he's done to her now. If you do nothing, like you've done nothing in the past, you're just as guilty as he is for what happens next."

"He didn't say where he was calling from," Mrs. Harmon said, her voice softer, less defensive.

She looked to Mr. Harmon. "For Lana's sake, tell me where you *think* he is."

Mr. Harmon pressed his lips tight and stared off into the distance where a group of officers and search and rescue people carried a basket gurney down a trail with the body of the woman who could very well be her sister. "My father, Rad's grandfather, has a property between here and Blackrock Falls. I spoke to my dad. He says he hasn't seen Rad. But there's a dilapidated outbuilding on the property no one uses anymore. It's a fair distance from the house. My dad drove by it and said he didn't see anything. But . . ."

"What's the address?"

Mr. Harmon gave it to her and instructions for how to find the outbuilding.

She made a note of the information in her phone. "Thank you."

"Cyn," Hunt called, waving her to come to him.

She tucked her phone in her pocket and braced herself for what came next.

Hunt pulled her into his arms and spoke quietly. "The other family that arrived to see if the woman is their missing daughter, they can't give us any definitive information for an ID that isn't similar to Angela's description."

They didn't want it to be their loved one. She understood that all too well.

"I looked, but I can't be sure one way or another because the body's been out in the elements too long. Is there anything you can think of that would make me be sure? Does she have a tattoo we don't know about? A scar or mark on her that would identify her? Anything you can think of."

She leaned back and looked up at him. "I'll know if it's her or not." She slipped past him and headed for where they'd placed the body behind a truck so the families didn't have to see it.

She felt Hunt right behind her as she approached the officers surrounding the gurney. They backed off immediately and let her pass. She kneeled on the ground, stared at the black body bag that had been left unzipped but still covered the person inside. There was an acrid odor that wrinkled her nose and turned her stomach.

She sat on her heels, her hands on her thighs, and gave herself a second.

Hunt squatted beside her. "You don't need to do this. We'll ID the body another way. This was just to help us determine who we should still be looking for. If it takes a few more days, it takes a few more days."

She reached up and put her fingers over his mouth to make him stop talking and let her do this. He kissed her fingers and held her hand. She took a couple of breaths and tried to feel if it was her sister, the way she felt her when they were together. But there was nothing.

Cyn tried to think of a way to know if this was Angela. "Angela has a beauty mark on her right earlobe right next to where her ear is pierced. Last I saw her, she was wearing the earrings I gave her as a push present when she gave birth to Lana. They're gold *L*s. She loved them and wore them all the time."

Hunt squeezed her shoulder and kissed the side of her head. He pulled the flap on the body bag up just enough to take a peek without Cyn seeing anything of the body. He gently laid the flap back down. "The ears are pierced but no earrings. Because of the state of the body, the dirt and grime and decomp, it's hard to tell if there's a mark on her earlobe."

She sighed, her stomach in a knot, a lump in her throat. "Let me see her hair."

"Cyn," Hunt warned without spelling out how much he didn't want her to see her sister or anyone like this.

"It's okay. I can do this."

"I don't want you to have to." But Hunt lifted the flap carefully, exposing just the top of the woman's head.

Cyn forced herself to look. "Angela's hair is two shades lighter. She has long bangs. This girl's hair is all one length and her roots are dark. This isn't Angela."

Hunt closed the flap and took her in his arms. "I'm sorry to put you through this, sweetheart. I promise you, I will not stop looking for Angela. We will find her." He held her tight and kissed her on the forehead.

"Please tell them I'm sorry for their loss." She pushed away from him, tears streaming down her face. "I'm sorry. I have to go."

"Wait for me."

She put her hand on his chest. "I need to go." She rose and ran away, her heart breaking for the family who lost their daughter, and the man who lost the woman he loved.

Rage washed through her that Angela was still missing and Rad refused to do the right thing.

She'd find him and make him.

# Chapter Twenty-Three

❧

Hᴜɴᴛ ᴄᴏɴꜰᴇʀʀᴇᴅ with the officer in charge of the search and gave him the information Cyn gleaned from looking at the body. He hated that she'd been so desperate for the truth that she'd put herself through that. He'd have spared her that if he could have convinced her to wait for the official identification from the coroner's office.

But Cyn showed her strength and perseverance and did what needed to be done.

And then she ran. He didn't blame her. She couldn't be here and see this and not think she might have to do it again for her sister.

He needed to find her and make sure she was okay.

The Harmons stopped him on the way to his car.

Mr. Harmon stuffed his hands in his pockets. "Was it her?"

Hunt shook his head and looked at the family across the way holding each other and crying together. "No. It was a missing hiker who looked a lot like Angela."

The Harmons sagged with relief. Mr. Harmon wrapped an arm around his wife and kissed her on the head. "Thank God."

Hunt eyed the man.

Mr. Harmon caught himself. "I just meant . . ."

Hunt got it. "You're relieved it wasn't Angela. But she's still missing and Cyn is still waiting and your son is nowhere to be found."

Mr. Harmon and his wife exchanged a look that spoke volumes without words.

"Do you know where he is?" Hunt asked, getting a bad feeling about Cyn taking off the way she did.

Her words rang in his head. *I'm sorry. I have to go.*

Damnit, she'd promised him she wouldn't go off half-cocked and run into trouble.

"Where is she going?" he asked the couple, who stood there looking unsure and uneasy.

Mr. Harmon sighed. "We don't know if he's there or not, but we think he could be on his grandfather's property, though my dad says he hasn't seen him at all."

"Where?" Hunt typed the information into his phone and ran for his car. He tore out of the recreational parking lot, hit the main road and pushed the gas pedal to the floor.

He was just about to call Cyn when his phone rang and the caller ID lit up with her name. "Damnit, Cyn, are you okay?"

"Yes. I'm sorry."

"You promised me you wouldn't do something reckless like this."

"I said I'd let you know if I did. I was out of my head. I need to find him and make him tell me where they are. I can't do that again, Hunt." Meaning look at another body.

"I get that, sweetheart, and I'm sorry you had to. But you need to pull over and wait for me to catch up to you before you go to that isolated property alone and confront Rad if he's there."

"Too late. I just found the outbuilding his parents told me about. It's old. Weathered. Just a shack, really. I think I see his truck's taillights just behind the building."

"Cyn, please, back out of there and wait until I reach you."

"Oh, shit. I'm sorry, Hunt."

The last thing he heard was a gunshot.

# Chapter Twenty-Four

⊱━━━━⊰

CYN CAUGHT the movement in the rearview mirror, looked in it, spotted Rad behind her car, gun raised, and grabbed the door handle and pushed the door open just as the shot rang out. She fell to the ground, scrambled up and ran around to the front of the car as another shot pinged off the front fender.

He was coming after her.

Her only hope was to run into the trees. She sprinted for them as fast as she could and heard his footfalls behind her, catching up. He fired again. She ducked and scrambled sideways, dodging trees and brush and rocks.

Another shot rang out and a fiery pain cut across her upper arm as bits of wood splintered off a nearby tree. Her foot caught on a root or stone and she went down hard, her hands sliding on the dirt.

Rad came up behind her, flipped her over, then stood above her, the gun pointed at her chest.

She glared up at him. "Where's my sister?"

"You're so close," he taunted. "But you'll never know." He pulled the trigger.

She expected the impact. The pain. The end.

Nothing happened.

He'd run out of bullets.

He chucked the gun at her head, but missed, and it went tumbling away.

Before she could do anything, he leaned down and grabbed her by the hair, yanking her up and dragging her back through the woods toward the shack.

"Hunt is coming for me." She stumbled along behind him, pain exploding along her scalp from his grip on her hair.

"Good. Then he'll be here to see I meant it when I said I'd make him pay by hurting you."

She tried to dig in her heels and struggled to get free by prying his fingers from her hair, but he just held on tighter. "Where are Angela and Lana?"

"Your stupid sister got what she deserved. Lana is not your concern. She's *my* daughter. No one is taking her from me."

Relief washed through her. Her knees nearly buckled, but he kept dragging her forward.

He pulled her up onto the cement pad in front of the barely hanging door and through it into a dark wide-open space filled with old farm equipment, horse tack, tools, gas cans, large water containers and a table strewn with miscellaneous stuff, including a pillowcase filled with jewelry, cash and other items, along with the ghost mask. Behind the table was a cot with a sleeping bag and a duffel bag of clothes.

She didn't see or hear the baby.

"Where's Lana?"

"She's not your concern." He grabbed a coil of rope hanging on a peg on the wall, walked her to one of the support posts in the center of the room, pushed her back against it and shoved her to the ground. "You should be worried about what I'm going to do to you."

"You kill me, Hunt will never stop coming for you."

"He already won't stop!"

She tried to scramble away, but he grabbed her wrist, pulled her back and shoved her down to the ground again.

He tied her hands behind her back and around the post. "You convinced her to leave me." He squeezed her chin so hard it stung. "She was the only good thing I had left. But she didn't want me anymore. She didn't want me around our daughter. She thought I'd hurt Lana, too."

"And did you?"

Rad grasped her by the throat. "I didn't mean to grab her that hard when Angela tried to leave with her. The baby started wailing. Then Angela went berserk and hit and scratched me. I had to defend myself!" The rage in his eyes promised death.

She couldn't use her hands because they were tied too tightly for her to get free. She gasped for air and tried to wiggle and back away, but she had nowhere to go.

Rad suddenly released her, a gleam of something merciless in his eyes. "What was it you said to me? You'd rather be set on fire than let me touch you? Yeah. I think that was it." He stood and grabbed a gas can.

Her heart raced and her vision blurred but didn't go out on her altogether. "Rad, please. Don't do this."

"Now she begs. Now she says please." He stared down at her. "Fuck you, Cyn. You ruined everything!"

"If you're going to kill me, then at least tell me where my sister is."

"You walked right over your sister's grave and you didn't even know it."

"Just tell me where she is!"

"You'll both be here together. That's what you wanted, right, Cyn? Wish granted." He dumped the gasoline on some empty bags in the corner next to a wheelbarrow and shovel, went to the table where an old kerosene lamp sat, grabbed a box of matches, lit one and tossed it onto the gas-soaked bags.

Cyn panicked. "Don't leave me here. You don't want one more death on your hands. Hunt knows about the burglaries. He knows you killed that man."

Rad grabbed the stolen items off the table, his duffel bag off the cot, and stood in the doorway. "He'll have to prove that, won't he? By then, I'll be long gone."

"You can't do this." She coughed as the flames rose higher, eating up the dry wood structure, filling it with smoke.

He grinned at her from the door. "You asked for it." He closed the door, leaving her to burn.

Tied up and helpless, she screamed at him, "Hunt's coming! You won't get away with this!"

# Chapter Twenty-Five

HUNT COULDN'T push the SUV to go any faster. He fish-tailed around a curve in the road and nearly slid into Rad's oncoming truck before he slammed on the brakes and came to a jarring stop. He leaped out of the vehicle and drew his gun.

Rad had miraculously stopped just yards away with his window down. He pointed back up the road. "Arrest me or save your precious Cyn? What will it be?"

Hunt turned and spotted the smoke rising through the trees up ahead.

Rad slowly rolled the truck down the road, calling out, "Better hurry if you want her back alive. But I'm pretty sure it's too late, asshole."

Hunt didn't think. He let Rad go, jumped back in his car, got on the radio and called for his fellow officers to try to apprehend Rad. That was a long shot since most of them were too far away at the site where the missing hiker had been found. He told the dispatcher he needed fire and an ambulance on scene immediately, though it would take a while for both to reach the remote prop-erty. During all this he raced down the road, his heart beating practically out of his chest, fear eating away at him that he'd be too late.

By the time he made it to the structure, half of it was completely engulfed in flames. Luckily, the wind was blowing the flames away from the rest of the building, slowing down the fire's progress, but he still had precious little time. He ran for the door and flung it open, coughing as a wave of smoke and heat hit him in the face. It billowed out of the building through the door and cracks in the dry wood. He pulled the T-shirt he wore under his uniform shirt up and over his nose, then raced in to find Cyn.

"Cyn, baby, where are you?" he called out, but didn't hear her respond back to him. "Cyn!"

Somewhere in the distance he heard her coughing.

He sank as low as he could to avoid the worst of the smoke and tried to see where she was as he bumped into a table, then some piece of equipment.

"Hunt," Cyn called out. "Are you here? Help me," she wailed, then got caught in a fit of coughs.

He pulled his flashlight from his belt and used it to scan the darker part of the room, the flames at his back. And there she was a dozen feet in front of him, lying on the floor, her arm bleeding, hands behind her back.

He fell beside her and softly touched her face. "I'm here."

She sighed out her relief as her pain-filled eyes met his and she tugged at her hands.

He pulled the knife from his belt, cut her free, then picked her up and ran out of the building with her. He took her to his car and set her on the grass beside it, cupped her face and kissed her hard. "Don't ever fucking do that to me again!"

Cyn's eyes rolled back in her head, and she passed out.

"Fuck." He caught her and gently laid her back in the grass, ran to his SUV, pulled out the first aid kit and went back to her. He used his knife to cut the sleeve of her sweater away from the bleeding wound on her arm. He guessed she'd been grazed by a bullet. He found a gauze pad, tore the wrapper off and pressed it to the wound.

Cyn started coming around, then sat bolt upright. "Angela."

Hunt held the pad to her arm with one hand and gently took her by the neck to steady her with the other, noting the bruising on her skin. "What about her? Is she in there?"

She pointed to the structure. "He said I walked over her grave." She pointed to the door of the building again.

He turned back to her. "Lana?"

Tears overflowed her eyes. "She's alive. I don't know where. He wouldn't tell me."

He pulled her into his chest, hugged her close and kissed her a dozen times on the head. She had a death grip on his sides. It took him a good long time to be able to let her loose. He only did so because she kept coughing.

He went to his car and got her a bottle of water. On his way back to her, he stopped dead in his tracks and stared at the busted-out window at the back of her car where Rad had shot through it. He didn't know exactly what happened, how she survived and got away somehow, but she was damn lucky to be alive.

And he was even luckier to have gotten to her in time.

He handed her the water. While she drank, he put a new pad on the gash on her arm and tied some gauze around it to put pressure on the wound and hold the pad in place.

Sirens sounded in the distance, soft, but growing louder.

He sat beside her and pulled her into his side; the relief that she was here with him, alive, overwhelmed him.

She stayed in his embrace and looked up at him. "Hunt."

He kissed her again because he needed to feel the connection they shared and know that she was real and alive and safe. "What?"

"I'm sorry."

"I know you are. The important thing is that you're okay."

Tears fell down her cheeks, leaving wet tracks through the soot on her face. "She's dead. He killed her."

He wiped the tears from her face. "You said she's here."

"He lit a bunch of cement bags on fire." She shifted and pointed to the cement pad in front of the mostly burned-down structure. "I walked over her grave."

He held her close and she dissolved into a fit of tears and grief so deep and consuming he could feel it all around him.

The ambulance and fire trucks pulled in behind them.

Controlled chaos erupted as the fire department let the structure burn while they put out the brush fire surrounding the building before it spread into the woods. The building wasn't worth saving.

The paramedics helped Cyn into the back of the ambulance and put an oxygen mask on her. Her $O_2$ levels were low due to the smoke inhalation but they said she'd be okay. They looked at her arm, determined she needed more stitches. She needed another trip to the hospital. But she refused to go until they found her sister.

The fire department had some heavy equipment on their trucks. Once it was safe to get near the building, they used a couple sledgehammers to pound the two-inch slab into chunks. Hunt helped move the pieces aside, then he took the shovel and dug down until he found Angela wrapped in a tarp. When he opened the tarp at her head and spotted the *L* earrings, he closed the tarp back up and laid his hand on Angela's head, then whispered, "Rest easy. We will find Lana. And I'll take care of Cyn and her for you from now on." He meant it with his whole heart.

Cyn stood with her arms wrapped around her, his jacket engulfing her slim frame, just outside the perimeter his fellow officers set up while they excavated the scene.

He walked right up to her and kissed her on the forehead, wishing he could tell her something different, and knowing this was what she needed to start healing. "We found her, sweetheart."

"Are you sure?"

"Yes. She's wearing the earrings you gave her."

The tears came again, but not in a torrent, more like resignation and relief. "Thank you, Hunt."

He didn't know if she simply didn't have the strength to cry anymore, or had simply run out of tears. She looked lost and pale and just so sad and done right now. He wished he could make it all better, but there was nothing he could say or do to bring her sister back.

"Lana is out there somewhere," she whispered. "Nothing matters now but finding her."

Rad had gotten away, but the manhunt had already begun, because while he recovered Angela's body, his fellow officers scoured the woods and found the gun Rad used to shoot Cyn and most likely used in the home invasion assaults and murder.

He was facing an insane amount of charges that would put him away for the rest of his life.

Which made him even more dangerous.

"I need to get you to the hospital."

"I'm fine."

"No. You're not. That gunshot wound needs to be cleaned and stitched. You're probably dehydrated again and you need to have your lungs checked after all that smoke you inhaled."

"My oxygen level is back to normal."

"Cyn." He stared down at her, waiting for her to make the right decision.

She looked up at him, confusion and something else in her eyes. "I don't know what to do now without her."

"Yes, you do, Cyn. You've already said it a half dozen times. We will find Lana. You will love and protect her and care for her. She needs you, sweetheart. And so do I. So please, let me take you to the hospital to get checked out."

Instead of moving toward his car, she leaned into him and buried her face in his neck.

He wrapped her tighter in his arms and they stood there as the firemen cleaned up their gear, the officers processed the scene and the stars stared down on them.

"Hunt?"

"Yes."

"I think I'm going to pass out again."

She fainted in his arms.

He didn't panic. He simply picked her up and put her in the back of the ambulance; the paramedic put in an IV because, yes, she was dehydrated again. As they hauled ass to the hospital, he held her hand and thought to himself that his life before Cyn had been dull and boring.

With Cyn, it was fraught with danger and fear and close calls that left him worrying that he could lose her. But there was also all the good stuff. The way she smiled at him and said his name. The honesty they shared and acceptance of each other for who they were, not something they wanted the other to be. The way she made him feel when she kissed him. The love and caring she put into every touch.

The way she surrendered to being with him with her heart open, even when they took another step deeper into intimacy and their relationship, because she knew he was right there with her, wanting the same thing. Something that would last.

She opened up to him in the same way he'd opened up to her.

He couldn't lose her.

They were just getting started.

But if they were going to have the life he wanted with

her, he needed to eliminate the threat that kept trying to take her away from him.

Rad was more dangerous now than ever.

Hunt vowed that this was the last time Rad ever hurt Cyn again.

# Chapter Twenty-Six

CYN STEPPED out of the shower and into the towel Hunt held open for her. It had been a late night at the ER. They wanted to keep her overnight. She wanted to be home with Hunt. If she kept going back to the hospital this often, they were going to have to just hold a room for her. It had taken hours for them to scan her lungs to be sure there was no smoke damage. The doctor told her that she was lucky—only minor inflammation. They gave her an inhaler to use twice a day for a week.

They numbed her arm, cleaned out the gunshot wound, then sewed her up. They checked the other stitches running down her calf and along her head and neck. Everything looked good. No infection. So, eventually, they let her go home.

Hunt gently rubbed the towel over her, drying her because she was simply too tired and grief-stricken to do it herself.

She looked down at the stitches in her arm. "The bastard ruined my tattoo." The stitches went right through Angela's butterfly, leaving only Lana's right above where the scar would be. It was like Rad had stricken her from this world and her arm.

Hunt kissed her right above the stitches. "You can get another one."

She went right into his arms and laid her head on his bare chest. "I don't have to get one for you."

"I don't expect you to, sweetheart." He hugged her and kissed her on the head. He hadn't stopped touching her in some way since she woke up in the hospital.

She looked up at his handsome face, his blue eyes filled with warmth. "I don't need to because your name is already etched all over my heart. It's like you're imprinted all over me. I felt it before, but then I watched those flames rise and come after me and all I could think about was that I'd never get another day with you. Thank you for saving me again, Hunt."

He scooped her up into his arms. "It was purely selfish." He walked out of the bathroom with her. "Because I can't stand to be without you." He laid her out on the bed, pulled the towel right off her and tossed it, then did the same with the one wrapped around his waist. His body covered hers and she welcomed him into her arms, the soft glow of the firelight dancing on his warm, strong body.

She brushed her fingers through the back of his damp hair. "I don't think I've ever been really *in* love. Have you?"

"Yes. Once," he said, kissing her softly before he looked her in the eye again. "I'm so in love with you, my sweet, kind, determined, stubborn, smart and sexy Cyn."

She smiled for the first time in what felt like forever. "I love you, too. More than I thought possible. My heart is so full with it at the same time it's breaking for my sister."

"I know. You'll get through this, sweetheart."

"I will, because you make me happy. You make me think of what we'll do together tomorrow, and the day after that, and the day after that."

He traced a finger down the side of her face. "Can we do things that don't end with us in the hospital from now on?"

She tried not to smile, but not very well. "I'll see what I can do."

"How about we do this?" He kissed her, his tongue sliding along hers in a kiss that spun out and made her melt.

At 2:10 in the morning, they were both exhausted. But it didn't stop them from making love with soft caresses, long, deep kisses and their bodies moving together in a sweet, urgent, loving joining that somehow, some way, made their intense connection deeper and stronger.

In Hunt's arms, she let go of the grief and trauma of the day and reveled in the love and life and joy he brought out in her in an elemental way.

And Hunt was a gift that kept on giving.

So she gave herself over to him and lost herself in their bodies moving together as his deep and even thrusts eased her tired body and washed her heart in comfort and warmth. Their joining reminded her she was alive and happy even in her grief and desperation to find her niece and make sure she was safe.

Hunt kissed her, touched his forehead to hers, his heart beating against hers. "It's going to be okay."

She placed her hand on his handsome face, a face she wanted to wake up to every morning for the rest of her life. "I know it is, because I have you."

Hunt overwhelmed her in the nicest way with kisses and his body caressing hers, distracting her from what happened, what she couldn't change, and reminding her of the precious things she still had in her life.

She clung to him, this moment, all the love overflowing her heart, and the pleasure that overtook her and her Wilde man.

And he wasn't done taking care of her. After they held each other and their breathing eased back to a normal rhythm, Hunt slipped out of bed, went into the bathroom and came back with the bandages and ointment for her wounds. She lay there, letting him tend her as the fire popped and crackled.

"Do you know how she died?"

"In the morning, Cyn. Let's just take a few hours for us. We need it." He lay behind her, pulled the covers over them, snuggled her back into his front and kissed her shoulder. "I almost lost you again."

"Never going to happen. Now that you caught me"—she gripped his arm banded around her middle, the tease about how often he caught her speeding and now he'd captured her heart, too—"you'll have to keep me."

"It's why I brought you, and no one else, here."

She caught his eye over her shoulder. "What do you mean?"

"Well, I brought a couple girlfriends here before the renovation. They hated the one-bedroom dump. They wanted to remodel and redecorate it into what they wanted. I already had a vision for what it could be. What I wanted it to be when I brought the woman I wanted to make a life with here."

"But you brought me here before we really started dating."

"You interested me long before that. I thought we'd be good together. And when you realized I was serious and didn't hesitate to open up and tell me what you wanted, I thought why not start where I want us to end up. And here you are. With me."

"I'm here, in your house, because a madman threatened to kill me, then tried to do that because I told him I'd rather be set on fire than let him ever touch me."

Hunt rose up on his elbow. "Is that why he set the fire and didn't . . . ?"

"Kill me another way," she finished for him.

"Damn. I knew he was dangerous, but that's a whole other level of revenge."

"He once gave my sister a black eye because there was a leftover spot of something on his dinner plate that didn't come off when she washed it."

"Then it's good you're here with me. At least I'm armed. Hopefully that will deter him from doing something else stupid instead of turning himself in."

"He's never going to do that. After today, he's got no way out. You might not have been able to get him for killing my sister and the burglaries before, but now you've got her body, my eyewitness testimony that I saw the mask and stolen goods in his possession and that he tried to kill me. His only out is to run, but we both know he's not going to do that. We want justice. He knows we won't stop until we get it. He'll have no peace because of it. And because he knows we'll never stop, and he blames us, like he always blamed Angela for the bad shit he did, he'll want his vengeance. He needs it, or he has to face the hard truth, that this is all his fault. And he will never do that."

"Then it's even more important for us to stay vigilant and for you to—"

"Not run toward danger with nothing to defend myself but my rage for him."

He settled behind her and hugged her close. "Yes. That."

"Have I thanked you for saving me?"

"Yes. But if you want to do it again after we get some sleep, I'm happy to join in."

Cyn didn't think she'd actually sleep, but then she woke up to a bright beam of sunlight spearing through the mostly closed curtains and Hunt kissing his way down her spine and squeezing her ass.

"Morning," she mumbled, pushing her bottom up into his hands.

"Your mom called. She couldn't sleep." Hunt brushed his fingers down her spine, over her rump, down the back of her thigh to her knee. "I wanted to let you sleep, but she didn't sound good, especially since she didn't get to see you at the hospital last night."

Cyn had a hard enough time dealing with her own emotions. All she needed last night was Hunt, holding her through the worst of her tears. His touch easing the aches and pains and heartbreak. His love filling her up and making her believe that everything was going to be okay.

They might be facing dark times right now, but he was the light she clung to, the joy she found even in the face of death. But she didn't know if she could face her mother's anguish and anger, even though she felt stronger now.

She didn't know if she could face it today. "Can we just stay in bed with the covers over our heads and eat chocolate, and the only decision we have to make is who is going to get up to stoke the fire? It'll be you, by the way."

She got the soft chuckle she wanted from him.

"That sounds like an amazing day, sweetheart. And being in bed with you in my arms is my very favorite thing."

"But you're going to work to see what's happening on the case and try to track down Rad."

"We need to find him before—"

"He comes to finish what he started yesterday."

"I was going to say before he disappears with Lana. Though it's going to be much harder for him to do that now. His picture and Lana's are all over the news. There's a statewide AMBER Alert. There's even a mention of anyone helping Rad facing charges."

"You're hoping that will make whoever's been taking care of Lana for Rad come forward."

"Yes. Maybe they don't know what they've gotten caught up in and will want to do the right thing now."

She rolled to her back, the sheet slipping down below her breasts.

Hunt sat beside her on the bed staring down at her. "You are such a temptation."

"And I'm all yours."

He slid his hand across her belly and gripped her side. "How are you feeling this morning?"

"Sore. Like my life has been turned upside down even though you make me feel centered and present and not lost in the shitstorm."

"Come have coffee and breakfast with me."

"I probably need to call my mom back. We definitely need to make arrangements for my sister. And I haven't been in to work in . . . I don't even know how long it's been at this point."

Hunt leaned in close. "Right now, you need to take care of you. And if you won't do that, you need to let me do it for you."

They had a very short staring contest. She knew she wouldn't win this argument and didn't know why she bothered trying when breakfast with Hunt sounded like it would probably be the best thing to happen to her today. Except maybe him making love to her again. Everything else she needed to do sounded like a lot of work and emotional upheaval ahead.

"You know what I love about you?"

"My exceptional restraint in not diving on top of you right now?" The deadpan look made it clear he was serious.

"And your ass," she teased.

"And me in my uniform and wearing my glasses."

"I'd take you naked in glasses happily."

He finally grinned. "You can have me any way you want me."

"That. Right there. The way you make it clear you're mine and I'm important to you."

"I am yours. And you are the most important thing to me." He traced his fingers just below the bandage on her arm covering the scar where she'd been shot.

"You're not going to lose me, Hunt. I won't let it happen. Because being with you is the best thing to ever happen to me."

"Same. So can you please just do boring, normal things from now on?"

"I'm never boring, Hunt."

He leaned down to kiss her, but stopped an inch from her lips. "No. You're not. But I could use a few days to recover from thinking I'd lost you again."

"I'll do my best."

"That's my Cyn." He finally kissed her, his tongue sweeping over her bottom lip, then sinking deep into her mouth. He tasted like coffee and desire, and she wanted to lose herself in his arms again and put off this day as long as possible.

But her phone rang in the other room, reminding her that there were things she needed to face and do today no matter how hard they seemed.

Hunt broke the kiss. "Get dressed. Let's eat."

"Shelby only brought me enough clothes for a couple days. My jeans are clean enough, but can I borrow a shirt?"

"Your jeans and everything else you wore yesterday smelled like smoke from the fire. I put all your clothes in the wash first thing this morning."

She tilted her head. "You washed my clothes for me?"

"Except for the dress you wore home from the hospital the first time. I wasn't sure that could go in the wash. It's hanging in the closet. You can wear that today. But you'll have to wait until after breakfast and the dryer to finish before you'll have some underwear and a bra to put on."

"Okay." She didn't know what else to say.

She'd had overnights at guys' places before, but none of them had ever thought to wash her clothes for her.

"Do you need help getting up? Go slow. You don't want to bring on a dizzy spell."

She'd completely forgotten about her lingering side effects. "I'm fine. A bit stiff. I'll go slow."

"I'll plate up the food. Meet me out there when you're ready." Hunt held his hand out to her.

She took it and climbed out of bed slowly, not rising too fast to overwhelm her system. Steady on her feet, she squeezed Hunt's hand. "Thank you."

"Happy to help." He headed for the kitchen.

She went into the bathroom to pee, brush her teeth and hair and wash her face. Feeling refreshed, she slipped on the dress she found in his big walk-in closet, not on the wall of empty space, but right next to his uniforms, dress shirts and suits. Slacks and casual pants were hung. His jeans, sweats, sweaters and other casual clothes were stacked in the cubbies. The closet smelled like him.

She thought about what he'd said about renovating the old building into a place he'd bring the woman he wanted to make a life with here. He'd thought of that woman and made the other side of the closet much bigger, with drawers and pegs to hang things like scarves and purses, and a full-length mirror.

"Cyn." Hunt startled her.

She turned to him. "You really did create this space with someone else in mind."

Hunt looked past her at the empty closet space. "I've heard women like big closets." He grinned at the innuendo that women liked other big things.

"What else did you do in this house for the woman you'd bring here?"

"Breakfast is ready." He tried to change the subject.

She wasn't having it. "Hunt. What else?"

"It's nothing."

"Then show me."

He held her gaze, shrugged after a moment, then took her hand and tugged her to follow him. "Fine. But don't get all weird about it." They headed up the stairs.

She'd never been up to the loft, though it looked like a cozy place to sit and read. She loved the floor-to-ceiling bookshelves and the huge windows that brightened the whole place. She stopped on the landing and looked out the windows. As far as the eye could see it was all grassy fields and woods in the distance. "Hunt, that view. It's gorgeous."

"I usually sit up here and drink my coffee when I have time to wake up slow in the morning."

"I can see why." And the comfy-looking chairs with ottomans he'd chosen seemed like a great place to relax and unwind. She easily pictured them there with a glass of wine in the evening, talking about their day.

He went ahead, passing an open door to a beautiful spare room that had dark wood furniture and a black metal bed with a white spread and pillows and black-and-white photos on the walls.

Hunt stood in front of the closed door and held the knob. "I told my family this room was for Eliza when I babysit her."

She raised a brow. "But that wasn't true?"

"No." He opened the door and stood with his shoulder against the doorframe looking in at the sweet nursery with a beautiful dark wood crib, dresser, changing table and bookcase, and a pale gray area rug on the hardwood floor to match the shade on the walls.

But it was what hung over the crib that held her attention.

"When did you do this room?"

"Before you were ever on my radar. When I got the furniture and decorated the room, it was one of those things where I thought, if it's here, maybe it will be a reality one day."

Cyn touched her finger to one of the butterflies on the mobile over the crib. Blue ones, green ones, orange, red, purple and yellow. "I love this."

"I thought a baby, boy or girl, would love the colors. It never occurred to me the coincidence that I picked that mobile and fell for you."

She turned to him. "If you build it, they'll come." That probably wasn't the exact famous movie quote, but it struck her how true it was in this moment.

"And here you are, Cyn. Maybe seeing those butterflies, how close we've gotten in such a short time, knowing this room represents the future I want, scares you a little. Truthfully, it does me. But you asked. So now you know it's here, and you, and this, are what I want for my future."

She looked at the mobile again and around the room. "I really wasn't expecting this." She looked at Hunt, who studied her with an intensity that touched her because of the raw need she saw in his eyes. "It's perfect."

The smile he gave her lit up her heart. "I'm glad you like it." He held his hand out to her. "Come with me. Let's eat."

She took his hand, glanced back one last time at the beautiful room he'd created for his child, then went into his arms and kissed him. "You're a very sweet man, Hunt."

He gave her a quick, hard kiss. "Don't tell anybody." He tugged her toward the stairs.

She chuckled and followed him down to the kitchen, where he'd left a mug of coffee on the breakfast bar for her and a plate of eggs, bacon and fried potatoes.

"How long have you been up?"

"Long enough to make you breakfast and reveal my little secret."

"On that note, I want to show you something." She picked up her phone where he'd left it charging for her on the counter. "I don't ever do this. Like never. But you and me . . . Well, it's different. It's real and I hope headed toward that." She held up her hand and pointed behind her at the baby's room upstairs. "So . . ." She turned her phone toward him and showed him the results of her blood work she'd asked the doctor to run while she was in the hospital the first time after drowning and Hunt saved her and she knew she didn't want to let him go any time soon. Which had now turned into her wanting to keep him forever.

"What am I looking at?"

"My test results. No STDs. I'm clean. Not that I thought I wasn't, but a guy like you, who likes facts and plays by the rules and all that, would want to see it in black and white. You always have a condom ready, which is great. I mean, you had a certain perception about me, so I thought—"

He kissed her midsentence. "Stop. The condoms were never about me thinking you had something."

"Safety first. That's you. I get it. And making sure you didn't get me pregnant. And you never asked if I was using anything."

"If you are, great, but it's still my responsibility, too, because things happen when it comes to the pill."

Right. Women didn't always take them properly, making them less effective. Antibiotics, which she was taking, rendered them less effective, if not ineffective. "I love that you're responsible and all that, but what I'm trying to tell you is that I can't get pregnant."

He went perfectly still. "Ever? Because we can adopt or use a surrogate. There are other ways to make a family."

She shook her head, loving him even more for coming up with a solution and being open to other possibilities and not even considering being with someone else who could give him a child. "I love you for that, but that's not what I'm saying. I can have a baby. At least, there's no reason to think I can't. I've never tried."

Hunt put his hand on her shoulder. "Cyn. What are you trying to tell me?"

"Sorry. I'm making a mess of this." She sighed. "It's simple. I don't have any STDs. I do, however, have an IUD, which prevents pregnancy. So if you didn't want to use condoms . . . I'm okay with that. With you." She didn't have any hesitation taking another step deeper into intimacy with him. Especially not after he'd bared his soul and showed her that room upstairs, letting her know exactly what he wanted.

Hunt grabbed his phone off the counter and started tapping his finger on the screen. "What is the damn password?" He tried typing something in again.

She touched his hand to stop him. "Are you trying to look up your records?"

"Yes." He looked up at the ceiling, thinking. "I had them run the blood work like ten months ago. It came back clean. Of course. And I haven't been with anyone since." He tried another password.

She took his phone and set it aside. "Okay."

He looked at her blankly. "Okay, what?"

"Your results were negative. Okay."

"You're just going to take my word."

"You have no reason to lie. And you're not a liar. I believe you one hundred percent. So we're good and can stop talking about all that. Unless there's something specific you want or need in our sex life that I can give you, then I'm open to the discussion."

Hunt's eyes went wide. "For real?"

"Yes. Making you happy, fulfilling your needs, that's important to me. How do I know if I am or I'm not if you don't let me know?"

"Is there something you want, Cyn?"

"I love everything we do. You're a generous and very attentive lover. And because of my injuries, you've been cautious."

"I don't want to ever hurt you."

"I know. I appreciate the restraint I sometimes feel in you. I hope, when I'm healed, you'll let loose that greedy side of you, because that would be a powerful thing between us."

"So you like things a little aggressive."

"I don't want there to ever be anything between us that holds you back from being you."

Hunt stood and cupped her face, looking down into her eyes, his ablaze with desire. "Believe me, Cyn, making love to you is the greatest pleasure. I don't care if it's slow and soft and sweet, or fast and hard and mindless, as long as it's with you. I'm glad we had this talk. I'm thrilled to have the only all-access pass. I only wish you'd waited until after you ate to tell me because now all I can think about is being inside you without any barriers separating us."

She slid her hand up his long, thick length and squeezed him in her palm.

He hissed with the sheer pleasure she read in his eyes, then pulled her hand away. "Eat your breakfast," he ordered, sitting next to her again. "Please. You're going to need your strength."

She giggled and picked up her fork. "You sure you don't want me to eat sitting on your lap?" She eyed him and put a forkful of eggs into her mouth and drew the fork out very slowly.

"Fuck, Cyn, you're killing me." He reached for her, but his phone rang. He didn't take his eyes off her when he growled again, then picked up his phone. "I wish I didn't have to answer this."

"Me, too, but it's part of your job." She understood that, as a cop, he was on call even when he technically wasn't.

He cupped her face in one hand. "Thank you for understanding."

"We're together. I like that too much to let the little things get in the way of us."

He gave her a quick kiss. "I don't know how I got so lucky." He reluctantly answered the call. "Wilde." He listened for a moment, then stood and walked away.

She took her plate, went into the kitchen, just as he closed the bedroom door, and put her plate in the microwave to reheat her food. She didn't mind that he took the call in privacy. She imagined there would be a lot of things he encountered at work that he'd need to keep confidential. Still, her curiosity was piqued, because she wondered if he was getting an update about her sister's death, Rad or Lana.

She sat back at the counter and ate the food Hunt made her even though her stomach went tight the moment he'd left the room.

Hunt threw the bedroom door open and rushed out. "Did you eat?" The urgency in his voice caught her attention.

She set down the glass of cranberry juice he'd left for her. "Yes. It was delicious. Thank you. Want me to heat up your plate?"

"No time. We need to go. Now. Finish off that juice. I have a water bottle in the car if you need it, too. Where are your shoes?" He started checking by the sofa, then by the door.

"They're in the bedroom next to the bed."

He ran back in there.

She started after him, but stopped short when he came out again, and shoved her shoes into her chest and hands. "Hunt. Slow down. What is going on?" She was talking to his back as he ran to the mudroom, disappeared for a moment, then came out carrying a pair of her panties and her bra.

"Put these on. You'll need a jacket or sweater." He disappeared into the mudroom again, then came out carrying a black zip-up hoodie. "This is clean. You can use it." He looked at her. "You're not dressing."

"I'm not moving until you tell me what is going on. This isn't like you."

He stopped in front of her. "I have a lead on Lana, but it's a dangerous situation. I don't want to do this, but it might be the only way to get her back."

"Why wouldn't you want to get her back?"

"I do, but it means putting your life on the line again."

# Chapter Twenty-Seven

HUNT PULLED into the bar's parking lot in Blackrock Falls and cut the engine an hour after they ran out of the house to his car. For all the rush he'd been in, inside he'd wanted to lock her in the house and never let her out again. Especially not to do this.

Cyn had spent all of the drive here on the phone with her mom, assuring her that she was fine.

Her mom sounded like she was in a bad place. And who wouldn't be? But Cyn calmed her down, they shared a few stories about Angela and Cyn promised to be there soon to help make the arrangements for Angela's funeral.

She never mentioned that they were on their way to hopefully get Lana back.

"I thought we were going to some biker club." Cyn stared out the window at the bar's neon sign.

He'd outlined the basic information he'd received. A guy who goes by Viper, in the motorcycle club, called the bar and told Lyric the baby was with the club's president's sister. Due to what happened yesterday and the press surrounding the case and manhunt for Rad, the baby was taken to the club so no one, including the cops, found out the woman had the missing baby. Viper didn't know how long they'd keep the baby there before they moved her, or did something else with her, because no one associated with the club wanted to be caught with a kidnapped baby.

"I need to check in here with my cousin who took the call."

She eyed him. "Your cousin?"

"Yeah. The family owns the bar." He slipped out of the car, not wanting to waste any more time.

Cyn met him at the front end and took his hand. "I need to get caught up on your family tree."

"They're Wildes. My dad's brother, my aunt and four cousins." Hunt walked in the front door to a bar that was bright with all the lights on because they were closed this early in the day.

Aria sat at the bar drinking coffee and doing paperwork. She turned at the sound of the door. "Finally. We're all so anxious about this."

At that, Lyric and Melody came out of the swinging door that led into the small kitchen and rushed him.

He braced himself for the three women to surround and hug him. He hadn't seen them in a while and it was good to catch them all in his arms and remind himself he had a lot of family support.

"Uh, Wilde, you want to introduce me?"

He turned to Cyn and caught the jealous and defensive look she gave him before she scanned the three dark-haired, blue-eyed Wildes.

Aria spoke before he could say anything. "How the hell did you get such a beautiful woman to like your ugly ass?"

"You like me," he pointed out, hoping to score some points with his pretty cousin.

She rolled her eyes.

He made the introductions. "Cyn. This is Aria, Lyric and Melody. Wilde," he added to ease her mind, though he liked seeing a little jealousy in her eyes. He looked at the girls. "Where's Jax?"

"Here." His cousin walked out of the back, yawning and carrying a mug of coffee. His gaze landed on Cyn and a slow smile broke on his lips. "Hello. Please tell me you're not with him."

Cyn grinned. "I'm with him."

He loved her immediate response and the way she moved closer to him. He wrapped his arm around her waist and pulled her close. "Tell me what you know and how we're supposed to do this."

Lyric took the lead. "A few of the biker club members like to come in here on the regular, even though they've got their club."

"They like the food," Melody said.

"And the women," Jax added, not meaning his sisters at all.

Hunt nodded for Lyric to go on.

"One of them, well, he's newer than the others. He's . . . intense." She waved that away. "Anyway, he called me this morning to tell me he overheard the president of the club say they were basically fucked if the Wilson baby was found with anyone associated with the club. Apparently, the president's sister knows Rad somehow. I think they dated, or were dating." She waved that away, too. "Rad has some kind of business going with the club."

Hunt exchanged a look with Cyn. "Maybe it had something to do with him pawning or selling off the stuff he stole. The club members would be able to move the stolen goods, presumably."

Lyric shrugged. "Anyway, the guy I know, Viper, said they were trying to get in touch with Rad for him to come and get the baby, but they'd had no luck reaching him. But they also wanted to get the baby out of there ASAP because the heat is on Rad and they don't want it coming down on them."

"Okay. But how did Viper know to contact you about the baby?" Cyn asked, trying to piece things together.

Hunt didn't get how they linked the baby to Lyric, which led to him and Cyn, either.

Lyric shrugged. "Don't know. Viper just asked if I could get in contact with my cop cousin in Willow Fork and get you and Cyn here."

Hunt eyed Lyric. "He seems to know a lot about your family and that I'm connected to the case."

Lyric shrugged again and didn't fill in anything from his leading statement.

"So why didn't your friend just bring the baby to you?" Cyn asked.

Lyric waved that away. "No one is supposed to know the baby is there. Viper didn't want the club to know he'd told me about the baby. He'd get in trouble for talking about club business with outsiders. They can't take the chance someone sees them bring the baby here either. Viper said the best plan was to make it seem like Rad sent you to get your niece."

Cyn sighed. "So basically you want me to walk in there and demand my niece back, saying Rad sent me, when we have no idea if they've been able to get in contact with Rad and could know that I'm lying."

"Yes." Lyric looked a little scared. "And if they know you're lying, you can't tell them how you knew the baby was there. I promised Viper that no matter what happened none of us would rat him out."

"Okay. So I'm supposed to bluff my way through this." Cyn turned to Hunt, concern in her eyes that so much of this could go wrong. Then she looked down at herself and back at his cousins. "I'll need something else to wear. I'm not walking into a biker club looking like I belong in a hipster coffee shop and can't hold my own."

Melody's eyes filled with delight. "I've got you covered."

"You mean uncovered," Jax grumbled, looking at Melody's purple tank top that barely covered her breasts, the white lace bra poking out the top of it and the skirt that barely covered her ass.

Melody waved Cyn to follow her down a long hallway. "I've got some stuff in my locker in the back. I never know when a fight is going to break out in here and I'm going to be covered in beer and booze."

"Every night," Jax called out to his retreating sister. "Usually because two cowboys are fighting over one of you."

Lyric shook her head. "No one's fought over me."

"That's because Viper glares at every dude who even looks at you."

She pressed her lips tight and shook her head. "No, he doesn't."

Jax's eyes narrowed. "Yeah. He does. Stay away from him."

"You're not the boss of me."

Aria bumped her shoulder into Hunt's arm. "Can I come live with you?"

Hunt chuckled. "You want three Wilde men being overprotective of you? Because me, Chase, and Max are just like him."

"Ugh! Save me from all Wilde men."

Cyn walked back into the main part of the bar with Melody on her tail.

Jax let out a long whistle. "Damn, cuz, you ever let her go, I'll keep her."

Hunt stared dumbfounded at Cyn, and said, "Never going to happen." He'd hold on to her any way he could for the rest of his life.

Cyn stopped in front of him and asked, "What do you think?"

"I should lock you up for being that beautiful and sexy." He growled and frowned at the skimpy clothes. "Didn't you promise not to get naked around other people anymore?"

"Only in front of your brothers. Remember?" she teased.

He'd given her the sexy black bra from the dryer this morning to wear under the maxidress she'd exchanged for a pair of black jeans with tears in the knees and thighs, showing off some skin. They fit her like a second skin and were probably a size too small. Over the black bra she wore a sheer red top that had spaghetti straps and draped over her ample breasts to just above her belly button. It left nothing to the imagination. To complete the outfit, she had on a pair of four-inch black boot heels. She'd also put on some red lipstick, dark eyeshadow and thick black eyeliner, giving her an even edgier look.

Jax checked her out from head to foot and back up again. "I'm not his brother. You can get naked with me any time you want."

"Shut it," Aria warned Jax. "Or Hunt will knock you on your ass."

"As long as I fall on top of her." Jax smiled at Cyn, pure teasing and taunting, nothing more. He obviously liked to relieve the tension in stressful situations with levity.

Cyn didn't take her eyes off Hunt. "I can do this," she promised him, knowing exactly how dangerous the situation could be.

He looked desperate to do this any other way than putting her in jeopardy again.

Cyn appreciated that he believed in her to get this done. She looked to Lyric. "Give me the address."

Lyric took Cyn's phone and put the address in the map app. "You'll know the guy who told me about the baby, Viper, by the compass tattoo on the back of his hand. Whatever you do, don't give it away that he helped you, but know that if things get bad, more than likely he'll help you."

Cyn frowned. "More than likely?"

"He's hard to read. He'll probably act like you're a pain in the ass like he does me, but since he called about the baby, presumably he wants to make sure this goes well. Get in, get out as quickly as possible. Oh, and don't be surprised if they search you for a wire or something. He told me to tell you that."

Cyn looked down at the transparent shirt. "Where would I hide one?"

Hunt took Cyn's hand. "You'll take my truck. I'll follow you with Lyric in her car. We'll park down the road and wait for you to come out." He squeezed her hand. "The thing is, I won't know if you're in trouble."

"You will. Viper said he'd send me a text if things went south."

Hunt glared. "We're relying on a guy named Viper, who is loyal to his club."

Lyric shrugged.

Cyn turned to her. "Do you trust him?"

Lyric bit her bottom lip, then shrugged again. "There's something off about him. I don't know if I trust him, but I believe he'll make sure you and the baby get out safely."

"Then I'll trust you." Cyn held her hand out to Hunt for the keys.

He hesitated in handing them over to her.

"Hunt, I'm going."

He dropped the keys in her hand.

She stepped into him and kissed him like it might be the last time she ever did, then hugged him tight and whispered in his ear. "I will come back to you."

He held on to her for another few seconds, then did the hardest thing he'd ever had to do and let her go, so she could walk into danger yet again.

# Chapter Twenty-Eight

CYN POUNDED her fist on the metal door for the third time, wondering if the guy who called Lyric was really telling the truth and expected her to come or not. She was about to knock again when the door nearly hit her in the face.

A huge dark-haired man filled the entire doorframe and glared at her. "What the fuck do you want?" He rubbed his fingers over his scruffy jaw.

She immediately noticed the compass tattoo on the back of his hand and played her part in this game. "Rad sent me to pick up my niece."

He gave her an almost imperceptible nod, then bellowed over his shoulder, "We got company." He barely moved out of her way when he waved her to come in and whispered so low she barely heard him. "Stick to that story."

She walked into a large square space with pool tables to the right and a bar with stools and a few tables on the left. Up ahead was a doorway, flanked on each side by pinball machines, that probably led to a storeroom or office.

The whole place smelled of cigarette smoke, pot, beer and sweat.

Her boots clicked on the cement floor as she moved into the room and closer to the six other men. She put a little shake in her hips and kept her shoulders back, breasts out. Three guys sat at the bar eyeing her. The other three sat at a table. The guy in the middle had a President patch on his leather vest with another wolf head over a skull and crossbones patch beneath it. That explained the many pictures and symbols of wolves around the space.

Beneath those patches, the name Lobo was stitched into the vest.

"You're a little early to be looking for a good time," Lobo said, doing the talking for all the others. "Who are you? And what are you doing here?"

"I'm Cyn," she purred, getting the attention of all the men in the room. She knew how to use sex appeal to get a man's attention and make her seem less like a threat and more a conquest.

The president leaned forward and braced his tattooed arms on the table. "Sin is what we do best."

She sauntered to the table, a sultry smile on her lips, planted her hands and leaned down, giving him a close-up view of her tits. "I bet you do. But I'm not here for a good time. I just want what I came for and I'll be on my way."

Lobo leaned back in his chair, grabbed his junk, adjusted his hard-on and smiled at her. "What is it that you came for?"

"She'll be coming for you soon," one of the guys at the bar said, making the others laugh.

She could feel Viper close behind her and took comfort in the fact he had her back. At least she hoped so.

Cyn kept her gaze steady on the man with all the power here, licked her lips, watched him adjust himself again and smiled. "I came to pick up my niece, Lana."

Everything changed in an instant. The room went deathly quiet. The president's lascivious gaze turned cold and menacing. "Search her," he ordered Viper.

The big man closed the distance behind her. She stayed perfectly still when he took her by the shoulders, pulled her up to standing straight in front of him, then took her hands and raised them over her head.

"Keep them up," he said for all to hear, but then he put his face in her hair and in that barely-there whisper said, "Sorry about this." His fingers raked through her hair, tousling her waves even more, then his hands skimmed down the sides of her breasts, over her belly, up over her breasts again, then down over her hips, one hand gliding between her legs so he could slide both hands down her thigh and leg and back up again before he did the same to the other.

She didn't show any sign that he'd hurt the cuts on her shin when he ran his hands over them.

"She's clean."

Cyn hated every second of that, but knew Viper only did it to put on the show the others expected. And so he could say she wasn't wired.

"Why would you think your niece is here?" Lobo asked, eyeing her.

She kept her answer short. "Rad sent me to pick her up."

The president studied her. "Word is he killed your sister."

She leaned on the table again. "He did. And believe me, he's going to pay for it."

The man stood and pulled a gun from behind his back and held it at his side. "Rad's a wanted man. Anyone associated with him and what he did could be implicated. You show up out of the blue asking about a kidnapped baby. Makes me wonder." He rounded the table and pointed the gun at the side of her head. "Why would you come *here*, to a place like this, alone?"

She tried not to show her fear, fisted her trembling hands and turned to him, putting the gun barrel right at her forehead. "I didn't come here to fuck you. I came to get my niece. That's all. She's mine now. And that fuck, Rad, can burn in hell for killing my sister. In fact, I'll send him there myself the next time I see him. Just give me what's mine and I'll walk out of here and you will never hear from me again."

Lobo stared her down for a long moment, then nodded to the guys at the bar. "Check all the windows. Make sure no one is lurking outside." He continued to stare her down. "If the fucking cops are waiting for you to come out so they can bust us . . . You'll wish I killed you quick."

She stepped into the gun, the barrel pressing into her skin. "I'm here alone. That fucker shot me and tried to burn me alive. I'm not here doing him any favors. He's stupid. I'm not. Which is why I'm not about to make an enemy out of you. You've got a problem I can solve. Give her to me and it ends here between us."

"What are you going to say when you show up with the kid?"

She couldn't tell him she had a cop on her side, willing to let her get the baby without coming after the woman or the club who had her.

"I got an anonymous call that I'd find the baby, alone, outside the abandoned bait shop I saw about three miles back down the road. As far as I'm concerned, I've never met any of you. Anyone says they saw me here, I'll say I stopped in for directions."

"I don't trust you."

"You don't trust anyone. But if you've ever lost someone you loved, then you understand how badly I want the only piece of my sister that is left in this world. That little girl is her blood. *My* blood. And I will fight to the death to get her back and make sure she is loved and cared for the rest of her life. You can trust that kind of devotion to family." She pointedly looked at the men surrounding him. "Now, please, give her back to me." Her voice cracked on the plea she hoped swayed him.

"She's right here," a soft voice called from the now-open door at the back of the room.

Cyn had a hard time not seeing the gun pointed right at her head, but stepped back and turned and ran to Lana, sleeping in her car seat. She fell to her knees, breathed a sigh of relief and leaned in and kissed her softly on the head. "Hello, beautiful."

"She's perfect," the woman told her. "She slept well last night. I fed her an hour ago. She'll be wanting another bottle an hour from now." She set the diaper bag Cyn had picked out with her sister beside Cyn. "Plenty of diapers in the bag, though that asshole Rad left me with a baby and little else. I picked up some formula. It's in the bag, too, along with a few outfits." The woman touched her shoulder. "I think she misses her mom. She cries sometimes for no reason."

Cyn looked up at the young woman. "Thank you for taking such good care of her."

"It was my pleasure. And my brother will let you go with no further concern."

Lobo growled behind her. "Fine. But if this comes back to bite me in the ass, I'm coming for you, Cyn. That new shop you're opening in town . . . Maybe you open it, maybe I make sure you don't."

Cyn didn't even acknowledge the threat or that he already knew who she was when she'd walked in the door. She stood and hugged the woman. "Anything you need, and I can help, you let me know. Obviously, you know how to find me." She notched her head toward the woman's brother.

She held out her phone. "Mind giving me your number? I'd love it if you shared pics of this little one. I've grown attached."

Cyn took the phone, put in her contact information, handed it back, picked up the diaper bag and her niece in the car seat and turned for the door. As she passed Lobo she nodded to him and said, "Thank you for the hospitality. And the directions," she added to let him know she'd keep up her end of the bargain.

Viper held up his hand toward the woman at the back. "Toss me your keys. I'll get the base for the car seat out of your car and move it to hers."

Cyn didn't stop walking. She wanted out of that place and to be back with her Wilde man.

She walked out the door and into the sunlight, squinting, Viper on her tail.

The second the door slammed behind them, he whispered, "You handled that perfectly."

"I've dealt with my fair share of controlling ass-holes." Her mother had brought enough of them home over the years.

"You okay? The whole thing with the gun . . . I didn't think it would go that far."

"I'm fine." She stopped by her car and looked down at her sleeping niece. "I just want to go home. Please."

"Sure. No problem." He raced to another car in the lot, opened the car door and pulled out the car seat base.

She had the truck door open and ready for him to put it inside. He did so efficiently and gave the base a good tug to make sure it was secure before he took the baby and latched the carrier to the base.

She tapped his shoulder to get his attention. "I don't know why you did this. I don't care. Thank you for getting her back to me."

"Will you do something for me?"

"Name it."

"Don't tell Lyric what I did to you in there."

She tilted her head and swore she saw regret and a plea in his eyes seconds before he masked all emotion from them again. "I won't say a word. And for what it's worth, I think you scored a lot of points with her by telling her Lana was here and to contact me." It dawned on her that she and Lyric weren't really connected. "How did you know she could get me here?"

"Smart women are always trouble." He closed the truck door. "We've seen you in town getting things ready to open up your shop. The club likes to keep tabs on people and what's happening around here. I saw you with the cop on the news. I got his name from someone

I know in Willow Fork. Since I couldn't risk calling the cop, I called Lyric."

"And put yourself on the line in doing so."

"Yeah, well, babies belong with their family. I'm sorry about your sister."

"Thank you. Do you know where Rad is?"

He shook his head. "No. But if I find out, I'll make sure he gets what's coming." He frowned again. "They're watching us. I'm going to move in like I'm going to kiss you. You shove me away and get out of here." He didn't wait for her to acknowledge that and leaned in close.

She put her hands on his chest, shoved him away, opened the driver's side door, got in and got the hell out of there, thanking her lucky stars for a man like Viper, who did the right thing even in the face of danger, because if his club knew he ratted them out about the baby, there would be consequences.

# Chapter Twenty-Nine

Lyric accepted the call as soon as her phone rang. "Is she okay?" she asked the formidable man she thought would be the last man who'd ever do something kind, even though he'd never actually done anything to warrant that assessment but be a force to reckon with just by existing.

"She's on her way back to you right now with the baby."

She breathed a huge sigh of relief. "Thank you." She never used that ridiculous name Viper. "I don't know why you did it—"

"I wish you did."

"—but thank you," she spoke over him. "Wait. What did you say?"

"Nothing. Listen, things got a little dicey. Make sure Cyn's okay when she gets there."

"What happened? Is she hurt?"

"No." He sounded defensive, then she got a softer, "Maybe. But not the way you think," that he quickly added in a gruff voice. "Lobo held a gun to her head. That kind of thing fucks with you for a long time."

She hated that it sounded like he knew that from firsthand experience. "I'm sorry that happened to her. And you," she added.

He didn't speak and the ensuing quiet pause held a world of something that pulled at her even as she wanted to deny it.

"If there's *ever* anything you need, anything I can do, let me know." She thought she heard a very faint whispered, "I need you," before he hung up, like he hadn't just twisted her heart up into a whirlwind of questions and emotions she didn't want to breathe life into, let alone acknowledge.

HUNT STARED AT his cousin, trying to read the uncertainty, longing and upset in her eyes. "What did he say?" His demand brought her out of her thoughts.

Lyric waved her hand, like she needed to symbolically wash away whatever she was feeling. "She's on her way. They gave her the baby. But . . ."

Hunt waited, but had to ask, because Lyric looked torn about telling him. "What?"

"Things got . . . complicated. They aren't the trusting sort."

"And? What does that mean?"

"Lobo, the president of the club, held a gun to her head."

Hunt swore. "I shouldn't have let her go alone."

Lyric shifted her weight and cocked a hip. "Trust me. It's better that she did. She held her own and got the baby. That's what counts."

"And what about how she had to go about getting the

baby? Do you have any idea what she's been through the last couple weeks?"

"I can't imagine, Hunt. And I feel for her. I do. But this was the only way that didn't end with the club getting rid of the baby some other way. Maybe they'd have dropped her at a fire station or hospital. I think the man who contacted me would have done that if he hadn't found the connection between the baby and me. But the others in the club . . . Some of them are ruthless."

"I still don't understand how he made the connection."

"It doesn't matter. Lana is with Cyn now, where she belongs. And with you, I guess, in a way. Are you two going to raise Lana together?"

Things were happening so fast, but he didn't hesitate. Not when it came to Cyn. "Yes. That's what I want. In fact, we had a talk this morning about moving things forward." God, had it only been a couple of hours ago he showed her the nursery and now they were bringing home a baby?

Unless Cyn decided to go back to her place once Rad was found.

They needed to have another talk.

Right now it had to wait because Cyn pulled in looking pale, her hand shaking when she took it off the steering wheel to open the car door. She ran for him, and he closed the distance, taking her into his arms and holding her close.

"I did it. I got her."

He wrapped her in his arms and held her tight. "You're safe, sweetheart. I knew you could do it."

"We need to leave. Just in case they followed me. I don't want them to see me with you and think I've called in the cops."

"Okay. We'll go. But first, look at me." He leaned back, but she didn't raise her face to his. "Cyn. Look at me."

She finally did and it tore at him to see the fear still in her eyes. "That was really . . . hard."

"But you did it. It's over. Lana is in the truck. We are taking her home. You are okay," he reminded her.

Lyric put her hand on Cyn's shoulder. "I'm sorry they scared you like that."

Cyn looked from Lyric to Hunt. "The guy called her to let her know about the gun to your head. I'm sorry I wasn't there to protect you."

"I knew he wasn't going to shoot me. It was a threat."

"A very real one," Lyric pointed out.

Cyn nodded and raked her trembling fingers through her hair. "I know. But I didn't think he'd do it. He wanted the baby out of there. He wanted to believe I'd take her and go and that would be the end of it."

"If they got caught with Lana, it could bring down their club."

"I'm sure they would have found a way out of it, but it would have shined a spotlight on them," Hunt agreed.

"Everyone is safe. That's all that matters. But to be sure, I think you two should head back to Willow Fork, so they're not spooked about you sticking around."

Hunt hugged Lyric. "Thank you."

"I didn't do anything. It was all . . . him." She looked confused about "him."

Hunt wasn't. He appreciated that Viper stuck his

neck out for Cyn. "Take care. If this blows back on your guy or you, let me know."

Lyric's concerned gaze softened. "I think it's all going to be okay."

Hunt exchanged a look with Cyn and the look in her eyes matched his thought. With Rad still on the loose, this wasn't over yet.

# Chapter Thirty

THE CLUB was packed with bikers and babes, the music blaring, pool balls crashing, pinball machines ringing, when Rad walked in and scanned the large open space looking for the woman who had what he wanted back.

Viper came out of nowhere, took him by the scruff of his neck and asked, "What the fuck are you doing here?"

"I came to see—" His head thumped against the wall, cutting off his words.

"You're a wanted man. Every cop in the state is looking for you and you show up here. You can't be that stupid." Viper held him against the wall.

Rad shoved against Viper's hand on his chest, but didn't gain even an inch against the bigger, stronger asshole. "I came for my kid."

"Lobo returned her to some purple-haired chick this morning."

Rad couldn't believe it. "No fucking way. Why the hell would he do that? His sister promised she'd watch Lana for me."

"It looked like you were never coming back, what with your face plastered all over the news, dumbshit.

And we're not an orphanage." Viper grabbed him by the shirt and dragged him toward the door, several of the other biker dudes taking notice. Viper shoved him outside and followed just enough to let the door slam behind him, the thumping sound of classic rock muffled by the metal door. "Your kid's not here. You don't belong here. I suggest you get as far away as possible because Lobo is out for blood since you put us all in jeopardy by ditching your kid here."

Rad took the warning to heart and ran back to the car he'd stolen from a parking lot in Sheridan, when he'd made a run up north to pawn the rest of his stolen goods. He needed the cash to get him and Lana out of the state and far away from Hunt and the Willow Fork officers hunting him down.

But when Rad climbed behind the wheel and peeled out of the parking lot, he knew he should cut his losses and get the hell out of Wyoming; instead, an unraveling happened inside him and all he could think about was what Cyn had taken from him. His girl, his baby. Now he'd never get either of them back.

It was all her fucking fault for meddling.

He had nothing left.

No way did she get to raise his daughter, keep Lana from him and live with Hunt all happy as a family.

Fuck that.

If he was going down, he was taking Cyn and Hunt with him.

# Chapter Thirty-One

CYN STOOD in Hunt's living room looking out the tall windows at the wide expanse of pastureland and woods beyond. She kept her arms wrapped around her waist. Her thoughts and emotions overwhelmed her. She tried to hold it all together, but everything seemed to have piled up inside her and she thought at any moment just one more thing could take her to her knees.

"What did the pediatrician say?" her mother asked behind her.

She'd called as soon as she and Hunt were on the way back to Willow Fork with Lana to let her mom know they'd found her. They arranged to meet at Hunt's house after they had Lana checked out at the ER and met with a social worker about Cyn keeping Lana. Because everyone knew Angela's story, that Rad was still on the loose, she was family and they were staying with a cop, it was a relatively quick process to get approved for temporary custody. On the drive back, she'd ignored Hunt's concerned glances and questions and called the lawyer about legal custody and adoption. She'd meant to call days ago but never got around to it because of all the things happening to her.

Since Cyn didn't answer, Hunt filled her mom in on Lana's checkup. "The doctor said she's in good health, though she's a bit underweight. She recommended a different formula than the one she'd been given lately. Cyn and I stopped at the store on the way home and picked some up, along with diapers and wipes. My brother's fiancée, Shelby, left a box of my niece's baby clothes for Lana on the porch before she went into work. Cyn spoke to a lawyer. They've begun the process for Cyn to get full custody of Lana. Once we have Rad in custody, we can pursue adoption."

"We?" her mom asked.

Cyn wasn't surprised by Hunt's blunt announcement. They hadn't discussed it. Then again, maybe they didn't need to. They'd taken another step closer to each other this morning when he'd shown her the nursery upstairs.

Had that only been this morning?

She had no idea what time it was right now, but it felt like this day would never end.

"If she agrees to it. Cyn and I are building a life together. Right now, things are new. We both know what we want. And it starts with us being there for each other through all of this."

Her mom sighed. "It's been a lot. I can't imagine what you've been through," her mom said to Cyn's back in a rare show of concern. "You found them, Cyn. Angela would be so happy to know you found her little girl and that she's with you now."

Yes. Cyn would raise Lana and do the best she could to be the mother Angela would have been to her. She'd tell Lana all about her wonderful mom.

But it wouldn't be the same.

Would it be enough?

Lana deserved to have her mother in her life.

Rad took that from her. He took Cyn's sister and Terri's daughter. He needed to pay.

"Cyn. Look at me."

She didn't want to look at anyone right now. She wanted to lose herself in the beautiful view and feel something other than the anger and pain writhing inside her.

"Cyn," her mother snapped.

She abruptly turned and glared at her mom. "What?"

"I'm sorry."

Cyn took a step back like she'd been struck with those words her mother had never said to her, even when her mom had made her and Angela's lives really hard.

"I put it all on you to talk to and watch over Angela, to fix this and make it right, to take that bastard down for what he did to Angela. I made it your responsibility to find them, while I sat back and did nothing but wait, hoping somehow that you'd pull off the miracle I wanted. Because you make things happen. You see what you want and you go after it and you get it. And you make it look so damn easy."

Stunned beyond words, it was all she could do to believe her mother was not only saying these things but meant them.

"You want a job that will support you and allow you to help your family, well, you put everything you are into school, working hard, building your own business. Your sister is stubborn and stuck in a bad relationship, you never give up on her. You fight for her. You make her believe there's better out there for her. You show her that you'll never back down, you'll never stop wanting the best for her, that you'll give it to her if she can't do it herself. You've done that for me even when I've gotten so caught up in my wants and needs and ignored the two of you. Lana loses her mama, you're on the phone, making sure she has the best mama a girl could ever want if she can't be with hers." Her mom glanced at Hunt, then back to her. "You want a good man, you have one."

Cyn hit the jackpot with Hunt for sure.

"I don't know how you turned out to be this smart, beautiful, kind woman who is so strong. It didn't come from me. Maybe it came from always taking care of your sister. You were better at that than I was, too. I wish I had more time with Angela and could see what I see now and make up for all I did wrong with her.

"I want you to know that I want things to be different between us. I want you to know I'm here for you, and I want to be a really good grandma to this little angel Angela left us." Her mom's eyes implored her to believe that she'd do better with Lana than she had with her and Angela.

"I want you to know how proud I am of you, Cyn, for everything you've accomplished, for the woman you've become and for standing up for Angela and stepping up to take care of Lana. With you as her mom, she's going to be an amazing woman, too."

Cyn stared at her mom, tears streaking down her cheeks unchecked. Her mom held Lana on her chest, a protective hand on her back, her cheek pressed to Lana's silky blond hair. Her mother had never looked so content or sorrowful. She hoped this newfound sense of family and thinking of others stuck with her mom.

Loss changed people.

It had changed her. It appeared to have changed her mom.

Parents shouldn't outlive their kids.

Lana should still have her mom.

It hurt Cyn's heart to think that Lana would never know Angela and the love her sister had for her child.

Cyn would try to give her all that, but it would never be the same. But Cyn would do her best and hope that Lana never doubted a day in her life that she was loved and cherished and wanted.

Hunt rose, came to her and cupped her face, brushing away her tears with his thumbs. He pressed his forehead to hers and looked into her watery eyes. "I know you're overwhelmed right now. You are everything your mother said and more. So much more, Cyn. You will get through this. One day soon, everything will be back to normal again and it will be you and me and Lana together, happy and safe."

"Angela's dead. She's not coming back." Saying it out loud made it all too real.

"I know, sweetheart. And I'm so sorry she's gone. I'm sorry we didn't get to her in time. I'm sorry you've had to live with not knowing and now you have to live without her. Grieve for what you've lost, but never forget what you still have. Lana. Me. And the life we can make together."

She put her hands over his on her face. "I know. I want it. I'm just . . ." She didn't know how to finish that sentence because it was all too much right now.

"I know, Cyn. Just focus on one thing at a time. I'm here to help. You're not alone in this."

Lana began to fuss and cry.

Cyn sighed. "It's time for her bottle."

Hunt didn't look away. "I'll make it. Sit with your mom. Spend time with the baby. Let the rest go for right now."

She nodded. "I'll try."

He kissed her softly, lingering with his lips pressed to hers, his eyes opened and looking right at her until one kiss turned into two, then three, and she closed her eyes and sank into him and he wrapped her in a hug, held her tight and whispered in her ear. "I've got you. You're safe. I won't let anything happen to you or Lana. I promise."

She loved him for making the promise, even though she didn't expect him to keep it, because Rad had proven to be difficult to catch and a lot deadlier than they'd expected.

The smart move would be to run.

But Rad didn't back down. He retaliated.

Rad wanted Hunt to pay for turning on him. He'd sworn Cyn would be his method of revenge against Hunt. Rad wanted her dead. Pure and simple.

"Cyn, baby, stop thinking whatever you're thinking and be here with me right now."

She shook off her dark thoughts and focused on Hunt. "I'm sorry. I'm here."

He held her gaze for a moment, then released her to get a bottle for Lana.

Cyn sat next to her mom, who was rocking Lana, patting Lana's back and cooing, "It's coming, baby girl," in a soft whisper.

"You're good with her," Cyn said.

"I've had some practice." Her mom met her gaze. "I miss Angela, too. So much." Tears welled in her already bloodshot eyes. "I wish I could make up for the past."

Cyn wrapped her mom and Lana in a hug. "Shh. It's okay. I know you did the best you could. I appreciate what you said about being proud of me. I needed to hear it, even though I know I've done well for myself. It means something to me that you see it, too. And I'm sorry I haven't been myself today."

"It's okay. You had a long day. You're going to have a lot of long nights with this one." Her mom patted Lana again.

Cyn leaned back and looked at her fussing niece. "I'm okay with sleepless nights, so long as I get to spend them with her."

"You and Angela were the best thing to ever happen to *me*. She'll miss Angela, but it will be you she knows as her mother. You will be the best thing that ever happened to *her*. You'll see."

"Oh, Mom," Cyn sighed, holding back tears.

Hunt held the bottle out to her mom.

"Um, I think this little one needs a new diaper." Her mom, tears in her eyes, patted Lana's little butt.

"I'm on it." Hunt plucked Lana from her mother's arms. "Back in a minute."

They watched Hunt take Lana upstairs to change her in her nursery.

"He's a good man, Cyn. They don't come better than that. I know. I never had one like him."

Cyn smiled at her mom. "He's more than I ever thought possible. I love him. He loves me back. It's new and it's wonderful and I already know it's forever. With all that's going on, all that's happened, he's the only thing I'm sure about right now."

"I don't think I ever had that with someone. I mean, there was love, sure, but not like I see when he looks at you and you look at him. That's rare, baby girl. That's something you hold on to and fight for to the end. That kiss he laid on you . . . I don't think a man has ever kissed me with that kind of reverence and love." Her mom bumped shoulders with her. "And he changes dirty diapers. That's gold, baby girl. Hold on to him."

"Oh, I'm not letting him go." She stared up at Hunt holding Lana protectively against his chest and kissing her on the head before he descended the stairs, his gaze immediately finding hers. The grin and satisfaction in his eyes told her how much he loved taking care of Lana and having them both here with him. "I'm going to keep you, Wilde man."

The grin turned into a broad smile that turned her gloomy heart bright with joy. "Good, because I'm not letting you go without a fight."

"There's too much love for you two to have anything to fight about," her mom said, taking Lana from Hunt, cradling her in her arms and putting the bottle into Lana's greedy mouth.

Cyn watched her mom feed the baby for a moment and marveled at the peace and love and sheer happiness that came over her mother. She felt it, too, when she looked at the baby.

Lana would be the light that kept Angela's memory alive for them.

Her mom looked over at her. "I made arrangements

this morning for Angela. She'll be cremated. I thought that maybe when this little one is older and understands that her mama is gone, we could scatter Angela's ashes at an appropriate place and time. What do you think?"

She took Hunt's hand as he sat beside her on the couch and answered her mom. "You and I can do something special when we get her ashes. Then we'll do something with Lana later."

A sense of peace washed over Cyn as she sat with Hunt, her mom and Lana as a beam of sunlight radiated across the room from the huge back windows.

She felt a soft brush on her shoulder, but quickly realized it wasn't Hunt, and that it had been something else.

Angela's spirit was watching over them now.

She felt it in her heart and sent up a silent message to her beloved sister. *Rest in peace, Ange. Lana is safe. I will love and care for her always.*

She pledged, *I will make Rad pay for what he did to you and took from Lana.*

# Chapter Thirty-Two

Hᴜɴᴛ ᴡᴀʟᴋᴇᴅ into Cyn's shop and smiled at the beautiful woman standing across the room behind her client in the chair, fluffing the woman's hair as she blew it dry. Lana lay sweetly against Cyn's chest in the baby carrier, her little fist on Cyn's breast, her face soft and peaceful.

Cyn had been quiet the last two days at home. She stayed at his place with his brothers watching over her while he went to work and she got Lana on a schedule. The little one seemed restless and fussy the first night. They chalked it up to her getting used to the new formula and being in a new place. It had to be hard on the baby to miss her mom and end up with different people every few days.

But for now Lana was with him and Cyn. He didn't know what Cyn thought about them practically living together and him making it clear that he wanted to be a part of her plans to raise and adopt Lana.

He'd always wanted a family. Now with Cyn in his life, he wanted it even more.

"There's my Wilde man," Cyn said, smiling at her customer in the mirror.

"There's my girls," Hunt replied, kissing Lana on the head, then stealing a quick kiss from Cyn. He wanted more, but she was working and he didn't want to delay her. He brushed his hand over her neck. "You got your stitches out."

Cyn smiled. "Chase took me to the doctor's office, like you asked him to do. The scar on my leg is still really tight and itchy, but they say the skin will stretch and the scar will fade over time.

"Want me to take her?"

Cyn turned off the hair dryer and set it in the holder at her station. "Thanks."

Hunt gently plucked Lana out of the carrier and laid her against his chest, then took the seat at the empty station next to where Cyn finished styling her customer's hair.

"If you tell me he changes diapers, too, I'm really going to hate you," the woman said, eyeing Cyn in the mirror.

"He does. And he cooks. He knows a couple of really sweet lullabies. Every time I see him with her"—Cyn shook her head—"I just want to jump him."

"If you don't, I will," the woman said, giving Hunt a flirtatious look.

He grinned at the woman who could be his mother. "Sorry. I'm hers."

The woman sighed.

Cyn grinned at him, and this time it was real, not tinged with the sadness clinging to her. "You might be too good to be true, Wilde."

"Why? Because I love you and this one and want to take care of both of you?"

Cyn turned to him and held his gaze. "Because you live up to the fantasy in every way."

"So do you, sweetheart. And though things have been really hard lately, I'm looking forward to some normal family time."

This time she sighed. "How have you just accepted all this so easily and gone with it?"

"I've nearly lost you twice. I'm happy and grateful you're still here with me, that we have this chance to be together and create something I've wanted for a while now." He kissed Lana on the head again. "If something had happened to Chase, and Shelby and Eliza needed someone, I'd have stepped up and been the uncle and dad she needed. Lana is yours now, which means she's mine. There's nothing else to do but give her a home where she'll be safe and loved. I know you have your place and a room set up for her, and if you want to be there when it's safe and we slow things down a bit, I'm fine with that if it's what you want, but I hope, eventually, we'll turn our two lives into a life we make together."

He and Cyn held each other's gazes.

"Marry him," her customer implored. "Men like him don't come around often. You've got to hold on to them when they do."

Cyn's vibrant smile warmed his heart. "I'm the luckiest woman in the world."

"I've got you beat, sweetheart," he assured her, because with her by his side, he knew he'd have a very happy future.

Cyn grinned. "I guess Shelby is going to have to find a new renter soon."

"It'll be easier for you to commute between your two shops, since my place is about halfway between here and your shop in Blackrock Falls."

"My sister lives out there." The woman beamed. "I'll be sure to tell her to go to your salon."

Cyn sprayed the woman's hair, handed her a mirror and turned the chair so she could see the back of her head in the mirrors. "What do you think?"

"Perfect. Now to knock my husband's socks off."

Cyn pulled the drape off the woman and she stood in a pretty dark blue dress. "Enjoy your anniversary dinner."

Hunt made a show of checking the woman out. "You definitely kill in that dress."

The woman blushed and waved her hand at him. "Oh, you. Thank you."

"It's the truth," Hunt assured her, then watched as Cyn processed her payment and showed her out the door with a smile.

She locked up and turned off the lights at the front of the store, then walked back to him, raking her fingers through his hair and leaning in for a soft kiss. "Are you done working for the day? Or are you on break between shifts?"

He hated to disappoint her. "Unfortunately, I'm on break for the next two hours. I thought I'd catch up with you here and we could have dinner together."

"I really should go through the paperwork that accumulated over the last few days and get a jump on running payroll. But . . . dinner with you sounds great. Mind if we order something and eat it at my place, though? I really need to stop by there to pick up some things and clean out my refrigerator. I don't even want to think about what I've left in there that's now rotten."

"It's probably not that bad. What do you feel like eating? I can go pick it up and meet you at your place." He didn't really want to leave her alone, but they both needed to eat and it sounded like she didn't have anything at her place they could make quickly before he had to go back to work for yet another double shift.

"Let's go together. We'll order pizza and have it delivered."

"Sounds good to me. You have everything you need for this little one?"

"I brought more than enough formula." Cyn checked her watch. "She needs to eat in about twenty minutes. So we can get home, order the pizza, and I can have her fed so you and I can spend a little time together."

"Are you going to stay at your place, or take her back to ours?"

She tilted her head. "You really do think of the house on the ranch as ours?"

"It finally feels complete when you're there."

She shifted her weight and stared at him. "Are we crazy for leaping like this?"

"Will we regret the missed opportunities if we hold off doing what I think we both want to do?"

"I do want to be with you, Hunt. All the time. When you're not with me, I'm thinking about you and anticipating when I'll get to see you again. But with all the good we've shared, we've had a lot happen in a short amount of time. We're still in the thick of things until

Rad is found. The last thing I want is for something to happen to you because of me."

"None of what's happened is because of you. I don't know what happened to the friend I used to know. I don't recognize the abusive, vengeful man he's become. I never would have thought he'd hurt a woman, let alone kill her. I never thought he'd dump his child with someone who was no more than an acquaintance. I never thought he'd break into people's homes and hurt them, let alone murder someone. I'd like to believe that somewhere inside him is the guy I used to know and that he'll turn himself in for the sake of his daughter and his parents, who are frantic and afraid he'll end up dead."

"You talked to them today?"

"His father called asking if there was any new information. He and his wife wanted to know if Lana was okay."

"Did you tell them I filed for custody?"

"Yes. They seemed fine with that and asked if you would be willing to let them see Lana."

She scoffed. "I don't blame them for what Rad did."

"I didn't think you would, but they fear that you'll punish them by not letting them see the baby because of Rad."

"I just want him caught. I want him locked up before he hurts anyone else."

He saw deep fear in her eyes. "What is it, Cyn?"

"I'm afraid he'll take or hurt Lana, especially because he knows there's no way out of this. What if he decides to end it and take her with him?"

"We won't let that happen. I've got officers, along with my brothers, watching you."

"I saw the officers drive by and hang out outside many times today."

"Everyone on the force is looking for Rad and more than happy to protect you and the baby."

"Which is the only reason you let me come into work today."

"I know this place is important to you and so is your independence. It's unlikely Rad would show up on such a busy street and risk being seen. He's not that stupid. But I'm not taking any chances with your safety."

"I appreciate it. I've been hyperaware of my surroundings all day. The other hairdressers who work for me are more than happy to get some extra shifts to cover for me. I just . . . needed something normal today."

"I get that. And I hope we find him soon so that you can get back to living your life without looking over your shoulder. I'm sorry Rad is coming after you because of me."

She cocked up an eyebrow. "Come on, Wilde, you know I gave him hell a thousand times while he was with my sister. I convinced her to leave him. That is why he's coming after me. Taunting you is just a bonus for him."

"Yeah, well, I'm not letting him get close enough to hurt you ever again."

"How long can he run? The money he got from stealing from those houses isn't going to last him long. Every law enforcement officer in the state is looking for him. His face has been on the news for several days. Someone is bound to recognize him and call the cops."

Unless he'd left the state. Hunt didn't understand why he didn't after he killed Angela. He'd come up with an almost believable story about Angela's disappearance. If he'd left, they'd have never found Angela's body.

"Did his parents say if they'd heard from him again?"

"They haven't. His phone battery either died or he's turned it off, knowing we can track him with it. We've got a cop watching his grandfather's place, though it's unlikely he'll go back there. And while his parents want their son back, they know they need to turn him in if he shows up there or they'll be in a lot of trouble. I think they've resigned themselves to that because they want to have a relationship with Lana and that won't happen if they don't do the right thing."

"It's sometimes hard to do the right thing when you want to protect someone you love. I wanted to kill Rad for hurting my sister. I wanted to forcibly remove her from him. I regret not doing either of those things. And at the same time I know that wasn't the answer. It wouldn't have solved the problem." She dropped her gaze to Lana. "And though I wish my sister had just left him like we planned, and I'm incredibly sad and angry that she's gone. I'm also ashamed to say that I'm glad he won't be in Lana's life. He'll never hurt her the way he hurt my sister. Lana won't grow up thinking she's not good enough, the way he made my sister feel. I want him to pay, but deep down I know the best revenge is that he won't be around to see his daughter grow up. He'll have no influence or significance in her life. He'll be the monster she's afraid of and hates for taking her mother. I hate that for her, but it's no less than he deserves."

"And that's why he's such a threat, Cyn. He can't stand the thought that he's screwed this up so badly and we will be the ones to raise Lana. The one good thing he did in his life is lost to him now. He wants us to hurt the way he hurts."

"I have a very bad feeling this isn't going to end well."

Hunt agreed, because he didn't see Rad turning himself in or going out without a fight.

# Chapter Thirty-Three

HUNT WALKED in behind Cyn to the house she rented from Shelby and flipped on the lights. Cyn put the baby seat on the couch, unbuckled Lana and picked her up just as Lana started to fuss for her next meal.

The door had barely closed behind him when a truck engine revved outside, tires skidded to a stop out front and a door slammed. Hunt turned to the living room window to check the street, caught sight of Rad storming around the front of his truck toward the house with a shotgun in his hands and turned back to Cyn. "Get down!"

The window exploded with the deafening sound of the shotgun blast. Glass and pellets pelted him in the back and arms as he ran toward Cyn and covered her with his body. Another blast rang out, hitting the side of the house, sending pellets and bits of drywall into him again.

He wrapped his arms around Cyn and the crying baby, held them down, then grabbed his radio on his shoulder and called for backup. "Shots fired!" He rattled off the address and pushed Cyn down to the floor with the baby protectively secure beneath her body. He hated to leave her, but stood, pulled his gun and turned to the door just as it burst open. Adrenaline pumping, he raised his gun just as Rad shot him with a nine-millimeter right in the chest, the impact making him stumble back.

Hunt got off a shot at the same time, but it went wide. Hunt hit the floor just as Cyn tucked the baby under the wood coffee table, grabbed the gun from his hand, spun around and without an ounce of hesitation shot Rad three times.

Hunt tried to get up, but the searing pain in his chest and a wave of dizziness kept him on his back as he tried to catch his breath. He managed to put a protective hand over Lana and glance down his body. Cyn kicked the gun away from Rad's hand as Rad coughed and tried to suck in air as blood spurted out his mouth and ran down his chin.

Cyn stood over Rad, the gun in her hand trained on Rad's head. "It didn't have to be this way!" she screamed at him.

Bloody bubbles rose from Rad's lips as he mumbled, "I want my baby."

Hunt managed to reach for his radio again. "Officer down. Assailant down. Send an ambulance."

Cyn's worried eyes found his. "You okay?"

"Vest," he managed to say on a ragged exhale. "Hard to breathe. Ribs."

"Look what you did," she said to Rad. "All this hurt and pain and for what?"

"Lana." Rad reached his hand out toward where Hunt lay next to the wailing baby.

Cyn sank into a crouch and stared down at Rad's pale face, the gun still in her hand and trained on him. "She's not yours anymore. You treated her the way you treated my sister, like she wasn't important enough for you to hold on to and love more than you loved yourself, you selfish, arrogant, stupid asshole." She pointed at him with the gun. "You could have been kind. You could have chosen to be happy with my sister, who for whatever reason found it in her heart to love you. She tried so hard to please you and you killed her because you couldn't control your temper and wanted to possess her instead of love her. She wasn't yours to own. She wasn't yours to punish for all the bad in your life that you took out on her." Cyn shook her head. "She was yours to love and you didn't."

"I did . . . love . . . her."

Cyn expelled a frustrated sigh. "You don't know what love is. And you'll never know what it is to be a father. The only thing you get that's worth anything right now is to know that Hunt and I will love Lana the way you couldn't and didn't. We will all be happy while you're burning in hell for what you've done."

The sirens outside grew louder.

Rad coughed up more blood. "I . . . want . . . to . . . s-see . . . her," he pleaded.

Cyn rose and came toward Hunt, kneeling beside him and putting her hand over his on his chest. "Don't you die on me."

He squeezed her hand. "Not happening. I'm fine." He'd finally gotten his breath back and his chest didn't feel quite as ferociously painful as it had moments ago, though he didn't attempt to sit up.

Cyn touched her forehead to his and closed her eyes. "Thank you for saving me again."

"I need you. I love you so much."

"I love you, too."

"Cyn." Rad's voice grew weaker. "Please."

She kissed Hunt softly, set the gun next to him, picked up Lana and turned toward Rad, who stared at his daughter and expelled his last breath.

# Chapter Thirty-Four

Cʏɴ ᴍᴀɴᴀɢᴇᴅ to make Lana a bottle even with her hands shaking and her heart racing while a female officer held Lana and questioned Cyn.

After telling what happened for what seemed like the thousandth time, she couldn't help but ask, "What was the point?"

The officer handed Lana to Cyn. "Of what?"

"Of all of it. Of any of it." Cyn put the nipple in Lana's mouth. "Why kill my sister? Why come after me? Why go after Hunt? All it got him was dead."

The officer leaned forward. "In my experience, some people get things into their heads and it becomes a gnawing need despite all the reason in the world that tells them what they're thinking is wrong. Some people just can't let things go. Even when they see doom coming, they race headlong toward it because they need to satisfy that thing inside them."

"Did he really think he could take Lana and that they'd have a good life after all this? He died for nothing."

"He died because he couldn't let it go and he didn't accept the consequences of his actions. He had a choice."

Cyn saw him in her mind's eye, dead on the floor. "He didn't give me one. He would have killed Hunt, and then me. I saw it in his eyes. Nothing but rage that things hadn't gone his way."

Lana finished the bottle.

Cyn put her up on her shoulder and gently patted her back. "I didn't want him to touch this little girl ever again."

Shelby put her hand on Cyn's shoulder. "Are you okay?"

Numb, she looked up at Shelby, wondering where she came from and who called her. Cyn frowned. "I'm so sorry about your house . . . What are you doing here?"

Shelby squeezed Cyn's shoulder. "The police called us right away. I came here as soon as they said it was safe, and I'm just so relieved that you're all okay."

Cyn looked past Shelby to check on Hunt again. "Where'd he go? Is Hunt okay?" She tried to stand, but Shelby held her down. "I need to see him."

Shelby patted her shoulder. "Chase is with him in the ambulance. They're taking him to the hospital. I'll drive you there as soon as you're allowed to go."

Cyn nodded, trying to make her mind work in some kind of order. "Okay. Let's go." She tried to stand, but Shelby pushed on her shoulder to hold her still again.

The officer stood instead. "I think I have everything I need right now. You'll need to come down to the station in the next day or two for some follow-up questions and to sign your statement." The officer looked into the living room where officers were taking pictures and cataloguing evidence. "But you won't be able to stay here for a while . . ."

"She'll be with us until Hunt is out of the hospital," Shelby assured the officer.

"How bad was he hurt?" Cyn asked.

"I'm not sure," Shelby admitted. "But he's going to be fine."

Cyn needed the assurance, even if Shelby didn't look one hundred percent positive, and Cyn wouldn't believe it until she saw Hunt for herself.

Shelby held out her hands. "Why don't you give me the baby? I'll put her back in her carrier and I'll help you clean and bandage those cuts on your arms."

"I'm fine," Cyn protested, but she handed Lana over to Shelby just the same, noting the spots and slashes of blood on her arms for the first time. She was so numb she didn't even feel them.

Cyn scanned Lana's body, looking for any sign she'd been hit by flying glass, too.

"She's perfect," Shelby assured her.

"We need to call his parents."

"Hunt's dad already knows he's been shot and that he's okay. He's at my place with Eliza."

Cyn shook her head. "No. Rad's parents."

The officer gave her a half frown. "Because of Hunt's relationship with the assailant and his family, he asked to be the one to make the call."

Cyn wrapped her arms around her middle. "I can't imagine how difficult that will be for him. Rad used to be his best friend. They have so much history together. It's sad that it ended this way."

The officer regarded that with a regretful shake of her head. "You're right, Cyn. It didn't have to be this way. Rad made it happen this way. He gave you and Hunt no other way to end this."

Shelby wrapped her free arm around Cyn's shoulders. "Come. Let's pack some clothes and anything else you'll need and we'll go see Hunt at the hospital. You need to get out of here."

Cyn followed Shelby back to the bedroom, pulled her suitcase out of her closet and started dumping everything from her dresser inside it.

Shelby laid Lana on the bed and smiled down at her but addressed Cyn. "What are you doing?"

"I'm sorry, but I don't think I can come back here again."

Shelby came to her side and hugged her. "Okay. That's totally understandable."

Cyn held tight to Shelby. "I need to be with Hunt. I belong with him. I can't be here anymore."

"Okay, Cyn. Hunt will be thrilled to have you with him. He loves you. And I know it feels overwhelming right now, and you're in shock, but you will get through this."

Cyn's hands shook at Shelby's back. "I know. I have to be strong for Lana. She needs me now. Everything's been happening so fast and all at once and I hoped we'd have time to figure it out so that we didn't go too fast and mess anything up, but now . . ." She looked at Shelby. "I can't be here. I have to be with him. I almost lost him. He could have died. What if we never got to be together the way we talked about?"

"You will. We're going to pack what we can take right now. Hunt and his brothers can come back and get the rest later. You'll be with Hunt and Lana and all of you will be happy together."

"Yes. That's all I want. And now Rad's gone. He can't ruin it, the way he ruined things with my sister." She pressed her hand to her belly. "He killed my sister."

Shelby cupped her face and brushed her thumbs over Cyn's wet cheeks. "Cyn. Breathe."

Cyn tried, but it felt like everything was crashing down around her.

"I said, breathe," Shelby snapped.

Cyn sucked in one long breath and then another.

"There you go. Now a couple more."

Cyn felt calmer.

"Okay. Now sit with Lana. I'll finish the packing. We will do one thing at a time. You'll feel better, more centered, when I get you to Hunt. You'll see that he's okay. And the two of you will hold on to each other and get through this together." Shelby wrapped Cyn in a hug again. "I am here for you whenever you need me."

Cyn hugged her back, feeling a little better. "Thank you."

"What are best friends for? And I have a feeling, someday soon, we'll be sisters by marriage."

Cyn found a wobbly grin for that, but somehow Shelby sensed her words made Cyn think about Angela.

"Oh, Cyn, I'm sorry. That was incredibly insensitive of me. I wasn't thinking."

Cyn shook her head. "I miss Angela. I will remember her every day, especially when I look at Lana. I'm not going to dwell on what I've lost, but appreciate what I have. You. My best friend, who is definitely like a sister to me. And Hunt. The man who makes my future look brighter than the brightest star. This will all pass. But Hunt and I . . . We're forever."

Cyn picked up Lana and held her to her heart. "We are so lucky, baby girl. You will grow up and only know Hunt's love and devotion to you and me. That's a gift, baby. And we will love him right back, and we'll be a family with Pancake Tuesdays and merry Christmases and happy birthdays and a million happy memories. We will always be together."

# Chapter Thirty-Five

~~~~

HUNT SAT in the back of the ambulance with the paramedic pulling out glass from his arm and cleaning the wounds. His brother Chase watching him closely. "What is it?"

Chase sighed. "You were shot."

"In the vest," he reminded his brother. "I'm fine." He pulled down his T-shirt to show Chase the bruise blooming across his pec and up toward his shoulder. He had no idea what his back looked like after being hit by the shotgun blast. It didn't feel that bad. Probably because Rad had fired from too far away to do a lot of damage. Not like the nine-millimeter shot. "It hurts to breathe. I probably have a couple cracked ribs. Otherwise I got lucky."

"Yeah, because if Cyn hadn't taken your gun and shot that bastard he'd have finished you off."

All Hunt could see out the open ambulance doors was the street beyond. He wanted to see her. "Where is she?"

"They're questioning her."

"She defended herself and me and Lana."

Chase put his hand on Hunt's leg. "I know that and

so does everyone else. You know the procedure. That's all this is, everyone on your team crossing all the *t*'s and dotting the *i*'s." Chase pulled the ambulance doors shut as the driver got behind the wheel up front. "Shelby will bring her to the hospital as soon as Cyn's allowed to leave."

"I can wait here for her. I'm fine." He didn't want to leave her alone.

"You need an X-ray and to have the pellets removed from the back of your shoulders and arms," the para-medic pointed out. "Not to mention all the glass in your arms and legs."

Everything stung at the moment. "Fine. Let's go. The sooner I get checked out, the sooner I can go home with Cyn and the baby." His mind started sharpening. "The baby. Is she okay?"

"Yes," the paramedic assured him as the ambulance pulled out and headed toward the hospital. "I checked her over. No cuts or bruises or any marks on her. She was in good health and ready to eat. Cyn was feeding her when we left the house."

Hunt settled into the gurney. "Okay. That's good." His thoughts turned to Cyn and what she'd been through. "She's got to be in shock after what happened."

Chase squeezed his leg. "Shelby's with them, so Cyn's not alone. You'll see her soon. Focus on taking care of you, so that you can be with her."

Hunt nodded and grabbed his uniform shirt from between his legs. He'd tossed it there, along with his bulletproof vest, so the paramedic could assess his chest wound. His phone fell out of the crumpled material. He pulled up his contact list and tapped on the Harmons' number.

"Are you sure you want to make that call right now?" Chase studied him.

"They need to know what happened to their son."

"I get that, but you're not exactly thinking clearly right now."

"I need to be the one to tell them."

Chase frowned and shook his head. "You take on too much responsibility sometimes."

"I just want to finish this so Cyn and I can be together without any loose ends." Hunt tapped the phone icon and the call went through.

"Hunt," Mr. Harmon said by way of hello. "Did you find him? Is he in custody?"

"Mr. Harmon, I'm afraid I have very bad news . . . the worst news . . . I'm sorry to inform you that Rad was shot and killed about half an hour ago at Cyn's home." Hunt felt his heart drop in his aching chest. No matter what Rad had done and turned into, it still sucked to lose a friend he'd known practically his whole life. He hated breaking Mr. and Mrs. Harmon's hearts.

"What? No. Why would he go there? That's not possible."

"Cyn and I returned to her house to have dinner after she got off work. We had Lana with us. We entered the house and had only just taken Lana out of her car seat carrier when Rad arrived and started shooting."

"What? He could have killed the baby."

"I don't think he considered that, though it's a blessing that Cyn and the baby weren't hit. I was by the shotgun pellets and I took a nine-millimeter round to the chest."

Mr. Harmon gasped. "Are you going to be okay?"

"Yes." Hunt tried to breathe through the pain. "I wish it didn't end this way. I wish I didn't have to make this call to you. Once the scene has been processed, they'll transfer his body to the morgue. You'll receive a phone call to make arrangements for him." Hunt rubbed at the back of his neck, wincing when his fingertips ran across a bloody cut. "I'm sorry for your loss, Mr. Harmon. My condolences to your wife as well. I hope, after some time has passed, that we can put this behind us and be the family that Lana needs us to be for her."

"I . . . I'm not sure how my wife and I feel about Lana staying with the person who killed our son."

Hunt tried to contain his rage. "I get that you're upset, but please try not to make things more difficult. Lana needs all the family she has left. Rad came armed and ready to kill me and Cyn and take the baby." To push his point home, he added, "I've just arrived at the hospital by ambulance. Cyn and Lana will join me here soon. Your son hurt a lot of people, Mr. Harmon. I'm sure the trauma Rad inflicted on Cyn will stay with her for a long time to come. Let it end here and now. For Lana's sake." Hunt hung up, hoping that the Harmons found a way to grieve their son and be the grandparents Lana needed without playing a game of tug-of-war over the baby. He didn't want to see things turn ugly between Cyn and the Harmons. He wanted them all to find a way to come together for Lana.

He hoped that once everyone settled down, they'd all do what was right for Lana. As she grew up, she'd learn the truth about her parents. If she had a steady childhood, she'd hopefully be better prepared to deal with the tragedy of what happened.

She deserved some peace and a loving home after all she'd been through and lost.

He wanted to give that to her and Cyn.

Hunt hissed in a breath when the paramedic pulled out another big chunk of glass.

Chase patted his leg again. "You handled that well. I'm sure they're both in shock. They'll come around to understanding it's about Lana now."

"I hope so. Because Cyn's been through a lot and I don't want her to have to keep fighting. After all she's been through, I really can't believe she's still sane at this point."

"She's strong and tough and she has you. During all the terrible days and weeks, she fell in love and has been loved by you. In all the bad, she had all those moments of happiness you two shared. Now that this is over, she's got a lot more of that to look forward to. If you're not a dumbass and you hold on to her."

"I'm never letting her go. In fact, I want to make it permanent."

Chase gave him a firm nod. "No time like the present."

Hunt gaped at his brother.

Chase shrugged. "When you've been through hell and survived it, heaven shouldn't have to wait. Believe me, I understand all too well nothing is guaranteed and it can all vanish in the blink of an eye." Chase had nearly died several times serving in the military overseas, then nearly lost his life to a prescription drug addiction. He'd finally overcome his demons and healed and was soon to marry the love of his life. He and Shelby may have known each other for years, but their real love affair and engagement happened quickly, because once they knew they never wanted to be apart, they made sure they never would be again.

Hunt felt that keenly right now, sitting in the back of an ambulance after being shot.

Chase nodded like he knew all of Hunt's thoughts. "Life is short, man. Don't waste time you could be spending with her."

"Call Shelby. Find out when they'll be here." Hunt lost track of Chase as the paramedics pulled him out of the ambulance and rushed him into the ER.

All he wanted was to see Cyn and Lana and make sure they were never separated again.

# Chapter Thirty-Six

CYN DASHED past a nurse and ran into the cubicle where Hunt was being treated. She threw her arms around him, hugging him fiercely, tears stinging her eyes. "Are you okay?"

Hunt held her close. "Thanks to you, sweetheart, I'm alive."

"I'll give you both a few minutes," the nurse said. "And I'll bring back what you asked for, Officer Wilde."

"Thank you," Hunt said to the retreating nurse, then rubbed his big hands up and down Cyn's back. His warm embrace assured her that they were both alive and well and right where they belonged. With each other. "I didn't want to leave you, but they made me come here to get checked out."

She leaned back and looked him in the eye. "What did the doctor say?" She ran her gaze over his chest, but couldn't see anything beyond the hospital gown he wore. Knicks and scratches marred both his arms.

"I'm fine." He pulled down the gown to show her the bright red and purple bruises covering the left upper part of his chest, spreading up toward his shoulder, the worst of the bruising about two inches above his nipple where there was an open wound.

"Oh my God, Hunt. Did the bullet go through the vest?"

"No. That's where the vest dented and the impact wounded me. The energy from the impact caused the rest of the damage. It's not as bad as it looks. Yeah, it hurts like hell. And I have two cracked ribs, but they'll heal with no lasting damage." Hunt held up his right arm. "The rest is all shotgun pellets and glass." Most of the wounds looked like small red holes that would scab and heal quickly. "There are a bunch on the back of my shoulders where the vest didn't cover me, too, but they're no big deal."

He took her hand and held up her arm, examining the few scratches she had on her. "You were barely touched by all that, thank God. The paramedic said Lana wasn't hit at all."

"No. She's fine. Out in the waiting room with your brother and Shelby." She wanted to throw herself back into his arms but stopped herself before she hurt his chest. "You're sure you're okay?"

"Yes. They're releasing me in a few minutes. We can go home."

"Yeah, um, Shelby's place is a crime scene now." She hated that her best friend's home had been damaged and that any of this mess touched Shelby in any way.

"We'll go to our place."

She loved that he always let her know, and made her feel, that the house at the ranch was their place.

Hunt squeezed her hand. "I'm sure I've got a frozen

pizza or two we can put in the oven. You must be starving."

"I have no idea. I feel numb, like none of this can be happening. It can't be real. I'll wake up any minute. Hopefully in bed with you."

"You will tomorrow morning for sure. But I'm sorry to say, this has all been way too real, sweetheart. How many times have I thought I could have lost you?" He kissed her palm. "I'm so glad it's over now."

The nurse walked in, followed by a man in a white coat. "As you requested, Officer Wilde." To Cyn she said, "This is Dr. Sutton."

Cyn looked to Hunt. "I thought you said you were okay. Why another doctor?"

"I'm not here for him," Dr. Sutton said. "Officer Wilde thought it might be a good idea if you and I talked about what happened tonight."

She eyed Hunt. "What? Why?"

Hunt pulled her a little closer. "Because my brother Chase has shown me the value in taking care of your mental health. Yes, Cyn, you made it out of there alive, but you didn't get out unscathed. You shot someone, Cyn. You did it to save us. It was necessary because of the dire circumstances. But that doesn't make it any easier to reconcile. It is not an insignificant thing. I know that. I've had to discharge my weapon a couple of times, but thankfully I've never killed anyone. I've seen Chase struggle with what he had to do serving our country. He was trained and still couldn't handle it. You've never been in the position to have to defend yourself like that. I hope you never have to again. But I don't want you to hold this inside and try to deal with it alone. I'm here for you. You can talk to me about anything. You can say anything to me. But I really think you need to talk to a professional who can help you cope with all the trauma you've suffered over the last several weeks."

"I'm fine," she assured him.

"Are you?" He held up their joined hands and showed her how she'd held on so tight her nails had bit into his skin and made him bleed.

She immediately tried to release him, but he held tight. "I'm sorry. I didn't mean to do that to you."

"You can hold on to me as tight as you need to, sweetheart. I can take it. What I can't take is seeing the sorrow and fear and desolation in your eyes. Please, do this for me."

"Of course I will. I'd do anything for you."

"Then make sure you're doing it for you, too, Cyn. Lana and I need you to be well."

She nodded several times. "Okay. I will be. I love you."

"I love you, too. Go with Dr. Sutton. Take as long as you need. I'll change into the clothes Chase grabbed for me out of my car before we came to the hospital and meet you in the waiting room. Then we'll go home."

She reluctantly let him go and followed the doctor out of the ER.

"We'll go upstairs to my office where it's quiet and we can talk." Dr. Sutton held the elevator door for her.

"I'm really okay," she assured him, wondering if she was trying to convince herself.

Dr. Sutton didn't comment, just held the door open for her again when they reached the third floor. She walked with him down the corridor to a set of double doors with his name on it. Since it was late, there was no one in the reception area. They walked through another door into his office with a large window that looked out over a greenbelt behind the hospital. The trees were gently swaying in the breeze. For a moment she got lost in the simple and pretty scene.

"Can I get you something to drink? Coffee? Water?"

She shook her head. "I'm fine, thank you."

"You'll probably find yourself saying that a lot over the next few days and even weeks before you actually do feel that way again." Dr. Sutton waved for her to take a seat on the small sofa. He took a seat across from her in a comfortable-looking club chair.

"A lot happened before tonight," she admitted.

"You lost your sister. She was murdered." The bluntness made her flinch. "Is it hard for you to hear that said out loud?"

"It shouldn't be. I know that's what happened. I knew the second I didn't find her at Rad's place. I never believed Rad's story that she left him. I knew for a long time if I didn't get her out of there, he'd kill her. I felt the inevitability of it in my bones and down to my soul. That's why I tried so hard to get her to leave him."

Dr. Sutton's head tilted. "Do you believe it's your fault?"

"No. Yes. No. Rad killed her," the angry words burst out of her. "I know that. I just feel like if I'd tried harder, or forced her to leave, none of this would have happened."

"Do you think Rad would have just let her go and that would be the end?"

"No. But maybe it wouldn't have come to this."

"It's difficult to watch someone you love get hurt by the choices they make. It's not easy to see the train wreck coming and not be able to stop it ahead of time."

"I understand that it was her choice to stay. But she decided to leave. I was supposed to pick her up the next day. We were going to live together. She would work for me. We'd raise her daughter, Lana, together. We'd be happy. He didn't just take her from me, he took that joy we could have shared. He took Lana's mother from her. He took the future Lana would have had with her mom and me. He erased any possibility that he could redeem himself and be the father Lana deserved. And for what? Why?" She really wanted an answer that made sense.

"There is no answer that justifies what he did or will give you an adequate explanation for why it happened."

She hated that, because she wanted it to make sense.

Dr. Sutton continued. "It's a tragedy that has a ripple effect on everyone who loved and cared about your sister. For those closest to your sister, like you and Lana, those ripples will feel like a tsunami crashing into your life, altering it irrevocably. You're already feeling it and seeing its effects. If not for what Rad did to your sister, what else might not have happened?"

"So many things."

"Hunt told me a bit about what you've been through and had to face recently."

The memories flooded her mind. Drowning. Staring at that poor hiker's dead body, seeing her sister, but knowing it wasn't her, but it was her sister's fate, too. The relief and anguish that she hadn't found Angela washing over her again even now. Rad shooting at her.

The flames growing and the smoke choking her as she faced certain death. Looking down the barrel of a gun at a man who lived on the edge and held little regard for anyone outside those he cared about. Rad shooting Hunt. The fear of thinking she might have lost him raced through her again. She hadn't paid attention that he wore a bulletproof vest under his uniform.

"I really thought he was mortally wounded," she confessed. "I didn't think. I just grabbed his gun and I shot Rad because I hated him for killing my sister and taking Hunt from me. I wasn't going to let him take Lana, too."

"That is a very real reaction to what you thought happened. Rad was a threat to you and Lana. You didn't know what he'd do next."

"I do. He would have killed me and taken her. He didn't deserve her. I would have given my life to keep him from taking her."

"How do you feel about shooting him?"

She didn't even think, just blurted out, "He deserved it. But it makes me sad."

Dr. Sutton tilted his head and studied her. "Why?"

"Because it didn't have to be that way. Because like my sister, he made all the wrong choices. In the end, she finally made the right choice to leave for Lana's sake. I wish Rad had done the same and turned himself in. That I would have respected. Maybe I'd have even forgiven him one day for what he did. Instead, he forced me to do something I never wanted to do. But I did it for Lana. For Hunt."

"Do you feel justified in shooting him?"

She didn't know if that matched her feelings or not. But she did know one thing. "If not for his actions, I wouldn't have had to do it. He came after us. He gave me no choice."

"Have you had, or are you having, any thoughts about harming yourself after all you've been through?"

"No." Not even a little bit. "I only want to be with Hunt and Lana. We're a family now. They're all I need. Yes, I'll grieve for my sister, but I will be happy with Hunt and Lana. Hunt and I will give Lana the life she deserves."

"How are you feeling right now?"

Her feelings were a jumble, but again she focused on what mattered most. "I'm anxious to see Hunt and take Lana home. I need to be with them, to remind myself that after everything that's happened, we are still together, and now we are safe. Being with them will make everything better."

"I think that might be the best kind of medicine you could get right now. But I'd also like to suggest that you come back and see me. The kind of trauma you've been through doesn't just vanish now that the threat is gone."

"I understand that. And yes, I think I could use the help to process my grief and the things that have happened. I know it will make Hunt feel better. And I want to be the best me I can be for him and Lana." Making this commitment felt like a step she needed to take to get there.

"I can help you do all of that." Dr. Sutton rose. "I'll have my office contact you tomorrow to make the appointments. Twice a week to start, then we can reduce that to once a week until you're feeling like yourself again."

Cyn followed the doctor out of the office. "Thank you for taking the time to talk to me tonight."

"My pleasure. It's why I'm here."

They rode down in the elevator and found Hunt in the waiting room alone.

"Where are your brother, Shelby and the baby?" Cyn took Hunt's outstretched hand.

"They took the baby home to get her ready for bed. I know how important it is to try to keep her on her schedule."

"You should have gone with them. I would have followed on my own."

Hunt shook his head. "I'm not leaving here without you." He glanced at Dr. Sutton. "Everything okay?"

Dr. Sutton smiled. "Everything is fine. We had a good talk. I'll see you both soon." The doctor left them alone.

Cyn looked up at Hunt. "Are you going to see him, too?"

He tugged her to follow him toward the exit. "It's police protocol after a shooting or traumatic incident. I'll meet with him twice a week for two weeks, or longer if I need it. Then he'll clear me to go back on patrol. Until then, I'm on paid leave until the investigation into Rad's death is concluded, then it's desk duty for a little while."

"I'm going to see Dr. Sutton again soon, too. It's all been a rush tonight and I feel like I'm fine, but I know it will come crashing down on me at some point."

"I'm here. Whatever you need."

"I know. I think that's what convinced him I was going to be okay, because all I wanted was to get back to you."

They walked across the parking lot to her car. "Chase and Shelby said they took all the stuff from your car and took it to our place with Lana."

"Okay."

Hunt pulled her into his arms beside the driver's side door. "I love you, Cyn. Don't ever fucking scare me like that again."

"Don't ever get shot again."

"I'm not making any promises, but I'm with you, that really sucked."

Cyn found she could chuckle about it now. "Get in the car, Hunt. I'll drive us home."

"That's the best thing I've heard all night."

She waited for him to join her inside the car before she said, "Well, I might be able to top that. At least, I hope you'll be happy to hear this."

"What?"

"I can't go back to Shelby's place."

"You don't have to if you don't want to," he assured her.

"I'm glad you feel that way, because most of my stuff is now at your place."

He took her hand, smiled, kissed her palm, then laid the back of her hand gently against his chest. "Our place," he clarified for the hundredth time, or at least it felt that way.

"Our place," she confirmed.

"That's the best thing I've ever heard in my life."

"I can top it."

He looked over at her. "You can try."

"I love you."

He leaned over, winced, but kissed her like he hadn't kissed her in forever. His fingers dove into her hair and he held her head to him, lingering over the kiss, their tongues gliding along each other's as they lost themselves in the connection they shared and the passion building between them. She was panting by the time he pulled back. "I love you, too. It's you and me and Lana now, Cyn," he promised. "Let's go home to our little girl."

She didn't know how her heart could be any fuller, but somehow Hunt found a way to build on the love they shared.

She let him rest on the drive home and focused on the peaceful night and the soft country music radio station that seemed to be playing nothing but love songs tonight. She held Hunt's hand, drove and let the perfect contentment of the moment wash away the stain of all the bad that happened tonight. It was hard to focus on that when she had so much to be grateful for, especially the man beside her.

She pulled into the driveway, cut the engine and squeezed Hunt's hand. "We're home."

Hunt rolled his head on the headrest and looked at her. "One day soon, I'm going to ask you to be my wife."

Yep, Hunt built the love inside her until her heart was bursting with it. "I'll be saying yes to that when you do."

His smile couldn't get any bigger or brighter. "Let's go see our girl."

# Chapter Thirty-Seven

HUNT WOKE up to the dim morning light seeping through the drapes. The fire from last night had burned out, leaving the hearth cold, but he was warm lying snuggled up to Cyn's soft curves, her rump pressed into his thickening cock. He had his hand on her thigh, his nose in her soft citrus-smelling hair. His chest still hurt after three days, but it got a little better each day.

He and Cyn had hunkered down at home with Lana, settling in together with a renewed sense of commitment to each other and their future. They didn't do much the last couple of days, except spend time together as a family. Cyn grieved Angela while getting to know Lana even better. He loved seeing a different side to Cyn. Her maternal side made him love her even more. She was sweet and tender and engaged with Lana as they both learned to take care of her.

The last few weeks had left Cyn quieter than usual, but she still found a way to smile when Lana cooed, or held her finger, or kicked her feet when she wanted to try to escape her dirty diaper. Every chance Cyn got, she touched him in some way to reassure herself he was still there with her. He was hers. He understood the need all too well, because he'd felt the same way after she drowned, after he pulled her out of the fire, and everything else. Mostly, though, they simply needed to show how much the other person meant to them.

All at once, he wanted to hold on to her and make a life with her. And he wanted everything right now. The urgency hadn't worn off after the danger had ended. The sense that time was short still permeated his thoughts and heart.

So he took advantage of the quiet morning and kissed his way from Cyn's shoulder down her arm as he slipped his hand between her legs. She immediately pushed her ass up against his hard dick and spread her legs so he could slide his hand down her panties and stroke and tease her soft folds.

"You're up early," Cyn teased on a soft whisper as she rocked her ass into his hips again.

"There's a beautiful woman in my bed, in my arms, and I can't think of a better way to start the day than making love to her."

Cyn rolled toward him and he thrust one finger, then two into her slick center, making her moan. "Baby, you can wake me up like this every morning if you want to."

He grinned right before he took her nipple into his mouth and sucked the pink tip. He loved that she slept in next to nothing. Her soft, warm skin brushed against him and set him on fire. And then she wrapped her hand around his thick cock and he sucked in a breath at the exquisite feel of her hand stroking him.

"Keep that up and this won't last long," he warned, licking her nipple and sliding his fingers into her again and again as her hips rocked into his hand.

"You started this," she teased back. "Now come here and finish it."

He loved that she didn't hold back. "You're going to have to take the top," he reminded her, because he couldn't hold himself up on his hands above her without it hurting like hell.

But Cyn had other ideas and shifted back to her side, catching his thick length between her legs. She guided him inside her and rocked her hips against his.

"Damn, Cyn, you feel so good." Making love to her with no barriers made the whole experience feel even better and upped the intimacy between them.

"You feel amazing." She didn't have a whole lot of ability to move, so he gripped her hip and pumped in and out of her. She slipped her hand down to where they were joined, her fingers sliding over her mound and spreading to the side of his cock as he thrust into her, increasing the friction and pressure. He slipped his arm under her and found her breast, plucking the tight bud and making her moan.

He increased the tempo, feeling his balls contract and the need to come coiling inside him.

Cyn slid her fingers up her wet folds and rubbed her clit as he thrust into her hard and deep. Her inner muscles clamped around him and he squeezed her nipple, thrust hard, and she brought herself and him to a climax that hit hard and fast and spasmed out for a minute that held them both enthralled.

His face planted in her neck and hair, his breathing ragged and uneven, he whispered, "Damn, baby, it just keeps getting better."

Her hand covered his on her hip. "Yes, it does." She glanced over her shoulder at him. "Are you okay?"

"Perfect." His chest hurt a little, but it was totally worth it to be with her. He nipped at her neck and shoulder. "How are you?"

"Perfect," she echoed him, but there was still that thing he heard in her voice the last few days. In time, her grief would wane, but this morning it felt like something more.

"What are you holding inside, sweetheart? You can tell me. You can say anything to me."

It took her a moment to respond. "I feel guilty." Her words stunned him.

"You have nothing to feel guilty about. That bastard deserved what he got."

She shook her head and sighed. "Not about that."

He leaned up on his elbow and looked down at her, though she stared across the room at the cold fireplace. "What, then?"

"I have everything."

He softly brushed his hand up her arm, understanding, but also wanting her to talk about it. "Why does that make you feel guilty?"

"Angela died so young. She never got the chance to find what I have with you. And she wanted it. She wanted someone to love her. She wanted Lana to have a good father. She wanted a simple, happy life. And she didn't get it. And now I have everything she ever wanted with you and her daughter."

"If Angela wanted those things for herself, don't you think she'd want them for you, too?"

"Yes. But—"

"But nothing, Cyn. She'd want Lana to be with you and me. She'd want us to love her and give her the happy life Angela wanted for her. We will grieve the loss of Angela. We'll find ourselves forever wishing she was here to see all the milestones Lana will reach. We'll miss her on birthdays and holidays and all the days in between. But it should make you happy to know that your sister loved you and knew that if she couldn't be here for Lana, you are the best mom Lana could ever get."

He kissed her shoulder. "In the end, Angela probably didn't think about what would happen to Lana. She knew you'd take care of Lana for her. What a comfort that must have been to her."

Tears slipped past Cyn's eyelashes and rolled down her cheeks. "I miss her so much. I was holding Lana last night upstairs in the nursery, rocking her back to sleep after her bottle. It was the most peaceful, beautiful feeling I've ever had in my life. I thought Angela probably felt the same way the weeks she'd had Lana at home. I knew those were probably some of the best moments of her life. I was so glad she had them when everything else in her life was so chaotic and sometimes scary." She looked over her shoulder at him. "I rage inside that she didn't get to leave him and be with me and find some happiness in her life. And at the same time, I'm so grateful that she brought Lana into my life and gave me that moment and a thousand others. I'll have a million more with her."

He wiped away a tear on her soft cheek with his fingertip. "And it makes you sad that Angela won't. It makes you angry that Rad took that away from her and Lana. I know, sweetheart. I feel the same way."

Cyn sighed and her eyes brightened with joy. "I think Lana smiled at me while I gave her a bath last night."

He grinned at her. "She's happy."

"That's all I want . . . to be enough for her that she is always happy."

"You are more than enough, Cyn. And she'll have the both of us."

Cyn turned and faced him. "Do you really mean that? You know, there have been a lot of changes in your life all at once. Us dating, me moving in here with you without you really asking me. I mean, I kind of just did it without us talking about it. I could have rented another place, but—"

He put his finger to her soft lips to stop her tumble of words. "I want you here with me. I like seeing your clothes in the closet and your stuff on the bathroom counter. I like that you helped yourself to everything in the kitchen and called this place your home. I want to see you settled here and feeling like it's your place, too. I don't feel like we're rushing, but making things the way we want them to be."

Cyn smiled. "That's a lovely way to think about it."

"I think so, too. And most of all, Cyn, I want Lana to live here with us and have cousin siblings to play with and grow up with on the ranch, the way I did with my brothers, running wild and feeling like nothing could ever touch us."

"Cousin siblings. I like that."

"We're a family. So let's just forget about the order of doing things and how they're supposed to be done in whatever amount of time and just be a family. After everything we've been through, we deserve it."

"You're right. I'm just working through everything in my mind. But the one thing I'm sure of, always, is you and me. Somehow, in all the crazy, we fell in love with each other."

"I think I might have loved you a little bit before you stopped thinking I was an asshole."

"I suppose it's a good thing you love me, because now when you catch me speeding you'll let me off with a warning."

He tickled her ribs. "I better not catch you speeding. You're with a cop now. You need to obey the law, so people won't think I'm giving you special treatment."

"But you are partial to me." She gave him a sexy smile and trailed her finger along his scruffy jaw.

He kissed her softly. "I love you. And if you're speeding, you're getting a ticket, so that you'll know I mean it when I say I don't like you speeding because I don't want anything to happen to you." He kissed her long and deep to keep her from arguing.

And right when things were getting hot and he had his hand between her thighs again, Lana's soft cries came over the baby monitor.

He broke the kiss and stared down at the beautiful woman he was grateful to have in his bed and his life. "I'll get her. You take a shower. We don't want to be late for Pancake Tuesday."

"Is that today?"

It didn't surprise him that she'd lost track of the days after everything they'd been through and the time they stole at home together the last few days.

"It's breakfast, then back to work for me. And the Harmons are coming by this afternoon to drop off all of Angela and Lana's things from Rad's place."

Cyn frowned.

"If you want me to be here when they come, I can use my lunch break and swing by."

Cyn shook her head. "No. I'm sure it will be fine. Difficult, but I can handle it." Cyn had proven she could handle just about anything.

"If you need me, all you have to do is call or text me and I'll be here."

"I know."

Lana's cries increased.

"She's hungry. Go get her." Cyn waved her hands to shoo him out of bed.

He stood up on the side across from her and watched her eyes roam over his naked body. "Having second thoughts about sending me upstairs?"

"I'm having wicked thoughts about you, Wilde."

"You can have your wicked way with me again later."

"Promise?"

"You make me want to beg for it." If Lana wasn't crying upstairs, he'd be diving back into bed with her.

"I'm yours, Hunt. Anytime. Anywhere. Always."

"I feel the same way, sweetheart. But our girl upstairs is demanding my attention."

Cyn gave him a mock frown. "Dumped for another pretty girl."

"Never." He pulled on his sweatpants and T-shirt, catching the disappointed look in Cyn's eyes when he covered up. He caught her in his arms when she slipped out of bed to head into the bathroom and kissed her softly. "You'll always come first, Cyn, even if Lana needs me, too."

"I don't mind sharing you with her." She smiled, then kissed him. "Hurry up. That girl is starving."

He reluctantly let go of naked Cyn and rushed to the kitchen to make the bottle before he went upstairs to get the baby. He heard the shower go on and Lana fussing upstairs and saw the dirty dishes from dinner in the sink and the blanket he and Cyn lay under on the couch last night on the floor by the coffee table. Cyn's coat hung on the rack by the front door along with her purse. She'd left a bag of double chocolate cookies on the breakfast bar.

He didn't mind the mess or having her here at all. In fact, the place finally felt like a real home where a family lived.

Cyn said she was his. Always.

For the first time ever, he knew what it felt like to love like that. "Forever's not enough."

Cyn and Lana just living here wasn't enough. He wanted to make them being a family official. And that meant he needed to make some plans.

# Chapter Thirty-Eight

CYN WALKED into the diner with Hunt for Pancake Tuesday, spotted the rest of the family already at the table and had a moment of clarity that she and Hunt would be doing this for years to come. Little Eliza and Lana would grow up surrounded by these Wilde men, and Cyn and Shelby would be best friends and family. It made her smile.

"I've missed that pretty smile." Hunt brushed his thumb along her jaw.

She looked up at his happy face. "I needed this."

"It's good to be with people who care about you."

She nodded. "It's better when they're family. Lana will have you and me and all of them."

Max walked over to greet them. "Hey, we weren't sure you three would make it." Max took the diaper bag from Cyn's shoulder and leaned in and kissed her cheek. "You doing okay?"

"A little better every day," she assured him.

Max shook Hunt's hand. "How's the chest?"

"Black and blue but getting better."

Max looked Hunt up and down, noting the uniform. "You're back to work today?"

"We're really short-staffed. So I'm in the office until I've healed and get cleared by the doctor."

"Come on, Shelby can't wait to tell you all about the wedding plans," Max said to them, then turned and immediately ran into a pretty woman with dark hair and green eyes, nearly knocking her down. He grabbed hold of her with one hand and let the diaper bag slip from his other and tumble on the floor, spilling the contents. "Kenna. Sorry." Max released the woman like touching her burned him. "Did I hurt you?"

"I'm fine," she bit out. "Excuse us." The woman and the guy she was with walked past them.

Max glared at the guy, but then his gaze softened on the woman again as she disappeared out the door and he watched her walk to the parking lot.

Cyn looked up at Hunt. "What was that?"

Hunt grinned. "Kenna is the one who got away."

"I let her go," Max grumbled, dropping into a squat to pick up the diaper bag contents littering the floor.

"I see." Cyn gave Hunt a knowing look, letting him know she understood that Max may have let Kenna go but he regretted that decision. Cyn also hadn't missed the flare of pain in Kenna's eyes when she looked at Max.

"Don't," Max said, opening the diaper bag to stuff in a handful of diapers.

"She's very pretty," Cyn pointed out.

Max growled something under his breath.

Hunt chuckled. "I'm going to set this little one down at the table." Hunt took Lana into the dining room and plunked her car seat atop a high chair next to Eliza's.

Cyn sank down to help Max. "You miss her."

"No, I don't." Max turned to grab the blanket and spare clothes from the floor.

"Maybe she misses you, too," she persisted.

"Looks like she's with someone new. Again," Max bit out.

Cyn tried to hide her grin.

"What?" Max snapped.

"Sounds like you've been paying attention to who is with her."

"It's a small town. You can't escape hearing about your ex with someone else." And Max didn't like it one bit.

Interesting. Cyn nudged him. "If you want her back, why don't you tell her that?"

"Trust me, that's never going to happen."

"Huh. I guess what I saw in her eyes when she looked at you is just on her part, then."

Max went perfectly still for a moment, then he grabbed the bag and stuffed in the pack of baby wipes so forcefully that when they caught on the edge of the bag, it tore. "Damnit, Cyn, I'm sorry."

She put her hand on his. "It's not a big deal." She could probably sew the seam back together.

Max poked at the torn seam. "Looks like someone tore this before and used some double-sided tape to repair it." He examined it more closely, then stuffed his hand down the hole.

"Max, you'll tear it more."

"There's something in here." He pulled out a thick envelope and handed it to her. "It's got your name on it."

Tears immediately welled in her eyes as she stared at her sister's pretty handwriting.

"Your sister hid that for you, didn't she?" Max took her arm and helped her stand up.

"Yes. I think so." Which broke her heart that her sister had thought to do so because of her fear of Rad. Her hands shook as she stared at the envelope.

"Come on. Sit down." Max steered her into the dining room and to the chair beside Hunt.

"What's wrong?" Hunt immediately put his arm around her. "What's that?"

Max hooked the diaper bag handle on her chair. "I found a letter from Angela hidden in the diaper bag."

Shelby put her hand on Cyn's shoulder. "You don't have to open it right now."

Cyn couldn't stand not knowing what her sister wrote. She opened the letter with the entire Wilde family watching her.

She read aloud . . .

My dearest sister, my best friend,

Cyn's eyes filled with fresh tears.

Hunt put his arm across her shoulders and rubbed her arm.

She found her voice again . . .

It's just after two in the morning and I can't help but sit by Lana's bedside, so I can watch her sleep. She's a month old today and I feel like I need to spend every second I can with her, because I fear that my time with her will be too short.

There's a constant image in my head of you holding Lana in the hospital. You were staring down at her with such a sense of wonder and contentment. In that moment, I thought, *They're perfect together,* and I knew that someday that's how it would be. You would raise our girl because I'm not here.

And if you're reading this, then it's come to pass and my worst fears have come true. I want you to know I planned to leave him. I just needed to do a few things before I risked taking her away from him.

I'm sorry I wasn't stronger, Cyn. I'm sorry I didn't leave the first time you begged me to stay with you or the tenth or twentieth or hundredth time you did. You never gave up on me. You never judged me. You always loved me. And I love you so much for always having my back. I know you do even now and that Lana is in the best hands. She will be loved above all else. She will never be afraid. She will be strong and resilient and independent and confident—just like her new mom.

I hope she has a little of your wild streak and grows up to be as fearless without being reckless as you. I know her heart will be as big as yours. And I hope she's as persistent as you in getting what she wants.

Whatever happened to me, I want you to let it go and remember me as I was with you, not who I became with him. Tell Lana I'm sorry. I loved her more than anything in this world. Tell her she was the best of me and that I never wanted to leave her. Teach her not to make the mistakes I made and that being in love doesn't hurt, but losing it does, and there's a difference between being loved by someone and being used by them. I know she'll know the difference because you won't settle for anything less than a pure and true love that is epic and she'll want that for herself.

Tell her I'm sorry I stayed with someone who didn't deserve us.

Find someone who deserves you, Cyn. I know that won't be easy, because you're the best person I know. Maybe that cop you're always grumbling about. There was something fierce in his eyes when Rad hit you, like he couldn't stand to see you hurt. And I could tell by the way you tried so hard not to look at him that you felt the sizzle between you, too. I really hope I'm around to see what comes of it, because I bet he's the one for you. And if he is, or some other guy is, I know he'll be the right one for Lana, too.

Be the mom I wanted to be. Make all the memories I wanted to have with her and know that I'll know she had the best mom and life I could have given her because she's yours now. I've made sure of it.

I wish "thank you" expressed how much I appreciate all you've done for me and all you'll do for my precious Lana. I love you and I wish you and Lana a happy, healthy and beautiful life together.

You were my everything, Cyn. Now you'll be hers. She's so lucky!

I love you,
Angela

Hunt leaned in, kissed her on the head, then whispered in her ear, "I'm so lucky."

Shelby hugged her from the side and said, "I'm so lucky."

Cyn turned into Hunt's embrace and let the tears fall.

"What did she mean . . . she's yours and she made sure of it?" Mr. Wilde asked.

Cyn wiped her tears with a napkin Hunt handed her, then shifted the letter off the other pages below and revealed the documents her sister had drawn up before her death. "She made a will and gave me custody of Lana. She made her wishes known that she wants me to adopt Lana and the letter is her telling me not to be just Lana's aunt, but to be her m-mom." Cyn burst into tears again.

Hunt helped her up from her chair and into his arms. "You guys go ahead and order breakfast. I'm taking Cyn outside for a few minutes. Shelby . . ."

"I've got Lana," she assured them.

Hunt grabbed the papers and led her out of the diner, where most of the patrons were watching them. She didn't really care.

All she wanted to do was be with Hunt and take a minute to really feel and understand all her sister told her in the letter.

Hunt walked her to the back of his car, leaned against it and pulled her into his arms. He held her until her tears subsided and she caught her breath again. Then he simply waited until she was ready to talk.

She stayed right where she was, her head on his chest, his chin brushing against her hair and their arms locked around each other. "She knew he was going to kill her."

"She was scared for herself and Lana. She wanted to be sure Lana would be safe and loved and she knew that would be with you."

"And you, apparently."

He moved his hand to her head and brushed his fingers through her hair. "It's nice to know she thought we'd be good together and that whoever you picked would be good enough for Lana, too. It's a comfort to me to know that."

"It is to me, too. I've been struggling with how to

proceed with Lana. She's so little. She doesn't know what's happening around her. I will be the only mom she knows. But I'm her aunt. What do I have her call me? Aunt Cyn, or Mom? I don't want her to ever think I took Angela's place."

"She won't. Because we'll tell her in ways that she can understand as she grows up that she was lucky enough to have two moms. One who gave birth to her and loved her dearly. And one who raised her as her own daughter, even though she's her aunt. That's what Angela wanted. When Lana is old enough, we'll show her the letter and that Angela wanted you to adopt her and be her mom. It's that simple, Cyn. Angela said it. Lana is yours now."

"Angela wanted more than that for us."

"I know. Did you look at the adoption papers she enclosed?"

"Not really."

Hunt let her loose and held the papers up for her to see. "She handwrote my name next to yours and initialed and dated it."

Cyn snatched the papers and stared at them. "That's the day she died. How did she know?"

"I don't know. Intuition. Clarity of thought in a time when she felt she was most vulnerable. Coincidence. Hope that you'd find happiness with me. Faith that everything would work out. Whatever it was, Angela believed you would choose what was best for you and Lana."

"You are everything I want and need for both of us."

He kissed her softly. "I know a judge who owes me a favor. I can ask him to make this a reality without us having to wait too long for it to move through the courts, especially since we have Angela's consent."

That fearless part of her Angela pointed out spoke without Cyn having to think about it. "Yes. Let's be a family and make all the memories Angela would have wanted to make with Lana if she could."

"I'll make the call. After breakfast." He kissed her again, then took her hand and led her back into the diner.

Everyone was at the table, talking among themselves.

Lana was tucked in sweetly in Mr. Wilde's arms. "She got a bit fussy, but Pop-Pop settled her right down."

Cyn's eyes teared up again.

How easily everyone accepted them into the family. How wonderful to belong.

Lana wouldn't just have a mom and dad, she'd have uncles, an aunt and a Pop-Pop to love her.

And Cyn would do everything she could to make sure the Harmons had a place in Lana's life, too, because she didn't blame them for what their son did.

Shelby took Cyn's hand and tugged her to sit down. "We ordered for you both. Your usual, Hunt, and the pancake special for you, Cyn, with extra butter."

Cyn smiled. "You know me so well."

"We're best friends and our girls will be best friends. That's how it will be, right?"

"Absolutely," Cyn agreed, then eyed Max across the table. "I bet we're going to like your Kenna," she teased him.

Max pointed his finger at Cyn, then Shelby. "Don't. Stay out of it. That's over and done. Not happening."

Cyn exchanged a look with Shelby and they burst out laughing. "I think he protests a little too much. What do you think, Shelby?"

"Yeah. There's something there."

Max glared at them, then turned to Chase and Hunt. "Call off your women."

Hunt and Chase both looked at Max, then her and Shelby, and shook their heads.

"Good luck with that," Hunt said, and Chase nodded his agreement and they both laughed at their brother.

Max groaned and picked up Eliza and sat her in his lap. "I've got all the girls in my life I need, thank you very much."

Cyn smiled and thought of her sister's letter and the documents she left behind. "I don't know, Max. If it's meant to be . . ."

CYN WAS STILL thinking about things that were meant to be that night when Hunt returned home and found her upstairs in one of the loft chairs feeding Lana her bottle before bed. "How was your day?"

Hunt kissed her, then kissed Lana on the head, and sat beside Cyn's feet on the ottoman. "Not good. Remember the guy we saw with Kenna this morning when Max ran into her?"

"Yeah. Tall guy. Dark hair. Cute, but not as handsome as you or Max."

Hunt shook his head and grinned. "Thanks. But I'm way more handsome than Max."

"Yes, you are," she readily agreed. "But what about the guy?"

"He died in a car accident after he dropped Kenna off at work this morning."

"Oh my God. That's awful. Poor Kenna."

"Yeah. She was upset when I spoke to her. They hadn't been seeing each other long. They'd only been on a handful of dates. Still . . ."

"Yeah. You never know what's going to happen or when."

Hunt picked up her foot and massaged it. "We've learned that the hard way lately. Did the Harmons stop by today?"

"I called and asked them to postpone until tomorrow morning. After getting Angela's letter, I wanted to just spend the day with Lana and let it all sink in."

"Are you doing okay? You've had to deal with a lot lately and that letter was really hard to read."

"It was. So I took the time I needed to let it settle and reimagine my life and what I want it to be from now on. I need to get back to work. My employees have been great at taking care of things in my absence, but I need to be there. So Lana and Eliza will go to day care together. Shelby raves about the woman who takes care of Eliza, so I feel comfortable taking Lana there, too."

"Sounds good. I can keep Lana on days I have off, because they might not always be the same as yours."

"I think Lana would love to be home with you."

Hunt rubbed his thumb up the center of her foot. "Well, that leads to the other thing I wanted to talk to you about. I spoke with Judge Evans and showed him all the paperwork your sister had drawn up through the legal document internet site. Most everything is in order, but we'll need a few small changes to the documents, which the judge was happy to help us do. So whenever we're ready, we'll go before him, and he'll sign off on everything."

"Perfect. When do you want to do that?"

"I'm ready now, but I'd appreciate it if you gave me a little bit of time. There's something I need to do first."

She tried to get a read on what he meant, but he didn't give anything away. "What?"

"Trust me." He tried to hold back a smile, but she saw the hint of it anyway. "It'll be worth the wait."

She had an inkling of what Hunt had in mind, and it took everything she had not to show the full extent of her excitement and anticipation.

# Chapter Thirty-Nine

Cyn was so grateful to have Shelby over this morning. Yes, she needed the distraction to help stave off the waves of grief, and someone who could answer some of her baby questions, because she wasn't prepared to be Lana's mom. She had some catching up to do. Luckily Shelby arrived ready with answers and a book that covered everything for a newborn up to one year. Cyn felt mildly better prepared.

"Thanks for spending your free morning with me."

"It's really no problem. Plus, I wanted to go over the wedding plans with you."

"I'm the worst maid of honor ever. I haven't helped you plan a damn thing."

Shelby put her hand on Cyn's forearm. "It's *my* wedding. And because I didn't have anyone to bounce ideas off of, Chase and I had a chance to really connect and create the wedding we want. Plus, it's not like it's a huge affair. It's just family and a few close friends." Shelby pulled a couple of photos out of her wedding folder. "I picked a couple of dresses I thought might suit you. Since blue is one of my favorite colors and yours, maybe you'd like one of these."

Cyn looked at the three choices. "I love them all. I'm happy to wear whichever is your favorite."

Shelby tapped her finger on the shimmery blue midi-dress with the cap sleeves, tight bodice, sparkly silver embellishment below the bodice and softly draping skirt that had a layer of see-through material. "This one is my favorite and the one I think will look fantastic on you, as well as go with your gorgeous hair."

Cyn laughed. "Everyone loves the purple locks."

"They're so you, Cyn."

"That dress is so me, too. Thanks for picking something I'll be comfortable in and can wear again."

"I want you to love it."

"I do," Cyn assured her.

"Okay, I'll order it."

"I'm happy to pay for the dress." After all, Cyn would keep it.

"The dress is on me. Eliza and you will match, though her dress is a different style, but the same color blue. I think I'll get her a silver headband."

"And I'll do her hair and yours. It's going to be so fun. And when you're my matron of honor, we'll do it all again."

Shelby eyed her left hand. "Is there something you want to tell me?"

"Not yet. But Hunt and I have talked about getting married. I mean, I live here now. We have a baby."

Shelby grinned, but her eyes were a bit wary. "A lot has happened to you recently, most of it traumatic. Are you sure you don't want to take some time now that things have settled down?"

"Nothing is going to change the way I feel about him.

After what happened at your rental, I couldn't go back there. But deep down, I also knew I didn't want to be without him anymore. I didn't want to spend a single day or night or moment away from him. When I'm with him, everything seems right. It's so perfect. And when I see him with Lana, the way he cares for her, I melt and think about how lucky we are to have him. For a long time now, I've wanted a husband and family of my own. When Hunt showed me the nursery he created upstairs for a baby that was only a dream to him, I knew he wanted what I wanted. A family. A place where we belonged, with people we love. Somehow in all the danger we faced and the desperation of trying to find my sister and Lana, we found that with each other. He was the calm in the storm. This house was the only place I wanted to be because he was here. At first, I fought the pull between us. But when I surrendered to it . . . I had everything I ever wanted."

Shelby put her hand on Cyn's shoulder. "You don't have to explain. I know just how you feel."

The doorbell rang.

Cyn sighed. "I hope *they* understand and accept that Hunt and I will be Lana's parents now."

"After what their son did, they should be grateful you're so welcoming of them in Lana's life."

"They're her grandparents. She's lost so much. I don't want her to lose them, too." Cyn opened the door.

Mr. and Mrs. Harmon stood on the porch. Mr. Harmon carried two big moving boxes. Mrs. Harmon had a wrapped gift.

"Hi. Can I take one of those boxes?" Cyn asked.

"Just point me to where you'd like me to set them down," Mr. Harmon said, his eyes a bit wary.

Mrs. Harmon looked even more insecure.

"Please, come in. Just set the boxes on the floor, there by the closet door." Cyn pointed to where she meant. She'd go through her sister's things later, when she felt stronger and capable of looking at them without falling apart. "This is my friend Shelby. She's marrying Hunt's brother Chase."

"And you're living here now?" Mrs. Harmon stared at her without a trace of whether she liked that or not.

"Yes. I was renting Shelby's house in town, but it needs repairs because of . . . And after what happened, I . . ."

Mrs. Harmon nodded. "I understand."

Mr. Harmon wrapped his arm around his wife's shoulders. "We wanted to get in touch with you sooner, but felt that maybe you needed some time."

"Thank you. I did. I still do." She quickly added, "But to grieve my sister, not because I don't want to see you."

They let out a collective sigh.

Mrs. Harmon held the gift out to her. "This is for Lana and you. A kind of . . . oh, I don't know, shower gift now that you're going to raise Lana."

"You know?"

The Harmons exchanged glances. Mrs. Harmon spoke. "We assumed you would want to keep Lana. We'd, of course, like to have some sort of visitation. Nothing formal or anything, but maybe set a time once a week to see her, so she gets to know us as her grandparents. If that's okay with you and fits into your schedule as well. We'd be happy to babysit anytime, too."

Cyn took it in and released her worries that this was

going to be difficult. "Yes. That would be great. I hoped we could work something out. I was afraid . . ."

"That we'd try to take her from you?" Mr. Harmon shook his head. "We talked about what's best for Lana. We think that's you, someone who is young and the next best thing to her mother. We know you love her and will take care of her. Despite what happened, you haven't shut us out and we appreciate that. We're here to help."

Cyn wanted everything to be clear. "Angela left a will and custody to me. She even had adoption papers drawn up for me."

Mrs. Harmon's eyes teared up. "She knew something bad was going to happen."

"Yes." Cyn didn't feel the need to sugarcoat it. "Hunt and I plan to get married and we will adopt Lana together. We will be her family, her mom and dad. We will tell her about Angela and your son in an appropriate way as she grows up, but for all intents and purposes, Hunt and I will be her parents from now on."

Mrs. Harmon gave her a firm nod. "She'll have a mom and a dad and a whole family of Wildes, plus us and your mom and stepdad to take care of her. She'll be surrounded by so much love, maybe it won't hurt so much to miss her mom." Mrs. Harmon's optimism matched Cyn's hopes.

"Open the gift," Mr. Harmon encouraged.

Cyn tore the paper away and handed it off to Shelby. She opened the box's lid, lifted the tissue paper and gasped at the framed photo inside of her sister smiling brightly, standing in front of a tree holding Lana up, their cheeks pressed together. Her sister looked happy and vibrant and beautiful.

Tears spilled from Cyn's eyes.

"I've never been good at taking pictures," Mrs. Harmon confessed. "I'm always too far away, things aren't centered or they turn out blurry. But this one came out perfect." Mrs. Harmon put her hand on Cyn's on the frame. "I thought maybe you could put it next to Lana's bed. Then she can say good night and good morning to her mom every day. She can see how happy her mother was to have her." Mrs. Harmon held Cyn's gaze. "I am truly sorry for what my son did to your sister. I am so sorry for your loss. I will spend the rest of my life trying to make it up to Lana by being the very best grandma I can be to her."

Mr. Harmon put his hands on his wife's shoulders. "I'm sorry, too, Cyn. For all of it. I wish we'd known the extent of what was happening and intervened. I wish we'd been better parents and Rad had turned out to be a different man."

Cyn choked back her tears. "From what Hunt told me about him, he was a good guy. I don't know what changed him. I don't know how he could treat my sister the way he did and do the things he did to her and others. I don't blame you for his actions as an adult. He made his choices. He suffered the consequences." Though Cyn thought he got off too easy, but she didn't say so. The Harmons probably knew that's how she felt. "Lana is all that is important now." She pulled the framed photo out and set the box on the breakfast bar, then faced the Harmons again. "Sounds like Lana is awake. Would you like to go up and see her? We can put this in her room."

"We'd love that." Mrs. Harmon smiled her relief and excitement to see Lana.

"You two head up," Mr. Harmon coaxed. "I'll bring in the rest of the things we brought from Rad's place." Mr. Harmon headed for the front door.

Shelby followed. "I'll help."

Mrs. Harmon started for the stairs. "We brought the high chair, playpen, all her clothes and the baby bathtub. You should be all set for a little while."

"We've been bathing her in the kitchen sink." Cyn reached the landing with Mrs. Harmon. "It'll be nice to use the tub. And the girl goes through clothes like you wouldn't believe."

"Don't we all," Mrs. Harmon teased.

Cyn opened the nursery door and Mrs. Harmon gasped, "It's beautiful."

"Hunt did it himself a while back."

"Did you recently add the butterflies?"

Cyn shook her head. "No. He found the mobile and thought a baby would love all the colors."

"How unexpectedly appropriate." Mrs. Harmon notched her chin toward the butterfly visible on Cyn's arm. She went to the crib and smiled down at a cooing Lana. "You started your life one way, but now you've got a completely new life. I just know you are going to fly."

Mrs. Harmon's words touched Cyn deeply and made her think of the life she and Hunt were starting together. A new beginning for all of them.

# Chapter Forty

HUNT PARKED his patrol car on the side of the road, facing out, so he could watch oncoming traffic. He and Cyn were heading over to Chase's place for a family dinner tonight before the wedding tomorrow. They were expected to be there in ten minutes, but Cyn was running late and he had something he'd been wanting to do for a good long time now.

The last month had been the best days of his life. He and Cyn had settled in together. They had a routine now. At least as good as one they could have with his hectic schedule, Cyn's businesses, including the start of the remodel of her new store in Blackrock Falls, and an infant. He loved coming home to them and just being together. He enjoyed his days off when he kept Lana home with him. Being a father to her made him happier than he'd imagined.

Cyn's grief had subsided, though it snuck up on her at times, especially when she was with Lana. But Cyn had embraced their new life together. She'd even bought a few things for the house. He loved the two new dark blue velvet chairs she bought to put in front of the windows in the living room, along with a round wood table. She loved to sit in the sunlight with Lana and enjoy the view. He loved to sit there with her in the mornings while they drank their coffee.

She'd added other touches around the house. Mementos and pictures from over the years. She didn't shy away from putting pictures of her and Angela up. They both wanted Lana to see her mother in the house, and that he and Cyn remembered Angela with love.

He silently thanked Angela a lot over the last month for all she'd given him, and promised her he'd always take care of Lana and Cyn.

And right now, he hoped to make Cyn's day.

Her car sped past him going at least ten miles over the speed limit. He hit the gas, turned on the lights and siren and sped after her with a grin that grew wider when he saw her spot him in her rearview mirror; she hit the brakes and pulled over to the side of the road.

He pulled in behind her, opened his door and anticipated the sparks she was about to throw off.

The second he arrived at her window, she looked up at him with anger flashing in her eyes.

He couldn't help but stoke that fire. "Do you know how fast you were going?"

"Wilde, I mean it, you do not want to do this."

"It's my job, sweetheart."

"Don't sweetheart me, Wilde. You cannot seriously be thinking of giving me a speeding ticket when I'm rushing to meet *you* for dinner."

He loved it when she got irritated with him and called him Wilde like that. "There is never an excuse to break the law," he pointed out. "Please step out of the vehicle." His cop talk only irritated her more.

She opened the door and stood. "Seriously, Wilde, this is ridiculous. Don't I get a warning or something? Doesn't sleeping with you get me a pass?"

He tried not to laugh. "No." He waved his hand for her to move. "Step to the back of the vehicle."

She did, folded her arms over her chest, raising her tantalizing breasts, and huffed out a frustrated breath. Then her gaze turned sultry. "Are you going to search me, Officer?" She unfolded her arms, spun very slowly, put her hands on the back of her SUV and leaned forward, pushing her really nice ass out toward him.

He nearly groaned and forgot why he'd pulled her over in the first place. He leaned in close, his body inches from hers, but begging to be pressed against her soft curves, and said, "Turn around, Cyn."

She did and leaned back against the car, arms folded again, anger flashing in her eyes and her mouth set in an adorable pout, though he wouldn't tell her he thought so. "This is not amusing, Wilde."

He opened his ticket book and started writing. "Speeding is dangerous, sweetheart. I'm just trying to keep you safe. Because I love you." He finished what he wanted to write and looked at her. "You're the most important thing in the world to me. I want to protect you and love you and be with you always."

She lost all trace of anger, dropped her arms and gave him a soft smile. "I love you, too."

Before she got angry again, he dropped to one knee and held up the ticket he'd written for her that wasn't a ticket at all, but a proposal. He'd scrawled in red ink across the page *Will You Marry Me?* With two boxes he'd drawn next to the words *Yes* and *No* beneath the question.

He held up the pen.

She shouted, "Yes!" knocked his arm aside, took his face in her hands and kissed him soundly.

He laughed and kissed her back. "You have to make it official."

She took the pen and marked *Yes*.

His rapidly beating heart soared.

"Sign it."

She took the book and with a wide grin signed her name at the bottom like she'd had to do on all the other tickets he'd issued her. This one they'd keep, maybe frame it and put it up on the wall in the house.

While she did that, he pulled the ring from his pocket and held it up to her. The second she saw it, she dropped the ticket book and pen and pressed her fingers to her lips.

Her eyes went wide and filled with tears. "Hunt. Where did you find something like that?"

He took her hand and slipped the ring on her finger. "I had it made from a design I saw online. That's why it's taken me this long to ask you." He kissed her knuckle above the ring on her finger and stood. "Do you like it?"

"I love it. It's perfect."

The butterfly ring was everything he hoped it would turn out to be. Three diamonds made up the butterfly body. And because Cyn loved blue, the bottom wings were pear-shaped sapphires and the larger top wings were marquise-cut London blue topazes.

"Custom-made just for you."

Cyn held her hand up with the other and stared at it. "I can't believe you did this."

"I'd do anything for you, sweetheart. I wanted you to have something special, something you'd love forever."

Her watery gaze settled on him. "I already have that, Hunt. I have you."

Stunned and touched beyond measure by her words, he took her in his arms. The kiss they shared was tender and sweet and went on and on because Hunt loved kissing his fiancée. He couldn't wait to make her his wife.

CYN WALKED INTO Chase and Shelby's home holding Hunt's hand, unable to contain her smile or excitement.

Shelby had picked up Eliza and Lana from the sitter earlier and walked to Cyn to hand over Lana.

Cyn raised her hands to take the baby, but Shelby pulled Lana back to her chest, her eyes went wide and she sputtered, "W-what is that?" She notched her chin toward Cyn's hand, then looked past Cyn at Hunt standing behind her. "You proposed without telling us first?"

Hunt chuckled. "I didn't think I needed to tell anyone."

"We could have had champagne or something to celebrate."

"Oh, I plan to celebrate." Hunt drew Cyn's back into him and kissed her neck.

Chase, Max and Mr. Wilde surrounded them.

Shelby took her hand and looked at the ring, tears in her eyes. "Oh, Hunt, it's perfect."

Cyn's heart raced and melted all at once. She'd never been this happy in her whole life. "It's amazing."

"Nice job." Chase smacked Hunt on the back.

"Congrats." Max smacked his brother on the back, too.

Mr. Wilde hugged Hunt. "So happy for you, son." Then Mr. Wilde hugged her. "Welcome to the family, beautiful girl."

She teared up. "Thank you."

Mr. Wilde released her and she took Lana from Shelby and tucked the baby into her arm and showed her the ring. "Look, sweet girl, Daddy got Mama a pretty ring. We're going to get married and be a family and one day soon you'll have a brother or sister."

Hunt kissed her on the head.

"So how did he propose? Tell us everything." Shelby handed her a glass of wine and Hunt a beer.

Cyn dramatically rolled her eyes. "He pulled me over and acted like he was going to give me another speeding ticket."

Shelby and all the others busted up laughing.

Cyn told them about the really lovely and well-thought-out proposal that was uniquely their story.

"If you want to see it, I captured it on my dash cam," Hunt pointed out.

Cyn shook her head. "That's why you asked me to move to the back of the car."

"I promise not to show anyone how you tried to seduce me out of the ticket."

Everyone laughed at that one, too, and Chase and Max, of course, asked for details, which Hunt respectfully kept to himself. Some things were just for them.

"So did you two talk about a date?" Shelby asked as she started setting dinner out on the table and everyone helped, then took their seats.

"Not yet," she answered, and Hunt said at the same time, "Soon."

He took her hand and kissed her palm, then rubbed Lana's back as she lay on Cyn's chest. "We've talked about doing something simple with the judge who is going to sign off on the adoption. I thought we could combine the two things, that way when we sign the adoption papers we do it as Mr. and Mrs. Wilde." He turned to her. "If you're going to take my name."

"I would love that," she admitted. "And then Lana will be a Wilde, too. She'll know she belongs to us."

"To all of us," Mr. Wilde added, holding up his glass. "To all the Wildes. Old and new. And the ones to come."

They all clinked glasses and settled into the family dinner in anticipation of Chase and Shelby's wedding ceremony the next day. Shelby would be the next official Wilde. And soon, Cyn and Lana would join the Wilde clan.

The evening was kind of magical. Cyn found herself engrossed in the family and how everyone talked and laughed with each other. Though she'd been to several Pancake Tuesdays, tonight's family gathering felt different. She felt like she truly belonged. She felt the bond she had with Hunt that extended to the other Wilde men and how her connection to Shelby felt even stronger.

And somewhere in the midst of all of it, she experienced a special moment where she stared down into Lana's bright eyes and Lana gazed up at her and smiled. And then she felt a soft pressure on her shoulder and it was like her sister was right there with her hand on Cyn to let her know she was with them, watching over everything. Sharing in the moment. And maybe Lana felt it, too.

The sense of peace stayed with her through their goodbyes to the family, getting Lana home and tucked into bed and her joining Hunt in theirs. The second she crawled under the covers, he took her in his arms and kissed her.

"I can't believe you're finally going to be my wife."

"I can't believe you pretended to give me a ticket."

"It's how we met." He rolled on top of her, braced himself on his forearms and stared down at her. "And who said I was pretending? I'm going to write you that ticket," he warned. "But maybe you can persuade me not to," he suggested, kissing one cheek, then the other.

She slid her hands down his back to his ass and grabbed both cheeks and squeezed. "Well, Officer, I think I can sway you, though I'm not sure that all my tactics are legal in this state," she teased.

Hunt's eyes smoldered. "You'll have to show me, just so I'll know exactly what you mean."

She put her hand on his shoulder and pushed him off her. He easily took her prompt and rolled onto his back. She flung all the covers off them and watched the firelight dance across his skin.

The bruising on his chest had healed. She leaned down and kissed the small scar left by the impact of the bullet into his vest. "You are a sight to behold, Hunt." She straddled his lap and brushed her fingertips over his pecs and down his washboard abs to where she covered most of his hard length with her already wet folds. She touched the head of his penis at the same time she rocked her hips and glided along his length.

His big hands clamped onto her hips. "Cyn." Just her name, spoken like a swear word and a prayer.

She smiled down at him. "You know, Wilde, being your wife isn't going to tame me any." She rocked against his length again and swirled her finger softly over the tip of his penis.

"God, I hope not." He bucked his hips up into her

as he held her down against him, creating a delicious friction that nudged at her clit, sending a swarm of sensations rippling through her.

"Let me in, Cyn." Hunt groaned as she rubbed against him again.

"Oh, Hunt, you're in my mind, my heart, my future. But right now, Wilde man, I want you in my mouth." She slid back, wrapped her hand around the base of his dick and took him in her mouth, deep.

"Fuck, Cyn. The things you do to me."

She did lots of wonderful things to him. Things to make him groan. Things to make him sigh. Things to make him drag her up his body and thrust into her and hold her there for a moment so they could both enjoy the feel of being a part of each other.

They took their time making love, showing each other and sharing how much love lived inside them.

By the time they came apart in each other's arms and she collapsed on top of him, the fire had burned low and the night had gone quiet until Hunt's deep, husky voice whispered into her ear. "I am yours." She found it poignant and heartfelt that he didn't claim her as his but pledged himself to her, and she easily gave him back the same oath. "I am yours."

# Chapter Forty-One

THEY CHOSE the perfect day to get married, though any day would have been perfect to marry the one you love. Still, Hunt rose to a glorious pink and lavender sunrise this morning and his smiling bride-to-be kissing him awake. They bucked tradition and made love first thing, not caring one bit that he wasn't supposed to see the bride before the wedding. He saw every bit of Cyn and made sure to touch and kiss and lick every lovely inch of her.

He popped the question six weeks ago. Planning the wedding had taken less time than it took Cyn to pick a dress. Luckily the one she fell in love with was available in her size. She had it shipped to Shelby's place so he wouldn't see it.

Their ceremony would be much like Chase and Shelby's backyard wedding. A simple gathering of friends and family. Because of the cold December temps, they'd have a quick ceremony in the garden where he and his brothers had strung lights and set up benches for their guests. He'd built a trellis for them to stand under while they said their vows. The florist had decorated it with bouquets of purple and white flowers, along with garlands and tiny white lights. After the wedding and celebration, he'd hang the bench swing his dad gave them as a wedding gift.

Inside the house, they'd moved furniture around to set up tables and chairs for the brunch after the ceremony. They had the caterer ready to go, the cake had been delivered and the florist had decorated the tables and hearth with dozens of floral bouquets and garlands, too. The whole house smelled like a garden.

The guests had arrived ten minutes ago and were seated on the benches lined up on both sides of a rose-petal-strewn path. The judge stood beside him as they waited for the ceremony to begin.

The music played. Max walked down the aisle with their cousin Lyric, who Cyn had gotten close to over the last several weeks while she worked on setting up her shop in Blackrock Falls.

Chase and Shelby, carrying Lana, walked down the aisle next. Shelby looked beautiful in a lavender dress that matched the color of the tiny gown they put on Lana. Chase wore a tux that matched Hunt's and Max's, down to the lavender bow tie and rose boutonnieres they wore.

Shelby stood across the aisle from him, while Chase took his place beside Hunt as his best man.

They all stood in their places with the judge at the center of them.

And then there she was at the end of the aisle, his beautiful Cyn in a white gown that nearly stopped his heart. Beautiful in its simplicity, the white satin hugged Cyn's curves, then flared out to a fuller skirt. A purple satin belt cinched her waist. The deep V neckline showed off the swell of her breasts, and the long lace sleeves were a touch of added elegance. When she took her first step toward him, he saw a hint of a purple high heel and grinned.

She'd kept her hair down, falling in soft purple waves, and added a single lavender rose tucked into her ear, holding back her hair on one side.

Cyn's mother stood beside her wearing a long-sleeved deep purple dress. She walked Cyn down the aisle. He couldn't take his eyes off his beautiful bride, not even when Cyn's mom put Cyn's hand in his and said, "Love each other always."

He'd love Cyn for eternity.

CYN STOOD BESIDE her handsome groom and smiled, letting him see how incredibly happy she was to be here with him today. "I love you."

Hunt chuckled. "Thank God, because we're about to get married."

Everyone present laughed, including Judge Evans.

Hunt cupped her cheek. "You are so beautiful. I love you, too."

Judge Evans took a step toward them. "And that is why we are here today, to share this special occasion with Cyn and Hunt as they pledge to share their lives together. Most couples have a cute or funny story about how they met. In this case, Hunt issued Cyn the first of many speeding tickets he'd give her before they finally saw that there was more between them than traffic laws and whether she'd obey them." The judge paused, then added, "Or not."

Hunt shook his head, agreeing that she probably wouldn't. Ever.

"Hunt admitted that he hated to write those tickets because they made Cyn glare at him all the time."

Cyn gave Hunt a lopsided grin.

He squeezed her hands and smiled back.

Their guests chuckled.

Judge Evans leaned in to her. "He was just doing his job."

Cyn rolled her eyes. "I know. He told me that a million times."

Hunt grinned even more. "And you kept speeding and I kept pulling you over."

"I kind of liked you chasing after me," she confessed.

Hunt chuckled. "Well, now I've well and truly caught you."

"Now I speed because I can't wait to be with you."

Their guests sighed.

Judge Evans continued. "And now you see why it was inevitable these two would end up together. When Hunt confessed his feelings, Cyn surrendered to her own and the bond between them grew. The love they shared saw them through some difficult and dangerous times, showing them how precious what they shared was and that they didn't want to waste a minute of the rest of their lives together.

"And so they stand before us today, ready to commit themselves, not just to being partners to each other, but also parents to their sweet Lana. Hunt and Cyn have written their own vows. Hunt, make your pledge to Cyn."

Hunt took the butterfly ring from Chase, along with a diamond band Cyn didn't know anything about. He took her hand and slid the slim band on her finger, then her butterfly ring.

"Hunt," she gasped. "It's beautiful."

"You're beautiful." He squeezed her hand, his gaze steady and filled with love. "Cyn, I promise to love you unconditionally, with patience and kindness, in health and sickness, good times and bad, to be your best friend, lover and partner in everything. As I join my life to yours, I promise to be loyal and faithful and to support and encourage you—even when you do something wild for all the right reasons and I'm afraid for you."

Cyn grinned and laughed under her breath.

Their guests, who knew her all too well, laughed with them because Hunt spoke the truth.

"In my arms and my heart you will always be safe. You will always be home. I will love you every day for the rest of my life," Hunt finished, and kissed the back of her hand, then continued to hold it as Cyn took the thick gold band Shelby handed her and held it up so Hunt could see the butterfly she'd had stamped on the inside of the band with a heart on both sides of it.

He smiled. "Cyn, that's perfect."

"You'll always have a symbol of me and my love with you." She slid the ring on his finger.

Touched by her words, he put his hand over his heart, then took both her hands in his as she returned the pledge he'd made to her.

After the initial vow, she added her own embellishment. "As I join my life to yours, I promise to be loyal and faithful and to support and encourage you. I also promise to seduce you out of writing me any more speeding tickets."

Hunt gave her a mock frown and shook his head. "Can't you promise not to speed anymore?"

"I promise to be truthful." She winked at him and he barked out a laugh.

Amused, she shrugged unabashedly, and finished the vows. "In my arms and my heart you will always be safe. You will always be home. I will love you every day for the rest of my life."

Hunt was still grinning at her, barely spared a glance at the judge and said, "I can't help it. I'm kissing her now." He pulled her into him and kissed her while the judge announced, "I now pronounce you husband and wife. Kiss her all you want."

Hunt did as their guests clapped and laughed.

Cyn was a little light-headed by the time Hunt ended the kiss with a soft brush of his lips to hers. "Mrs. Wilde," he said reverently. "I love you."

"I love you. Now you really are my Wilde man."

"Always," he assured her.

"And now, we have one more joining to make on this exciting and momentous day." The judge held out the folder with the adoption papers. He handed the pen to Cyn. "Cyn Wilde, do you promise to love, protect, care for, support and encourage Lana all the days of your life?"

"I do," she pledged, signing the document.

"Hunt Wilde, do you promise to love, protect, care for, support and encourage Lana all the days of your life?"

"I do." Hunt signed the document.

Shelby handed Lana to Cyn, and she stood with Hunt and their daughter in front of the judge.

"You are now, and forever more, Lana Wilde's mom and dad." The judge motioned for them to turn to their guests. "I present to you, Cyn, Hunt and Lana Wilde. A family made of love and devotion."

Their guests clapped and Hunt kissed Cyn again, then they both kissed Lana on the head. Lana slept through the whole thing. But they had sweet pictures of everything, so one day when she was old enough to understand, they'd tell her the story of how her mom and dad met, married and promised to love each other, and her, forever.

Keep an eye out for the next novel in the
Wyoming Wildes series

# Max Wilde's
# Cowboy Heart

By Jennifer Ryan

Coming soon from Avon Books!